m w

"No—s
away."

Andrew
open. When his tongue touched the inside of
her lips, slowly savoring the taste of her, she
found herself yielding to his erotic demands.
"Julia, let me hold you. Let me touch you. Let
me show you how you make me feel."

Julia knew she should resist, force him to leave,
but under the edge of her gown, his hand was
stroking her, while his insistent mouth invaded
the soft warmth of her body. Desperately she
sought for a last measure of control. "No, Andrew
. . . it's wrong."

"It can't be wrong. Not for me, and you'll see,
not wrong for you either." And as he seared
her silken skin with caresses, even the very stars
seemed to melt in the fires of love that sent
her spiraling into a new uncharted place she
would never want to leave. . . .

THE EXILED HEART

Torrid Historical Romances from SIGNET

The Exiled Heart

BARBARA KELLER

A SIGNET BOOK

NEW AMERICAN LIBRARY

NAL BOOKS ARE AVAILABLE AT QUANTITY DISCOUNTS WHEN
USED TO PROMOTE PRODUCTS OR SERVICES. FOR INFORMATION
PLEASE WRITE TO PREMIUM MARKETING DIVISION, NEW
AMERICAN LIBRARY, 1633 BROADWAY, NEW YORK, NEW YORK
10019.

SIGNET, SIGNET CLASSIC, MENTOR, PLUME, MERIDIAN and NAL BOOKS
are published by New American Library,
1633 Broadway, New York, New York 10019

First Printing, October, 1985

1 2 3 4 5 6 7 8 9

PRINTED IN THE UNITED STATES OF AMERICA

To my best editor, my husband, Jim

PROLOGUE

Cape Horn, November 1870

Through the gray afternoon a ship sailed steadily, breasting white-capped waves. From the southwest a great slate-colored cloud drove down on the square-rigged vessel. Beneath the threatening sky the once sturdy-looking brig seemed too frail to challenge the surging ocean. Lashed by swirling winds, the sea rose in giant swells, and flurries of hail began to pelt the straining sails.

At the cry for all hands on deck, a woman holding a child moved hastily away from the railing. From beneath a dark shawl strands of wet red hair whipped across her face as she struggled to a companionway and to a tiny cabin below. She thrust the child to the back of a narrow bunk and climbed in next to the small body. Pulling the shivering child close to her, she braced herself against the sides of the bunk.

Would the terrible effort to round the Cape never end? After each morning's respite, the war with wind and sea began. As she clung to her child, she wondered if she were being punished. Her sin had been great, but surely not worth the suffering inflicted on the sailor whose ribs had been broken last night, or the young man, scarcely more than a boy, who had been swept overboard. And she had already been bitterly punished. God could not be so unjust.

Her cabin was completely dark. Fortunately the child slept, but she dared not relax; she must fight against the shuddering roll of the bunk and keep them both safe.

In these unfriendly seas, ships often lost the battle for passage from the Atlantic to the Pacific. Had she fled, only to have them both die? But remaining behind would have meant another kind of death.

She must believe that she had done the right thing; that they would find a safe home. To soothe herself she deliberately forced her thoughts back five years, when home was a secure place and the future bright.

1

South Carolina, September 1865

In the afternoon sun a row of immense oak trees stretched their dark shadows across a dirt road. Where the rutted tracks ended, a mixture of oaks, cotton-woods, and pines sheltered the weathered outbuildings and yard of a shabby two-story plantation house. Tall white columns rested on a lower porch which had been newly repaired, but the upper balcony sagged like a fatigued old man. Bullet holes pockmarked the wood framing of a scarred front door, testifying to the vio-lence and poverty of four years of civil war. On a sign swinging from a splintery post, freshly painted letters read "HUNDRED OAKS."

Some distance away, where the road circled the edge of an outlying field, a mule plodded, a young woman on its back. She rode astride, a flounced russet cotton dress bunched halfway up long legs, bare feet dangling. Around her flushed face, where dark lashes framed golden-brown eyes, tendrils of coppery red hair curled damply. A full sensual mouth set over a determined chin suggested a passionately willful nature. The top buttons of her lace-trimmed bodice were unfastened, and beads of moisture glistened at the base of her throat. Across her slender back the silky cotton clung in damp patches. Her black shoes, laces tied together, were draped like a crude necklace around the mule's neck.

Julia Rayford dug her heels into the animal's sweaty sides. "Violet," she coaxed, "you can go faster than this." The mule's pace quickened momentarily, then returned to its placid rhythm. Julia sighed in guilty exasperation. She shouldn't have gone to inspect the west field this late in the day, and despite the heat, she should have resisted the temptation to wade in the creek. At age twenty she ought to be more restrained.

To her right a movement caught her attention as a man on a bay horse rode up the path from the river. She shaded her eyes and saw a tall, broad-shouldered man with black hair showing below a white hat. He rode with an easy grace that piqued her admiration and curiosity. Julia had never seen him before, but she knew it could be Andrew Langdon, Richard Langdon's son. They had arrived today, accompanying Papa back from Charleston.

Julia thought of her appearance and knew Mama would never forgive her if a guest saw her as she now looked. He wouldn't speak to her, the Southern code demanded that a man pretend not to see a woman doing anything undignified. But even she, who chafed at the necessity of being a lady, was embarrassed. Turning the mule to the sheltering bulk of an oak, she waited as hoofbeats sounded louder, then faded. When she peered around the tree, she discovered with relief that the rider was gone.

It was getting late and Mama expected company for dinner. With only a few black servants left at Hundred Oaks, Julia had to help with many tasks slaves had done before the war. She urged the gray mule back into motion.

Over the next rise, she pulled abruptly on Violet's reins, shocked at what she saw ahead of her. A small buggy stood in the road, a stocky brown horse in the shafts. Nearby, a short, paunchy man in a dark claw-hammer coat and trousers pointed across the field. Beside him a young black man in the hated blue Yankee uniform nodded in apparent agreement with something the white man was saying.

Anger lent strength to the kick Julia gave Violet, propelling the mule forward. Everyone in the district knew the sight of that despised buggy. It belonged to Willard Deavers, a Yankee from Washington, supposedly checking on unpaid taxes, but really trying to steal land. He had no right to trespass on Hundred Oaks, and Julia felt her stomach tighten with fury at the man's daring.

The two men turned as she slid off Violet's back and spoke with a voice that shook from rage. "What are you doing on our land?"

Deavers looked surprised, then removed his hat and made a stilted bow. Tiny broken veins mottled his florid cheeks. "Now, now, miss, no need for difficulty. My duties include inspecting this property. I have Mr. Rayford's permission—"

"You lie!" Julia clenched her fists, shouting. "Papa would never allow you on Hundred Oaks."

The veneer of courtesy disappeared as Deavers stepped toward her threateningly, his voice a snarl. "Haven't you people learned yet that you're beaten? No rebel girl can tell me what to do."

"Rebel!" Julia put into her voice all her contempt for the men who sought to profit from the South's suffering. "I wouldn't bother to rebel against the likes of *you*! Now, get off this land."

Deavers gave an ugly laugh and raised his arm as if to

strike her, when another voice, deep and cold, interrupted. "I suggest you honor the lady's request."

Julia whirled and saw the stranger on the bay horse.
Dismounting, he strode toward them, his tall form pro-
jecting a reassuring strength. Her racing hearbeat slowed
as she faced Deavers again and found his bullying stance
replaced by wary courtesy.

For a moment the tax agent stood his ground; then,
with a sullen look, he gestured to the silent black
corporal behind him and climbed into the buggy. The
young soldier joined him and, taking the reins, swung
the vehicle around in the road. Dust billowed behind
the wheels as the buggy rolled away.

A sudden feeling of nausea made Julia's throat burn,
and her stomach heaved precariously. She had felt such
anger in the past and she recognized its aftermath. No,
she thought miserably, she mustn't retch. Closing her
eyes against the feeling, she felt herself sway. The
stranger's arms caught her, and an alarmed voice asked,
"Are you ill?"

She willed her stomach to calm. As the threat of
sickness passed, she became aware of the man holding
her. His coat smelled faintly of tobacco and another
scent that reminded her of fresh-cut wood; she felt the
buttons of his shirt press against her breasts, the warmth
of his chest, and even the beating of his heart. Or
perhaps it was her own.

For a moment she leaned against his comforting
strength, until a strange sensation—different from her
recent fury—began in her stomach. She felt a fluttering
of excitement, of anticipation as she hastily opened her
eyes and pulled free of the supporting arms. "Thank
you—I'm fine now."

"You're sure?" His deep voice sounded worried. "You
must have been frightened."

"No, just angry." Julia stepped back, struggling to regain her composure, and found she had to look up at him. She was tall, but this man stood a head taller. He had a strong face framed by thick black hair, which curled over the edge of his high collar. Under the broad-brimmed hat dark brows contrasted with intense blue eyes still mirroring concern. Only an angular jaw and slightly irregular nose saved his face from being too handsome. He wore a loose tan coat, open in the heat, and brown trousers that emphasized heavily muscled thighs. Under the coat a white shirt stretched across the broad shoulders and chest of a man accustomed to activity. She guessed his age at close to thirty.

Brushing a loosened strand of hair away from her face, she was suddenly aware of her disheveled appearance—the bare feet below her dusty skirt, her partially unbuttoned bodice. A blush burned her face as she spoke. "Thank you for defending me, though I believe he would not have dared remain on Hundred Oaks."

He smiled, and the strong angles of his face softened with unexpected charm and warmth. "I'm sure you're a match for any Yankee, but I wished to make sure he didn't harm you." Small lines deepened around his eyes and full mouth, as if he wanted to laugh. "I apologize that we've not been correctly introduced." He glanced at the flaming red hair which everyone noticed. "I think I recognize you, Miss Rayford, from your twin brother's description. Perhaps James will present me properly later. I am Andrew Langdon."

He *was* Richard Langdon's son, Julia thought, realizing they had the same unusual height, dark hair, and blue eyes. Both were strikingly handsome men, though Andrew seemed more relaxed and open than his father. She felt her skin flush at the admiration his eyes conveyed.

How ridiculous we must look, she thought, comparing Andrew Langdon's clothes and formal manner to her rumpled dress, smelling faintly of her mule. She began to laugh, and the mirth she'd seen in Andrew's eyes joined hers. Mockingly she curtsied low and held out her hand. "Of course we must wait for a proper introduction." Andrew took the grimy hand she offered, but he didn't kiss it. Aware of the streaks of dirt on it, she understood why not, and laughed again. Suddenly she found herself wondering what his lips might feel like against her skin, but startled at her own reaction, she drew back.

He gestured toward Violet. "May I help you mount?"

She hesitated, knowing how she'd look riding bareback and astride, but it was too late for embarrassment now. Andrew didn't offer his hand for her to step on; instead his hands encircled her waist and lifted her to Violet's back. His touch felt strong and sure, and a shiver of excitement mingled with her discomfort at showing her bare legs.

"Thank you." She didn't look at him as she nudged Violet forward, but she knew he watched her as she rode away.

As the mule plodded toward home, Julia's thoughts returned to Deavers. Despite what she'd said to Andrew, she had been frightened as well as enraged. She'd seen too many tax-foreclosure notices all around Hundred Oaks lately; they brought back her terror that Papa might have to sell their home. But since Great-Uncle Francis had died and left Papa his money, Papa could pay the taxes and restore Hundred Oaks. She and James would each receive a small legacy on their twenty-first birthday. Men like Deavers couldn't harm them now.

She reached the first of the sheds behind the house,

slid off Violet's back, and retrieved her shoes. A vigorous slap started the mule toward the barn and the stableboy. The dust beneath her bare feet felt soft and warm, and momentarily she squeezed her toes in pleasure. Then she hurried past the kitchen building to the small side door. After peering cautiously up the dark steps and seeing no one, she ascended noiselessly to the upper hall and slipped into her room.

As she pulled off her stained clothes and poured water into the large china washbasin, she thought of Andrew. With a flush of pleasure she remembered his inviting blue eyes, the strength of his arms when he'd held her. Certainly he was an attractive man, but was he like his father?

Something about Richard Langdon made Julia uneasy, and she usually avoided him. The Langdons had lived in Brazil for the last ten years, untouched by the War Between the States, though Richard had made regular visits to the South. She didn't understand why Papa had spent so much time with Richard Langdon recently. And Papa had seemed tense and excited before his trip to Charleston to meet Richard and his son. Well, Andrew had helped her, and her dislike of his father didn't matter. Besides, the Langdons would be leaving tomorrow.

After she finished washing away the dust, she put on one of her few presentable dresses, a figured yellow muslin with a full skirt, and began to brush her heavy hair. Humming to herself, she coiled the silky strands at the back of her head, capturing almost all of the reluctant curls. From beside her bed she took the letter from Philadelphia which had arrived last week, the first word from Nathan in almost a year, its edges already worn from rereading. She started to unfold it, then

replaced it, not needing to look at the memorized words
to feel a glow of pleasure. For a moment she pictured
his brown hair and gentle eyes. Nathan was alive, and
he still loved her as he had before the war interrupted
her visit with Mama's family.

She made a laughing face at herself in the mirror
before she turned to leave the room. The war was over,
Nathan loved her as she did him, her only problem now
would be to explain to Mama why she was late coming
to help in the dining room.

The evening light was beginning to fade before Julia
finished setting the long damask-covered table and
slipped out on the columned front porch. She loved this
time of day, when a compassionate dusk brushed its
patina of gray over the scars of war. In the half-light she
could imagine the house as it had once been, with clean
white paint sparkling beside green shutters, the fan-
shaped panes of glass above the front door uncracked.

Below her on the gravel walk at the foot of the steps a
tall figure paced restlessly—Andrew Langdon. She
paused, suddenly feeling both excited and self-conscious.
Would he say anything about their earlier meeting? As
he turned and looked up at her, she found her breath
suspended, waiting for him to recognize her.

From the walk below, Andrew stared, fascinated, at
the young woman above him, and at her lustrous red
hair, its color still brilliant even in the early-evening
light. Except for that fiery hair, he thought, she hardly
looked like the furious young woman he'd found con-
fronting the carpetbagger several hours earlier. He
watched her move across the porch, her full skirt swaying
around her tall slender figure, accenting her small waist.
Her pale yellow dress left part of her neck and shoulders bare, and even with its modest cut, he could tell

that her breasts were small but invitingly rounded. The earlier glimpses of her legs when she'd been on the mule promised an enticing body.

As she reached the rail, he could see her face clearly where the last light touched it. Its even planes and straight nose looked serene, but the full mouth suggested tempestuousness. What would it be like to kiss that mouth, feel her lips soft with passion? Thick lashes shaded the brown eyes he remembered from the afternoon. Above her slender neck, escaping curls destroyed the severity of her restrained hair, subtly inviting him to pull it loose.

Caught in the intense scrutiny of the man below her, Julia felt almost relieved when a voice called, "Andrew . . ." She turned to see her twin brother coming up the path from the river. To her surprise she saw that James wore his gray Confederate officer's uniform, the empty right sleeve pinned to the shoulder, the coat loose around his thin frame. What startled her even more were the illegal insignia and buttons, the latter obviously recently shined, on his uniform. Why was James making this gesture of defiance to Yankee rules?

James reached the tall man on the walk and briefly clasped his hand. "Come, I'll introduce you to my sister." He bounded up the twelve stairs to the porch, and Andrew followed. When they reached the top, James put his left arm around Julia and hugged her. He was almost the same height as she, but his blond hair and gray eyes made him look more like their mother than did Julia, his twin. He turned toward the man behind them. "Julia, I wish to present Mr. Andrew Langdon."

Now was the time to acknowledge she'd met Andrew earlier, but Julia didn't want to explain to James what she'd been doing that afternoon. Instead she extended her hand and demurely said, "Welcome to Hundred Oaks, Mr. Langdon."

"Thank you, Miss Rayford." Only the barest hint of amusement in Andrew's eyes betrayed what he must have been thinking as he raised her hand to his mouth. His lips were warm against her hand, and she felt again that strange flutter in her stomach that had been so pleasurably exciting when he'd touched her that afternoon. The blue of his eyes suddenly deepened, like a lake when sunlight fades, telling her he felt the same attraction between them that she did. Hastily she withdrew her hand; her emotions confused her—she didn't expect to feel that way toward anyone but Nathan.

His voice held no trace of anything but courtesy when he spoke. "I've been admiring your house, Miss Rayford. It must have been magnificent before the war."

She felt the rush of delight she always experienced when someone praised her home. "Oh, yes, it was."

James laughed. "You've chosen Julia's favorite topic, Andrew. If you let her begin about Hundred Oaks, you'll hear nothing else."

"I'd enjoy that," Andrew responded politely, but Julia could almost see his reluctance. He probably expected her to talk about household activities instead of the things that usually interested men—the selection of crops, planting methods, and the other work which was the lifeblood of a plantation. What would he think, she wondered, if he knew that those were her interests too? Most men didn't want to hear of women's work, but neither did they like women knowledgeable about what they considered their sphere.

A clatter of hooves sounded from the drive on the opposite side of the house. "Excuse me," James said, "I'd better see who's arrived. I'll be back." He disappeared around the corner of the veranda.

Julia smiled at Andrew. "I'm not sure if I thanked you properly for helping me—and for not mentioning it to James. I'm afraid he doesn't always approve of what I do." Andrew's mouth quirked in answering amusement, which invited Julia to tease him laughingly. "I can tell you'd like to know what I was doing and why I looked so disreputable."

He laughed in return, his blue eyes sparkling. "I admit to curiosity."

"I wanted to see whether the west field had been cleared yet." The surprise she could see on his face challenged her to startle him more, and she continued talking of the plantation work which she loved, losing herself in the intensity of her enthusiasm.

Suddenly she realized that her reply had become a lengthy monologue, and she stopped, embarrassed. "But I'm sure you don't want to hear all those details. James warned you not to let me start."

Andrew still looked faintly surprised, but certainly not bored or uncomfortable. "I assure you, Miss Rayford, I'm very interested in what you've been saying."

They strolled along the porch to the corner that looked out toward the river. He lounged against the rail, his hands in his pockets, his full mouth curved in a smile that was warm and inviting. "Your interest in running the plantation, Miss Rayford, is somewhat unusual."

In the anonymity of the growing dark his relaxed pose and the interest with which he listened to her loosened the restraint which she tried to maintain, the pretense that she felt only frivolous, ladylike emotions. She spoke intensely, hurriedly. "Hundred Oaks means everything to me. I've always loved it, but the last two years of the war Papa was recovering from his wounds and James was away fighting. So I had to run Hundred Oaks."

She looked out over the dark trees, seeing in her mind the fields that surrounded them. "I suppose I shouldn't admit it, but I never cared for 'women's work.' Even with the war, I loved managing the land. That's where I'm really happy. Sometimes when I'm planning the next day's work, I feel like a drunkard with a bottle." She paused, then said passionately, "Men are so lucky—everyone expects them to do what women are only allowed when no man can do it for them."

Andrew spoke soberly. "I understand your desire to be out working, but you should realize that an unprotected woman may encounter men such as that Yankee today—"

She interrupted, letting her voice express the scorn she felt for the tax agent. "That trash—he can't touch us now. But he can corrupt the Negroes. That young man was born on the Scotts' plantation next to ours, and now he is coerced into helping a robber . . ." She clenched her hands. "I can't talk about it—I get too angry."

"But only at the Yankees, not at the blacks? With all your family suffered . . ."

His words stirred the grief she always felt when she thought of the tragedies of the past years—her two older brothers dead, James losing his arm, Papa ill for so long, but she responded calmly, "We must be fair to the colored people. Slavery was an evil that white people forced upon them, so we can't blame them for what the Yankees did."

His black eyebrows arched in questioning surprise. "This is an unusual opinion of blacks to find in South Carolina, Miss Rayford."

She thought of Philadelphia and Nathan. "I lived two years with my mother's Quaker family before the war began, so I have a different view of slavery from many other Southerners. And we're going to hire freedmen to restore Hundred Oaks."

For a moment Andrew looked at her with a strange expression, almost as if he knew something she didn't. When he said nothing, she continued, "But you must tell me of your home in Brazil, Mr. Langdon."

His face relaxed again, and he answered enthusiastically, "It's as beautiful in its way as Hundred Oaks. *Deus naceu em Brasil*, which means, 'God was born in Brazil.' "

She was still too caught up in the emotions of their previous conversation to resist a question, though she knew it sounded rude. "And do the slaves in Brazil say that also?"

Before he could reply, she heard a feminine voice behind them call, "Julia . . ." Sally stood in the front entrance. When she saw Andrew, she gave him a dimpled smile and came toward them.

As Andrew straightened from his relaxed position against the rail, Julia made the introductions. "Sally, I wish to present Andrew Langdon. Mr. Langdon, this is my cousin and James's betrothed, Miss King." A flirtatious upward glance of Sally's blue eyes accompanied the hand extended in response to Andrew's bow and greeting.

Watching them, Julia found herself wondering what a man saw when he looked at Sally. She was small but well-rounded, with pink and blond coloring which contrasted sharply with Julia's brilliant hair and eyes. Would a man like Andrew respond to the blond prettiness and smoothly practiced but meaningless coquetry? Somehow Julia wanted to think he wouldn't.

"Julia, I just hate to take you away from this lovely gentleman, but you know Aunt Mary simply can't get along without you. We'll have to enjoy Mr. Langdon's company at dinner." A swing of pink flowered skirts and another smile over Sally's shoulder promised future flirtation.

"Please excuse me, Mr. Langdon. I've enjoyed visiting with you." Julia realized that she truly meant the polite phrase.

"And I with you, Miss Rayford." Andrew's response sounded equally sincere, and she felt a warm glow as she followed her cousin into the candlelit central hall.

Why, she wondered, had she talked to Andrew so freely? After their earlier meeting it seemed silly to stick to the generally inane conversation considered appropriate for young women. He'd appeared genuinely interested in her feelings, and perhaps knowing he would leave tomorrow made her more candid.

With a pleasant feeling of excitement she remembered the appreciative look in his eyes. The strength of her response when he'd kissed her hand had disconcerted her. Since she loved Nathan, she shouldn't be so affected by another man. But, she assured herself, it was only natural to enjoy admiration from someone as handsome as Andrew; her reaction meant nothing more than that.

From the open door to the study she heard men's voices and glanced inside, recognizing several of their neighbors and her father's stocky figure. William Rayford's red hair had once glowed like her own, but now white had dulled its brilliant color. Beside him stood Richard Langdon. Seeing her father's animated face across from the enigmatic bearded one, Julia felt her usual uneasiness with Richard Langdon. His manner seemed not quite real, his words too polished, his face too ready to smile.

"Julia," Sally called from the dining-room door, "Aunt

Mary wants you to come help." Julia hurried to the double doors. Her mouth watered at the smells from the dishes on the sideboard—ham, roast chicken, candied yams, bread made from real wheat flour, canned peas, and other almost forgotten treats. No cornmeal mush and turnip greens tonight! All this thanks to Great-Uncle Francis.

He had moved to England before Julia was born, so she couldn't feel grief for his death, and she loved having his money. She almost danced into the dining room.

Candlelight softened the faces of the men and women seated at the long damask-covered table. Julia turned her wineglass, watching it catch the light from the silver candelabra. It reminded her of the frightening night when she'd hidden the family valuables under the floor of a slave house before the Yankees came. Thank God those times were behind them and she'd never have to face a hostile army again.

Across the table from her, Andrew admired her graceful movements as, at a nod from her father, she rose to get a decanter of wine from the sideboard. God, she was a beauty! And even more—she had vitality and exuberance. Her conversation had surprised and intrigued him. During dinner he'd talked more than usual about Brazil, and her eyes hadn't glazed over. Recognizing the physical attraction between them, he almost wished he were going to be here longer. But he couldn't do more than flirt very cautiously with the daughter of his host, and besides, soon he'd be back in Brazil enjoying Lele's dark beauty.

Julia looked lovingly at her father as she crossed behind him where he was holding court at the head of the table. She was proud of the way the other planters turned to him for leadership. In spite of the frayed cuffs and threadbare collars they wore, some of them were still powerful men. Of course, everyone here had suffered from the war—everyone but the Langdons.

While she moved around the table, filling glasses from the decanter of claret, she wondered why Papa had asked all the women to stay at the table for more wine. Usually by now the men had been left to their brandy and cigars. She smiled to herself; Papa must have some surprise to announce tonight—he was a man who loved drama.

Watching Julia bend gracefully over the wine decanter, Andrew was also thinking about the announcement to be made this evening. Judging from their conversation outside before dinner, William Rayford had told his daughter nothing of his plans. Mary Rayford had a weary air; probably her husband no longer amazed her with anything. But Julia didn't look submissive. From what she'd said about Hundred Oaks, Andrew guessed she would be extremely upset. Suddenly he wished he didn't know how much pain she would feel.

Julia reached Andrew and felt again the admiration in his eyes as she filled his glass. He had his own particular scent, different from the tobacco and brandy she associated with her father, but very masculine. Would he have noticed, she wondered, the fragrance of roses that was her favorite? Standing behind him, she could see the way the black hair curled at the back of his neck, making him look somehow very young. Suddenly she wanted to reach out and touch that hair above the high white collar, feel it spring back against her fingers. Hastily she walked on around the table to return the decanter to its place, hoping no one could see the flush she knew had crept up her face.

"Gentlemen . . . ladies." Her father stood and waited

until others rose also. Julia lifted her wineglass and turned toward him. "With the help of Mr. Langdon and Andrew, arrangements been completed for my family to move to a new land. I hope that many of you will join us when"—he paused, his eyes showing clearly his enjoyment of the moment—"we leave Hundred Oaks to live in Brazil."

The crash of breaking glass halted the murmur that had begun. Julia looked down and saw that the wineglass she had been holding lay shattered on the oak floor at her feet. Red splatters of wine stained the hem of her pale yellow dress. Dazed, she stared at the pool of wine and shards of glass, unable to believe what her father had said.

Beside her she saw a black hand pulling her back a step. Serena had a cloth in her hand and was bending to clean up the wet glass. Julia looked at her father, trying to focus on his face, but it blurred before her eyes. The room seemed like a distant stage on which something was happening that interested her but didn't really affect her.

Richard Langdon's voice cut into the silence that had followed the sound of splintering glass. "Well, gentlemen, I am pleased that Andrew and I can act as your agents."

Julia dimly heard those words—"Andrew and I"—and her shocked mind focused on them. Richard Langdon had persuaded Papa to move to Brazil. But not just Richard—Andrew also. How could this be true?

Papa, beaming with proud pleasure, like a little boy who has just accomplished a difficult trick, was addressing Richard again. "We are grateful for your assistance with the emperor's government." He held out his hand to the tall man before him. With murmured agreement the other men in the room offered their hands in turn.

William picked up his glass. "Gentlemen, the Confederacy. Broken she may be here, but her spirit will live on in a new land."

"The Confederacy," echoed through the candlelit room.

"Mr. Rayford . . ." Still unwilling to believe what was happening, Julia turned toward another voice, Andrew's, and heard irritation—almost anger—underlying the polite surface.

Excitement sparked in William's eyes as he responded. "Yes, Andrew."

"May I propose an additional toast?" Andrew didn't wait for assent. "To that new land where many spirits flourish. To Brazil."

Rainbows burst from the tiny planes of crystal as the ruby wine was lifted again, but Julia did not wait for the glasses to be emptied. With her heart full of a pain she thought had ended with the war, she turned and fled along the hall.

Julia gripped the railing along the wide front veranda where she had been pacing for what seemed like hours, struggling with her dismay and rage. Leave Hundred Oaks? Leave all that her two older brothers had died for? How could Papa even consider it?

James had known, but he'd told her nothing. Her twin, the person closest to her in the world, had betrayed her. Earlier he had stood right here, introducing her to Andrew Langdon as a friend. And all the time James knew that the Langdons had persuaded Papa to give up land that his great-great-grandfather had torn from a swampy wilderness. How she wished she hadn't explained to Andrew how she felt about Hundred Oaks. Her confidences must have embarrassed or even amused him. Shame added to her fury.

Well, she'd not leave Hundred Oaks. Never! She

pounded on the railing, and the resulting pain in her hand felt almost good.

She heard sounds from the side entrance and moved farther along the porch. Guests were leaving, taking their carriages and horses, but she didn't want to see any of them. At footsteps echoing behind her, she turned and saw candlelight from the hall silhouetting two figures—Andrew Langdon and James.

Julia called to her brother. "James." She couldn't bring herself to speak to Andrew. "I must talk to you."

"Julia, of course." He turned to the taller man. "Andrew, excuse us, please."

"Certainly. Good night, Miss Rayford." Andrew's voice sounded almost sympathetic.

Hypocrite, she thought furiously as he vanished into the hall.

James joined Julia and put his arm around her. "Hey, Julie Ann, don't be so upset."

At her brother's use of his pet name for her, she felt tenderness mingle with her anger. Thank God he had been in the war only during the last two years and had returned, missing his right arm, but at least alive.

His face looked older than twenty now. She remembered his homecoming, the exhausted figure trudging slowly up from the ferry, not even enough silver in his pocket for the ferryman. Her father had ridden back to pay the fare.

But she couldn't let sympathy for her twin distract her now. "James, I can't believe Papa wants to move to Brazil!"

He gestured excitedly. "Yes—the Scotts and some others want to emigrate too. Oh, Julia, I knew you wouldn't like it, but it's a great idea."

Her anger rose again. "You approve! Oh, James, how can you think of leaving Hundred Oaks?"

Turning away from her, he looked out into the night shadows, his words taking on the bitter edge she'd heard in so many voices this last year. "What's here for us? Our Hundred Oaks is gone, Julia. How could we live here—ruled over by the Yankees?" His face twisted with contempt. "Would you have me sign the oath and crawl to the Yankees? Swear loyalty to the government that killed our brothers, tried to ruin us? Could Father ever do that?" He faced her again, the passion fading from his thin face. "Besides, you'll love Brazil. Andrew's been telling me—"

"Andrew! I wouldn't believe anything Andrew Langdon or his father said!"

James frowned, his wiry form tensing. "You don't know what you're talking about, Julia. You have to leave decisions like this to men."

"To men!" Her voice was scornful. "I suppose you've spent so much time with Andrew that you include yourself with him. Well, I don't trust him or his father."

James stepped back, his face stiff. "I'm not going to talk to you now. You don't want to be reasonable." He turned and strode back into the house.

Julia started to call after him, but stopped, bitterly hurt by his desertion. Papa probably wouldn't listen to her alone, she thought despairingly. He petted her and indulged her up to a point, as he had when he'd let her spend the two years with Mama's brother and his family in Philadelphia, even though he disliked their Quaker ideas. But now . . . She shivered in the warm night air.

She stared out at the dark trees, hardly seeing their outlines for her turbulent thoughts. Approaching Mama wouldn't do any good; Julia had always been closer to her father than to her mother and had seldom gone to Mama with her problems. She knew Mama considered her willful and tempestuous, though she'd tried hard to gain more control over her own passionate nature.

Angrily she wiped away the tears which threatened to fall as she turned and went slowly back into the house. Its familiar walls seemed to reach out and embrace her. She couldn't leave here and go to Brazil, she thought desperately. Tomorrow she'd talk to Papa—he *had* to listen.

But she knew her father too well. She closed her eyes, her determination not to go blazing inside her, and the wild tears she'd been holding back flooded her face.

2

Julia dreamed she was riding in a swaying black carriage; on a high seat in front of her, two dark-cloaked men with whips were flogging wildly straining horses. She looked behind them and saw, across desolate brown fields, the burned shell of Hundred Oaks. Struggling forward, she clutched at the drivers' arms and their faces turned toward her—Richard Langdon and Willard Deavers. She woke with her throat tight from an un-voiced scream.

When morning finally arrived, she sent a message downstairs with Sally that she felt too ill for breakfast, though she knew her mother wouldn't believe it—Julia was never sick and hated inactivity. But being hungry and confined in her room was less punishment than having to be polite to the Langdons. She spent the next hour planning what to say to Papa and pacing her bedroom, the full skirts of an old blue dress swinging nervously around her. The softly gleaming oak furni-ture, the faded rug her grandmother had hooked, the lace curtains at the windows—all the familiar surroundings seemed alien at the thought she might have to leave them.

The noise of a carriage coming to the side entrance

drew her to the window, where below she could see the top of a black head. Tobias, one of the few former slaves who had stayed with them after the Union victory, was carrying a large leather case from the door to the carriage, followed by Richard Langdon and her father. As they paused on the steps, she could hear their good-byes. Finally the Langdons were leaving! She could go downstairs now, perhaps get something to eat, and find her father.

Nervously she tucked a stray curl back into her chignon. Then, closing the bedroom door softly, she crossed the open hall and descended the stairs. Through the dining-room doors she heard Serena, Tobias' wife, humming as she cleared the table. It was too late for food there, but maybe she could wheedle something in the kitchen.

At the bottom of the stairs she turned toward the back of the house and almost collided with Andrew, coming along the hall. Startled, she drew back. In her stomach she felt a knot growing, the residue of anger mingling with shame at the attraction and freedom she'd felt with him the previous day. Reluctantly she noticed how handsome he looked in a blue morning coat that emphasized the intense color of his eyes and contrasted with his black brows and curling hair. Ignoring the sense of masculine power his size and height gave him, she spoke coldly. "Mr. Langdon . . . I thought you had left."

His wide mouth showed no smile, but the blue eyes looked amused. "I'm sorry if you are disappointed, Miss Rayford. In a few minutes I'll fulfill your hope."

He was making fun of her, she thought furiously, and made her voice as icy as possible. "I did not mean to suggest you should have departed, Mr. Langdon, only that I thought you had."

No amusement lingered in his eyes now. "Have I offended you in some way, Miss Rayford?"

The social requirement to conceal her antagonism warred with Julia's natural impulsiveness. Candor won. "Yes, Mr. Langdon, you have offended me, praising Brazil as if it's a paradise where everyone should go." Julia clenched her hands with the effort of keeping her temper under control. "Well, I don't believe you. No place could be as marvelous as you describe. And I think my family should stay at Hundred Oaks where we belong!" She was glaring at him now, not caring about manners.

"I agree."

Julia felt as if he'd dropped her into a cold stream. Speechless, she stared at him.

"Yes, Miss Rayford, I think your family, and your friends, should remain here."

Shocked, she wondered if he were mocking her. "But you helped convince Papa to move."

He frowned, his mouth sober-looking, the lines around his square jaw almost grim. "I'm afraid your father gave me credit I don't deserve. Brazil can be everything I have described, but it is not South Carolina. I fear your father and his friends have expectations that can never be satisfied."

Confusion replaced her anger. Indirectly Andrew was questioning her father's judgment, and in loyalty to William and James she had to reject this unexpected support of her own position.

She raised her chin and spoke in the tone she had heard her mother use with offensive tradesmen. "I think you and I do not agree after all, Mr. Langdon. I'm sure my father understands the situation in Brazil very well. My objections are to leaving our heritage here—a concern which apparently you do not appreciate."

He looked at her steadily for a moment; then a smile lightened the severe lines of his face. "If that heritage includes beautiful women who understand how to run a plantation and speak their own minds, I most assuredly do appreciate it. Unfortunately, I can't stay longer to discuss this most interesting subject. Please excuse me." He bowed briefly and strode past her to the front hall.

Feeling strangely bested, she watched the tall figure go through the wide doors onto the veranda. Just outside, he turned, the morning sunshine outlining his thick black hair, shadowing his face so that she couldn't see his expression. "Good-bye, Miss Rayford." Julia felt her face flush; then she whirled and continued along the hall and into her father's study.

Restlessly she walked around the familiar room. The scarred oak desk with its untidy heaps of papers reminded her of the times she'd faced her father across it and waited for his temper, as quick as her own, to subside. She'd known that if she could get him to laugh, her misdemeanor would be forgiven, or at least lightly punished. Even the time she'd lured Sally up into her brothers' treehouse and then taken away the ladder, her father had eventually pardoned her in a gust of laughter. He understood how exasperating her orphaned cousin could be.

Today the issue was not an escapade like dressing in boy's clothes or swimming in the river. Her family's future—*her* future—was being settled. Papa had to listen, had to realize they mustn't tear out roots put down over a hundred years ago.

A noise in the hall stilled her agitated movements. She took a quick breath, then released it as the door opened and her father appeared, his ruddy face smiling and relaxed.

"Julia." He gave her cheek a warm kiss before he

crossed the room and sat in the worn chair behind the desk. "You wanted to see me?"

"Yes, Papa." Suddenly unsure how to begin, she watched his blunt fingers pull a pile of papers toward him. He looked up, waiting.

She leaned against the desk, gripping the edge, and anguish freed her tongue. "Papa, please . . . please listen to me. We mustn't go to Brazil—Hundred Oaks is our home. We can't leave it."

His lined face stiffened, his brown eyes growing stern. But before he could speak, she hurried on. "I know the Langdons made Brazil sound wonderful, but now that the war is over, Hundred Oaks can be almost the same again."

He rose and came around the desk. "You don't know what you're saying, Julia. Can you forget what the Yankees did here at Hundred Oaks? Forget the struggle just to stay alive?" His flashing eyes and flushed face prevented her from interrupting. "You think the war is over—didn't you learn anything from our trip to town last week?"

Julia stared at her father, but instead of his face she saw again the main street of Wayneville. Papa had not allowed her or her mother to accompany him on trips to town for several months because of the Yankee occupation. But Mama needed to see Dr. Butler in his office, and Julia had been allowed to go with them. After the visit to the doctor she begged Papa to walk along the central street.

The pleasure of visiting familiar places and people had been marred by the pain of seeing the evidence of the hated new government. Posters announced the hours at which the townspeople could be on the streets. Through the open doors of a saloon she saw men in blue uniforms, already drinking, although the afternoon sun still scorched the dusty buildings. That some of the men were black, she knew, further enraged her father.

Ahead on the boardwalk two Union officers emerged from an open doorway and came toward Julia and her parents. One officer was heavy, his face flushed and his uniform wrinkled; the other, a slight young man with a drooping blond mustache, wavered a little as he walked. She could feel her father's hand stiffen where he held her elbow, and saw him draw her mother closer on his other side.

As the distance shrank between them and the Yankees, it became obvious that the two men would not step aside. The older officer stared at Julia, his eyes raking her in an insulting manner. Her father's grip tightened until her elbow hurt. Then he turned abruptly and left the sidewalk, propelling them all across the swirling dust of the street.

He pulled them into the shaded doorway of the Wayneville General Store before his hands released them. When he finally spoke, his voice was hoarse. "If I had my sword . . ."

Now, facing her father in his study, Julia felt helpless to ease his bitterness. She understood his terrible anger, but nothing warranted giving up their home and heritage. She put a pleading hand on his arm. "Papa, it's because of all we've lost that we mustn't give up and leave. It would be like letting the Yankees win all over again. And they won't be here forever . . ."

A look of patient understanding replaced the anger in her father's face. The change dismayed her; she could counter her father's anger, but patience relegated her to the role of an incompetent daughter.

"Julia, nothing here will be the same." He gently stroked her cheek. "The life my father and his father knew here is gone, buried as deep as William Henry and Francis." As he spoke the names of her dead brothers, his voice shook. "Buried by the Yankees."

He went to the window and stared out for a long moment, then turned back to her, and she saw that he had regained control of himself. He spoke enthusiastically. "But we can have our life in Brazil. The Emperor Dom Pedro understands the economics of agriculture, the need for slavery. He knows the coloreds need white supervision to take their places in the natural order."

Julia stopped listening to the familiar arguments, the justifications for slavery she'd heard so many times before. She didn't want to argue with Papa now about that topic, because she needed him to listen to her pleas.

Unwillingly she embraced the idea she'd rejected when Andrew presented it. "But, Papa, Brazil sounds so different from South Carolina. How can you be so sure we'll like it?"

An irritated frown creased her father's forehead. "Julia, you don't understand." She gritted her teeth to suppress an outburst at the hated phrase. "I know leaving Hundred Oaks will be hard for you, just as it is for your mother. But I confess I'm grateful you're not married and will go with us. Mary will need your help and support, and I expect it." He paused for a moment; then lines deepened around his mouth and his eyes looked sad. His arms went about Julia and he held her close.

She was almost as tall as he, and her head rested next to the familiar cheek. She smelled the odors that had represented love and security all her life: tobacco, his shaving soap, and the farewell glass of brandy he must have shared at breakfast with Richard Langdon. He spoke in the voice that had settled the outlines of her life for twenty years. "Julia, your mother is not as well as I would wish. I thank God that she has you with

her." At a tremor in her father's voice, Julia pulled her
head away and looked up at him. In his eyes she
thought she saw the beginning of tears. Then he smiled
and continued in his normal voice. "Go on. Find your
mother. Mary can provide plenty of work to keep you
from brooding."

Julia closed the study door behind her and fled out
the back entrance, forcing back her own tears of frustration. Talking to Papa had been useless. He thought
Mama was not well, but he always worried over his
wife's every little cold or sniffle. What about her, his
daughter? Bitterly she reminded herself that an unmarried daughter had few choices at any time, and even
fewer now because of the war.

The war—always the war. If not for that, she might
have finished her education, perhaps even married
Nathan.

Nathan! She stopped in the shade of a laurel tree that
bordered the kitchen garden. If she were married, her
place would be with her husband.

As Julia stared at the green and brown rows, she
thought of Philadelphia—how far away it seemed. She
might have been a different person, laughing and teasing with her cousins and Nathan, their foster brother.
From the time she'd seen his smiling hazel eyes and
tousled brown hair, she'd felt almost as close to him as
to James. Together they'd gone to parties, been caught
in a snowstorm, argued all the way home from an
abolitionist meeting. By the end of those two years in
Philadelphia, she'd realized she loved Nathan and he
loved her.

When Fort Sumter had been fired on in 1861, Julia
had returned home, and Nathan, just finishing medical
school, had joined the Union Army. Though he'd worn
the hated Yankee uniform, he'd been a medical officer,

saving instead of taking lives. In spite of the difficulties
with mail, they'd written, shared their despair at the war
and their hopes for the future, and her love for him had
grown in spite of the separation. Then a year ago, his
letters stopped, and Julia hadn't known whether he was
alive. But last week her uncle's letter had arrived with a
note enclosed from Nathan, returned unscathed from
the war. The news had filled Julia with joy. Eventually,
she felt sure, the terrible gulf the war had created
would be bridged, because Nathan still loved her. They
hadn't actually spoken the words, but she knew she
hadn't misunderstood his feelings. Now, if she moved
to Brazil, she would never see Hundred Oaks or Nathan again.

Surely if he knew how she needed him, he'd be
willing to come to Hundred Oaks. Though he had never
farmed, he could learn, and while he practiced medicine, she would do the principal work of running Hundred Oaks. It was what she most longed to do anyway.
She brushed at a buzzing fly, excitedly wondering how
to approach the subject of marriage with Nathan. I'll
write, she decided, and tell him how desperately I want
to stay in South Carolina, even without my family.
He'll read between the lines, know how I need him,
and propose. My dowry can be the house and part of
the land; the rest we'd take care of for Papa.

Suddenly the morning seemed fair, the sky smiling as
she sneaked into the kitchen building, temporarily deserted in the between-meal lull. On a covered plate she
found a square of cornbread and ate it as she hurried to
the main house. Her mother thought she was in her
room and wouldn't be looking for her to do chores.
She'd write to Nathan now.

*   *   *

An hour later Julia sighed and shifted her birch writing box from her lap to the bed beside her. On it was a half-written letter, and three crumpled pieces of paper lay by her feet. The words to Nathan still lodged in her mind, obstinately resisting her pen. She liked direct speech, not the hints she was trying to compose.

Sighing, she rose and walked restlessly to the window and looked out. Below, she saw her mother with Duncan Scott, the young son of their nearest neighbor. Julia admired her mother, but Mama had so many virtues that Julia felt mean and small sometimes by contrast, and she knew her tempestuous nature troubled Mary.

I wonder, Julia thought, if Mama knows how hard I've tried to be the sweet daughter she'd like to have. But I can't be what I'm not, just as I can't give in and go to Brazil because Papa says so.

She leaned over the windowsill as Duncan mounted and rode away. Her mother looked up and called, "Julia, I need to see you. Please come to the morning room."

Julia decided she'd listen to Mama and then talk to her about Papa's plans. It probably wouldn't do any good—Mama never opposed Papa in anything—but Julia had to try.

She went downstairs to the sunny room used for sewing and keeping household accounts, where her mother was already seated at her small desk. Julia spread her full blue skirt around her and sat on the wooden bench. "Yes, Mama?" Mary straightened an already neat pile of notes before she finally turned to her daughter.

In the sunlight Julia noticed that her mother's face looked pale, her gray eyes dull. Her blond hair, now mixed with strands of white, her colorless face, and blanched skin all made her seem small and faded. Why, Mama does look ill, Julia realized, her worries about Brazil momentarily set aside. "Mama, are you all right? You look . . . not well."

Mary looked away from Julia as if unsure how to answer. Then she faced her daughter again, speaking hurriedly, as if afraid she might not be able to say anything if she hesitated. "Julia, I've not been feeling myself recently."

Her mother's strange tone frightened Julia. "But what's wrong, Mama? Is it something serious?"

Mary managed a smile, but it was strained. "Oh, I hope not. But it means I'll need your help here in packing, and especially when we arrive at our new home."

With a rush, all Julia's concern about going to Brazil returned, overriding her fears about her mother. "Mama, I don't want to leave Hundred Oaks. And if you're not well, you must want to stay here too—not go to some far-off place you don't even know."

Mary spoke wearily, as if Julia's passionate tone suggested a battle she had fought many times before. "Your father has decided, and that is the end of the matter." She continued reprovingly, "It is not your place to question your father's decisions, Julia. Taking care of us is his duty, and ours is to accept his judgment."

Julia jumped up and stood in front of her mother, the anger she'd tried to subdue flooding her. She clenched her hands to keep from screaming. "But Papa was the one who taught James and me to ask questions. If Papa discusses things with James, why not with me? I'm just as old, just as smart. How can Papa take advice from the Langdons and ignore me?"

Mary raised her hand as though to prevent the torrent of words. Her face looked flushed now, her eyes strained as she spoke. "Julia, I hadn't wanted to tell you this because Papa and I didn't want you and James to worry. Dr. Butler says that . . ." Her voice thickened and softened until it was barely more than a whisper. "He says . . . it's something in my chest . . . I may be quite ill, though of course I hope he's wrong."

As much from Mary's stricken face as from her words, Julia recognized that her mother's illness was serious, and fear drained her anger. Though rebellion against leaving Hundred Oaks still simmered inside her, she realized she had a duty she couldn't escape. Sally, though warmhearted, was flighty and couldn't be depended on.

Julia leaned over and put her arms around her mother's stiff figure, hugging her almost compulsively. "Mama, I'm sure you'll get well soon. Of course I'll help you all I can."

Mary returned the embrace. "Yes, I know you will." Tears filled the pale eyes as she held Julia close. When she released her daughter, her face was calmer. "Go on, now. I'll talk to you later about what we have to do."

Too full of pain to do more than nod, Julia turned and left. Slowly she mounted the stairway and entered her room. From the writing box on the bed she picked up the half-finished letter to Nathan. For a moment resentment engulfed her at having to put her parents' desires before her own. Then guiltily she pushed the thoughts aside, reminding herself of all her father and mother meant to her. She had to go to Brazil; her love for her family as well as her duty to them had trapped her. With a sudden jerk she tore the letter through.

3

Brazil, December 1865

Julia woke to the familiar noises of creaking wood and waves lapping against the hull. Above her, sailors' footsteps mingled with a slap of the deck being swabbed. For a moment the lulling motion of the ship invited her to return to sleep, until her stomach tightened painfully.

Before yesterday morning she had still felt as if she were on a cruise which would end in Charleston harbor, but then the *Columbia* had steamed past Cape Frio, and by evening they had sighted the Organ Mountains. Today they would dock in Rio de Janeiro; Hundred Oaks lay behind them.

She could hear Sally's regular breathing in the bunk below, and across the narrow stateroom Mama still slept. Julia lay awake, stemming the tears which gathered just behind her lids when she thought of her home. No, she scolded herself, I won't give in and hide here.

Quickly she slid from her berth and found one of the two brown cotton dresses she had worn most of the four weeks since sailing from South Carolina. As she brushed her hair, she tried not to worry about Hundred Oaks. At least Papa hadn't found a Southern buyer, and he refused to sell to Yankees. Because he'd never allow the land to be lost to the hated Union government, he'd pay the taxes, and his attorney would act as caretaker for the plantation.

Also, she reminded herself, when I'm twenty-one next August, I'll have the thousand dollars from Great-Uncle Francis and I can go home before anyone buys Hundred Oaks. By then Mama will be settled in and surely feeling well enough that she won't need me. I'll marry Nathan and then I'll remember this trip as just a holiday. Fastening her hair into a coil at her neck, she picked up a shawl, eased the stateroom door shut behind her, and climbed the steep companionway to the main deck.

The conical peaks of the Organ Mountains loomed above her, shrinking the ocean. Steep slopes dropped almost to the water's edge, leaving only a slender strip of white beach along their base.

"By your leave, ma'am." A harried-looking sailor waited behind her. Julia moved out of his way and joined a familiar one-armed figure at the railing.

James was dressed in dark trousers and white shirt with a tan coat, and despite her own feelings about Brazil, she was glad for the animation in his thin face. "James, I see you're happy we've arrived."

"Of course." He kissed her, then gestured excitedly toward a narrow opening between two masses of rock. "The harbor entrance."

A warm breeze pulled at her hair, reminding Julia that south of the equator, summer began in December. She loosened the shawl.

The ship passed a fort, where a green-and-gold Brazilian flag whipped in the breeze, and steamed through the rocky portals. An azure bay stretched ahead like an immense lake, dotted by islands and enclosed by layers of hills in a hundred shades of gray and green. Masts of dozens of ships swayed and dipped, as if nodding to each other, and sailors shouted back and forth in a garbled mixture of languages. The pungent smell of the salt water reminded Julia of seaports in South Carolina.

Along the western side of the bay, the city of Rio de Janeiro spread in a crescent. Church steeples and minaretlike towers mingled with red tiled roofs and balconied houses; palm trees thrust up between the buildings like languid sentinels. James pointed above the city to the sharp peak of Corcovado and the bleak flat-topped rock called Pão de Assucar, Sugarloaf.

The glowing morning soothed Julia. For almost the first time in her life she had not shared her plans with James. Though he knew of her love for Nathan, she'd said nothing to him about her determination to marry soon and use her legacy to return to Hundred Oaks. But, reassured by her secret intentions, she could share his enjoyment today. Suddenly she felt exhilarated, as if she were truly on a holiday. "Oh, James, I can't wait to go ashore and see everything."

James hugged her, his gray eyes alive with pleasure. "I knew once you got here you couldn't resist an adventure—you never could. Just think—it's our new home." Even that phrase hardly bothered Julia now.

A bell clanged, reminding her of the time and that Mama would need help. Reluctantly she turned to go below, not wanting to leave the bustling excitement. James spoke consolingly. "You won't miss anything now. We won't be disembarking until after breakfast."

"Will Papa be meeting us?" She'd hardly seen her father since the day she'd learned of her mother's illness. He'd come to Brazil soon after that, leaving James to complete arrangements at home and accompany the women.

James answered cheerfully, "Yes, Papa will be here, and probably the Langdons too."

Do I want to see the Langdons again? Julia wondered as she descended to her cabin. She still resented Richard Langdon's influence over Papa, and embarrassment made her flush when she thought of all she had told Andrew, but she also remembered his dark good looks and intense blue eyes, looking at her as if there were some special link between them. If I'm honest, she told herself, I have to admit I was attracted to him even though I shouldn't be. She pushed the confusing thought aside as she entered the tiny stateroom.

Two hours later Julia stood by the rail again, this time with Sally and Mama. Behind Mama, Serena hovered, her black face watchful, with her husband, Tobias, nearby. Julia was glad they'd agreed to accompany the Rayfords to Brazil; Mama would like having the familiar English-speaking servants with her.

Julia brushed a strand of soft hair back from her face, now properly shaded by a bonnet, enjoying her lime-green cotton dress with its full skirt, the material so fine it felt almost like silk. The darker green of the lace trim at her neck matched her bonnet, and she knew it complemented her coppery hair.

The *Columbia* maneuvered close to a large stone quay where small tenders, crude sailboats, canoes, and rowboats jostled each other. Shouts of sailors to black men on the dock accompanied the raucous complaints of winches as nets of baggage swung over the side of the ship and were lowered to the wharf.

Sally clutched Julia's arm. "Julia, where is James? When will Uncle William ever get here?"

Julia was annoyed with her cousin's seeming helplessness. If no man were around, she expected Julia to take care of her, and Julia usually did. Sally acted childlike, even though she was eighteen.

Julia answered as patiently as she could. "James is making sure our luggage is unloaded, and Papa will be here soon." She turned back to watching the dock, where gaudily dressed women and men exchanged fervent embraces. In the brilliant sunlight, crimson hats and orange shawls that should have clashed seemed appropriate, extensions of the scarlet poinsettias and blue and yellow begonias beside the buildings along the shore.

"Mama," James said behind them, "Papa's coming."

Julia looked toward her brother's pointing finger and saw her father's white-suited figure, followed by two black-haired men, also in light suits. As she recognized Andrew and his father, her heartbeat accelerated.

The three men pushed their way through the crowd on the dock, and Julia could see her father's broad smile and vigorously waving arm. She stood on tiptoe, gesturing wildly in return. Next to her, Mama's gloved hands clutched the rail, and Julia could see that Mama's pale face had regained some of its old color. Gleefully she hugged her mother.

William left the other two men and bounded up the swaying gangplank, embracing first Mama, then Julia and Sally, as boisterous in his greetings as the Brazilians around them. The familiar voice and hug filled Julia with joy. After William greeted Serena and Tobias, they all descended the unsteady ramp to the dock.

"Welcome to Brazil, Miss Rayford." Richard Langdon's polite smile concealed any genuine emotion as he bowed to Julia.

"Thank you, Mr. Langdon." At her cool voice, his usually impassive eyes looked momentarily irritated before he turned to Sally.

"May I add my greetings?" Julia looked up into Andrew's face, where his eyes, so like his father's in color, smiled with obvious warmth. A strange combination of both heat and cold began in her stomach and spread up into her chest. "I think you'll find Brazil even lovelier than you expected," he continued.

Before she could decide whether he was teasing, he took her hand, his touch turning her chill to flame. Hoping that her face did not betray her agitation, she pulled her hand away. Her voice at least was steady as she replied, "You may be correct, Mr. Langdon, especially since I do not expect much."

He laughed. "You're determined not to like us. We'll see. May I escort you to your carriage?" The others had already started along the dock. Without waiting for her reply, Andrew took her arm and they headed toward the end of the stone quay.

As they walked, Julia realized that Andrew's height, several inches over six feet, made her own five feet, nine inches seem small. Being as tall as most men often gave her a comfortable feeling, and she wasn't sure she liked the sensation of vulnerability with Andrew. But she did appreciate his strength as he made a way for her among the crowds of blacks unloading cargo.

When they reached the carriage, Andrew handed her up. Good-byes were said, and the Langdons and James left with Tobias to pick up luggage from the customs-house. When the carriage moved off on its way to their hotel, Julia realized Andrew had said nothing about seeing them again. Irritated with herself for noticing his omission, she concentrated on the sights around her.

The area near the docks looked dirty and disorderly. A gutter ran down the middle of the narrow street; from the odious smell it obviously contained human waste. Farther away from the port the streets were wider and well-paved, and the scent of tropical flowers drifted on the air. Buildings had an appealing picturesque quality, with orange, pink, yellow, and even turqoise walls interspersed among the more usual white. Balconied windows jutted out into the street, and women leaned on the sills, calling back and forth like brilliantly plumed birds chattering between sunlit cages.

Half-naked black men, as straight and firm as bronze statues, carried heavy loads securely on their heads. Mules laden with baskets of fruit and vegetables reminded Julia of Violet. Two padres dressed in long brown cassocks and square hats passed by. On a curbstone a black woman sat, her tattered clothing barely covering her glossy skin, a naked child asleep across her knees. By the time they reached the wrought-iron gates in front of the hotel, Julia felt as if the ride had lasted hours, so strange and congested did the city seem.

The carriage turned into a curving driveway and stopped in front of a white stucco building surrounded by trees with large deep-colored oranges nestling among glossy green leaves. From behind the two-story hotel she heard a gentle pulse as the ocean worried the pale sand. Suddenly the alien sights and sounds brought a bitter ache to Julia's throat. Hundred Oaks seemed impossibly far away.

For the next three days Julia spent most of her time watching the waves of the bay spend themselves on the shore. By the third morning she was irritable from the inactivity she hated. So far she'd seen no more of Rio than the immediate area of the hotel and the Larangeiras road, the "orangery," where Mama took her daily drive. Purple or orange bougainvillea climbed the white walls that surrounded houses along the road, and an occa-

sional wide gate gave glimpses of people sitting in the
gardens with children playing near black nurses.

These vignettes only tantalized Julia, making her even
more restless. Since the hotel catered to English-speaking
guests, almost no Brazilians came there, and the daily
Portuguese lessons took barely an hour. She had dragged
her cousin out for walks along the beach until Sally, in
unusual rebellion, had refused to go again. Each day
James and Papa rode into the main section of the city,
but they had claimed the need to take care of "business" when Julia pressed to go with them.

She scuffed at the sand, kicking up a shower of glistening granules. Tomorrow night they were all to attend a musical evening at the palace of Emperor Dom
Pedro, an honor that Richard Langdon had arranged.
Sally was wild with excitement and had spent most of
the last two days debating what to wear. Julia welcomed the prospect of meeting the emperor, but most
of all she wanted to get out and see more of Rio.

Since their arrival, Richard Langdon had not reappeared, nor had Andrew come to see them. Julia disliked herself for feeling disappointed. Instead of a tall
black-haired man, she concentrated on picturing brown
hair over a loving face, the youthful eyes filled with
sadness, as Nathan had looked the day Julia left Philadelphia in 1861. That was more than four years ago, but
she still loved him, her feelings strengthened by his
letters.

Though he had never specifically written about marriage, his words had done everything but say directly
that he loved her. Phrases from those wartime letters,
cherished and memorized, comforted her. "You keep
me company on lonely nights . . . only the image of
your face drove away my despair . . . I know you understand what was in my heart. . . ." And in the very

last note, telling her of his safe arrival home, he'd written, "I'm impatient to get settled here so that I'm free to say to you what I've dreamed of so long." In the glow of her memories she could assure herself that she thought about Andrew only because she was restless and bored.

As she turned back toward the hotel, she saw James standing on the hotel terrace. It was barely noon, but since he was back now, perhaps he would take her somewhere. Anywhere! Lifting her long skirts, she ran toward him.

The open carriage rocked on the rough paving of a street near the center of Rio. It had taken only a few minutes for Julia to tell Mama she was going with James and to change to a coral-and-green flowered dress with the parasol, bonnet, and gloves her mother insisted on. Sally had preferred to wait for the hotel seamstress to alter a dress for tomorrow's evening at the palace. But at last Julia and James were away, with a black Brazilian driver, who spoke a little broken English.

During these days when James had been with Papa, she'd missed seeing her brother. She felt a flash of envy that he was included in business affairs when she, who had run Hundred Oaks for two years, had to remain behind with Mama and Sally, but the freedom of being out was too delicious to spoil. She put her hand on his arm. "Tell me what you and Papa have learned about plantations here."

"Opportunities for cotton planting are superb!" James responded enthusiastically. "The land that Papa purchased near São Paulo can raise fine cotton as well as coffee and tobacco. Sugar too."

Julia listened eagerly as James discussed details of markets and shipping. She hoped that the plantation, or *fazenda* as it was known here, would prosper—both for her family's sake and so there'd be less opposition to keeping Hundred Oaks.

The carriage came to a large open market with rows of stands tended by blacks. Some tables were covered with oranges, bananas, and guavas, while others held orchids, which ranged from ivory and pale lavender to deep purple, as well as brilliant blossoms Julia didn't recognize. She was fascinated by the costumes of the women. Most wore high muslin turbans and had long bright-colored shawls draped across their chests and shoulders.

"James," Julia said, "let's stop here and walk around the market. We could get Mama some fruit or flowers." When James looked doubtful, she added, "And Sally would like one of those bracelets." She pointed to a display of jewelry made from bright-colored beads.

The carriage stopped, and Julia stepped down before her brother could help her. Much as she loved him, sometimes his adherence to all the rules of conventional behavior made her impatient. She did wait to take his arm as they walked through the narrow aisles between the stands. Around them men and women strolled and chattered, their Portuguese beginning to sound familiar.

As James paused before the array of bracelets, Julia noticed a nearby flower display and then a man's head, towering over the people around him. She recognized the angular face under the thick curling black hair and felt a sudden rush of blood which made her pulse beat faster. "James"—she nudged his arm—"there's Andrew Langdon."

James turned and his gray eyes showed surprised pleasure. "It *is* Andrew! I haven't seen him since we arrived." He started in Andrew's direction, then suddenly stopped.

The crowd parted, and they could see Andrew was not alone. A woman stood beside him, her gloved hand resting on his arm. He had on a cream linen suit of the sort many Brazilians wore during the warm weather, but the woman's dress could have come from South Carolina, with its tight waist and full skirt with lace-trimmed top. However, the vivid colors, turquoise with orange braid, looked Brazilian, and her face, smiling at Andrew, had velvety dark skin and sultry black eyes.

James stiffened, starting to pull his sister back; at the same time Andrew turned and looked directly at Julia and James. The woman with him turned also, and they faced each other.

For a moment Julia felt a pain she could not identify; she only knew she wanted to retreat from the handsome couple before her. Instead, she moved forward, smiling politely. "Mr. Langdon, how remarkable to run across someone we know in a city this large."

He hesitated; then he slipped his arm from his companion's grasp and took a step so that he was slightly in front of her. When he spoke, he sounded completely at ease. "Miss Rayford and James, it's a most pleasurable coincidence." He bowed briefly to Julia, then nodded to James, who returned the nod stiffly.

Julia scarcely followed the pleasantries the two men exchanged. Though she kept from staring, all her attention was on Andrew's companion. She looked perhaps twenty years old, and had a striking dark beauty. Midnight-black hair peeked around the edge of her bonnet.

Andrew's voice reclaimed Julia. "I look forward to seeing you again." A warm smile accompanied the words, one that softened the angular lines of his face but did not quite explain the amused look in his eyes.

"Yes, of course." Julia felt James pulling on her arm,

but she deliberately included the dark woman behind Andrew in a smiling good-bye. She saw a flash of surprise on Andrew's face as she gave in to James's grasp and went with him back to the carriage.

"Julia!" James almost shoved her into the vehicle, his glowering face matching his voice as he followed her and waved the driver to go on. "What were you thinking of, speaking to Andrew under those circumstances?"

Julia's anger rose to meet James's. "And what circumstances are you talking about? That Andrew Langdon didn't introduce us to his friend? How was I to know he wouldn't?"

"You know very well why he didn't," her twin hissed. "You're not so naive as that. You shouldn't have spoken to him at all when you saw him with his . . . with her."

"With his mistress. Is that what you were going to say?" Even as she heard her defiant tone, Julia knew what was upsetting her; she was jealous of the beautiful woman with Andrew. The realization appalled her.

"Julia!" James's voice was shocked. "You mustn't say such things."

It was a relief to vent her feelings on James. "You're being ridiculous. Am I supposed to pretend that I don't know that mistresses exist? Just as we were to pretend that Andrew either was alone or not there at all?"

"You shouldn't talk about . . . about arrangements that men occasionally make," James reprimanded angrily. "And yes, pretending we didn't see Andrew is exactly what we should have done. You would understand that if you weren't so impulsive."

"And you think I should also refuse to notice she's a mulatto?" Julia continued defiantly.

"Keep your voice down. We won't discuss this." James reached forward and tapped the driver. "Return to the hotel."

Julia hardly looked at the scenery as the carriage retraced the route she had enjoyed only a short time ago. Could she really be jealous of a woman with Andrew Langdon? No, it must be some other emotion. She hated to quarrel with her brother, and the outing was ruined. Surely that was why she felt so miserable.

Carefully lifting the front of her hooped silk skirt just enough to avoid tripping, Julia followed her parents up the curving steps that led to the palace reception hall. Sally and James followed behind her. Inside, hundreds of candles in wall sconces multiplied their glow in the polished marble walls of a high-ceilinged room. Green-and-gold crossed flags hung below the candles; their colors were repeated in green velvet draperies and table covers with gold fringes. Clustered in groups around the room, men in dark suits and officers in bright blue uniforms lavishly trimmed with gold braid chatted with women in formal gowns of brilliant silks and satins. On the far side of the hall an archway showed a smaller room with rows of empty chairs.

Richard Langdon, his bearded face carefully welcoming, was walking purposefully toward them, and William and Mary stopped to greet him. As Julia stood beside James and Sally, she looked curiously at the animated faces, many with black hair and eyes, but a surprising number with fair coloring she hadn't expected. A general air of waiting suggested that the emperor and empress had not arrived.

Across the room another tall figure was moving toward them. As Julia recognized the confident stride and easy grace, she felt her face begin to warm. Hastily she looked away, trying, but not quite successfully, to erase the discomfort she felt at remembering their meeting yesterday. What must Andrew be thinking of her today after the way she had so boldly spoken to him, and nodded to his mistress?

Andrew had noticed how Julia's glance skittered away from him. He hadn't planned to attend the emperor's musical evening, but after the encounter with Julia and her brother yesterday, he'd been curious to see them again. Now, watching them, he remembered with amusement James's obvious distress at his sister's unconventional behavior. Of course he wouldn't introduce Lele to the Rayfords, but Julia's conduct intrigued him. He wasn't sure if she were bold or naive. It reminded him of the confrontation with her as he left Hundred Oaks. Maybe red hair did mean a volatile temperament, he thought, if Julia could be used as evidence.

As he made his way through the crowd, he decided James must like Sally's dainty white dress and blond hair, but he much preferred Julia's dramatic coloring and the exciting way her russet silk gown outlined her slender waist and small but womanly breasts. Her erect carriage and the glowing hair piled on top of her head, with only a few curls beside her face, made her look as if she should be wearing a royal crown. How would she greet him this evening? He'd enjoy finding out.

When he reached the Rayfords, he bowed to Mary and kissed her hand. "Mrs. Rayford, I am delighted to see you again." He nodded to William. "Mr. Rayford."

Mary's face looked pale, the skin tight over her cheekbones, but she smiled warmly. "Andrew, how pleasant to find you here."

He turned to find Julia's sherry-colored eyes on him. He'd forgotten until he saw her again how beautiful she was. Although she appeared composed, he saw a faint pink color rise in her face. So, yesterday's meeting must have embarrassed her after all—or else James had scolded her thoroughly. Probably both, Andrew guessed, seeing James's somewhat strained smile.

He extended his hand to the younger man. "James, I'm sorry we haven't had an opportunity to talk together, but I think we can remedy that soon. Miss Rayford, Miss King . . . I hope Rio has welcomed you properly."

James's face relaxed a little. "Yes, we must see each other before we leave next week for São Paulo."

At James's almost casual announcement, Julia felt first shock and then an envy so intense it was almost a physical pain. Apparently her family's departure for São Paulo was settled, but nothing had been said to her or Sally, and perhaps not to Mama either. Yet only six months ago Papa had been conferring with Julia, depending on her for the daily management of Hundred Oaks.

She looked away from James, and found Andrew watching her. To her mortification she could feel a blush in her face again. She stared back at him defiantly. Women were supposed to lower their eyes, to be modest, but at this moment she didn't want to be womanly. If he laughs, she thought furiously, I'll kick him! But his deep blue eyes looked questioning rather than amused.

A bustle at the doorway distracted her and she turned to see a man and woman entering. No particular fanfare announced them, but women all around Julia dipped in low curtsies and men bowed. The couple must be the Emperor Dom Pedro II and his wife, the Empress Tereza.

Julia had never before seen anyone who held the title of emperor, and she had not known what to expect. He was as tall as Andrew, with blond hair and eyes that even from a distance looked bright blue. His hair had receded slightly, giving him an appropriately majestic forehead. A bushy blond beard covered much of the lower part of his face, but his mouth and smile looked gentle. She remembered that his fortieth birthday had been celebrated just a week before.

The Empress Tereza was a short, stout woman with none of her husband's attractiveness. As she moved forward on Dom Pedro's arm, Julia saw that she walked with an ungainly limp. She looked older than her husband.

The contrast in the couple's style of dress surprised Julia. Dom Pedro had on a simple black suit, more appropriate for a businessman, but his wife, despite her bulky figure, wore an elaborate wine-colored silk dress with a glittering collar of diamonds and a jewel-encrusted tiara.

The emperor spoke courteously but gravely to people near him. When the empress smiled, her plain face became gracious and animated, and the answering smiles from the Brazilians around her appeared to express real affection.

Richard Langdon approached the emperor and bowed, then turned back toward the Rayfords. "Your Majesty, I would like to present Mr. and Mrs. William Rayford and their family, Mr. James Rayford, Miss Julia Rayford, and Miss Sally King. They have come from the United States to live in Brazil."

Dom Pedro inclined his head and spoke in faultless English. "Welcome to Brazil. Mr. Langdon has spoken of you and the contribution you can make to the prosperity of our country."

As she joined her mother and Sally in a low curtsy, Julia heard Papa say, "I thank you for your most gracious welcome and assure you of my intention to do all I can to merit it."

She turned to follow the crowd moving behind Dom Pedro and Dona Tereza and found Andrew at her side. "May I have the pleasure of escorting you?"

She hesitated. A picture came to her mind of Andrew and the beautiful dark woman who was his mistress, but Julia banished the ridiculous feelings that seemed like jealousy. Andrew meant nothing to her, so she had no reason to behave differently to him than to any other man she knew casually.

"Yes, thank you, Mr. Langdon." She smiled and put her hand on the arm extended to her. Like most of the other men there, Andrew wore a lightweight suit with frock coat rather than the more formal knee breeches and boots. She supposed that was in deference to Dom Pedro's conservative taste in clothing. Under the navy-blue cloth of his jacket his arm felt hard and muscular, and as the heat from his arm warmed her hand, a shiver of excitement surprised her.

"Please, could you call me Andrew?" His eyes sparkled at her as he added, "I think you know me well enough."

Julia decided to ignore the possibility that his words had a double meaning. She hadn't known him the socially prescribed time to use first names, but she disliked the coy pretenses of South Carolina society. Besides, this was Brazil. "Yes, of course, Andrew, and please call me Julia."

They followed her family and his father to one of the rows of chairs with graceful bentwood backs and cane seats; Julia sat between James and Andrew and looked around curiously. Wine velvet draperies hung beside double windows which led outside to a moonlit terrace. On a raised platform at the front of the large room was a small piano; beside it several musicians in formal evening wear were tuning their instruments—a violin, a cello, and a flute. Julia felt disappointed; she'd hoped for more exotic sounds.

At a nod from the emperor, the musicians began, playing several familiar selections by Mozart and Vivaldi. Then the cellist, a slight white-haired man, took from behind him a five-stringed instrument which looked a little like a banjo, and the pianist, a very dark-skinned young man, produced a small drum. He began to play, an irregular syncopated rhythm, and was joined by the older man, strumming a plaintive melody. Julia felt caught up, her heartbeats paced by the players, as the violinist briefly joined in and the music accelerated to a crescendo. Applause, led enthusiastically by the emperor, filled the room.

Julia had to wait a moment to catch her breath before turning to Andrew. "What was that music?"

"Adaptations of some native songs, favorites of the emperor. You liked them?"

"Oh, yes," Julia responded, still feeling the intoxicating rhythms.

The air was warm with the effects of the many candles in the crowded room. As they stood to return to the reception hall for refreshments, Julia patted her moist forehead with her handkerchief. In the moving crowd, she and Andrew were separated from James and Sally.

The tables now held decanters of red wine and amber brandy beside platters of small cakes and bowls of purple grapes. A short black man in green-and-gold livery offered glasses of sparkling pale wine which Andrew took for himself and Julia, but she shook her head to a plate of sugar-dusted cakes.

"Would you like to look at the official portraits?" Andrew motioned toward the far end of the room.

"They're in a corridor where the air may be a little cooler."

Julia hesitated; if Brazil was the same as South Carolina, she should stay near her family, but the desire to see more of Dom Pedro's palace won over propriety. A servant took their wineglasses, and Andrew's hand under her elbow guided her across the crowded marble floors to the hall. Recessed windows, open to the moonlit air, faced a row of full-length pictures illuminated by candles positioned around the frames.

Only four other people were in the corridor, two young men in military uniforms, a bald-headed man who was talking in a low voice, and a young woman who giggled playfully every few moments. The group moved along the hall, paying no attention to Andrew and Julia, and she felt almost as if they were alone. Momentarily she wished she could ask him about their meeting the previous day, but she didn't need James to tell her she mustn't. Instead she concentrated her attention on the portraits.

The first was obviously Dom Pedro II, without a crown, but holding a tall scepter in his right hand. Over a lace-trimmed white shirt and form-fitting breeches a belt held an elaborately decorated sword. A large ermine cloak billowed from beneath a short embroidered cape. The emperor appeared majestic and very serious, almost sad.

"The emperor is very handsome," Julia commented. "He was gracious to welcome us in English."

"Dom Pedro speaks nine languages fluently and reads and writes fourteen," Andrew responded.

"How extraordinary," Julia said admiringly. "And I protested at having to learn Latin and French in school."

Andrew laughed, but from the admiring look in his eyes as he watched her, Julia decided that his mind was not on the emperor. She was both pleased by his attention and annoyed with herself for feeling that way. Hastily she continued, "Does his wife speak English also?"

"The empress, like the proper wife she is, seldom speaks at all when her husband is present."

Julia would have liked to challenge him about what he thought a proper wife would be, but considering the almost caressing way he was still looking at her, she decided to be more discreet. "Was it an arranged marriage?"

Andrew's eyes crinkled in a teasing smile. "Are you a romantic, Julia? If so, you might have much in common with the emperor. A story says he had thought his wife-to-be pretty from the picture shown to him by his ministers and looked forward eagerly to her arrival from Sicily. When he met her on board a ship in the harbor, he was very disappointed. He was only seventeen at the time and wanted to break off the match, but his ministers said that would cause international complications. So they married."

Julia felt sorry for the handsome monarch and his too plain wife. The empress couldn't help her appearance and must have been bitterly hurt at his reaction. "Then they have been unhappy?"

Andrew laughed again, this time almost boyishly. "You're indeed sentimental, Julia. Not all arranged marriages lack romance. At first, it's said, he didn't love his wife, but he had his father's example to warn him. So he persisted and now prizes her virtues as a devoted wife and mother—and one who does not meddle in politics and other activities unsuited for women."

Julia's back stiffened. He sounded as if he were mocking her interest in managing Hundred Oaks, but, still determined to be polite, she ignored his last remark. "What did you mean about his father's example?"

"Come see." Andrew took her arm, and they moved to the next portrait, which showed a handsome man in full military uniform. Above the medal-covered chest, intense dark eyes and a narrow mustache gave a wicked cast to a rakish face. "The first Dom Pedro also had an arranged marriage," Andrew continued, "but he found his consolations in different ways. Or I should say, in many different ladies."

Julia knew she shouldn't listen to such talk from a man, but she'd already practiced all the restraint she could muster. The corridor, lit only by candles and moonlight slanting through the open windows, seemed like a room in a dream where nothing really counted. The other people had disappeared, and this man in this unfamiliar and exotic setting made ordinary rules less important. Recklessly she questioned, "Do Brazilians take after the present emperor, or do they imitate his father?"

Andrew moved closer and lightly ran one finger along her bare arm. A hot spark followed his touch. She started to step back, but he took her shoulder and pulled her into one of the recessed window enclosures.

His voice was soft, almost tender, as with one hand he gently touched the side of her face. "I can't tell you what most Brazilians do, but if you were the consolation, I'm sure any man would choose the way of Dom Pedro I."

Julia felt a shiver begin in her stomach and spread into her chest. The shadowed face moving closer seemed to mesmerize her until she could see only the mouth above hers. Then she felt his warm lips, sending a tremor arching down to meet the constriction in her throat. She moved her lips against his, feeling heat building in her body, savoring the excitement of his kiss.

Her senses whirled, then slowed as sanity returned. Yesterday she had seen this man with his mistress, and now she was letting him kiss her! She pushed violently against his chest, breaking the spell. He let go of her, and she took a long breath, hoping he would not hear from her voice how shaky she felt inside. "Mr. Langdon. You presume too much."

He made no effort to touch her again, but his eyes, warm and inviting, held hers, and his voice caressed her. "Must we go back to formalities?" When she took another backward step, the warmth changed to mocking amusement. "Do you want me to think you're surprised I kissed you? Hadn't you already decided I'm not a gentleman?"

Resentment toward his confident manner mixed with dismay at her own behavior. Julia whirled and started along the hall, when he called softly after her, "You don't wish to rush back alone, do you, Julia? How would that look—to return without your escort?"

Why hadn't she slapped his face! Without looking back, she spit words over her shoulder, "Anyone who noticed would think I had finally used good judgment." His laugh followed her.

Quickly she slipped inside the main reception room and looked around. Her parents were not there, but near the end of a long table she saw James and Sally. Taking a steadying breath, she walked unhurriedly through the thinning crowd, pausing to let a small man, whose uniform had so much braid it looked as if he would topple over, escort an extremely fat woman toward the door.

When she reached James, he turned and frowned impatiently. "Julia, I've been looking for you. Mama is

very tired, and we must leave." The frown depeened.
"Where have you been?"

Julia ignored his question. "I'm sorry to delay you.
Shall we find Mama? Do we say good night to the
emperor?"

"No. Dom Pedro and Dona Tereza have left." He
took Sally's arm, and Julia followed them across the
high-ceilinged room. When they arrived at the entrance, her mother and father were outside, with Andrew beside them. For a moment Julia hesitated, then
continued on to join her parents.

Mary smiled happily, her face tired but animated.
"Julia, I have told Andrew how confined you and Sally
have been with me and how much you want to see Rio.
He has offered to take you all on a sightseeing expedition around the city tomorrow."

Julia felt dismayed. She had no way to explain a
refusal when she had complained about not having a
chance to do just what Andrew was suggesting. As she
looked at him she could tell from his expression that he
guessed what she was thinking. Suppressing the temper
that threatened to destroy the manners her mother
expected, Julia spoke as pleasantly as she could. "Yes,
of course, Mama. That will be delightful, Mr. Langdon."
She forced her mouth to smile at Andrew, but hoped
her eyes sent a different message.

4

The morning after the emperor's reception Andrew woke to the delicious feel of a tongue circling his left nipple and a hand caressing his penis. Fire arched from his hardening shaft up through his belly. As he opened his eyes, a cascade of silky black hair spilled across his face.

Lele raised her head, her obsidian eyes glowing with passion, and he lifted her over him and positioned her for his thrust. Within minutes she cried his name and he exploded into her dark warmth. When his heartbeat slowed, he pulled her to his side and slept again.

Several hours later a cup with the last of his breakfast coffee sat on the marble-topped dresser. He straightened a narrow bow tie around the high collar of his shirt and checked his black hair in the mirror, where he could also see the reflection of Lele's pouting face.

"Mas, Andre, quero ir—"

So she wanted to go with him. The brandy he'd drunk after the reception had left him with a faint headache, and despite the pleasurable awakening, he was not in a patient mood. "In English, Lele."

She stamped her foot, the pout now a scowl. *"Não."*

He picked up a broad-brimmed straw hat. "You'll

never learn English, Lele, if you don't try to speak it."
She'd asked him to teach her his language, but she was
lazy and didn't want to make the effort. This morning
he wondered why he bothered, because even if she
repeated her request in English, he wouldn't be taking
her out today. Slipping his hand inside the front of her
ruffled muslin robe to caress her breast, he kissed her
lightly and then turned toward the door.

She grabbed at his arm, her voice taking on a faint
whine. "*Onde . . .*" She stopped, then resumed in barely
recognizable English, "Where you going?"

Andrew frowned; he should probably have left her in
São Paulo, where she had activities to fill her time
when he couldn't see her. She'd begged to come with
him, but he disliked the demands for his constant attention. One of the sugar planters he knew liked to say
that white women were for marriage, Negro women for
work, and mulatto women for fucking. Lele certainly fit
her role.

Shaking off her hand, he went out through the small
enclosed garden of the house he had rented for the
three weeks in Rio. Life might be less complicated if
there were a woman who could fill all three roles, but
he'd never wished for a simple life.

As he waited for his manservant to bring around the
hired carriage, he thought of the impulse which had led
to the outing today. Something about Julia Rayford
invited challenge. He grinned, remembering the look
she'd given him last night after she'd had to agree with
her mother's acceptance. When he'd met her in South
Carolina, her interest in history and politics had surprised him, and for a moment he wondered if she might
be a woman who would fit all three of the sugar planter's categories for women. The way she'd returned his
kiss last night, without all the preliminary courting

most *gentle* women required, suggested she could be a passionate lover.

The carriage arrived and he swung up and took the reins. Despite her occasional whining, Lele suited him very well. He had blacks of all kinds to work on the *fazenda*, and he didn't want a wife.

Julia settled her muslin petticoat over the stiff crinoline, pulled on a striped white-and-lime-green skirt, and buttoned a matching top that fit snugly over her breasts and waist, flaring just above the skirt. In the humid morning the high neckline even of the light cotton already felt warm, but the whalebone cage let air circulate around her pantalets.

The shy Brazilian hotel maid had finished combing Sally's blond curls, and Julia sat on the carved wooden bench before the dressing table, pleased that she had learned enough Portuguese to supplement the black girl's English. She watched in the mirror as slender fingers arranged her burnished tresses in a coil at the back of her neck.

She looked at her reflected mouth and thought again of Andrew. How could she have let him kiss her, and even worse, responded to him so shamefully? No one had ever kissed her quite like that, his mouth open, his tongue touching her lips. Was she fickle, or even wanton, attracted so easily to a man she hardly knew, one with a mistress he flaunted? No, perhaps that wasn't fair; he couldn't have known he would see James and her that afternoon.

But she couldn't excuse her own behavior—kissing one man when she loved another. And she did love Nathan, would love him for his idealism and dedication, even if he didn't represent her chance to go home to Hundred Oaks. As soon as she returned from the sightseeing trip, she'd write to him again.

A knock at the door preceded James's voice. "Sally, Julia—Andrew is here."

She perched a small green hat swathed in delicate veiling on top of her hair and picked up a matching parasol.

"Julia," Sally disapproved, "you'll spoil your skin without a bonnet."

Forcing gloves over her damp hands, Julia replied impatiently, "You know I don't even freckle, so please don't scold me." She opened the door and smiled at James, then left him to wait for Sally.

In the sitting room of her parents' suite, Andrew greeted Julia with a completely correct bow, nothing about his manner suggesting they'd shared a kiss the previous night. His cream-colored suit appeared to be of a thin material which moved easily with his body, emphasizing the muscles of his shoulders and chest and the smooth movements of his thighs. For a moment her breath seemed to catch in her chest, but she forced herself to nod calmly, determined to maintain her composure. She kissed her mother farewell and accepted Andrew's offered arm.

Outside, Andrew handed Julia into the carriage, but he didn't release her hand immediately. He spoke so softly that James and Sally, just behind them, couldn't hear. "Will you renew your permission for me to call you by your first name?" His blue eyes suggested a secret amusement that only the two of them understood. "I promise to be a gentleman, Julia."

Reluctantly she felt drawn to the shared warmth, and though she intended to sound aloof, his beguiling eyes coaxed her into responding in a teasing tone. "You don't fear that such a restriction will put too much strain on your nature?"

He laughed as he swung up beside her and took the

reins. "That is something you may discover during our day of exploring Rio."

Behind them James settled Sally. With a flick of Andrew's strong wrists, the carriage moved away.

As morning became afternoon, Julia found the handsome man beside her a charming and interesting guide. He took them past magnificent public buildings and through areas where markets and small shops crowded together. Julia enjoyed watching the people on the streets and hearing Andrew's occasional wry comments. She noticed one black woman dressed in white, with bare neck and arms, her sleeves caught up with some kind of armlet. A large white turban covered her head, and a long saffron-yellow shawl passed crosswise under one arm and over the other shoulder, hanging almost to her feet in back. Behind her walked a simply dressed girl carrying a bulky bundle and holding a parasol over the older woman's head. Julia touched Andrew's arm. "The woman and girl—is the girl a slave?"

He looked and nodded. "Probably."

Julia watched as the two entered a small shop. "How do you suppose the mistress feels? I used to wonder why some of the free blacks at home owned other blacks."

Andrew's dry tone suggested her question was unsophisticated. "They probably have slaves for the same reason white people do." She wasn't sure she agreed with him, but it would be ungracious to argue about slavery with him today.

In another street she saw a tall black woman who seemed to be in a great passion. Gesturing violently, she flung her shawl wide, throwing out both arms, then drew it suddenly in and folded it about her. Opening it once more, she shook her fist in the face of another similarly clad woman.

As the carriage moved slowly on, Andrew grinned
and nodded admiringly toward the quarreling women.
"The very tall blacks are from Mina in West Africa.
They're Muhammadans, and they seem very spirited."
Did he value similar feelings in all women? Julia won-
dered. Was his beautiful mulatto mistress "spirited"?

Along the residential streets she was startled to hear
the sounds of pianos everywhere, some harsh and dis-
cordant, others clear and melodic. Her face must have
shown her surprise, because Andrew lifted a questioning eyebrow. "You didn't expect to encounter this kind
of 'culture' here? We Brazilians love music."

"I didn't realize you think of yourself as a Brazilian,
Mr. Lang . . . Andrew."

He glanced at her in the laughing way she was beginning to find familiar. "Certainly—at least when I'm
playing my piano."

The image of him seated before a piano was appealing, and as the swaying carriage moved on, she realized
that she was seeing sides of Andrew she wouldn't have
guessed. His admiration for Brazil had been obvious all
along, but some of his interests surprised her. Did she
want to know him better? Part of her nature said yes,
while the other—she hoped her more rational side—
said no.

Julia stood with James beside the stone wall that
rimmed the mountain peak called Corcovado. Over two
thousand feet below, Rio de Janeiro and the waters of
the South Atlantic locked in a convoluted embrace, separated by a chaste line of white foam. From this height
she could look down on the immense harbor with its
many islands and then up at the circle of mountains
where shy clouds leaned softly against the nearer peaks.

An impertinent wind pulled loose a silky strand of

hair from under her hat and whipped it across her face.
She reached for her brother's arm and held it companionably, letting him shelter her from the strongest gusts.

The carriage had been left at the terminus of the
Larangeiras road, and they had transferred to horses for
the ascent by a winding narrow path which led through
a fragrant forest, passing occasional brooks or small cas-
cades. Though she silently groaned at the sidesaddles
provided for "ladies," Julia welcomed the exercise. She
loved the way the wind rustled the stiff palm leaves and
shook the silvery foliage of the giant candelabra trees.
The path steepened sharply at a little station called the
Paineiras, and they dismounted there. Sally had refused to walk the fifteen minutes to the top, so Andrew
remained below with her while James and Julia climbed
the last steep ascent.

She hadn't liked leaving Sally and Andrew behind,
even though they had plenty of company from other
travelers resting at the station. Fleetingly she wondered if she were jealous, then dismissed the idea. It
was Sally's behavior that worried Julia, indeed had concerned her increasingly over the last few months.

James had been so busy before they left South Carolina that he'd spent little time with Sally and hadn't
seen, as Julia had, how Sally flirted with men who came
to Hundred Oaks. Julia felt sure that Sally meant no
harm; the younger girl loved admiration and was impulsive and thoughtless. Once when Julia had warned her
cousin about speaking to a visiting neighbor more frequently than she should, Sally had been immediately
contrite, but soon she was carelessly seeking attention
from another man. Both Sally and James were young,
but they had been betrothed for three years, and she
needed the security of marriage.

Julia touched her brother's hand with a loving caress.

"James, do you think we should rejoin Sally and Andrew now?"

He turned and smiled at her. "Yes, if you wish, but I hate to leave this place. It's so beautiful. And right now we have it all to ourselves."

They walked slowly toward the path. Julia hesitated, then decided she must ask about his plans. "When do you think you and Sally will marry?"

James stopped; under his wind-ruffled blond hair the lines of his thin face deepened, giving him the haunted look Julia had seen when he first returned home from the war. "I don't know—we need to get settled here first."

She turned him to face her. "I think you shouldn't wait longer. Sally needs to take her place as your wife, and she deserves it also." Julia didn't feel as sure as she wished that Sally did deserve to be James's wife, but loyalty to him didn't let her voice the thought.

His response was strained, his gray eyes anguished. "But, Julia, I can't marry Sally until I'm sure that I can manage a man's work with only one arm."

Surprise left Julia momentarily wordless; then compassion for her twin filled her as she protested, "You've taken care of everything you needed to do since you recovered your strength."

He looked away from her before he spoke, his voice so soft she could barely hear. "Sally loves beautiful things, Julia. How will she feel when she sees . . ."

Julia's eyes filled with tears as she put her arms around her twin and held him close to her. "Oh, James, she loves you. However you look, she'll think you're handsome."

He returned her embrace and they stood, getting warmth and strength from each other until he pulled away and laughed shakily "Come. Sally and Andrew will be sure we've fallen over the precipice."

Her heart full of the tears she hadn't shed, Julia almost clung to James's hand as they went down the steep path. She knew how hard it must have been for him to speak of his fears, even to her, for it showed the intensity of his pain. But she would help Sally, Julia resolved fiercely; nothing must hurt her brother that she could prevent.

When they reached the Paineiras, Sally and Andrew were sitting well apart on a bench. Sally greeted James animatedly, but Julia thought Andrew's eyes looked a little glazed, and he left abruptly to get their horses. Sally must have talked the whole time, Julia thought with amusement. As the younger girl laughed and chattered with James, Julia relaxed, glad she'd spoken to her brother. All would go well for him—it must.

The ride down the hill seemed short, the singing rivulets and whispering trees left behind too soon. When they reached the carriage, Andrew said they would be going out to a home on a small island in the bay. "It belongs to Baron Saia," Andrew explained as he drove. "The baron is one of the most influential men in Brazil. He's built an enormous fortune through railroads and other business enterprises."

As they neared the dock area, Julia noticed an old wall, several feet wide, covered with vines and overhung with thick foliage, that seemed to be a stand for vendors of fruits and vegetables. A powerful-looking young man lay at full length on top of the wall, looking over into the street. His jet-black arms rested on a huge basket of crimson flowers, oranges, and bananas, but he appeared too indolent to lift a finger to attract a customer.

"There's a man who lives in *carioca* style." Andrew's

voice sounded teasing. "Do you think you could learn
to be a *carioca?*"

Julia was already familiar with the word that meant
the inhabitants of Rio. "If you mean would I like to
while away my days with little to do, my answer is no."

His blue eyes danced at her. "And if I meant, could
you love Rio?"

She responded without hesitation, "It's not home."

"And home is still Hundred Oaks?" A note of sympathy softened his deep voice.

"Yes, and I'm going back."

At his questioning look, she added defensively, "I
have a plan . . ."

A surge of homesickness gripped Julia so acutely that
she couldn't continue, and suddenly the colors around
looked garish, the faces alien. The pretense of a holiday
in Brazil was bitter—she must go home as soon as
possible!

Ahead of them, carts, buggies, and men with mules
tangled in a noisy brawl; the resulting congestion focused Andrew's attention on handling their horses. By
the time the carriage halted at the dock, she had recovered her composure.

A pinnace took them out to the island, where a black
man in loose cotton pants and shirt showed them to a
sprawling house. Julia was surprised to see that the
outside was plain and the adjoining chapel modest, and
she turned questioningly to Andrew. "Did you say the
baron is very wealthy?"

"Yes, but he wasn't always a baron. He says he likes
to remember his humble origins and to live simply, so
the house is large enough for his eleven children, but
not ornate."

The servant ushered them across a shaded veranda
and into a high-ceilinged entry hall, where Julia and

Sally left the men and followed a black woman into a large garden. Coconut and banana trees guarded their fruit beside a path outlined with seashells; passion-vines climbed over a wall, with here and there a dark crimson flower gleaming between the leaves. Marble statuary, mostly of religious subjects, occupied every corner. Beyond the garden in another hall a young girl in a plain blue dress met them.

"I am Flavia," she said in a soft voice with only a trace of accent, "the oldest daughter of our family."

Julia was glad to use English rather than the meager Portuguese she could manage. "I am Julia Rayford and this is my cousin Sally King. We are so grateful for your hospitality."

A shy smile lit Flavia's dark eyes as she motioned toward open double doors farther along the hall. "Please come meet my mother. We will have refreshments before you rest."

Julia and Sally followed Flavia into an airy room with tall windows looking out into the garden. Woven bamboo chairs and settees with colorful cushions were scattered about the room, and at one end a white cloth covered a large round table set with heavy red pottery dishes. This must be the sitting and dining room for the women of the Saia family, Julia realized. She knew from her reading about Brazil that upper-class women were closely guarded by the men of their families; to meet the baroness in her own rooms was a privilege which James and Andrew couldn't share.

Flavia presented the two visitors to a small black-clad woman. Julia curtsied low and said, "*Muito prazer encontrar a senhora*," hoping her words meant they were happy to meet their hostess.

Apparently all was well, because the baroness smiled and responded, "*Muito prazer*." Her plain face with

black hair pulled tightly back into a bun seemed friendly
and welcoming. Flavia then introduced five more daughters and two small boys before the baroness led them
all to the table.

Servants in gray dresses and sparkling white aprons
served platters of oysters, prawns, and crabs. Julia found
she was extremely hungry and enjoyed the seafood and
the thin cakes of manioc or *farinha,* followed by bananas, pineapple, and sweetmeats.

When the meal was over, Julia rose and curtsied to
her hostess in thanks for her hospitality. Then she and
Sally followed Flavia to a bedroom where slatted wooden
shutters darkened the windows but still let air through.
After indicating she would return later, Flavia left them.
As Julia gratefully removed her dress and crinoline, she
felt the air cool her damp skin, and realized how refreshing the Brazilian custom of *sesta* was.

Dusk shrouded the garden as the same silent woman
led Julia and Sally back to the entrance of the Saia
home. It hardly seemed possible to Julia that she had
slept three hours. No wonder *cariocas* seemed indolent, if the climate had this effect.

Just inside the open front door, James and Andrew
were waiting with a small but stiffly erect man in a dark
business suit. Thinning black hair fell over his forehead
and curled over the tops of his ears; heavy eyebrows
and deep lines from his nose to the edges of a thin
mouth gave his face a serious, almost somber look.

Andrew spoke. "Julia and Sally, may I present Senhor Vasconcelos Silvera de Queiroz, Baron Saia. Baron
Saia, Miss Rayford and Miss King."

The baron bowed to Julia and Sally, his brooding
eyes faintly lit by an austere smile. "I hope you find
much pleasure in your new life in Brazil. Thank you for

visitng my home." His English combined Portuguese and British accents. "Mr. Langdon tells me that you are interested in hearing our native music."

Julia realized Andrew must have remembered her enthusiasm for the last pieces at the emperor's concert, and glanced gratefully at him before replying, "Yes, Baron Saia, I would love to hear some Brazilian music."

The baron smiled more warmly and turned to Sally, who spoke in her usual breathless voice. "And I most certainly would also."

He offered an arm to each woman and led them out the door. "I cannot say that what you will hear is Brazilian. The slave trade was abolished fifteen years ago, so most of our blacks were born in Brazil rather than in Africa. They have adopted some music from our Indians and imitated a few of the Portuguese popular songs, but most of their songs and dances are really African."

They took a path which led around the house and toward the island's small dock, then stopped at a cleared area where a group of black slaves were gathered in a circle around a fire. "They are going to do the fandango," Baron Saia explained.

The men wore loose white pants and shirts but no shoes. Though the women were also barefoot and their skirts were white, their blouses and headkerchiefs ranged from vivid crimson to deep purple, as if the colorful plumage of birds had been reversed from male to female. Some had dark, almost blue-black skin, and a few looked very fair.

A tall man in the center, who seemed to be the leader, began a chant, addressing each person in turn as he passed around the circle. At regular intervals the others joined in a chorus of rising and falling notes. Julia could hear an occasional word of Portuguese, but most of the language sounded unintelligible to her. Three young men came up to one side of the chanting slaves, each with a small drum which he began to play.

The baron excused himself and left, but Julia was too fascinated by the scene before her to do more than offer a brief thanks to him. The slaves had begun to dance, the same black man in the center of the circle. He looked young and was powerfully built, with muscles that bulged in his shoulders and thighs. Dampness had molded his loose white pants and sleeveless shirt to his body; sweat glistened on his bare arms and dripped from the ebony skin of his neck.

The momentum of the dance increased, accompanied by the cries and exclamations of the participants. Their legs blurred with short, jerky, loose-jointed motions, while at the same time the upper parts of their bodies and arms swayed rhythmically from side to side, almost like Spanish dancers Julia had once seen in Charleston.

The bonfire lit the circle of dancers, and now darkness shrank the world beyond the fire so that they all, the four visitors and the dancing slaves, seemed contained within a small universe. When someone put more wood on the fire, sparks and flames shot upward. Julia felt as if she were being drawn into the dance; she could feel the cadences of the chanted music reflected in her heartbeat; the drumbeats seemed to be reverberating along her breastbone. Suddenly she longed to be free of the constrictions of corset and crinoline, to wear the loose skirts and vivid blouses she saw on the women of the circle, and to join in the increasing frenzy of the dance. The whole enormous country of Brazil seemed compressed into this firelit center, distilled in the rhythms stirring her.

A touch on her arm startled her, and she looked up at Andrew's face. Light from the bonfire illuminated the angular bones of his cheek and glinted on his black hair, but left his eyes in shadow. Swept up by the chanted rhythms, she swayed toward him, her body ready to follow his into the dance.

His voice broke the spell. "We must leave now, Julia."

She jerked back, embarrassment flooding her. Had he noticed her motion toward him? What had her face told him? She turned and saw James and Sally waiting. Her heart still pounding, she hurried after them as they started along the path to the dock. Behind her she could hear Andrew's footsteps.

The short ride back to shore over the darkened waters did little to restore Julia's serenity. Those moments when the dance and music had seemed to capture her were difficult to shake off. She had a vision of Brazil, an enormous looming figure, weaving a magic which enslaved not just the blacks dragged so miserably to her shores, but people like her, who thought they could control their own destinies. And somehow Andrew Langdon seemed part of this magic, a sorcerer who had the power to enchant her.

Through the carriage ride back to the hotel on the Larangeiras she sat quietly, warding off James's inquiry about her unusual silence with the excuse of fatigue.

When Andrew reined in the horses, she gave her hand to James to help her down, ignoring the questioning look the torchlight showed in Andrew's face. She heard her brother expressing their thanks to Andrew, and though she knew she was being rude, she turned and fled into the building. As she found her way to her room, she realized she would be glad to leave Rio after all—to escape from the city that spread its flaring gaslights around the bay, and especially from this man whose presence seemed to make her act like a person she didn't know.

As Andrew rode away from the hotel through the warm night, he thought of Julia's response to the fandango, and desire stirred in him again. She'd looked unbelievably exciting, with her hair like flames that burst upward in sparkling surges and her eyes enormous with emotion. The passion in her face had aroused him; he'd wanted to pull her into the concealing shadows of the trees, to kiss and caress her until he could lose himself in her. For a moment she'd swayed toward him as if she too felt that overwhelming urge to join her body to his. But when he'd spoken, she'd drawn back, and during the return to the hotel she'd hardly glanced at him.

Best that the moment had ended when it did, he reminded himself. If he held her as he'd wanted to and expressed the desire he could still feel when he thought of her, it would only mean trouble. A spoiled Southern belle, particularly one who wanted to go home, was no wife for a man who had all the riches of Brazil beckoning him. And involvement with a woman like that meant taking her for a wife.

No, regardless of how exciting it might be to make love to Julia Rayford, Andrew knew he'd stay away from her.

The creak of leather harnesses mingled with the raucous chatter of birds in the thick forest and with the shouts of the *tropeiro* who alternately lashed and swore at the troop of eight pack mules. Restlessly Julia shifted her weight on the cushioned seat of the enclosed cart where she rode with her mother.

It seemed more than a week since she had gone to

the Saia island and watched the fandango dance, and she wondered wearily if they would ever reach the São Paulo *fazenda* her father had purchased. What would it be like? Papa talked so excitedly of the five thousand acres, ninety slaves, and a hundred and twenty-five head of cattle. He'd bought it and all its furnishings for ten thousand dollars from Baron Perante, who was now Minister of Agriculture and lived in Rio. The fifty-mile boat trip from Rio to Santos had been pleasant, the breezes refreshing after the humid heat of the capital. Santos had been interesting, with all the colorful activity of a bustling port, but the climb from the coast to the plain beyond São Paulo in the mule-drawn wagon seemed to be taking a month instead of two days.

A sudden jolt sent an ache up her back and stirred the dust which coated her hair and mottled her brown cotton traveling dress. Miserably she longed to be riding even one of the scraggly mules—anything to be out of the cart. She looked at Mama, who was sitting uncomplainingly in the opposite corner, her eyes closed, and felt contrite. Mama looked so ill since they'd left Rio. Papa had arranged for this specially constructed cart, which was supposed to make the ride easier, and they moved at an excruciatingly slow pace. Even so, Julia could see her mother was suffering.

She reached for the water pouch that hung beside the door and dampened her handkerchief. Sliding across the seat, she wiped her mother's forehead.

Mama's eyes opened and she murmured, "Thank you." Her pale lips attempted a smile. "Julia, you are such a good daughter. I don't know how I would manage here without you."

Julia smiled in return, but then busied herself putting the handkerchief away. If Mama only knew how little she felt like a good daughter! Guiltily she hoped her face didn't reveal her feelings.

Mary shifted against the cushions, then spoke softly. "Julia, you should get outside, change places with Sally, and let her ride with me for a time."

For a moment Julia thought longingly of accepting her mother's suggestion, but though Sally meant well, she was little help to anyone who was sick. "No, Mama, I want to be here with you." Watching the sad face across the cart, Julia felt filled with a wistful tenderness and truly did want to stay inside.

In the light filtering through the bamboo-shaded windows, her mother looked almost like a stranger. Julia realized she wasn't sure she really knew this woman whom she'd often resented, and she remembered a question which had bothered her during her visit in Philadelphia. "Mama, why did you leave your home to marry Papa when your family hates slavery so much?"

Mary looked surprised, then smiled. "Because I loved him. He didn't feel the same way about slavery. He was raised with it and it seemed natural and right to him."

"But didn't it bother you? Even after only two years living with Uncle Daniel, I could see that slavery is wrong."

Mary sighed, but her voice sounded affectionate. "Julia, you're so young and so impetuous. When you love a man and marry him, you have to accept his way of doing things and his beliefs."

"And give up your own?" Julia felt the temper rising that her mother had tried so hard to teach her to suppress. "But, Mama, I couldn't do that, no matter how much I loved someone."

"And do you think you would have been so easily convinced of Quaker beliefs if Nathan hadn't been doing the persuading?"

Startled, Julia gaped at her mother. She hadn't thought Mama had paid enough attention to know about her feelings for Nathan.

A blast from the horn of the guard on the coach made words impossible for a moment; then Mary leaned forward, her voice intense. "Julia, your father loves you very much, and he may need your help. A man, even one as strong as William, sometimes must depend on a woman. If anything should happen to me, remember you must be a true and faithful daughter."

Julia's stomach churned with warring emotions. Love and apprehension for her mother mingled with the fear that such feelings were the bars of a cage that could trap her here in Brazil.

When the cart arrived at the *fazenda* late the following day, Julia had briefly relinquished her place in the cart to Sally. She had been so worried about her mother that she'd hardly seen São Paulo as they passed through. Now, at her father's shout, she reined up beside him and saw a large house of stucco with marble trim and iron grillwork, situated on a knoll just in front of a mountain. This was the *casa grande*, or big house. A long stone-paved terrace, outlined by a balustrade, surrounded the building; on one side she glimpsed the rainbow-colored spray of a fountain.

They stopped at the bottom of a long sweep of stone steps which led up to the terrace. Under Papa's direction, Tobias and several slaves brought a litter to carry Mama from the cart to the building, through an echoing central hall and up polished curving stairs. Julia followed close behind and along a hall where, to her distraught mind, red wallpaper above mahogany wainscoting seemed like a tunnel to a satanic underground.

For the next week Julia saw little more than the large

room with the high canopied bed where Mary lay. Tall
windows let in cooling breezes, but they seemed to
give the sick woman little relief. Occasionally Julia stood
and stared out at lush green growth that sloped away
from the house, but she had not yet gone outside. She
knew from Sally's reports that Serena, with the help of
a slave who knew English, had taken charge of the
household staff. Sally also talked excitedly of a banana
room and of a music room with a grand piano, but Julia
was too anxious and tired at night to do more than crawl
beneath the embroidered cotton coverlet of her own
bed.

Then came a night when Mary's shallow breath faltered, and the doctor from São Paulo shook his head
hopelessly. Julia held James's hand in a grip so tight
that she could feel her nails digging into his skin; the
candlelight wavered in the tears that filled her eyes.
William gave a hoarse cry and fell to his knees beside
the bed. Mama was dead.

The doctor picked up his bag and went out into the
hall; James and Julia followed, leaving their father alone
with his wife. In the red corridor they clung to each
other and to a weeping Sally.

The bedroom door opened and William emerged, his
steps shaky, and reached out his arms. Julia let go of
her brother and embraced her father, his face distorted
with tears. "Julia . . . Julia. My Mary is gone."

James took Sally into the darkened room as Julia
continued to hold her father. Brokenly he spoke again.
"Thank God I have you still."

Later, when Julia lay on her bed, the terrible weeping for her mother finally stilled, she thought again of
what her father had said. Through the grief and sorrow
for her mother crept the painful awareness that the
doors of her cage had closed.

5

Below the stone balustrade at the edge of the large terrace stretched a blur of moon-tipped trees and silver fields. Julia stood savoring the scented air and the feel of her aqua silk dress. She loved the way it glistened in the moonlight and the soft caress of the cloth where it circled her bared shoulders. Four months had passed since Mama's death, and today the dark clothes had been put aside. Papa might have wished for a whole year of mourning, but with James and Sally's wedding only a month away, tonight all the family except Papa wore bright colors for their first party at the *fazenda*. After dinner Julia had made sure the visitors were all pleasantly content before slipping outside for a moment to herself.

Mama would have been proud, Julia knew, of the way she'd managed arrangements for the many houseguests. In three months of taking over her mother's duties, Julia had discovered how much work running the plantation house required and how confining it was. Mama, I didn't appreciate you, she thought regretfully.

A warm breeze stirred the loose tendrils of hair that had escaped from the ribbon tied high on the back of her head, and she had to remind herself April meant winter, not summer, was coming; the nights would soon be cool. The pungent smell of damp earth from an afternoon shower reminded her of South Carolina. As the grief of her mother's death abated, her hopes for returning to Hundred Oaks had risen. Papa, though sad, was more himself, and after the wedding Sally might take over the household management. Then Julia could leave.

Sighing, she turned to go into the house. Sally probably wouldn't change that much with marriage, and in any case, hostess duties remained tonight.

Although this was the Rayfords' first formal entertaining, the Americans living nearby, including several of their neighbors from South Carolina, had already gravitated to the Rayford *fazenda* informally to talk and play cards. Tonight someone had suggested holding a mock tournament tomorrow, like the staged medieval jousts which had been popular at home. As she crossed the terrace, Julia thought impatiently that the men's time needed to be spent learning about their plantations instead of leaving everything to the Brazilian overseers. But Papa didn't ask her opinion here as he had during the war years at Hundred Oaks, and she'd been so busy in the house, she knew little about the work outside.

Julia paused by the fountain, which sent ghostly sprays into the moonlit night, reluctant to return to the crowded house. Instead of using the great carved doors of the front entrance, she walked around the corner to the courtyard at the side. As she pushed open the double iron gates, she saw Tobias inside near a window that opened onto the court. Thank goodness for him and Serena, she thought gratefully. Julia's Portuguese had progressed rapidly, but it was a relief to deal with familiar faces and language for some of the many tasks which had fallen on her.

The shadows of the clipped cedars held one side of the court deep in shadow as she crossed, her soft kid pumps soundless over the smooth paving. As she neared the side door, she saw a tall form silhouetted against the white wall and stopped, her heart suddenly beating faster. It was Andrew Langdon.

She had encountered him briefly once since her mother's funeral, when he had come to see her father. The Langdon holdings had turned out to be close to the Rayford *fazenda*. Richard Langdon had spent a great deal of time with Papa, but Julia had avoided him as much as she could, unable to overcome her initial distaste for him. Today Richard had come early, as had most of the guests, but Andrew had not appeared for dinner.

Julia stepped forward, and stopped again as a slight figure moved close to him and a girlish voice floated clearly across to her. "I'll wait for you in your room."

Shock froze Julia. The voice was Sally's. Julia heard Andrew's low response, but his words were indistinct. Without thinking, she whirled and sped silently back through the iron gates, pausing only after she had rounded the corner of the building.

She stood, her hands gripped across her knotted stomach, her pulse pounding wildly in her throat. How could Sally? Flirting had been bad enough, but going to a man's room was insanely reckless. Andrew must have suggested it, and Sally brainlessly agreed. Painfully Julia remembered how skillfully he'd flirted with her and kissed her.

She realized she should have stayed in the court, interrupted them right then. Why hadn't she done that? It was the shock of seeing them together, hearing a plan that could cause such harm to James—to all of them—that made her flee. She must go back, confront them, and make Sally see how foolish and scandalous her behavior could be.

Resolutely controlling her angry trembling, she ran back to the side court, but it was empty. When she hurried on into the large music room, Sally was not among the women chatting lazily around the piano. As she turned to continue searching, Mrs. Wetherly's reedy voice called, "Julia, you must tell us how you managed all that delicious food."

From a chair next to her birdlike friend, Mrs. Scott also smiled at Julia, her round face and body showing how many meals she'd appreciated in her forty-five years. "Yes, indeed, Julia. I'm just groanin' from all those mouth-waterin' things. Why, I haven't had both fried chicken and chicken creamed in patty shells at the same meal for years."

Trying not to let her impatience show, Julia reluctantly joined her South Carolina neighbors. Mrs. Wetherly bounced her white curls emphatically as she took up the praise. "Just like a feast at home—okra, spoonbread, biscuits, fig and damson preserves. I swear we're lucky these Brazilians eat pork and ham and rice, but where did you get butterbeans?"

"Why, the Scotts brought them." Julia made herself smile at the plump woman who had been their closest neighbor at home. "And Serena was responsible for the custards and light puddings."

Mrs. Russell, a thin woman from Alabama, began to talk about the difficulties of managing Brazilian house slaves. As Julia waited impatiently for a break in the conversation so she could excuse herself again, she saw Sally come in, alone. Her cousin's eyes looked unusually animated as she joined the circle of women.

Before Julia could think of an excuse to take Sally aside, the men entered from the dining room where they'd lingered over cigars and brandy. Andrew was with James, and Julia felt her stomach begin to knot again.

Andrew stepped forward and bowed, the darkly handsome face smiling, his long body gracefully relaxed in his tailored formal clothes. "Good evening, Julia. I offer my sincere apologies that I couldn't arrive earlier. A problem with some machinery."

You hypocrite, she accused inwardly, behaving so politely to me and James when you're trying to seduce his fiancée. She could only manage a stiff nod as she replied, "We're always happy to have a friend of *James's* here, Mr. Langdon." When she turned back to the chatting women, she could see her brother's surprise at her tone, but he said nothing as he and Andrew moved off to join a group around William.

Mrs. Wetherly played the piano for her older daughter, a thin, nervous-looking girl, to sing several Stephen Foster songs in a soprano voice that was not quite on pitch. After polite applause—whether for the songs or from relief at the end, Julia wasn't sure—the men left for the card room to begin the drinking and gambling which constituted male diversions at most parties. Julia relaxed a little when her cousin stayed with the women, but she had trouble following the conversation around her, waiting for bedtime and a chance to speak to Sally.

Finally yawns announced it was late enough to retire, and Julia thankfully led the way to the upper floor. But when she reached her room, she heard Mrs. Scott's motherly voice behind her. "Julia, I'll just come in your room for a visit while you get ready for bed. My own dear Willhelmina and I used to have such nice little talks after a party."

Julia watched in dismay as the short, plump woman sailed into her bedroom and Sally disappeared down the hall. She realized that their former neighbor was missing the married daughter she'd left behind in South Carolina and probably trying to substitute for Mama, but she wished desperately that the older woman had chosen to look after Sally instead. Not until Julia had put on her white batiste nightgown and hurried through brushing her hair did Mrs. Scott conclude her motherly chatter with a kiss and leave.

Julia waited only a few moments before pulling on a wine-colored silk wrapper and going to the door. After looking quickly down the hall, she eased her bedroom door shut behind her and stood motionless, listening. Candlelight from a wall sconce shed soft light on the embossed russet wallpaper and mahogany wainscoting. No one disturbed the silence.

Holding up the skirts of her wrapper and gown, she hurried down the corridor, bare feet soundless on the polished floor. At the fourth door she stopped and rapped softly. No one answered. Carefully she opened the door. Light from the hall penetrated only dimly as she moved across to a high four-poster bed.

"Sally?" she whispered, but the bed, covers turned down for the night, was empty, the mosquito netting looped to one side. Her cousin was gone—out to the small house set aside for unaccompanied male guests, Julia thought grimly.

Fury gripped her stomach in a throbbing knot. Tonight she didn't know if she truly cared what happened to Sally, but James, not her cousin, would be the real victim, and Julia couldn't stand for her twin to be hurt more.

She wondered if she could find Sally in time, and knew immediately she must. Slipping out of the bedroom and back past her own door, Julia stopped at the wrought-iron railing of the galleria above the entry hall and leaned down, listening to sounds below. A laugh and the murmur of low voices told her the men were still in the card room. Probably Andrew played with the others; coutesy required that no one leave the gambling tables until the host did so. But her father had looked tired tonight; the games might not continue long.

She realized she should put her clothes back on, but dressing would take too much time. Her wrapper concealed her nightgown and was dark enough not to be easily seen outside. She'd cover her loose hair and don shoes.

Inside her room she slipped on flat black shoes and snatched a gray shawl from the wardrobe; now anyone outside might think from a distance that she was a slave. She paused only long enough to snuff the candle she'd left burning.

At the end of the hall opposite the galleria a door opened onto a marble balcony from which a narrow stairway led down to the back of the house. Julia almost tumbled down the steep steps, but at the bottom she hesitated. What if Andrew had found some excuse to leave the gambling early and had already gone to his room? Her heart pounding, she moved softly across the square flagstones of the back terrace, around a corner, and approached a window recessed into the foot-thick wall. Keeping to one side so that her face remained in shadow, she peered inside the card room.

Cigar smoke drifted upward toward the candles which burned above black-suited shoulders. She heard the murmur of voices, a laugh she recognized as her father's, and the clink of a glass. James sat at a near table, his blond head bent over his cards, and she saw a glimpse of her father's mixed red and gray hair beyond. To one side Tobias moved around the seated men, filling glasses from a glittering decanter. Frantically she looked for a man who would be taller than the others. Across the room, black hair framed Andrew's strong face where he lounged in a chair at one of the gaming tables. Relief let her breathe a little more easily. Now she must find Sally.

Swiftly Julia moved across the terrace, wanting to run but fearing to attract attention. She saw no one as she hurried down stone steps and along the path which led through the garden to the bachelor quarters.

In the dim light from the moon the guesthouse looked pale and shadowy as she stopped in the shelter of a small tree and listened. The low building stood silent, a soft glow coming from candles in the central hall, and suddenly all Julia wanted to do was return to her own room. James, James, she cried silently, why must you love Sally? Why couldn't you want to marry someone else?

She couldn't hesitate now. Nervously gripping her shawl, she walked silently along the corridor to the last room. Taking a trembling breath, she pushed open the door. A figure whirled and faced her, and Julia recognized the slight outline immediately.

"Sally!"

"Julia!"

The two names collided with each other.

"What are you doing here?" Sally's whisper grew shrill. "You're following me, spying on me. Go away, Julia. Leave me alone!"

Julia stepped forward and grasped her cousin's arm. "No. You have to get back to your room *now*, before anyone else knows you're here." Though as slender as the younger girl, Julia was taller and stronger. Sally tried to pull away, but Julia held fast.

"Let me go. No one will find me." Sally's voice began to quiver. "You're not in charge of me. I'm not hurting anyone."

All of Julia's anger surfaced. "It's insane for you to come here. I heard you in the court, planning to come here, and if I heard, someone else might have also. What would Papa say—and James? Do you remember that you're going to marry James?"

Sally's resistance began to crumble as Julia pulled her cousin into the hall and to the outside door. "But, Julia, this has nothing to do with James. It was just a joke with Andrew—it didn't mean anything."

Julia paused outside and looked around. She saw only the flagstone path. Nothing moved. "Why is being in a man's bedroom a joke?" she asked incredulously as she propelled Sally forward. "Men have killed each other over less. Do you want James and Andrew to fight a duel?"

Sally began to sob as she stumbled along, her arm still firmly in Julia's grasp. "Oh, Julia . . . I know you're right . . . I shouldn't have gone. But really, it just seemed like a game. Nothing would have happened. I didn't think about someone seeing me." She sobbed harder. "Nothing's ever fun or exciting anymore. Since the war . . . this awful place . . ."

They were nearing the main house. Julia gripped Sally's arm hard enough, she hoped, to be painful. "Be quiet! We can't talk now. Someone might hear us." The sobs subsided.

Suddenly Sally stopped, almost pulling Julia off balance, her whispered voice frightened. "My shawl! Julia, I left my shawl in Andrew's room!"

Julia wanted to cry in dismay. She should have noticed that Sally's hair was shining even in the faint moonlight. Seeing the panic in the other girl's face, she decided instantly what to do. The shawl mustn't be found in Andrew's room, but her cousin would never be calm enough to retrieve it.

In front of them the large house was serene, muffled noises drifting from the windows, but no voices or steps outside. Taking off her own shawl, she hurriedly draped it over Sally's head, and spoke urgently into her cousin's ear. "Go on up the back stairway into your room. Get in bed as fast as you can." She gave Sally a push as she whispered, "I'll go back for the shawl."

Waiting only a moment to see that her cousin hurried on, Julia turned and ran back to the guesthouse.

No human sounds or movements disturbed the quiet. Barely breathing, Julia pushed open the door to the room where she'd found Sally. When she heard and saw nothing, she released her breath and entered.

Light from a candle in the hall penetrated a short way into the room, but not enough to see clearly. On a small table beside the door she found a partially burned candle. She listened again. Nothing. Taking the candle, she lit it from the flame in the sconce in the hall and by its flickering light surveyed the bedroom.

Mosquito netting hung around a large bed; next to the bed stood a carved washstand with a painted china basin and pitcher on top. In front of the fireplace centered in the remaining wall stood two wooden chairs.

Something hung over the back of one chair. Hurriedly Julia crossed the room and held her candle closer. The sheen of a blue-and-green peacock design caught the faint light, revealing one of two identical shawls her father had brought for her and Sally from São Paulo three weeks before.

Julia picked up the silky wrap and started back to the door, when she stopped, frozen. From a distance came the sound of a high-pitched laugh that she recognized immediately as Duncan Scott's. The men must be returning to the guesthouse.

For a moment Julia couldn't think; then reason returned and she blew out the candle and put it down. Swiftly moving to the door, she pushed it almost closed, leaving only a crack. Her heart pounded so that she was afraid she wouldn't be able to hear, but she put her ear to the narrow opening and listened.

Apparently the men had stopped at the entrance to the hall. Again she heard Duncan Scott's laugh and then another voice that wasn't low enough to be Andrew's—it sounded like old Mr. Fitzpatrick.

Julia strained to hear more as she tried frantically to remember who was staying in the guesthouse. Another laugh, almost a giggle, would be Mrs. Wetherly's youngest son, but no voice that sounded like Andrew. Perhaps he was still at the main house. She leaned against the wall to keep her legs from shaking.

On the walk from the main house Andrew had slowed his steps to let the other men go before him into the guesthouse. God, how tired he was of their incessant talk about the Confederacy. They expected to reproduce in Brazil the life they'd known before the war. They couldn't—or wouldn't—see the incredible beauty and promise of this land, its richness in its own way. Clinging to the past, they thought of themselves, not even as Americans, but as Southerners. Drinking, gambling, mock tournaments were all right as entertainment, but not for full-time occupations.

He stopped and watched the three men ahead of him as they lingered in the doorway. Well, let them bury themselves in outworn ideas; inwardly he laughed at them. They thought of him as American too, but he wasn't. He was at least as much Brazilian now, and he lived in the present and the future. That's what they should be working for—a new life in a new land.

"Mr. Langdon." Mr. Fitzgerald's white head was turned toward Andrew. Reluctantly he joined the others in the doorway. "I trust you will afford me the opportunity to challenge you at cards another time."

Andrew smiled politely and nodded at the older man. "Yes, Andrew," drawled Duncan Scott, his pudgy face admiring, "you had the devil's good fortune tonight—as usual. I suspect you've made a pact with Mephistopheles. Cards . . . women—even your plantation runs too well for ordinary luck."

Andrew joined the general laugh and suppressed the disdainful reply he would have liked to give. If Duncan Scott and his brother and father had spent as much time as he learning about Brazil and its inhabitants, their *fazenda* might flourish also. When the newcomers arrived in Brazil, he'd tried to pass on what he'd learned in ten years here, but only William and James Rayford had listened.

Andrew murmured his good-night and let the others go ahead to their rooms. As he walked down the hall to the farthest door, he loosened his silk cravat and unbuttoned his jacket. Fatigue weighed on him—not the welcome tiredness of a long day's riding around his fields, but the weariness of too much liquor and gambling, of boredom.

He opened the door to his room and instantly recognized the odor of a recently snuffed candle and of another scent—perfume. A motion caught his eyes—a female figure at the end of the bed.

Anger rose in him as he hastily closed the door behind him. By God, the silly bitch had meant what she said. Two steps took him next to her. He kept his voice barely more than a whisper. "I thought you understood when I told you not to come in here!" He reached for her shoulders, and she shrank back against the bedstead.

He stopped, startled. This woman was too tall for

Sally! His hand brushed across a silk sleeve and fastened on her upper arm. She gasped as he pulled her across the room to the window. With his free hand he pushed the drapery away from the window and let the declining moon illuminate her face.

Light fell on tumbled hair which betrayed its red color even in the half-dark. Wide anxious eyes stared at him above a flaring nose and trembling mouth. Julia Rayford!

Surprise loosened his grasp on her arm as they faced each other. Julia—beautiful and appealing, but cold and distant since their meetings in Rio. They'd hardly spoken to each other the time he'd seen her since then, and she'd given him an icy reception earlier tonight. Why was she in his room?

Julia, finally recovering from the shock of his entrance, whirled and started toward the door. Instantly he grabbed her arm again. She struggled, but he pulled her against him until her face was only a few inches below his.

"No!" He breathed the words against her ear. "You don't leave until I find out why you're here."

Rage inflamed her that he, who had caused so much trouble to her family and James, should be questioning her. Furiously she whispered, "As if you didn't know, you despicable—" She choked on her own words, unable to say more.

Startled, Andrew found his temper rising to meet hers. Why was she angry at him? He hadn't sought her out—she'd come uninvited to him. Again she struggled to free herself, but he held her close. Her efforts made him aware that he felt, not the rigid cage that usually encapsulated women of her station, but soft breasts against his chest. He ran his hand down her back and below the slender waist to a swelling hip. She stiffened instantly, but he felt the beginning of sexual passion grow in his body.

Suddenly he didn't want to remember the reasons why he'd decided in Rio to stay away from her. This warm woman with little clothing and soft curves excited him enormously. Why she was here became less important than her presence in his arms.

Her perfume, like crushed roses, filled his nostrils. In the moonlight her eyes were deep brown pools, reflecting now, not uncertainty, but rage. She moistened her lips, as if to speak, and her partly open mouth glistened irresistibly. He kept his voice barely audible. "Is this what you came for?" If she had an answer, his lips smothered it as he pushed her back against the wall and kissed her.

For the first strained moments she struggled; then she softened, her mouth hesitantly yielding to the insistent warmth of his. Her breasts enticed him as they pressed lightly against his hard chest, as if asking for his touch. He held her closer as his tongue circled her lips and tasted the inner surface of her mouth.

Julia felt amost drugged by the sensuality of his kiss. Tentatively she touched the black curls that had tantalized her ever since their first meeting. The hair felt silky under her fingers. She leaned against him, and his hand traced the curve of her hip.

The touch shocked her into sudden awareness. She wrenched her face away from his. "No! Let me go!" She gasped the whispered words and began to push frantically against his chest. But her strength couldn't match the muscular arms that held her close to his tall body.

Andrew could feel her legs twisting, trying to kick at him, but her struggles only made the thinness of her clothing more obvious. Whatever her seeming protests, she had come to his room dressed in a way that was an invitation; the thought added to the excitement of her body next to his. He knew she must be able to feel his penis, hard against her abdomen. Caution vanished in his growing passion. With the arm that encircled her he pulled her hips more strongly against him. His other hand found her breast and brushed across its soft fullness, then cupped it in his palm. His breathing came harder, blocking out sounds around him.

The rap on the door shocked him. "Mr. Langdon . . . Andrew. This is William Rayford. I'm sorry to disturb you, but I must speak to you."

At the sound of her father's voice, Julia wrenched herself free from Andrew's loosened grasp and stepped back. She could hear his breath, harsh and rasping in the momentary silence, and felt her own chest heaving in shallow gasps.

The enormity of her father's presence in the hall outside paralyzed her. As thought returned, she looked frantically around, but nothing offered cover. Darkness concealed the expression on Andrew's face as he turned toward the door. Perhaps he wouldn't let her father in and she might still go undiscovered.

The opening of the door dashed her hope. Her father stood in the doorway with James beside him, a lighted taper in his hand. Andrew could only step aside and let the two men enter the room.

William's eyes stopped on Julia and his face went rigid. The same shock appeared on James's countenance, but then the muscles of her brother's face relaxed, and she was sure she saw relief in his eyes. Instantly she guessed he had feared to find Sally here.

Her father's low voice, harsh with shock and anger, erased all other thoughts. "Julia!" William stepped farther into the room and motioned to James behind him. "James, please close the door."

No one spoke as James shut the door behind him. In the wavering light of the single candle the faces of the three men looked like masks from a Faustian drama. Julia began to feel as if nothing was real, that at any moment she would waken in her bed with the cocoon of mosquito netting drawn protectively around her.

But William's barely muffled anger brought back reality. "Mr. Langdon, I did not believe what I was told a few moments ago, but I find to my bitter regret that it was true. I wish an explanation of my daughter's presence here." Julia clenched her hands at her sides and looked at Andrew, dreading his answer.

Behind his carefully expressionless face, a furious question pounded in Andrew's mind: had Julia planned for her father and brother to find her here? Bitterly he recognized he had only one possible response to her father's demand. With an effort he kept his mounting anger at bay as he spoke. "I'm sorry, Mr. Rayford, but I have nothing to say."

Even in the half-dark Julia could see the flush of rage in her father's face as he turned to her. "Julia. Since Mr. Langdon will not oblige, I am waiting to hear from you."

Julia felt as if she were choking on her own silence, but she could think of no words to defend herself. She looked at James and saw in his eyes bewilderment, but not pain. She thought of the fears he'd expressed to her that day on Corcovado—his feelings of bitterness and despair. How could she tell what had happened and wound him? She couldn't. Whatever disgrace she brought on herself, she had to protect James, and that meant shielding Sally.

She conquered the tears that threatened to overwhelm her, but when she finally spoke, her words came out in a whisper. "I'm sorry, Papa."

"And that's all you can say?"

Unable to look at her father, she curled her trembling hands into fists and hid them in the folds of her robe as she stood silent.

Abruptly William turned and strode to the door, then faced the room again. In his manner no trace lingered of the father she had so often cajoled. "James, please escort your sister to her room. Julia, you will remain there until I send for you. Mr. Langdon, even though the hour is late, I ask you to accompany me to my study."

Julia felt James take her arm as she started toward the door; then the enormity of Andrew's position struck her. Duels were illegal but were nevertheless fought. Fear of what her father might demand forced her to turn back. She couldn't leave without saying something.

"Papa, it wasn't what . . . I mean, Andrew isn't to blame for—"

"Julia." Her father had never sounded so angry. "I will speak to you later."

As she silently accompanied James from the room, she seemed to feel both Andrew's and Papa's eyes searing her back. The tears she had been containing spilled two scalding drops down her face.

When they passed the closed doors, Julia cringed inwardly. No matter how quiet the confrontation in Andrew's room, others must have heard something. She and James left the bachelor quarters and walked silently toward the main house.

Suddenly she stopped, pulling on his arm until he halted and turned to face her. "James, why did you and Papa come to Andrew's room?"

The moonlight fell on his forehead and cheekbones, turning his eyes into dark smudges that gave her no clue to his thoughts, but his voice sounded strained.

"Tobias heard Andrew and . . . someone in the court-yard earlier and spoke to Papa."

The hesitation in his sentence told her what she had feared. She stared at him silently before he whispered, "Do you want to tell me why you were in Andrew's room tonight, Julia?"

No—she didn't want to tell him, ever. He may have guessed, but he couldn't be certain. Surprised at how calm she sounded, she replied, "Does it matter?" Holding rigidly to her outward composure, she moved past him to the narrow back stairs and slowly ascended the steps she'd hastened down only a short time before. But, she thought bleakly, long enough to be caught in disaster.

Andrew couldn't remember when such anger had burned his gut. He knew now all too well why Julia had been in his room, and he'd acted like a boy who couldn't think about anything but his prick. Silently he swore a list of obscene oaths in both English and Portuguese as he followed William Rayford through the darkened house and into the older man's candlelit study.

Did Julia's father or brother know about the trap she'd laid? Somehow he couldn't believe they did. When William turned and faced him, the tired confusion in the older man's face confirmed his belief. No—Julia had managed it with the help of her frivolous little cousin, and probably one of the black servants who'd come with them from South Carolina. And he'd thought Sally fool-ish but harmless.

"Andrew . . ." William stopped and cleared his throat before he recovered his frosty dignity and spoke clearly. "I had not expected this kind of behavior from you. Without any reasonable explanation, I can only ask for satisfaction."

Bitterly Andrew wanted to shout that her father should question Julia's behavior, but he forced down his rage. Only one course lay open to him. He hated duels, thought them a vestige of an insane code, but he knew the rigidity of the standard William had left his own country to uphold. If it were only a matter between him and William, he might choose to be called a coward and leave, but that wouldn't satisfy the question of Julia's honor.

Rigorous self-control kept his voice even. "I regret that my actions this evening were precipitate. I wish, of course, to ask for Julia's hand in marriage." For a moment he thought he would gag on his own words.

"I see." William sighed heavily. "Yes, well . . . of course I would have preferred to have heard this request without . . ." He seemed not to know what to say next. Instead he reached for a decanter of brandy and partly filled two glasses. Extending one to Andrew, he continued, "Let's forget the events tonight. I shall speak to Julia in the morning. I can only conclude from . . . well, that your offer will be favorably received."

Andrew took the glass of brandy, his anger blunted somewhat by William's obvious distress. He liked James and William both; they seemed like men who might profit in Brazil. If Julia had the honor of the rest of her family . . . But futile to think of that now. He could only hope something would happen to prevent a marriage he didn't want and couldn't imagine why she did either. The first swallow of brandy almost lodged in his throat. Trapped by one of the oldest tricks ever—and he hadn't even had a chance to earn the penalty. When the liquor did go down, it did not burn as fiercely as his rekindled rage.

6

Morning sunlight crept down the white lace curtains, brightening the roses that forever bloomed on wallpaper vines. Gaining strength, it enticed gleaming reds from the polished brazilwood wardrobe and in a golden glow pierced the mosquito netting which swathed the four-poster bed.

Julia groaned and turned away from the probing light, trying to protect herself from the dull aching behind her eyes. After James left her at her door, she'd lain awake until dawn, alternating between bitter resentment at Andrew and Sally and futile wishes that she had acted differently. Now the warring thoughts returned. She should have left the shawl—retrieved it this morning. When Andrew returned she should have hidden . . . No, that was impossible. And those moments in his arms, the kiss, his strong body pressed against hers—unwillingly she remembered the evidence of his arousal and her own jagged streaks of pleasure at his touch. Her face burned now at the memory; she only hoped he hadn't known the effect he'd had on her.

Resolutely she sat up, brushed back her tangled mass of hair, and pushed aside the mosquito netting. She must stop tormenting herself with futile regrets and instead plan what to say to Papa.

A soft tap sounded at her door; it opened and Sally slipped inside. Her blue flowered morning gown was rumpled, as if she'd dressed without her usual care, and her eyes looked red and puffy. She hesitated by the door. Then tears began to flood her cheeks, and she rushed across the room to collapse on the bed beside Julia.

Her words came in gasping sobs. "Oh, Julia, I'm so sorry—I can't tell you how terrible I feel." She took Julia's hand, pressing it to her wet face. "I was waiting, listening at my door, and I heard you, and then I almost died when I peeked out and saw James behind you, and . . . Oh, Julia, this morning I went down and Uncle William said you were sick, and I knew something dreadful happened, and it's all my fault—"

"Sally, Sally, stop crying." Julia pulled her cousin into her arms and held her until some of the wrenching tears lessened. In the ten years Sally had lived with the Rayfords, Julia had learned to love the warm-natured girl, though she'd been angry and exasperated with her countless times. Seeing how truly contrite Sally was this morning, Julia lost some of her resentment. She knew that Sally never intended any harm; she just didn't consider the effects of her actions.

Julia pushed the blond hair away from the troubled face and spoke as calmly as she could. "You might as well know. Andrew came back to his room before I could leave with the shawl, and Papa and James found us there." She wouldn't tell Sally about Andrew's embrace because she didn't want to think about that herself.

"Oh, Julia, no! But . . . I mean, why—?"

"Tobias heard you in the courtyard."

Sally's eyes were anguished as she whispered, "What did you tell them?"

"I didn't tell them anything."

"What did Andrew say—what did you tell him?"

"Nothing."

"But then they must think . . ." Sally pulled away from Julia and sat silently. On her face Julia could see guilt change to frightened determination as she stood and said in a shaking voice, "I'll go talk to Uncle William right now."

Julia rose also and grasped Sally's shoulders. "No, Sally! You won't say anything to *anyone*. Not now or ever!"

"But, Julia, that's not right. I ought to. You shouldn't be blamed for what I did."

Julia gripped Sally tighter. "And who would be most hurt?" Fiercely she answered her own question. "James!"

Suddenly the fatigue of the night made her legs tremble. She pulled Sally back to the bed and sat down, holding the smaller hand in her own. "Sally, do you love James?"

"Yes . . . yes, I do. I know it's hard to believe now, but truly I love him."

Julia cut off the sobs that were beginning again. "Sally, listen carefully to me." She must betray a confidence, and only hope Sally could understand. "James told me something I think you should know, but you must never tell him that I told you. Do you promise?"

The nod from the wide-eyed face beside her didn't satisfy Julia. "*Do you promise?*"

"Yes," Sally whispered, "I promise."

"James loves you very much, but he has delayed your marriage because . . ." Julia had difficulty getting the rest of the words out. "Because he's afraid his amputation will bother you."

Sally gasped, her doll-like eyes dismayed. "I didn't know—he never said anything."

Relentlessly Julia continued. "Will it, Sally? Can you accept what his arm looks like?"

Sally buried her face in her hands so that Julia could barely hear the muffled words. "I want to. Oh, Julia, I want to so much." She raised her head and spoke through returning sobs. "I'm not like you. I wish I were, but I know I'm not. Sometimes I think I'm not good enough for James—but I do love him and I'd never want to hurt him."

As Julia pulled her cousin close to comfort her, she felt ashamed of the times she'd thought just what Sally was saying now. "Sally, if you love James, you'll be strong enough to make a grand wife for him. I know you will," she continued, hoping she was right. "But you see, don't you, why you can't say anything about being in Andrew's room last night?"

As Sally dried her eyes, she nodded. "Yes, I understand, and I'm so ashamed and sorry. I don't even know why I went to Andrew's room. It just seemed exciting . . . and he's handsome and teases—I didn't think."

Yes, I know the way he leads you on—probably the same way with anyone, Julia thought, resisting the pang Sally's words gave her.

"But, Julia, what will you do?"

Julia managed a small laugh. "Get dressed. Wait to talk to Papa." She rose and went to the window, looking out. "At least maybe the idea for a damned tournament has been dropped." She turned, and was amused at the shocked expression in her cousin's face. "Sally, don't you ever swear?"

"No—and I don't think you should, but I guess after last night, I shouldn't blame you for anything you do."

Julia laughed aloud, glad to feel something other than

anger and despair. "Sally, you'll never completely approve of me. I wouldn't recognize you if you did."

For a moment Sally clung to Julia. "But I do love and admire you, Julia. I always have. And I'll try to be the best wife I can to James."

As Julia heard the warmth in Sally's voice and felt the affection of her embrace, she hoped that perhaps she and Sally could be closer, more like sisters. Maybe something good would come from last night.

Sally left the room, promising to return with a breakfast tray. As Julia dressed, her mood darkened again. James would be safe, but convincing Papa that nothing had happened would be difficult. Maybe events would be smoothed over and eventually forgotten, but she couldn't persuade herself that would happen easily.

If only she could tell Papa the truth—but it would wound him almost as much as James, and even more, it might jeopardize James's marriage to Sally. At the least it would damage Papa's feeling for the daughter-in-law he'd be living with for many years, and it wouldn't restore Julia's reputation.

As she wandered restlessly to the window and looked out into the Brazilian morning, she felt more fearful of the future than at any time since she'd left Hundred Oaks.

When Andrew entered the sunlit breakfast room, the pungent smell of coffee, diluted by the fragrant sweetness of pineapple, greeted him from the sideboard. Beyond the array of red and gold fruits and the tempting browns of crusty breads, the doors onto the terrace were open; he could see men gathered around two white tables, the graceful ironwork of the legs partly hidden by an array of dark trousers. William sat with the others, but Richard Langdon was standing, facing the tables.

Ordinarily Andrew would have been amused to see his father placed that way; Richard stood whenever possible, using his impressive height to gain subtle advantage over others. Andrew couldn't criticize that tactic—he'd employed it at times himself. But this morning it only reminded him that he didn't know why Richard had worked so diligently to persuade the Rayfords to come to Brazil. Whatever devious plans went on behind his father's bearded face, he wished grimly that they had failed—that Julia and her family had stayed at Hundred Oaks.

Distastefully he turned away from the silver covers which concealed the meats and fish he ordinarily enjoyed, and added hot milk to a cup of steaming bitter coffee. He could have had the beverage brought to his room, but he'd decided he might as well face the others now. It had been a long time since he'd paid attention to what others might be thinking about him, but the sheer gaucherie of being found with a woman in his room—like some callow boy—was humiliating. Arranging a noncommittal expression on his face, he took his coffee outside.

The faces that turned at his step were as carefully pleasant as his own. Only in his father's familiar eyes did he see a hint of the amusement he probably would have been feeling at someone else's plight.

General "good mornings" greeted him as he took a seat beside Mr. Fitzgerald; then Hubert Scott, his round face already perspiring in the morning sun, continued the previous discussion. "But the emperor surely doesn't agree with the views of a radical like Jãoquim Nabuco. And that a respectable newspaper like the *Correio Mercantil* publishes that abolitionist cant astonishes me."

His high voice became even more shrill. "We didn't come to this country just to hear more blasphemous attacks on slavery."

"Gentlemen," Richard broke in, "you can be sure that Senhor Nabuco represents only a minority here, but because he is considered a leading intellectual, he gets a hearing. The emperor thinks of himself as an intellectual also, but he chooses highly practical men as his ministers, so I believe that shows us he will ultimately stand with us on this matter." Richard gestured to include not only the men before him but the surrounding land as well. "That is why we must work closely together, so that the government knows how strongly we intend to maintain our position here."

Could that be what his father was doing, Andrew wondered, collecting support for his pro-slavery position? That would hardly seem worth all the effort to encourage American immigration, when nearly all the major Brazilian planters agreed with him. Andrew speculated whether any of the men here besides his father realized how much abolitionist sentiment existed in Brazil. They wouldn't hear it from the large *fazenda* owners to whose society they gravitated, but in any gathering with Brazil's small but growing merchant and industrial class they'd find the same antislavery arguments they had fled.

For some time Andrew had been hiring more immigrant labor for his *fazenda*, anticipating the time when slavery would disappear in Brazil. He thought about saying this to the men around him, but mentally shrugged, cynically sure they didn't want to hear anything that challenged their beliefs. Besides, he realized uncomfortably, he didn't want to draw any more attention to himself this morning.

When William rose, signaling the end of the breakfast gathering, Andrew found his father at his elbow. "If you're going back to your room, Andrew, I'll accompany you." Nodding his assent, Andrew crossed the stone terrace with the tall man whose appearance so much resembled his own, yet whose opinions so often clashed with his. Silently they followed the flagstone walk through the garden where flowers boldly paraded their vivid blossons. When they arrived at the farthest room of the guest cottage, Andrew motioned his father ahead of him. Following inside, he closed the door, then waited until Richard had seated himself in one of the two chairs before taking the other.

Andrew had never felt close to his father, and during the ten years he'd lived in Brazil, he'd seen little of his parent. Though Andrew's *fazenda* adjoined the older Langdon holdings, it belonged to him alone, purchased with money which had come to him on his twenty-first birthday from his barely remembered mother's family. In those eight years, the independence which had always been fiercely important to him had found outlet in managing his own affairs, and not for many years had Richard commented on his son's behavior. What would he say now? Andrew wondered with grim amusement. Well, his father would have to begin; he wouldn't provide the opening.

The repressed laughter Andrew had noted earlier returned to Richard's eyes. "Well, Andrew, is it true— what the servants are saying?"

The anger which so far this morning Andrew had kept in abeyance began to rise, but he allowed none of it to spill into his voice. "I don't listen to servants' gossip. You'll have to be more specific."

A smile crept from the eyes to the bearded mouth. "That you and Miss Rayford—with William's urging, or should I say insistence?—have an understanding."

Andrew could feel his face flushing with an embarrassment he hadn't felt before his father for years, but he
maintained a calm tone. "Have you come to question
me?"

"By no means." The smile broadened. "I wish to
offer my heartiest congratulations. Ah, I see I surprise
you." Richard rose and rested his hand on his son's
shoulder. "Would you expect me to disapprove? I admit I was astonished at your being discovered, but then
Julia is a beautiful woman and very spirited—at times
unconventional, I would guess. She ought to make marriage interesting for you. And an alliance with the
Rayfords will be an excellent thing."

"For you, perhaps, but not for me." Unconcerned
that his anger was showing, Andrew rose and shook off
his father's hand. "And I'm sure it doesn't surprise you
to know that I don't care whether you approve or not."

Richard's eyes sparkled with evident enjoyment, add-
ing to Andrew's bad temper. "Yes, I realize that, but
since the marriage will take place anyway, I feel free to
be pleased at the prospect."

His patience ended, Andrew walked past his father
and pointedly opened the door. "Don't count on this
'alliance' just yet. Nothing is settled." As his father
left, he wished morosely that he could be sure he was
right.

Morning had approached noon before Sally came to
say that William wanted Julia in his study. From her
window she'd heard carriages leaving. Because everyone would be returning in four weeks for James and
Sally's wedding, guests had come for just one night,
and obviously the idea of a tournament had been abandoned. To her relief she met no one as she descended
the curving front stairs and walked along the hall to the

corner room, her shoes clicking nervously on the blue-tiled floor.

At the carved mahogany door she paused to wipe her damp hands on her handkerchief and calm her rapid breathing. She had put on one of her favorite dresses, a white sprigged muslin with tiny yellow flowers and pale lace that edged the round neck and loose sleeves. Over only a single ruffled petticoat, the dress fell around her in simple lines. With her unbound hair drifting in waves along her shoulders, she hoped she looked young and innocent, deserving of Papa's compassion.

As she raised her hand to the wooden panel, she heard her father's voice, and sudden panic stilled her. Was Andrew with him? She resisted the instinct which told her to flee, and forced herself to knock.

Tobias opened the door and, his dark face expressionless, stepped aside to let her enter before leaving and closing the door behind him. A rapid glance around the room found only her father, and her heart slowed its furious pounding.

William stood beside his desk; behind him a window, recessed into the thick wall, had opened its shutters to the warm midday breeze. His face looked tired and his graying hair tousled, as if he had been running his hand through it. Ordinarily Julia liked this room, with its clutter of books and papers testifying to her father's messy habits, but now the white walls reminded her of the offices of the port officials in Santos with their suspicious authority.

"Sit down, please." He gestured to a carved wood chair with an orange cushion. She sat, feeling like a prisoner in the box, her anxiety increasing when her father remained standing. Then anger rose to help her. She had actually done nothing wrong; at the same time, she knew that among the people who were important to her family, appearances meant almost as much as actions. She had been in Andrew's room, wearing a nightgown and robe, and she couldn't explain her behavior. Still, knowledge of her innocence straightened her back and strengthened her voice. "Yes, Papa?"

Her father's stern expression didn't soften as he looked at her. "I discussed this matter with Andrew last night, but now I want to hear your explanation."

Julia began with the only half-truth she had been able to think of during the long night. "I wanted to get the shawl which . . . was accidentally left in Andrew's room. Earlier yesterday I was in the guesthouse checking everything . . . and I remembered, and I didn't want it lost . . ." At her father's disbelieving frown, she faltered, the jumble of truths unpalatable on her tongue.

"Don't lie to me, Julia!" Disappointment deepened the lines around his mouth and harshened his voice. "You want me to believe you went to a man's room in your nightwear in the middle of the night to get a forgotten shawl? No matter what else you've done, I've always been able to count on your honesty before this."

At his bitter tone she felt her throat constrict with threatening sobs. "Oh, Papa, I don't know what to say. Haven't you ever done something foolish and you didn't even know why?"

His eyes flashed with the temper for which he was known among his fellow planters, but she didn't dare hope this anger would vanish as easily as it usually did. "Don't try to divert me, Julia. We're discussing your conduct, for which you are responsible, and not my mistakes."

"But, Papa . . ." Julia stood and took her infuriated father's arm. "Nothing happened." She brushed away the memory of Andrew's embrace as her fingers tightened on William's sleeve. "I know it looked bad, but truly nothing happened."

He shook off her hand, his face flushing crimson. "You call the loss of your reputation nothing? The slur on our honor nothing?"

Julia recoiled from the man who at this moment was almost a stranger; never before had he been so angry with her. At her motion, he appeared to make an effort at control, and when he continued, he sounded more like himself. "Andrew has asked for your hand in marriage, which I assume from your behavior last night is what you wish."

A gigantic fist clasped Julia around her ribs, squeezing all breath and voice from her. She stared at her father's rigid face for a long moment before she could manage a shocked whisper. "Marriage! No . . . no! That can't be. I don't want to marry Andrew and he doesn't want to marry me." At her father's disbelieving look she hurried on. "It was all a mistake—he doesn't have to offer marriage."

The tide of red returned to William's face as he grasped her shoulders as if to shake her, then let his clenched fists fall to his side. "Are you saying he's never made any advances to you—that you went to his room without any encouragement on his part?"

Memories of the emperor's musical evening stilled Julia's denial; she could feel the flush that must look guilty to her father. Andrew had "made advances" to her, and though he hadn't expected Julia in his room, she wouldn't have been there unless he had also made some overtures to Sally. Why should she protect him now, take on herself all Papa's anger and the terrible pain of his disappointment? But marriage to Andrew—no, she must think of another solution.

"Papa, I don't need to marry Andrew." She put her

hand urgently on her father's arm. "I'll go home to Hundred Oaks—I've wanted so to do that—and in a little while all this will be forgotten."

Some of William's anger faded into a stern calm. "No, Julia, that's impossible. Even if your reputation didn't matter, a single woman—"

"But I won't be single—I'll marry Nathan," she interrupted, her voice light with relief at the thought of a solution that fit all her desires, "and he'll come to South Carolina. I can use the money from Great-Uncle Francis—"

William's surprised voice broke in. "Nathan? Nathan Holt, Daniel's foster son?"

"Yes, Papa. I know he hasn't written to you yet, but we've been in love since before the war, and I know from his letters that . . ." Something in her father's face—dismay, almost pity—stopped Julia.

Gently he covered her hand with his own. "Julia, my grown daughter who is sometimes so young, marriage means much more than 'being in love.' It involves duties and obligations, not just to yourself, but to your family as well."

The sympathetic look in his eyes frightened Julia. "What do you mean?"

"Yesterday Mr. Wetherly brought mail sent on by Mr. Glennie from the consulate in São Paulo. A letter came from Philadelphia I didn't have an opportunity to show you last night. Your Uncle Daniel has been gravely ill, so much so that his life was in question. You know, of course, that your cousin Cecil was killed in the fighting at Bull Run."

He paused and cleared his throat as if almost reluctant to go on; growing dread kept Julia silent as he continued. "Daniel wanted your cousin Purity safely married to someone who would look after her and oversee the family affairs. And so naturally he turned to Nathan."

As if to separate herself from what her father was saying, Julia stepped backward. "No . . . Nathan loves me. He wouldn't marry Purity."

"Julia, honey, Nathan owes Daniel a great deal. Even if he loves you, he has a duty to his foster father."

She stared blankly at the pearl buttons on her father's white shirt as she felt a wrenching pain in her chest, but she spoke defiantly. "I want to see the letter. I won't believe this until I see it."

William picked up a thick brown envelope from the desk and gave it to his daughter. Taking it to the window, she pulled out two folded sheafs of paper. The spidery writing of her Uncle Daniel, even more shaky than usual, covered one. Swiftly she glanced through the details of his illness and partial recovery and the explanation of his worries about his business affairs. Halfway down the last page, her eyes stopped at the sentence she'd been dreading: *"And so on Saturday last, I knew the contentment of watching my precious Purity and Nathan recite their vows as man and wife. If God grants me but a short time yet to live, I shall go to my Maker easy in the knowledge my beloved daughter will be in the care of the man who has been the next thing to a son to me."*

While her mind cried denial, her stunned hands unfolded the second packet, addressed to her in Purity's delicate script. Steeling herself against her increasing distress she began to read. *"My dearest Cousin Julia, You will be so pleased to know that Nathan and I were married . . ."* The pages began to blur as Julia reached the end and found a few lines in Nathan's familiar writing. His stilted words told her more clearly than anything else that it was true; he had put his duty to Uncle Daniel before his love for her.

Numbly she returned the letters to their envelope and dropped it on the desk. Ignoring her jumbled emotions, she faced her father. When she could be alone, she'd think about Nathan; for now she must fight for herself, convince Papa she need not marry Andrew.

But as she looked at William's lined face, the aging effects of her mother's death clearly evident, doubt made her hesitate over the defiant words on her tongue. He was right; not just her reputation but his honor would be stained by her actions. In the closed group of American immigrants, honor was supremely important. Brazilians, of the class who would be her family's friends, guarded their unmarried women even more closely than did Southerners. Her heart seemed to shrivel into a sharp lump that was lacerating her chest in bloody gashes.

Seeing the pain in his daughter's face, William pulled her close, stroking her red-gold hair, wishing he could absorb her hurts himself. However, he knew that this time she had gone beyond the reckless but harmless escapades of the years before the war. Even if it were wise, he couldn't protect her now, and after the shock of finding her in Andrew's room had worn off, William knew he was not really displeased. Andrew was a strong man, and while marriage to him might not be easy, his beautiful Julia was strong too. They don't realize it yet, William thought, but they are well-suited to each other.

Though he wanted to comfort, not discipline Julia, he pushed her away and looked at her sternly. "I've asked Andrew to speak to you before he leaves today." Ignoring the way her face whitened and the beginning of a storm in her golden-brown eyes, he went to the braided bell pull and gave a sharp tug. After a few moments of uncomfortable silence he heard Tobias rap and went to the door. "Tobias, please ask Mr. Andrew Langdon to come to the study."

At his words Julia felt the blood rush to her face, but she could tell from the stiff posture of her father's back and the set of his jaw that nothing would prevent this interview. But, she tried to comfort herself, if I can talk to Andrew without Papa, the situation still may be saved.

"Will you stay here, Papa, or are Andrew and I to be alone?"

For the first time a trace of William's usual humor appeared. "Under the circumstances, I think I can leave you unchaperoned with him in midmorning."

Relief at her father's lightened mood struggled with dread of seeing Andrew and hope he might think of some solution. Returning to the orange-cushioned chair, she waited silently for the knock at the door.

When the sound came, Julia heard her father greet Andrew and offer him a chair before she could look at him. Chagrined, she saw that though her heart was pounding apprehensively, he appeared composed and at ease. In a tan morning coat with white shirt and dark trousers, he looked as if his only concern were his elegant clothes. At the same time the bold lines of his face and the waiting strength of his broad shoulders and muscular body made Julia think of a partly tamed panther, needing only a single provocation to spring into action. When she forced herself to look directly at his face, his penetrating blue eyes under the black brows intensified her feeling of incipient danger.

Determined to retain her composure, she nodded, but a polite greeting seemed false under the circumstances, so she said nothing. Despite her resolution, she found her breath catching in her chest and something like a shiver along her spine. Damn him, she thought, her anger reviving. If he weren't a rake, none of this would have happened. A man like that has no right to be so handsome.

Andrew noticed the flush of color which rose in Julia's face and the sparks of emotion in the eyes that looked as if they might blaze furiously at any moment. But what right did she have to be angry at him? he asked himself. She, not he, had brought about this farcical situation. And yet Andrew found himself admiring Julia's beauty and remembering the feel of her pressed against him last night. God, he concluded gloomily, I almost wish she were thin and frumpy, except that I really might have to marry her.

Julia saw the glowering look that came over Andrew's face and defiantly raised her chin. Clearly he was as unhappy with her as she was with him. Good! Surely that would make him eager to find a way to avoid marriage.

William spoke pleasantly, as if this were no more than a social occasion. "I believe, Andrew, that you have something to discuss with Julia, so I'll leave you."

At his departure, the room suddenly seemed stifling, and Julia rose and pushed open the shutters of another window. When she turned around, Andrew was standing with his arms folded across his chest. He spoke in a sarcastic drawl. "I trust you won't insist on my being on my knees."

Julia felt her face burn. "Since I don't want a proposal from you, you're safe."

"Your father, however, has quite different wishes, which can hardly surprise you." His arms dropped and his eyebrows came together in a scowl, angry contempt in his voice. "Tell me, Julia, how did you manage that compromising scene last night? And for God's sake, why?"

Julia gripped her hands, wanting more than anything else right then to hit him. "I didn't manage anything. If you hadn't been so eager to seduce Sally, none of this would have happened."

He grasped her arm and pulled her away from the open windows, his hands pressing painfully into her skin. "Seduce Sally? What the devil are you talking about? I've never done more than speak to your empty-headed cousin."

She felt rage radiating from him, but she wouldn't give ground. "I heard . . . in the courtyard last night, I heard her tell you she'd meet you in your room."

"The next time you decide to eavesdrop, you should listen better." His low voice seemed louder than a shout. "If you had, you would have heard me tell her what a stupid idea that was and to *stay away from me*."

A memory from last night returned to Julia that in later events had been pushed aside. When he'd entered his room, the first thing he'd said was something about having told her not to come there. At that time he'd thought she was her cousin. Dismayed, she stared at him. Had he tried to discourage Sally, and she still persisted in meeting him? Was he really not to blame?

He continued relentlessly, "But this still doesn't explain why I found *you* in my room."

She licked her suddenly dry lips. "I wanted to make sure she hadn't gone there."

Sarcasm narrowed his mouth to a hard line. "So instead of looking for her in *her* room, you came to mine, and when you didn't find her, you stayed until I arrived, perhaps to tell me good night?"

"No . . . no. It wasn't like that," she protested, knowing she was on the defensive now, hating the guilty color he must see in her cheeks.

"Tell me, then, just how it was."

Silently she stared at him, her mind whirling. She'd have to tell him Sally had been in his room and why no one must know. Otherwise he'd never understand. But when she tried to speak, the memory of James's agonized face when he'd told her of his fears kept her silent. No matter the cost, she couldn't betray her brother's vulnerability to this man whom they both knew so little.

Yet what could she say that would protect Sally and James and still excuse herself? Despairingly she wanted to give in to the sobs bottled in her throat, to throw herself into Andrew's arms and cry until his accusations turned to sympathy. Appalled that she felt like seeking comfort from him when only moments ago she'd wanted to attack him, she spoke haughtily. "Sally happened to be out of her room . . . for a moment, so I looked for her, and unfortunately you returned sooner than I expected."

His eyes seemed to penetrate her brain, evaluating her words and, from the icy tone of his voice, judging against her. "And your father and brother, also *unfortunately*, felt compelled to come to my room at just the right time? That's very hard to believe."

"But it's true," she cried. "Tobias was beside the window of the court—I saw him there—and he heard you and spoke to Papa."

"Which you, although you know him well, never expected."

She flushed at his sarcastic tone. "No. I mean, yes, I know that Tobias would tell Papa something like that, but at the time I didn't know he'd heard. Oh!" She glared at him in frustrated rage. "You don't want to believe me. But can't you at least understand that no matter how it happened, *I don't want to marry you?*"

At her impassioned words, he responded even more angrily. "Yes, I quite understand you wouldn't wish to marry a man you claim to believe would betray his friend by trying to seduce the friend's bride-to-be. However, your wishes are no longer the principal issue. Your father, again most *unfortunately*, is determined you and I must marry."

Seeing the contempt in his darkly handsome face, Julia felt an almost nauseating pain. Then a surge of strengthening fury revived her courage. Though she couldn't explain to him what had happened, she would not let him browbeat her. "Yes, I know what Papa thinks, but you could refuse. He can't force you to marry me."

His raised eyebrows punctuated a grim smile. "No— not unless you call proposing a duel forcing me. Quite aside from the question of my honor. You, Julia, are equally free—at the cost of your reputation—to reject me."

A lock of black hair slipped down over Andrew's forehead, giving his face a rakish cast. Suddenly Julia couldn't look at him, and turned away, staring instead at the books leaning drunkenly against each other on the shelves. He was right, of course. His good name meant as much to him as Papa's and hers did to her family. Though she wanted to blame Andrew, to hold on to her anger, miserably she recognized he was as caught as she.

If she were honest with herself, she knew that no matter with what fierce courage she might ignore others' opinions, she did want love and regard, and a family of her own. She shrank from the prospect of disgrace, of being a social outcast—of having a reputation that meant no respectable man would want to marry her. While an engaged couple were indulgently forgiven if they overstepped prescribed behavior, unmarried women were not. And memories of transgressions—especially interesting ones—lasted a long time. Worst of all, the final disgrace fell not just on her, but on the man who was supposed to be guarding her—her father.

Andrew watched Julia's shoulders slump and her proud stance soften in defeat. When she slowly faced him again, he could see the conflicting emotions in her face—the pained eyes above the full mouth that struggled not to lose its defiance. As he looked at her, his anger diminished, and for the first time he wondered whether marriage to her would be such a bad thing. Eventually he'd want to marry and have children. She was beautiful, and intelligent—maybe too intelligent and independent for comfort. If only she hadn't maneuvered him into this proposal; that's what stuck in his craw. But had she? Something about the events of last night still puzzled him.

What was clear, what was coming back to him so vividly that he could feel stirrings of desire, was the memory of the passion which had momentarily flared when he'd held her close and caressed her. Probably she'd deny it, but he'd known too many women not to recognize the ardor of her response. Yes, marriage to her might have many benefits, especially having her in his bed, awakening the nature he was almost sure lay under that usually contained exterior.

From the softening of the lines around his mouth and a change in the rhythm of his breathing, Julia could tell when Andrew's thoughts turned from cold accusations to warm desire. Startled, she stepped hastily backward, but his arms caught her and pulled her against him.

She could feel her heart begin to accelerate, pushing her heated blood against her skin. His eyes trapped her, their blue intensifying as he said huskily, "Arranged marriages are common, Julia; perhaps ours has just been arranged in an unusual fashion. It may even work out better than we dream now."

A sensuous smile curved his lips as he ran one hand along her arm, pushing up her sleeve, sending tremors across her shoulders and down to her breasts. With the other hand he lifted her chin and bent his head until she could feel his breath against her lips. "If I'm to pay the penalty for having eaten, I should at least taste the fruit."

Alarm prompted her to push against him, but it melted in the warmth of the mouth that covered hers. Gently at first, then with growing insistence, his lips opened hers, then tasted them with a thrust of his tongue. The heat from his kiss raced through her, making her blood pound and surge beneath her tingling breasts, awakening an ache in her abdomen so that she no longer wanted to move away from him. Instead, the hard bulge under his trousers, which she could feel through her soft skirt and petticoat, seemed to feed a confusing hunger deep inside her. The hand that had made her arm tremble dropped to the round of her breast, cradling and then gently rubbing the now sensitive orb, stroking the nipple and setting it on fire to match her blood.

His hands moved to encircle her hips and lift her against him until she was standing on her toes, the throbbing juncture of her thighs fitting against the strained cloth of his trousers, his hard shaft pressing on that most sensitive center. She felt as if her body were alive as it had never been before in her life, as if it were

in control of her actions, her will lost in the sensations
Andrew was arousing in her.

Suddenly he released her hips, letting her slide down
his body, and held her almost tenderly against him. She
could hear his rasping breath and feel the rapid pounding of his heart and knew that her own pulse matched
his. Bewildered and uncertain, she looked up at him.

His eyes were dark with passion, and he smiled
almost ruefully. "I'm afraid the taste leads too easily to
a feast, but this isn't the time or the place." Gently he
raised her head again and kissed her lightly, then released her and stepped back. Without thinking, she
looked at the front of his trousers, which still showed
the extent of his arousal. At his laugh, she turned
hastily away, her face hot with embarrassment.

Amusement lingered in his voice as he asked, "Do
you wish to tell your father that you've agreed to my
proposal, or shall I?"

She was amazed to find that she could speak without
her voice revealing the trembling she still felt inside.
"I'll inform Papa you knelt and I accepted."

Laughing again, he swept her a bow. "Tell your
father also that I'll call on him soon. And on my
promised—and very promising—bride. I hope you can
contain your impatience until then." Jauntily he bowed
again, kissed her hand, and left.

As the door closed, Julia felt as if she were waking
from a spell. At the thought of her response in Andrew's arms, shame and confusion swept her. She had
agreed to marry a man whom she hardly knew, who
might have been betraying her brother, and she had
acted as if he, instead of Nathan, were the lover she
had been eagerly waiting for. She knew Nathan was lost
to her, and with him all the dreams she'd had about

their future together. But that didn't excuse her response to Andrew's embrace.

Suddenly a memory came to her of Andrew and a dark beauty before a flower stand in the open-air market in Rio. His mistress! How could she have forgotten that?

Burying her flaming face in her hands, Julia gave way to the exhaustion and distress of the last night and day. What did the future hold for her, with a man she didn't love and probably should despise, but who stirred elements of her nature she hadn't known existed?

7

"Miss Julia, those custards are just settin' up."

At Serena's voice, Julia pulled her hand hastily back from the corner of the white cloth which covered the silver bowls on the scrubbed oak table. For a moment she was a small girl at Hundred Oaks, being scolded for snitching food so she could sneak off outside to the fields. Serena crossed the large kitchen and put her hand soothingly on Julia's arm. "You go on now, and relax. You've done a fine job, and the weddin' will go just as smooth as cream tomorrow afternoon. If you carry on like this, you'll be so fussed folks will swear you're the bride."

Julia smiled at the familiar face. "You're right, Serena. I think I'll slip outside until it's time for supper."

The terrace fountain was lazily stretching its shadow in the waning sunlight as Julia closed the double entrance doors behind her. All the women guests had been welcomed and were resting, or primping, in their rooms. Sally had fluttered along the upper hall, nervously accepting the compliments due tomorrow's bride. Thanks to Julia and Serena's planning and preparations, for a short time nothing needed Julia's attention.

Grateful to be alone, she walked along beside the

THE EXILED HEART 129

stone balustrade, looking out over the valley which sloped away below. An occasional yellow tree reminded her that though it was May, the season was autumn, but the unvarying green of the shrublike coffee trees covered most of the landscape. She pulled her shawl closer around her shoulders where her heavy silk dress left her skin bare.

Purple was an unusual color for someone with her red-gold hair, but she liked the vivid colors young Brazilian women wore, and this dress with its full skirt and low-cut bodice became her. An inset of matching lace kept the neckline from being too daring, but the top of her high breasts showed more than Mrs. Scott or Mrs. Wetherly would approve. Let them, she thought defiantly; they probably disapprove of me now anyway.

Where the stone railing curved sharply above the garden, she saw a tall black-haired man. He had his back to her, and he was dressed almost casually in a loose dark jacket and pants, but she recognized the broad shoulders and easy stance. Andrew! Her throat felt suddenly tight.

As everyone who had been invited to this wedding undoubtedly knew, their engagement would be announced on the third night after the marriage ceremony, just before James and Sally left for their three-week honeymoon. Since the confrontation in Papa's study a month ago, she hadn't seen Andrew. He had come to call on Papa, but she'd been in São Paulo with James and Sally to do the last shopping for Sally's trousseau. Julia had enjoyed the two days in the bustling city and couldn't decide whether she was relieved or disappointed at missing Andrew.

She'd questioned Sally about why she'd gone to Andrew's room that night, but as time passed, Sally's memory of events faded. She insisted that Andrew had flirted with her, but Julia knew he might only have mouthed the meaningless phrases conventional in Southern society. Guilt made Sally uncomfortable, and though she wanted to be repentant, she preferred to forget anything she might be blamed for. Just how much Andrew might really have led Sally on and how much the flighty girl had misunderstood, Julia couldn't tell.

If she knew Andrew was at least as much to blame as Sally, she could still be angry at him, and anger would protect her against the scary feelings of their embrace in the study. But reluctantly she gave up trying to question Sally when the last discussion ended with Sally's protesting, "Oh, Julia, why are you worrying? Everyone says he's such a good catch."

At least in the question of a marriage settlement, Papa had listened to her, and Andrew had accepted the terms. Half of the land at Hundred Oaks would be her dowry, and the money which would come to her on her twenty-first birthday would remain hers alone. Though Julia wasn't sure how Brazilian law treated women's property rights, she knew that her South Carolina land would become her husband's. Andrew had no interest, as far as she knew, in returning to live in the United States, and he had agreed that he wouldn't dispose of that land without her family's consent. At the thought that a special place remained which she truly called home, she felt better.

Now, annoyed with herself for hesitating, she approached the tall figure and said, "Good afternoon, Andrew."

When he turned, the low rays of the sun struck his face. He made a sweeping bow and responded, laughter dancing over a mustached mouth, "You have made a very common mistake, Miss Rayford."

Had Andrew grown a mustache? Suddenly Julia realized that the eyes sparkling in the familiar face were not blue—they were midnight black! Startled, she drew back and stammered, "But . . . you're not Andrew."

The man who both was and yet couldn't be Andrew threw back his head with a shout of laughter. "Dear Julia, you cannot regret that any more than my family has often done. I, my sister-to-be, am Roberto, the disgraceful second Langdon son."

Andrew's younger brother? No one had ever mentioned another son. From the lighthearted grin on the handsome face, Julia didn't believe this man felt disgraced, but if his family wasn't proud of him, perhaps that's why she hadn't known of his existence.

As she looked more closely at him, she could see that he was not identical to his older brother, though the resemblance was exceptional. They had the same impressive height and muscular bodies, though his hair was more unruly-looking and his skin darker. He appeared to be five or more years younger than Andrew, perhaps even close to her age. The mustache which, obscured the shape of his mouth, and the color of his eyes were all that readily distinguished his face from his brother's.

When he spoke again, she could hear a flavor of Portuguese in his English. "Don't worry about staring," he assured her gaily. "Everyone does that. Richard stamps his mark on his sons at birth."

She realized that she had indeed been staring, but in the face of his good humor, it didn't seem to matter. "I'm sorry I didn't know who you were, especially since you seem to recognize me, Mr. Langdon."

"But of course, you are the beautiful red-haired Julia. Please—we will be sister and brother—call me Roberto, and may I call you Julia?" At her nod and smile he continued. "I'm not surprised that Andrew hasn't mentioned me. He and Richard would prefer to forget I exist."

Julia wondered if she imagined a bitter undercurrent in the jesting manner. "It's not that. Andrew and I . . . well, we aren't very familiar with each other yet." At his attempt not to laugh again, she realized what she'd said and felt her face grow warm. "I mean, I don't know much about his family," she added.

He did laugh finally, but so unrestrainedly that she couldn't be embarrassed. "Julia, I know I'm going to like being related to you."

With a pleasure that surprised her, Julia agreed with him. His calling his father "Richard" surprised her, and she decided that although he looked like his brother and father, he didn't seem to be much like either of them. Both Richard and Andrew intimidated her, Richard because she distrusted his feelings, and Andrew because he made her distrust her own. In Andrew's unfamiliar house, which she would live in but hadn't yet seen, a friend, even so unorthodox a one as Roberto, would be welcome.

"Please," she said as she moved to stand beside him at the railing, "tell me about yourself and your family."

"If I confide in you, will you tell me something special in return?" As he spoke, his eyes surveyed her thoroughly, lingering particularly on the top of her dress and the curves showing through the lace.

She pulled her shawl closer about her and saw a mischievous smile flicker around his mouth, but she couldn't feel the annoyance she should at his impertinent perusal. "Very well, but I don't promise anything exciting."

He spread his arms dramatically. "Before you stands a live *bandeirante*."

It took Julia a moment to remember the stories she

had read of the bands of adventurers who, in the previous century, had traveled into the interior of Brazil, subduing the scattered natives and claiming large territories. Settlements had been founded, often rough and brawling, and mining enterprises had been set up by these soldiers of fortune, who had become heroic figures.

"I didn't know *bandeirantes* still existed today."

He grinned boyishly. "*I* certainly do. Sometime when you are my sister and we have a long winter day together, I'll tell you of all my adventures. But you also asked about my family. What wicked secrets do you want to know about us?"

The question Julia would most like answered flashed through her mind: did Andrew still have his sultry mistress? Though she quickly suppressed it, some of her concern crept into her query. "Do you all live on the *fazendas*, or do you or Andrew . . . stay sometimes in Rio and other cities?"

Roberto studied her, trying to decide how he felt about her. To charm people, especially women, was one of the challenges he liked best, and this woman would be worth knowing well even if she didn't belong to Andrew. That just added to the excitement. Now, in her eyes, Roberto sensed a question Julia wasn't asking, and he began to probe, hoping to uncover more.

"Richard travels to the United States frequently, and when he does, I'm expected to look after his property." He gave her the half-innocent, half-devilish smile he knew women found so disarming. "But one of the advantages of having a brother like Andrew is that if I don't stay to look after Richard's business, my responsible and capable elder brother will step in and save the family fortunes." Suppressing a sly smile, he added, "Andrew is a very determined man; even if he's off enjoying himself, he rushes home. He doesn't like to give up anything that belongs to him."

At the color that rose in Julia's face he guessed that she knew about Lele. Should he say more? he considered. He had spies everywhere. Anyone so dependent on the whims of others needed lots of information. He knew of the tears Lele had shed when Andrew had told her he was to be married, and of her screaming tantrum when he'd said he would no longer keep her as a mistress. Roberto even knew the amount of money Andrew had deposited with his banker to settle Lele in a place of her own in Rio and provide her with an income until she found another protector.

Should he hint to Julia about Andrew's provisions for Lele? No, that particular bit of news might upset this fascinating new relative, and he could still use it—or whatever part of it seemed to his advantage—later. Besides, he realized with some surprise, he didn't want to disturb the responsive smiles with which Julia had received his earlier teasing. Roberto tried to be unfailingly honest with only one person—himself. As he watched the expressive face with the changeable eyes which seemed to have captured the last sunlight, he knew somewhat ruefully he didn't want her hurt, not by him, not by his brother.

Curiosity led him to risk an audacious question, but he knew the circumstances surrounding Andrew and Julia's engagement and had wanted to meet the woman who had trapped his wary brother. However, she didn't fit the role of a predatory female, and he felt sure more was involved than he'd heard.

He smiled in his most winning manner. "Now it is your turn to answer a question. How did my brother have the good sense to snare you as a bride?"

At his question, Julia suddenly didn't quite trust the

candor which seemed to shine innocently from the black eyes. How could he not have heard the story which she'd been sure everyone knew? Before she could decide, a deep voice behind her answered for her. "I'm the one you should ask, Roberto."

She turned, startled at his silent approach, and found Andrew beside her. His clothes were dark like Roberto's, but the well-tailored fit was formal; the two brothers looked like portraits of the same man at different ages: Roberto the still-rebellious youth, Andrew the mature adult. Andrew took her hand, and then, before she realized what he intended, he pulled her close and lightly kissed her mouth. She could feel a tremor which was more than surprise at so intimate a gesture. Then, as casually as if it were an everyday occurrence, he put his arm around her shoulder and drew her to his side before facing his brother.

"You see, Roberto, I can appreciate more than land and money. Much more."

Apparently unruffled by his brother's sudden appearance, Roberto spoke lightly, though again Julia thought she heard a harsh undertone. "I agree thoroughly, my brother, and I see that with your usual perception—or luck—you've appropriated the most beautiful and appealing woman to appear in our land for a long time." He spread his hands in mock despair and added dolefully, "I suppose now I must relinquish her company to you. But, Julia, wait. He can't keep you from me all the time." With a motion which was more a salute than a bow, he turned and sauntered around the edge of the house.

Conscious of the warmth of the arm around her shoulders, Julia stepped back and looked up at Andrew in the fading light. "I was surprised to meet your brother.

At first I thought he was you, particularly since you've never mentioned him."

"He's been away for several months, and I just didn't think to tell you about him," Andrew replied, taking her arm and turning to walk along the terrace toward the broad steps which led to the garden. "Often we don't see each other for long periods of time."

Julia stretched her stride to keep up with Andrew's long legs. "He told me he's a *bandeirante*, but I'm not sure whether he was teasing. I thought the *bandeirantes* had vanished now."

"Most have, but a few free souls, particularly here near São Paulo, go off on expeditions which imitate the exploits of their grandfathers. Roberto likes to think he's one of them."

They reached the top of the steps, and Andrew started down, but Julia stopped, halting them both. "I think I should go back inside now and see whether guests are downstairs."

"Come, Julia," Andrew declared, "others can do without you, and we need to talk." Firmly he pulled her down the stairs to the carefully tended riot of color below.

Shadows from the tall acacia trees that ringed the garden deepened the twilight, obscuring the view from the house. Julia followed Andrew to a marble bench, and, as they sat down, asked curiously, "Please tell me about your family. Is Roberto your full brother, and are there others?"

"Roberto is my half-brother, my only brother, and I have no sisters. My mother died when I was five. My father had already acquired some land here, and when he made a trip to Rio after my mother's death, he met and married the daughter of an old Brazilian family.

The next year Roberto was born, but his mother died in childbirth."

For the first time, Julia felt sympathy for Richard Langdon. "How terrible for your father, to lose two wives. He was very unlucky."

"Perhaps, though the amount of land he received through his marriages might lead some to think him very lucky."

Uncertain how to interpret Andrew's dry tone, Julia returned to the subject of his brother. "Did you and Roberto know each other when you were boys?"

"When I was nine, I came to Brazil with my father on a visit, but Roberto was only two, and I wasn't much interested in a small child. By the time I returned to live here when I was nineteen, I was involved in running the Langdon *fazenda* during Father's absences and then my own plantation, and Roberto was busy playing, something he's continued to do."

Julia thought of the undercurrents she'd sensed earlier. "I think Roberto envies you."

Andrew's mirthless laugh surprised her, but his words startled her even more. "Then we're even, for I envy him."

He rose restlessly, his highly polished black boots rasping on the graveled walk. "At times I'd like to be like Roberto, going freely where he wishes, with no thought for responsibilities."

Her throat tightened so that she had to force the question which his words demanded. "If you feel that way, why did you give in about marrying me? You sound as if freedom means more to you than honor."

He turned and looked down at her assessingly, and when he spoke his voice had a cold edge. "Are you still trying to bargain your reputation for mine? I thought we'd settled that."

As she jumped up to face him, the anger she'd hoped for returned. "You certainly are suspicious. Is it just of me, or do you distrust everyone?"

His eyes gave no quarter. "You'll admit it wouldn't take a suspicious man to wonder about your actions."

Incensed, she swung around to leave, but he caught her arm, his voice conciliatory when he spoke. "Wait, please. I didn't mean to start a quarrel today. It's just that Roberto is a subject that often provokes me."

Reluctantly she turned back, and the smile he gave her made the resemblance to his brother even more pronounced. Both men, she thought warily, could be charming, and Andrew certainly could be infuriating. Perhaps Roberto was not the open person he seemed to be either.

As Andrew pulled her back to the bench, she realized that she, too, was weary of quarreling and was willing to risk giving up the barrier of anger. She tried to relax and not worry about the overwhelming feelings he might arouse. If they had any chance of making a marriage work, they must try to know each other. Maybe tonight could be a start.

"Julia, what do you expect from marriage?"

Surprised, she looked at his face for some suggestion of mockery, but he was regarding her seriously. Her plans for her life had centered around Hundred Oaks and then Nathan for so long that she realized she hadn't thought about what marriage meant with Andrew. He didn't know about her feelings for Nathan—and she wouldn't mention them. But what did she want?

"Is that such a difficult question?" A hint of a smile had appeared in the watching blue eyes, suggesting one answer he had in mind, and Julia felt the unwelcome warmth in her skin. *I can't seem to do anything but blush with him,* she thought, trying to ignore a vision of the two of them sharing a bedroom as husband and wife.

She looked away from him, as if attracted by the darting of a small green-and-yellow parrot in the nearby trees. "I suppose I expect marriage to be like Mama and Papa's life, managing a plantation, taking care of a family." She faced him again, and her voice strengthened. "But I'm not like Mama, and I couldn't stand the life many Brazilian women seem to lead, leaving everything to slaves and doing almost nothing themselves. I don't know if you remember how I felt about Hundred Oaks. I only did what I had to in the house—I loved the real plantation work, and I was good at it too," she concluded defiantly.

"Yes, I remember." His eyes were definitely amused now, but in a friendly way, as if they were both included in some entertaining joke. "Are you suggesting you would like to be the overseer on my *fazenda*?"

The humor in his face took the challenge from his question, and she smiled in return. "I could be. Want to let me try?"

He reached for her hand and held it, turning it over so that her palm was up. The warmth from his skin stole up her arm as he touched her fingers, curling and uncurling them. He sat silently, and she could hear the sounds of small insects that were venturing out into the shadowy air. Then he looked at her, and although he didn't move, the intensity of his gaze seemed to draw her close. "You said a family. Do you want children, Julia?"

A tide began deep inside her that swept upward and filled her with anticipation until she could hardly breathe. "I . . . I suppose I expect to have children someday. Do you . . . want children?"

He laughed, and the tide swelled until she felt as if

she might shatter into a hundred pieces, and they weren't talking about children—they were talking about being a man and a woman together, bound in sensuality.

"Yes, Julia, I want children eventually, though I'm more interested now in begetting them than in being tied down by the responsibilities for them. And how could you ride through the fields, overseeing the coffee harvest, when you're enormous with my child?"

She pulled her hands away from him and rose hastily, her response blocked by his specific reference to a subject which she wasn't sure men and women ever talked about even after marriage. And his teasing tone suggested he hadn't taken seriously what she'd said earlier about the kind of work she longed to do. Well, if he expected her to be a docile wife, accepting whatever role he thought appropriate for her, he was mistaken.

Andrew watched the changing emotions as her eyes flared and the lines of her mouth straightened, losing the softness of moments earlier. What had put her back up? he wondered irritably. Was it his reference to not wanting to be tied down? She had seen Lele once. Did she think his remark meant he would keep a mistress after they were married?

Julia stood stiffly, beautiful in the brilliant purple dress, her breasts rising and falling with the agitated emotion she obviously was feeling. "I must go, Andrew. Guests will be waiting for me. Please excuse me."

As she turned, her skirts swung in an arc which, as much as her rigid back, told him that some of the ground he thought had been gained was lost. He really didn't want to do battle again, but remembering her reactions to his embraces in her father's study, he felt confident his offensive weapons were effective.

Strolling behind her hurrying figure, he admired the slender waist and imagined the seductive hips beneath the full skirt. He could have told her he'd dismissed Lele from his life, but a gentleman didn't discuss a former mistress with his betrothed. Besides, he was damned if he'd let her think she was going to control his actions.

He mounted the stairs, seeing Julia already disappearing inside the house where candles now gleamed through the windows. He'd cut his ties to Lele because his marriage would have a difficult enough beginning without his keeping her, but the wedding to Julia wouldn't be for a few months, and he didn't relish being without a woman for that long. Plenty of black women were available on his *fazenda*, but he'd always disliked the coercion implied in a master bedding a slave. Besides, he preferred intimacies with women whose company he enjoyed. Maybe he'd been too hasty in sending his bed partner off to Rio, he thought irritably, though she'd begun to bore him and he'd kept her as much from habit and a measure of loyalty as any real desire for her accomplishments.

As he reached for the ornate door and remembered the gaggle of women inside who would be watching him and Julia this evening, his frown smoothed. Did the wait for the wedding have to be so long?

Though she was determined not to let anyone guess her apprehension, Julia had been dreading the first time the Southern immigrants who formed such a close circle would see her and Andrew together after that scandalous episode in his room. Tonight she was braced for the sidelong looks, either sniffily disapproving from some of the women or slyly knowing from the men.

As she circled the large parlor that evening, speaking to guests, making sure everyone was comfortable, she found she had a buffer against either disapproval or curiosity. Soon after dinner Roberto made himself her escort, and Andrew was also at her side most of the time. Obviously others besides Julia had not known of a younger Langdon son, and the startling resemblance between the two men captured everyone's attention.

Mrs. Scott made the same mistake Julia had made, addressing Roberto as Andrew. Winking at Julia over Mrs. Scott's ample shoulder, Roberto reassured the amazed woman that he understood her error and flirted with her until she fluttered her fan like an enamored sixteen-year-old.

When the men carried James off for a final, probably drunken evening as a bachelor, Julia escorted the women upstairs, apparently forgiven for snatching one Langdon son because of the availability of such a charming substitute. When her engagement was announced, a few uncomfortable looks might come her way, but in the face of the rather formidable manner Andrew could assume, nothing would be hinted; the worst was over.

Later, she lay in an unfamiliar bed which had been set up in a small room normally used for storage. It was at the end of the hall, beside the door to the balcony and the back stairs. The house overflowed with guests, and she preferred this temporary bedroom to sharing her own with Mrs. Wetherly's giggling daughters.

Would Sally sleep well tonight? she wondered. Her usually carefree cousin seemed nervous, and James also showed the strain of waiting. They wouldn't have to undress together tomorrow night; Julia had overheard Southern matrons brag that their husbands had never seen them naked, but even in her ignorance, she didn't believe James would behave that way.

Oh, James, Julia thought, I want a happy life for you as much as for myself, since you've always been like a part of me. Giving a prayer that Sally's naturally loving disposition would sustain her, Julia settled down to sleep.

Fragrance from the banks of vivid blossoms which had made a garden of the large music room drifted to the entrance hall, where Julia waited the following afternoon. The estate chapel seemed the perfect place for a wedding to her, but only Catholic ceremonies were held there, and the Southern immigrants were staunchly Protestant. Rows of chairs brought that morning from around the *fazenda* were all occupied, and some of the male guests stood around the edge of the room. At the other end of an aisle between the chairs, she could see the Reverend Henry Shackelford. Soon James and Duncan Scott would join the Episcopalian minister. Duncan was not James's closest friend; that had been Duncan's older brother, killed at Antietam, but James, like her, Julia thought, had to accept a substitute.

On the left the three Langdon men stood together, and Julia could see that Andrew was slightly taller than his father or brother. She felt sure more than one female was covertly watching the striking trio. As if responding to her gaze, Andrew turned and looked at her, and a smile lightened his angular face.

After their aborted conversation in the garden, she had expected him to be cool toward her, but he had acted the perfect escort and bridegroom-to-be all the previous evening. The glance that lingered on her now held pleasure and approval, and she felt an unexpected glow at the warmth in his eyes.

Suddenly she was glad that her golden shot-silk dress heightened her coloring, emphasizing her eyes and setting off her hair. A narrow ruffle of darker gold outlined narrow sleeves and the neckline which circled her bare shoulders and dipped low over her breasts. The tight bodice extended below her waist, where the silk flared over her stiff crinoline to more ruffles at the hem. The *fazenda* seamstress had painstakingly fashioned gloves of the same dark gold silk.

Feeling too conscious of Andrew's scrutiny, she glanced back at Sally, standing beside Papa, and watched Serena fuss over the drape of one of the many layers of white lace which made Sally's dress float around her. Then Mrs. Wetherly began the music, James and Duncan moved to their places, and Julia was walking steadily forward, hearing the rustle of turning heads, and finally stopping to one side of the three men.

Words surrounded Julia, the sonorous tones of the minister, Papa relinquishing the bride, James's familiar voice, and Sally's breathless responses. Suddenly the meaning of those phrases she would be repeating so soon jolted her. If only her reputation didn't reflect on her family, she thought despairingly, she'd leave Brazil and go home to Hundred Oaks. But she stood, a silent participant, and then took Duncan's arm to follow James and Sally to the main drawing room to accept congratulations.

As she watched her brother's face, looking relaxed at last, her resentment and fear dissolved in love for him, releasing a burst of lighthearted joy. His relief and happiness transformed the afternoon, and when Andrew bowed over her hand, she smiled at him, welcoming the admiration in his eyes. She greeted Roberto with a teasing laugh, appreciating his exaggeratedly correct attire and manners.

Andrew, watching his brother flirt with Julia, felt a familiar irritation that Roberto could elict with shallow charm the attention most men earned. Then he dismissed his annoyance. One of the traits he admired in

Julia was her forthright and discerning intelligence. She'd soon know Roberto for his real self.

Roberto, noting the unaccustomed expression on his brother's face, guessed that Andrew was feeling a jealousy he wouldn't recognize. Delighted, he gave Julia a surreptitious wink and was rewarded with a suppressed giggle. The time was overdue, he gloated, for Andrew to be jealous of him.

For a moment an old wound reopened, and Roberto was again a romantic seventeen-year-old, waiting until a beautiful mulatto was old enough that he could persuade his father to agree to their marriage. In his mother's heritage, as in most Brazilian families, was a mingling of black blood, and he'd been confident his father would eventually agree. But Andrew hadn't waited, and had taken Lele for himself, as a mistress, not a wife. Probably he hadn't even known of Roberto's passion for her.

Now the inexperienced boy was buried in the cynical man, and the rage Roberto had felt five years ago was too old to upset his outward good humor today. As he flashed another barely decorous smile at Julia, he saw with satisfaction a tiny line tighten around Andrew's mouth. Yes, this marriage of his brother's had much to offer.

For Julia the remainder of the day passed in a pleasurable whirl. After the congratulations, the guests followed James and Sally out onto the terrace, where the gathered house slaves showered the bride and groom with rose petals. Then everyone returned to the dining room and the long table spread with foods of all sorts, tempting unwary diners to eat until waistcoats and laces had to be furtively loosened. The Southerners exclaimed over such remembered delicacies as guinea hen, Jerusalem artichokes, and hot mustard pickles. Local guests found the black beans and rice sprinkled with manioc meal that were always served, as well as fish and turtle and a variety of meats. The Brazilian sweet tooth was well supplied with custards and confections and gallons of orangeade. Serena and her helpers had prepared both the traditional Southern fruit cake and *pao delor dos anjos*, angel's sponge cake. Julia savored the taste of *aluá*, a drink made from rice flour which had been fermented in a clay vessel with sugar and pineapple rind.

She might have feared the potency of the *aluá* had it not been for the vigorous dancing which began at dark. The furniture had been removed from the large drawing room, and the polished floor reflected black boots and swaying skirts as whirling couples fluttered the candle flames along the blue papered walls. Julia floated through reels and waltzes with a succession of partners, enjoying the music and the admiration in both adolescent eyes and lined faces.

About nine o'clock the dancing paused while everyone filled the terrace to watch rockets and fireworks shower the sky with rainbows of color. When the dancers returned inside, Julia joined James on a settee at one end of the long salon.

James didn't dance because he feared his impaired balance would make him clumsy, but he looked at ease, now that the ceremony was over and he and Sally were committed to each other. He and Julia sat quietly, not needing to talk to know each other's feelings.

Julia hadn't yet danced with Andrew, though Roberto had been her partner several times and Richard once. Earlier she had noticed Andrew waltzing with Sally, but she hadn't seen him since, and supposed he was in the game room. It surprised and, she realized, annoyed her that he'd so quickly abandoned the role of attentive escort. Now, when he approached, she nodded coolly, still piqued by his indifference, but he returned her greeting with an inviting smile before addressing James.

"May I dance with your sister? I've been restraining myself to allow others their chances, but my unselfish nature has reached its limit."

James grinned and made a gesture relinquishing her. "Of course, Andrew—she's yours."

Julia's first impulse was to refuse; she was not James's to give and didn't intend to forget Andrew's neglect so easily. But his firm hand overcame her resistance.

The black musicians began a waltz, and though Andrew held her at the proper distance as they circled the room, Julia felt as if some power he gave off had closed the space between them so that they were dancing in an intimate embrace. She could feel her skin tingling and hoped no one, especially Andrew, could observe her agitation. He danced gracefully and easily, and when they neared the far end of the large salon, he skillfully whirled her through the entrance hall and outside.

As the chilly May air brushed her bare throat and arms, she stopped. "Andrew, wait—what are you doing?"

Ignoring her protest, he pulled her around the side of the house, where Scizira, the young slave who acted as maid to Julia and Sally, waited. She held out one of Julia's cloaks, a dark gray wool with a warm flannel lining.

"*Obrigado*, Scizira," Andrew said, and wrapped the cloak securely around Julia's shoulders as the black girl nodded and slipped away.

"The dancing in the *casa grande* tonight is not as exciting as the celebration in the *senezala*," Andrew told her, taking her arm and leading her across the back of the terrace to the path which led from the big house to the slave quarters.

"But, Andrew," she protested, "I can't leave the guests."

He laughed joyously, continuing to guide her along the dark walk. "That's why I waited so late to come for you. Even if you're missed, the beverages which have been consumed so freely will ensure that no one will mind." He cut off further objections by saying smugly, "Besides, Julia, the beauty of our situation is that whatever we do is probably no worse than what everyone thinks we're doing."

From the carefree tone of his voice, Julia decided that he, too, had consumed a good portion of those beverages, and her own lighthearted capitulation to his urging could perhaps be due, she rather fuzzily thought, to the delectable taste of the *aluá*.

Flaring torches lit the terrace and part of the path to the slave quarters, but now it was dark, and she stumbled over an uneven stone. Andrew caught her around the waist, lifting her in his arms and carrying her along in his smooth stride. Her cloak slid back, and cradled against him, she could feel the heat of his body through her dress and his formal suit. Around her legs the hoop skirt billowed awkwardly.

"Andrew, put me down." When he showed no sign of releasing her, she added, "Please." He laughed, an exuberant, almost gleeful chortle, and continued down the dark path. She could only fasten her arms around his neck and cling to him, hoping the alcohol he'd drunk wouldn't combine with the uneven ground to trip him.

She began to hear ahead of her the beating of drums and the sounds of music she knew was popular with the slaves. When they arrived at the first of the small cabins, he put her down. She could see dark figures silhouetted in the glow of a large bonfire and hear

clapping and singing. Andrew kept her close beside
him as they moved forward and stopped just at the
edge of the shadows; then his arms encircled her, holding her with her back against his chest.

As at the dancing she'd watched on Baron Saia's
island, men and women had formed a circle around a
leader. To one side several musicians crouched. One
held an instrument made from a skin-covered gourd
with two strings which he plucked with his fingers;
another pulled a bow across the single string of a similar
instrument. Three men had small drums, and one player
sat astride a drum about five feet long which lay on the
ground. The dancing must have been going on for
some time, because in spite of the cold, most of the men
had abandoned their shirts, and sweat ran down their
dark shoulders and backs.

The dancers seemed to imitate the motions of the
flames as they leapt and writhed. Around them other
slaves chanted and clapped, swaying in time to the
rhythm. A young woman, her head swathed in a gleaming white turban, her emerald blouse and turquoise
skirt swirling about her, bounded into the center and
began to dance opposite the leader. Snapping her fingers first at her sides and then high over her head, she
advanced provocatively, her breasts thrusting toward
her partner, only to retreat in the face of his response.
Faster and faster she advanced and whirled backward,
her skirts flying high around her bare legs.

Julia gasped, not just at the sight of the half-nude
woman, but also at the same response she'd felt when
she watched the slave dances so many months ago in
Rio. The open sensuality of their movements captured
her, drawing her out of herself. Only the hard arms
around her held her to reality, but those arms seemed

not so much to restrain her as to weld her to the heartbeat she could feel thundering against her back.

She twisted and looked up into Andrew's eyes and saw there the same desire that was being acted out before them. Pulling her into the deeper shadows of the nearest cabin, he murmured into her ear, "Does this stir you as you stir me?" He kissed her, and she felt consumed by the fierce demand of his searching lips.

No thought of restraint marred the shivering pleasure of his mouth on hers, his arms holding her pressed close to him. His hand first stroked her back and neck, then moved under the cloak to the low neckline of her dress and one breast. She felt as if the bonfire had leapt the circle of swaying dancers and flamed inside her, scorching her skin and sending streaks of fire from her lips to her breasts and deep inside to a core which was melting in its heat.

She could hear ragged breathing but could not tell whether it was she or Andrew who gasped for air. He gently imprisoned the other breast and stroked the throbbing nipple while with his arm he strained her against him as if trying to banish the barriers of their clothing. She grasped his shoulders and slid one hand through the thick hair on the back of his neck, wanting nothing so much as to feel him closer.

With a half-shudder, he released her breast and pulled her cloak around her, holding her, but no longer insistently. She could feel a burning deep inside, but the raging fire began to die, the highest flames smothered. He spoke, his voice low and unsteady. "Julia, Julia . . . you drive me beyond propriety—but at the wrong time. We must go before I disgrace you."

Too stunned by the depth of her responses to speak, Julia held to the strong arm which supported her as they retraced the path to the big house. When they reached the terrace, Andrew paused at the edge of the light and opened her cloak. Startled, she drew back, but he laughed and only straightened the upper edge of her dress where it was askew. "Give me your cloak, and I'll return it to Scizira. No one will know you've been away."

As he lifted the cloak from her shoulders, he pressed a brief kiss on the tender skin where her neck joined her bare shoulder and whispered, "Think of me later, Julia."

Crossing the terrace to slip back inside the room where couples still revolved in what now seemed sedate dances, she knew that she would be thinking of him.

8

A few minutes after Julia returned to the big house, Andrew followed her for one very chaste waltz before Roberto claimed her. At midnight the musicians gathered their instruments and left.

After the men and women escorted James and Sally separately to their elaborately decorated bedchamber, Julia slipped away to her small temporary room and gratefully let Scizira release her from her dress and crinoline. Before sinking into the feather mattress on the bed, she saw her gray cloak hanging on one of the pegs along the wall.

Andrew had been among the men escorting James upstairs, and he disappeared with the others. Now, watching the stars through the small window near her bed, she relived the moments in the *senezala,* remembering the sensuality of the slaves' dance and Andrew's caresses.

Confused by the sensations still so new to her, she turned restlessly. How had he felt? Recalling his ragged breathing and pounding heart, she realized that however much he'd aroused her, she'd had at least as much effect on him. Is he thinking about me right now? she wondered. No—he was probably gambling at monte or laughing over a glass of brandy. Determined to put him out of her mind, she covered her head with her pillow and finally slept.

Below on the terrace Andrew watched the glow of his thin cigar and calculated how much longer the drinking would last. Too long for his taste, but he felt compelled just now, he realized irritably, to abide strictly by the Southern code, and that included remaining a participant and upright as long as liquor was served.

Honor—the plague and strength of the American South. A man should revere his father, drink, gamble, respect women but yet be successful with them, and defend himself, violently when necessary. If he also made money, that added to his status, but being poor didn't disqualify him as a gentleman. Probably the similarities in codes between Brazil and their previous home appealed to the displaced Confederates, though the Brazilians seemed a little more carefree and tolerant with each other.

He tossed his cigar in an orange arc over the railing and thought of the excursion tonight to the *senezala*. He'd been foolish—Julia's father might yet take a pistol to him for his recklessness, but the blacks celebrated with an exuberance he'd wanted Julia to see. He'd remembered how stirred she'd been when she'd watched the dances on Baron Saia's island, and the greatest excitement had been holding her in his arms, awakening her passion.

He heard a step behind him and turned to find Roberto. "What, Andrew, not totting up more wealth at the expense of your new neighbors?"

At his brother's faintly goading voice, Andrew curbed a familiar irritation, wishing that Roberto had land of his own; then his jealousy of Andrew might lessen.

Outwardly imperturable, he replied, "I was just waiting to pit my skills against yours."

As he walked with Roberto back to the card room, he thought wryly that most meetings with his brother seemed to end with some kind of contest.

When Julia finished her duties in the house the next day, she changed into a two-piece brown-and-tan taffeta dress suitable for the afternoon's entertainment. No chore seemed onerous after her glimpse of Sally's happy face at breakfast that morning. Now Julia picked up a large Brazilian straw hat and settled it over her chignon before hurrying down to the front terrace. Two clusters of women waited for her, the Southern immigrants and the few Brazilians from nearby *fazendas* maintaining an uneasy separation.

Julia noticed one of the Brazilian women gesturing animatedly, obviously the center of attention in her group. She was Senhora Carlota Pereira, a young widow who lived with her sister's family on the nearby Bernanos *fazenda*. Last night Senhora Pereira, who appeared to be in her late thirties, had easily attracted admiration from the men with her flirtatious dark eyes, sensual mouth, and voluptuous figure. Now she was entertaining her appreciative female audience with sprightly conversation, but she spoke too rapidly for Julia to understand. A burst of giggles, followed by sly looks at the Americans, made Julia guess that Senhora Pereira had been making fun of the Southerners.

Annoyed at the senhora's unkind influence over the otherwise friendly Brazilians, Julia walked quickly to the tittering women and smiled graciously. Using her best Portuguese, she spoke to the oldest guest, the black-clad elderly mother of Senhor Bernanos. "A Senhora Bernanos, I hope you and the other senhoras are

ready to ride to the field for the games." At the tiny
woman's smile and nod, she turned to include the
Southerners, and the two groups descended together to
the drive, where black coachmen stood beside the waiting carriages.

The conveyances, looking like circus wagons from the
many brightly colored hats and parasols, drove down
the slopes where coffee trees with their red berries
disguised themselves as shrubs, then across sugarcane
fields where new green shoots pushed up through the
still-scorched earth. Soon they arrived at a large cleared
area; the men, who that morning had gone hunting for
wild turkeys and pigs, were clustered around the horses.
When the carriages stopped, the men came to help the
women down and escort them to benches where bamboo shelters had been erected.

After the last of the other passengers had preceded
her, Julia found Roberto at the carriage, ready to help
her descend. He saluted her gloved hand before encir-
cling her waist and lifting her from the seat. His almost
bold manner made Julia step quickly away from him as
soon as her feet felt the ground. Her thank-you sounded
stiff to her ears, but Roberto smiled serenely and offered his arm.

"Thank you, Roberto," Andrew said behind her, "you
seem to be looking out for Julia regularly. But no need
now." Julia thought she saw a flicker of muted anger in
Andrew's face, but he smiled affably at his brother and
tucked her hand in the bend of his elbow. Both men
wore Brazilian-style riding clothes, loose pants and shirts
with waist-length soft leather jackets and broad hats
held on with leather thongs. The similarity in dress
emphasized their strong physical resemblance.

As she walked with Andrew to the benches, he looked
down at her, and the expression in his dancing eyes

took her back instantly to their embraces the previous
night. "You slept well, Julia?"

"Yes—very well, as I assume you did?"

He laughed, and she knew he'd understood her question as she had his. He'd intended her to think of him,
but she wanted him to know she expected him to have
been equally visited by dreams of her.

Games occupied the rest of the afternoon, beginning
with the match races between horses whose owners
challenged each other and rode their own mounts. None
of the Langdons participated in these contests, though
Julia thought Roberto must be wagering, from the activity around him.

Next the men tried their skills at *canas e argolinhas*,
reeds and rings. This Brazilian pastime delighted the
Southerners because of the resemblance to the mock
tournaments and jousts staged at home. The riders
used reeds as lances; on horseback they charged at the
rings, suspended from tall poles, and attempted to catch
a ring on the end of the reed. Laughing and cheering,
the spectators bet on the outcome of each trial.

Andrew and Roberto entered the competition, Andrew riding a sleek brown gelding and Roberto cavort-
ing on a small, wiry mare. Both men captured their
share of rings, but Julia was fascinated by the difference
in their styles. Andrew rode effortlessly, with no wasted
motions, as if man and horse were a single fluid animal.
Roberto, on the other hand, seemed to be playing the
part of a jester, riding carelessly, looking as if he might
overshoot his goal or even fall off his horse. Yet at the
last moment he recovered in time to snare his ring.
What sort of deviltry did Roberto harbor? Julia wondered. Did Andrew have devils too, but ones that were
better concealed?

After the rings had all been claimed, the men began

to gather around a small roped area to one side of the benches. When Julia saw a slave holding a rooster while another slave laced spurs, like tiny sword blades, to the bird's feet, she realized the next entertainment would be a cockfight. She hastily rose and left the benches, knowing she couldn't stand to watch the two birds slashing at each other, but several of the Brazilian women eagerly joined the growing cluster of men waiting to wager on the outcome.

The older Senhora Bernanos also rose and came to stand by Julia. In her soft Portuguese she asked, "You do not wish to watch?"

Julia tried to look polite as she replied, "No, I don't enjoy cockfights."

"Oh," the tiny woman urged, "you should at least see the canaries. My daughter-in-law's sister, Senhora Pereira, likes to watch the male canaries fight most of all."

For a moment Julia thought she had not understood the word *canario*, but she realized that the elderly woman did indeed mean canaries. Sickened, Julia quickly asked the senhora about São Paulo winter weather, hoping by the inconsequential chatter which usually bored her to blot out the vision of those small singing birds in a bloody tangle. When the enthusiastic shouting of the engrossed spectators died, she glimpsed a slave carrying something that dripped red, and when the women who had been watching rejoined her, Julia could hardly stand their looks of satisfied pleasure. Just then she saw Andrew returning from the far side of the field and realized with relief he had not been watching the cockfights. She waved happily to him, and he returned her greeting with a dazzling smile.

As the carriages returned to the big house, the men rode their horses alongside, like an honor guard escorting medieval ladies back to the castle. Julia gladly saw the women upstairs for *sesta,* though she rested only briefly before dressing and going to see that Serena had not had any emergencies. Everyone gathered for the evening meal, but after the women left the dining room, the men soon went directly to the card room for the usual evening of dicing and cards.

Julia wondered how much money had been won and lost that day; Brazilians seemed as crazed to gamble as most of the Southerners. She asked Mrs. Wetherly's daughter to sing for the women, preferring the dubious music to more gossip, but instead of listening, she thought that the next night everyone would again dance and visit to honor the announcement of her betrothal to Andrew. A constriction in her throat spread to her stomach; tomorrow she would be publicly committed to marriage.

Across the wide music room, she heard a happy laugh and saw Sally, light from the branched candelabrum on the piano highlighting her sparkling eyes. Obviously the wedding night had quieted her fears. Julia wondered how her own face would look after her first night of marriage. At the thought, she felt a shiver that could have been either anticipation or fear.

She woke from a dream of bonfires and drums, feeling vaguely as if something were wrong, and looked up for the overhead canopy until she remembered she was in the small room at the end of the hall. Reassured, she turned to look through the nearby window at the stars floating in the night sky. Suddenly she heard a movement, the shush of a boot against the braided rug. She sat up, straining to see in the dark. A tall shape loomed beside the bed, and a hand swiftly stifled the scream on her lips.

"Softly, softly, Julia."

Shock throttled a second scream as Andrew cautiously pulled his hand away from her mouth. For a moment she gaped at the dim figure which knelt beside her bed.

"Andrew!" Her aghast whisper sounded like a shout in the still night, and she made her voice as quiet as she could. "What are you doing here?"

"Scizira told me where to find you."

Momentarily she thought her senses were betraying her, that he couldn't have done something so outrageous. But his soft laugh convinced her of his reality. Anger turned her whisper into a hiss. "You must leave, right now!"

He slipped one hand around her head and brought her ear against his lips as he barely whispered, "I haven't seen you all evening, hardly all day. I couldn't go to bed without a proper good-night."

Before she could respond, his fingers turned her face to his, his lips moved to her mouth, and he was kissing her. Surprise robbed her of thought or protest as he kissed her again, his lips warm and inviting. His mouth moved hungrily, forcing her lips open. When his tongue touched the inside of her lips, slowly tasting her mouth, she found herself yielding to the erotic pressure. His lips released hers, only to plunder them again, lingering, leaving her trembling. As he moved downward to taste her throat and then lower to the opening of her batiste gown, her senses erupted in a streak of flame. Struggling to control the sensations his kisses were building, she pushed at him, forcing his head away. "No . . . stop. Someone will find you here. Go away."

His finger on her mouth stilled her whisper. "No one will hear us in this room. Before, you came to me. Now I return the call." Laughter threaded through his hushed voice, and she could smell the mingled odors of brandy, tobacco, and a fresh, almost forestlike scent she recognized as being particularly his.

"You've been drinking!" Determinedly she pushed back from him, but he followed her, sitting on the side of the bed, gathering her close and brushing her loose hair away from her face.

"Yes, but what has intoxicated me is the memory of your gleaming hair and the fire in your eyes which matches it. And most of all the passion that hides in your beautiful body, just waiting for me."

No one had ever spoken that way to Julia before, and the whispered words infused her like a strong aphrodisiac. He pulled her across his lap and held her against him as he pressed brief kisses on her eyelids, her ear, the tender skin along her neck. "Julia, let me hold you. Let me touch your skin, so soft and silky I can hardly believe it's real. Let me show you how you make me feel."

She knew she should resist, force him to leave, but under the edge of her gown, his hand stroked her shoulder, while his lips sought hers again, smothering her, possessing her. She felt as if the stars from the night sky had swooped down and were burning furiously in her chest. Desperately she sought for a last measure of control before slipping into the chaos her sensations had become. "No, Andrew—it's wrong."

"It can't be wrong. Not for me, and you'll see, not wrong for you either." His soft words came to her faintly through the welter of new and overwhelming feelings his hands and mouth were creating.

Andrew could sense that fear mingled with Julia's growing passion. Keeping a firm grip on his own surging desire, he shifted their bodies until he was stretched out beside her on the bed. For long moments he held her close, stroking her back, tenderly kissing her forehead where the hair curled in soft wisps, soothing the lines he could feel in her confused face.

When he felt the tense muscles of her back relax, he allowed himself to follow the path his longings demanded. Pushing aside her loose gown, he gently caressed the curve of her breast, taking pleasure from her soft gasp. When he touched the already erect nipple, he felt his own swift intake of air as fire shot through his loins, making his rigid shaft throb. Struggling to remember her inexperience, he forced himself to be content with gently teasing the hard bud until he could wait no longer to capture it with his mouth.

Julia felt the wet heat of his lips searing her breast; she shuddered as a new and intense sensation filled her, enveloping not just the breasts which he suckled, first one and then the other, but the throbbing which had begun deep in her belly. Some great hunger possessed her which could not be appeased in any way she had ever known.

He shifted away from her, and she felt abandoned and cold. Then he was lifting her, pulling her gown off over her head, and swiftly ridding himself of his clothes.

At the cessation of his touch Julia's raging sensations dimmed. When he slipped back into bed beside her, she shrank back, exposed and vulnerable to the naked body against hers. As if he knew this, he only held her close, smoothing her hair, murmuring softly, "There now, don't be frightened. Just let me touch you, show you, teach you some of the pleasures we can have."

Reassured more by the sound of his voice than the words which she could barely understand, she began to lose her fears. Gradually the heat of his body, the pressure of his hard chest with its hair gently brushing her soft breasts, and his unhurried caresses rekindled her unsatisfied longing. Again he gathered the pulsing stars within her, wooing her with his mouth and hands, caressing her hard nipples, restoring her greedy straining for something more.

His hand moved farther down her body, awakening nerves in her skin she hadn't known were so alive, caressing her hip, her barely rounded abdomen, her thighs, and finally touching the soft juncture of her legs, where suddenly all sensation was concentrated. When his fingers stroked the soft curls, then parted them to stroke again, the terrible new hunger made her moan and arch against his hand.

More insistently his fingers caressed her, building the sensations until she felt as if all the stars that had captured her were transporting her up into the night sky. From a distance she felt his mouth tugging on her breast as his hand continued its movements, sending her even higher into the black universe; then all the stars melted in an explosion of fire that swept her spiraling into space and falling back to an earth which was Andrew's arms.

She lay sheltered by his length, trembling with the last of the intense shudders which had flung her so far. He held her tightly, tension still obvious in his powerful body. Though her hunger had been appeased, she could tell from his rasping breath and the way he pressed her hips against him that his passion demanded more. Bold in the aftermath of the radiance he'd created, she brushed her fingers across his firm chest and felt the erect nipples in his springy hair. He turned slightly away from her so that she could more easily discover his impatient body.

Hesitantly she moved her hand down the rippling muscles of his chest to the flat belly, following the line of hair that first narrowed, then widened. Suddenly ashamed of her overtures, she started to draw back, but he caught her hand, breathing into her ear, "Yes, yes—touch me, hold me."

He guided her hand downward until she felt the thick nest of tight curls and his hard, pulsing penis, standing rigidly out from his body. As her fingers curled around his shaft, he groaned, and she stopped. But he brought her hand back and guided her until she was stroking his stiff phallus, touching the tight orbs beneath.

Andrew knew he couldn't wait much longer. He must either leave with Julia's virginity technically intact and his passion painfully unslaked, or he must go on. When he'd come to her room, he'd first been challenged by the imprudence of such a visit. He'd intended only enough preliminary lovemaking to give them both additional pleasure and a foretaste of what would come. Once with her, however, he'd been unable to resist the tremendous longing to know more of her, to have her naked beside him, to touch all of her, and finally to give her the tumultuous release that had provided him almost as much pleasure as would his own.

When she reached out to caress him, he hadn't been able to resist her touch, and now her tentative hands were driving him beyond restraint. He rolled her over on her back and again found her sensitive center of pleasure. His lips close to her ear, he breathed, "I want to be inside you, Julia, be part of you." He felt her pulse pounding as his mouth again found her breast and he continued to probe her velvet opening with his fingers. When he thought he would explode with longing, she shifted and parted her thighs wider. Lost to everything but his throbbing need for her, he moved over her soft center and with a swift thrust buried himself in her tight heat.

Julia felt a cutting pain and bucked against him. Instantly he stopped, his breath rasping in her ear, his heart thundering against her chest, and gradually the pain subsided. When she softened and moved, wanting more from him, he thrust again, and the hunger of her center was renewed in the pressure of him inside her.

His voice was a groan. "God, God—you're wonderful. That feels so good." He filled her, intensifying her desire with each accelerating motion, until he arched against her with a series of convulsive shudders and was still.

She lay beneath him, not wanting him to be finished, trying instinctively to rotate her hips against his. He turned to his side, slipping out of her, but before she could voice the protest which rose involuntarily, his hand found her still-pulsing opening. Quickly his fingers filled the void left when he separated from her, and he first nurtured, then appeased her passion as she came to a second blinding release.

Cradled against him, she rested while her breathing returned to normal; she could feel his heartbeat slowing as well. Her other senses began to operate again—the stars resumed their glittering outside the window; she could see the shadows and lights of the bones of his face. The fading odor of brandy mingled with a musky, strangely exciting scent which must come from their lovemaking.

With the waning of the overwhelming sensations of her body came the realization of what they had done, bringing in its wake all the prohibitions of twenty years. "Andrew—"

His lips stopped her, then he said softly, "No, Julia—no regrets."

"But we're not married—it's wrong."

"Such pleasure can't be wrong. What would be wrong would be to refuse what we can give each other. And we'll be married soon."

Shame warred with the wish to believe him and deny the distress she would feel otherwise. "But tomorrow—how can I face everyone?"

He murmured soothingly, lightly caressing her neck, "We've done no more than most of them believe has already happened."

Bemusedly she realized he was right, but no longer would she have the certainty of her own innocence to sustain her. Tears seeped from her eyes, tears of confusion and dismay; she tried to move away from his embrace, but he refused to release her, kissing her tears, rubbing her back until she relaxed against his warm length.

To her astonishment, she felt a hard pressure against her thigh and realized that his penis had swollen again. He gave a soft laugh, kissed her quickly, and rose from the bed. Finding her nightgown, he slipped it over her head; then he picked up his own clothes and put them on. Though she could see him only dimly, she thought a bulge still strained the front of his trousers.

He turned and leaned over her, his voice faintly amused. "You see that I could happily stay with you all night, but you'd be much too sore in the morning. Sleep well, my beautiful Julia, and never waste regrets on such joy." After one more brief kiss, he slipped silently out of the room.

Fearfully Julia waited for the alarmed cry that would tell her Andrew had been seen. When nothing disturbed the silence, she lay back and tried to sift her bewildered emotions, but the task seemed too much. All she could know coherently was that she had experienced feelings so strange but so pleasurable that she would never be the same again. And if she had held any secret hope that the marriage to Andrew could somehow be avoided, she abandoned that hope now.

When Andrew reached the bottom of the staircase from the balcony outside Julia's room, he glanced back at her dark window and then silently made his way to the bachelor quarters. Though his body had experienced intense satisfaction, he did not feel sated. He truly could have spent all night with her, made love to her again and again.

As he slipped into his bedroom, this time the closest one to the outside entrance, he thought of how much he had exposed her by going to her bed tonight. Reluctantly he recognized that he had deliberately seduced her. Though he hadn't consciously intended to go so far, he should have known that once he was with her, holding her so intimately would overcome his self-control. With awareness came an unaccustomed feeling of guilt. A gentleman would not have done as he had tonight, and though he knew he could be ruthless, he usually acted more honorably.

He removed his clothes and slid into the cool sheets, still pondering his behavior. Had he gone to her because she'd trapped him into marriage—as a kind of revenge? No—he was no longer sure that she'd intended to be found in his room. He didn't know just what had happened a month ago, but somehow he believed she wouldn't resort to a plot of that kind. And he didn't need or want a "conquest" to prove his masculinity; that kind of challenge didn't interest him. Why, then, had he made love to her tonight?

An unbidden answer forced itself on him: he wanted to ensure that she would marry him. Startled, he considered the idea, but the agreement had been made; he didn't need to bed her to establish a claim. Roberto's face intruded into his thoughts, Roberto smiling at Julia, flirting with her.

Restlessly he turned over. He didn't worry that Ro-

berto would influence Julia in any way. The simplest
explanation must be the best—she was a beautiful and
exciting woman; he found his desire awakened too often
when he was with her to want to wait for a wedding
ceremony. That was all.

The sound of soft voices and laughter disturbed Julia's sleep. She opened her eyes and then closed them
against the sunlight which filled the small window.
Groggily she pulled the pillow back over her head; then
memory jolted her awake. The events of the night
flooded over her—Andrew's sudden appearance, his
careful lovemaking which overcame her fears, the incredible sensations. But stronger now than memory
were shame and guilt.

How could she have been so acquiescent—so abandoned! She should have resisted longer. What would
Papa think of her if he knew? And Andrew—had he lost
all respect for her, as she'd been told any man would if
she "gave in" before marriage? And what about pregnancy? She shuddered and clutched the pillow, wanting
to hide behind it forever. Longing for her mother assailed her; though she couldn't have talked to Mama
about this, knowing she was dead seemed to make it
worse.

Slowly she pushed the comforting darkness aside and
stared up at the ceiling, where sunlight, reflected from
the polished floor, shimmered wavelike over the bleached
boards. Nothing could change what she'd done; she
must have the courage to face whatever might happen.

As she forced herself to leave the bed and pour water
from the pitcher into the china basin, she tried to think
more calmly about what had happened. Last night hadn't
changed her reputation, nor her commitment to mar-

riage with Andrew. Only they knew that now a wedding was as appropriate as everyone had assumed.

With her hands on the edge of the basin, she stopped. If she had to give up those wonderful, scary sensations, would she want to do that? Was she that ashamed? She didn't know.

She let the nightgown fall to the floor and washed in the cold water before putting on the flowered morning dress which Scizira had left hanging from a peg last night. The maid might guess Andrew had been here last night, but maybe she wouldn't gossip about it to the other slaves. Examining the rumpled bed, Julia found a pink stain on the sheets. Hastily she pulled up the covers, as if momentarily someone would burst into the room and search for evidence of her lost virginity. She'd have to manage to take the bed linens to the washhouse herself; once they were gathered with all the other laundry, no one would know where those particular sheets had come from.

Anger swept her at the need for this kind of deceit. If Andrew hadn't forced himself on her . . . No, though her distressed spirit longed to blame him for her misery this morning, she knew she'd accepted his lovemaking, perhaps even welcomed it.

As she brushed her hair, she couldn't banish the unreasonable fear that she looked different now. Apprehensively she picked up the tiny wood-framed mirror that stood on the dresser, but it reflected a face that seemed just the same as yesterday—thickly lashed golden-brown eyes, straight nose, almost too-full lips, and a jaw James said showed how stubborn she could be. She turned the small mirror facedown so forcefully she heard it crack.

When she descended to the small dining room, most of the women guests were already drinking coffee and brushing away the crumbs of the sweet rolls served for the light breakfast. No one looked at her with more than ordinary interest.

Mrs. Scott beamed and patted the seat next to her. "Julia dear, please do tell us what you think about this new fashion of leavin' off crinolines at formal entertainments."

Fortunately Mrs. Wetherly was too anxious to express her disapproval of such an inelegant idea for Julia to have to answer. She felt relieved, but almost disappointed that a discussion of hoop skirts interested the group more than possible evidence of dissipation on her face.

Another hunting expedition had taken the men away, and for the remainder of the morning household activities required Julia's attention. Gratefully she concentrated on solving the problems which arose daily on even the most scrupulously planned occasions. One of the kitchen girls cut her hand badly; Julia attended to the stitching and binding of the wound. The door to the smokehouse had been broken open and a crock of pork taken which was the staple for the slaves. Though the overseer would try to trace the thief, Julia saw that the smokehouse was put back in order and the stores for the meals in the slave quarters replenished. She wondered how well Sally would manage in the future, but these and other minor tasks kept her too busy to brood about Sally or muse painfully on her own wicked nature.

When the female guests retired to their rooms for an early-afternoon *sesta*, Julia managed to slip away for a Brazilian-style bath in the stream which splashed down the hill behind the garden. Because she couldn't go alone, she decided to take Scizira with her. Serena needed all the kitchen help, and the other maids would be busy pressing the elaborate dresses for the evening.

Reluctantly Julia sought out the young black woman, but Scizira's face was impassive as she listened to Julia's directions and went to collect soap and towels.

With the maid following, Julia went through the garden and along a path where purple and lavender orchids festooned the heavy foliage. She found her favorite bathing spot where the stream, after dropping steeply over some boulders, curved back upon itself, forming a deep pool beneath the cascading waterfall. Thick growth along the banks provided an effective screen, with the only access the path from the gardens. Stationing Scizira along this trail, Julia undressed and slipped into the water. At first the cool water made her shiver, but vigorous splashing soon warmed her.

Enjoying the sandalwood scent of a bar of special soap, she bathed and washed her hair, then lay back where sun had warmed a shallow swirl of water. Looking at her long bare legs, she thought of the difference between her and Andrew. His body had been so firm, the surface of his muscular arms and legs smooth and hard, such a contrast to hers. She'd been so caught up in her sensations last night that only now did she wonder what he had thought of her.

She sat up in the water and looked at herself as if seeing everything new. Though she was very slender, and her breasts small, they stood up firmly, the rose nipples distinct against her white skin. Andrew had groaned when he caressed them last night; had he felt as much pleasure as he gave her?

"Sinhazinha!"

At the sound of Scizira's soft call, using the affectionate name slaves gave their young mistresses, Julia started, a spray of water from her hands making tiny rainbows beside her. *"O que deseja?"*

Scizira's gesturing hands punctuated her rapid Portuguese. "The men have returned from the hunting, and some of them are coming along the path, going to the lower pool."

Julia scrambled from the water. The men would not ordinarily come near this part of the stream, since it was reserved for women, but the drinking began early at these extended parties, and some of the guests might refuse to be guided by the servants and wander upon her. Scizira helped rub her partly dry and gathered the damp red hair into a curling fall down her back. Julia pulled on her shift and soft dress over her still-damp skin and raced up the path. Though she was dressed, she shouldn't appear before any man in the informal garb which clearly suggested she'd been bathing.

She thought she'd regained the back of the house safely. Halfway up the steps to the terrace, she looked up and saw Roberto, in the casual clothes of their first meeting. He stopped and waited at the top of the stairs. Realizing she couldn't go back, she continued upward, wishing he'd turned away, as a Southern gentleman would have done. Uncomfortably aware of her revealing dress and disheveled hair, she reached the top.

He smiled winningly, as if they were meeting in the most formal salon. "Julia, you're looking especially beautiful." His black eyes admired her as he gave an obviously fake sigh. "I wish I could think meeting me had produced this radiance, but I'm afraid not. Has some magic spell charmed you? If so, I wish it were mine."

At his bantering guess, Julia felt the guilt which she'd barely controlled knot her stomach. Fearing that if she tried to respond, tears instead of words would emerge, she brushed past him and fled across to the back stairs, leaving his surprised face behind.

When she reached her tiny room, the weeping which she'd resisted all day engulfed her. When the torrent subsided, exhaustion took its place, mercifully enfolding her in dreamless sleep.

"Andrew, what do you think of the talk that Baron Saia will be Minister of the Interior? He's a friend of yours, isn't he?"

Andrew hadn't seen Julia since he'd left her room last night, and he found, to his annoyed surprise, that he was watching almost anxiously for her arrival in the drawing room where guests were gathering for dinner. Now he looked at Hubert Scott, reluctantly focusing his attention on the pudgy face. "Yes, Mr. Scott, I know the baron, and I admire his abilities. He'd serve the emperor very well, I believe."

Richard joined the discussion, in his usual disagreement with his son. "But I understand Baron Saia has associates among the Liberals who have recently been pressing their questions about slavery in the General Assembly."

"Baron Saia has friends from both political parties," Andrew responded, hoping to avoid becoming involved in another argument about abolitionists.

Behind him he heard William's voice. "Gentlemen, the ladies are with us. Let's put aside our political discussions until later."

Although Andrew welcomed the release from the conversation, he felt a familiar irritation at the assumption that politics was a subject only for men. Some of the women he knew, his father's mistress for one, and probably Julia for another, could understand the intricacies of political power better than several of the men here.

Through the door to the front hall he could see only the bottom of the steps which led to the upper floor. As he unobtrusively watched the entrance, he saw the

sway of an ice-blue skirt on the curving stairs. As the
wearer of the silky dress descended, he saw next a
slender waist and a tight bodice, hugging the high
breasts he recognized.

He turned away, not wanting Julia to know he'd been
waiting for her. What would he find in her eyes—
accusations of dishonorable behavior, which he uncomfortably felt might be justified? But when he heard the
swish of her full skirt and faced her, she seemed poised
and gracious, a pleasant greeting in her smile. He found
he was angry; even some outrageous reaction would
please him better than this apparently cool indifference.

As soon as she entered the room, Julia had seen Andrew.
She'd rehearsed their meeting a dozen times, both
disappointed and relieved each time she'd been downstairs after her *sesta* but hadn't seen him. Whatever
she'd been prepared for—a leer, a look of disgust for
her easy surrender—she was taken aback by his relaxed
calm, as if nothing unusual had happened between
them. She felt the muscles of her back stiffen and her
face seemed like a mask. Determined that nothing would
give away her inner turmoil, she smiled as serenely as
he.

For an instant she thought she saw in his eyes a hard
glint, but then he was bowing to her, only polite attention in the angular face. Behind him William stood.
Though she'd been dreading her first encounter with
her father, in her agitation she smiled at him in her
usual way.

Gratefully she heard Tobias at the door, announcing
dinner. Richard Langdon offered his arm, and for once
Julia gladly accepted him as her escort.

Following a short interval of brandy and cigars for
men and gossip for women, dancing began in the drawing room. Dances with all the male guests prevented

Julia from more than one waltz with Andrew, and she was relieved that when they danced, he had as little to say as she.

The candles in the wall sconces and silver candlelabra had burned halfway down before William called Julia and Andrew to his side and signaled for the musicians to interrupt their playing and the servants to refill glasses of champagne. Julia gripped her tulip-shaped crystal glass as conversation stopped and expectant faces turned toward the two men and her.

William's voice rang out in the stilled room. "Ladies, gentlemen, senhoras, senhors. I feel both sorrow and joy at the toast I am about to offer. Sorrow that my beloved daughter before long will leave me, and joy that she will find much happiness in her new life." He raised his glass with a dramatic flourish of the sort he so much enjoyed. "A toast to my daughter, Julia, and her future husband, Mr. Andrew Langdon."

As glasses were emptied and the congratulations began, Julia held her wine, thankful she didn't have to drink to a marriage which seemed so uncertain to her. Despite the intimacy she'd shared with the tall man at her side, she felt more unsure than ever what life with him would be like. She didn't love him, nor he her. They didn't know each other well enough for love, and their feelings had been as much resentment and rage as anything tender. Forlornly she wondered whether she had really loved Nathan or if she had just convinced herself of it. Otherwise, how could she have had so much pleasure in Andrew's arms? Was lust so powerful that it could overcome animosity and distrust?

She looked at Andrew and found that he was gazing intently at her. Did the enigmatic look in his eyes mean he, too, felt as if they were like the *bandeirantes* his brother claimed to be—setting out for an unknown country?

9

The parrots the next day seemed to Julia especially raucous, as if maliciously broadcasting the secrets they'd collected in shadowy corners and dark bedrooms over the past three days. In the drive below the big house, she exchanged polite pleasantries with the assembled guests, giving each one a ribbon-tied packet of rice to throw at James and Sally as they left. Soon the celebration would end, and she could be alone to think about the troubled state of her life.

William, watching Julia, worried about the faint lines of strain in her face. She looked as if she hadn't slept well, and when he'd spoken to her, she'd seemed reluctant to look at him. Uncomfortably he wondered if she had noticed his attentions to Senhora Pereira. Only five months after his wife's death, he shouldn't be noticing another woman, but the flirtatious widow had made him smile and feel like an attractive man. Julia wouldn't understand that despite his grief for Mary, he still loved social occasions; besides, he also missed the physical side of marriage. Well, considering the circumstances of her engagement to Andrew, perhaps she knew more of sexual needs than he wanted to recognize. Shifting his glance to Andrew, he wished he knew how the self-confident, almost arrogant-looking man really felt about Julia.

Under William's scrutiny, Andrew shifted his weight, his collar suddenly tight, and he barely resisted loosening his maroon cravat. For the last month, he'd been intermittently plagued with awkward feelings that hadn't bothered him since he was in his teens. Dammit, Julia had started all this, and though he couldn't reasonably blame her for his behavior night before last, this morning his irritation with her grew. They must talk before he could escape to the work on his *fazenda*, and only the way her soft green dress clung to her curves offered any consolation for his discomfort.

Julia turned thankfully at the sound of laughter from the top of the steps as Sally and James appeared, she with one hand on her ribbon-trimmed bonnet and the other holding James's elbow. At the glowing smile on her brother's face, Julia's spirits lightened. When they reached her, she embraced them both, and James let go of Sally long enough to give Julia a hug and kiss that told her how happy he was.

Rice showered over the couple as they went on to William's good-byes and then descended to the decorated coach which would take them to São Paulo. A scream from Sally led to a scramble before a toad, hidden in the coach to assure a fruitful honeymoon, was thrown into the bushes. Laughter and good-bye waves followed the departing vehicle.

A short time later other carriages lined up to take away the wedding guests. Julia stood beside William, accepting thanks and hoping her pasted smile would last. When she had waved to the last visitor, she wearily followed her father back to the house.

In the deserted entrance hall she heard a familiar

deep voice coming from the drawing-room door. "Julia, I'd like to speak to you before I leave."

Realizing they were alone for the first time since he'd come to her bedroom, she turned to face Andrew and reluctantly looked at him. To her surprise, she saw a faint flush under the bronzed tan of his skin. Somehow that disconcerted her more than the disdainful familiarity she'd feared, or the self-assurance he usually showed.

She motioned toward the back of the house. "We can go into the family sitting room."

"I'd prefer somewhere more private."

She thought of what had happened the last time they were alone and felt a dismaying clutch of excitement in her chest. As she hesitated, the melodious sound of bells reverberated softly. "We could go to the chapel," she suggested. "It's usually deserted this time of day."

"Fine." he responded, and offered her his arm.

She barely rested her fingers under his elbow as they walked through the courtyard where she'd overheard Sally that disastrous night and along a graveled walk to the *fazenda* chapel.

A bell tower, reached by narrow stone steps, guarded the small whitewashed building. Here bells rang each day for morning Mass, to mark the noon hour, and in the evening for vespers. William had kept on the *fazenda* priest, since all of the house servants and many of the field slaves were Catholic. Julia loved to slip into the back when it was empty and enjoy the opulence of the gold and silver service and the purple altarcloth.

When she led Andrew inside and turned to face him, light from the windows touched his black hair and eyebrows but left his eyes in shadow, masking his expression. He waved his hand, indicating their surroundings. "Do you feel safe from me here?"

She felt her legs tremble and knew she couldn't

battle with him today. "Please, Andrew, I'm very tired. What did you want to talk about?"

Now that the moment had come for an apology, Andrew found he couldn't say the words. He'd never believed in apologies; only actions could remedy mistakes. If he'd wronged Julia, which he wasn't sure he had, he'd have to make her trust him by what he did from now on. "I could say I'm sorry for the other night, but it wouldn't be true. You're a very desirable woman, Julia, and my only regret would be if you hadn't received as much pleasure as I."

Golden sparks flared in her eyes, and he realized she wouldn't let go easily of all the fears and prohibitions Southern girls were taught. Doggedly he continued. "If you're worried about pregnancy, let me reassure you that it's unlikely." He smiled, hoping to tease her into a more relaxed state of mind. "After all, any doctor can tell you that first babies take from two to nine months. After that, they all take nine months."

Offended that he would joke about something so serious to her, Julia glared at him. "That may seem funny to you. You're not the one who would be disgraced."

Instantly his face lost its smile. "I'm as involved as you, Julia, in whatever we do. No one would doubt my responsibility for a child we would have, but I think it's best our marriage take place soon."

Surprised, she could only remember the weeks of planning that preceded Sally and James's wedding. "But the preparations—"

Impatiently he interrupted. "Do you want an elaborate ceremony?"

She thought of the past three days and answered fervently, "No!"

"I have business in Santos in mid-June. If we were married before then, we could honeymoon by the ocean."

Mid-June—only a month from now; Sally and James would barely have returned. If the Rayfords didn't have another lavish wedding, their friends and neighbors might be affronted, but suddenly she didn't care. She'd had to accede to too many pressures from others in the past year; if she didn't want three days of festivities, she wouldn't have them. At this moment nothing of this marriage warranted a celebration. But perhaps a Brazilian-style ceremony would suit them. "What about local weddings, Andrew, are they simpler than ours?"

The light caught on the crinkling lines around his eyes as he tilted his head back in laughter. "Brazilian wedding parties last for six or seven days, with customs you probably wouldn't like." Grinning, he touched her cheek lightly, not quite caressing, not quite teasing. "The groom abducts the bride, or pretends to, and Brazilians are sometimes bawdier than Americans about the kinds of jests they enjoy."

Fatigue and exasperation combined to make her voice snappish. "I certainly don't want pranks, and now that . . ." She checked herself, unable to refer to their intimacy. The amusement in his eyes sparked all the anxiety and shame she'd felt in the last day and a half into furious anger. "I suppose you're proud of yourself—and you think now I'll be meek and humble and thank you kindly for wanting to marry me soon."

He stiffened, his voice cool. "I'd never be so foolish as to expect humility from you, but for you to be reasonable doesn't seem too much to ask."

"Yes—reasonable from your point of view!" Even as she heard her voice trembling with rage, Julia knew she wasn't making sense. Why was she so angry with him? He wasn't having his way any more than she was, but it seemed as if he had some advantage over her just by being a man. Wearily she controlled her temper. "Yes, Andrew. Let's have a very small ceremony in early June."

"Good." He sounded as impersonal as if they'd decided on a business arrangement. "Will you let me know just what day you decide on?"

She nodded, and turned abruptly, leaving him in the chapel with the dust motes, dancing in the light from the window, reluctantly settling behind her.

Slowly Andrew followed her, watching the graceful movements of her tall, slender figure as she hurried toward the big house. Why did they have such difficulty when they tried to talk? The suspicion she might have manipulated him into a marriage proposal galled his pride and still stood between them. Andrew realized that having a distant and often absent father who yet tried to dominate him had fostered a fierce independence that at times overrode good judgment.

As he turned toward the stable to get his horse and make sure his servant had ridden on ahead with his bags, he decided that holding her was much easier than talking to her, and more enjoyable by far. Perhaps she'd chosen the chapel to prevent his touching her; maybe she feared his ability to arouse her. But when they embraced, she held equal power over him.

He heard steps and found Roberto walking beside him. "I saw you and your bride-to-be leaving the chapel. Did you pledge your sacred trust to each other?"

Andrew glanced at his brother, noting the indolent smile. "The Catholic Church is your domain, Roberto. Would your priest sanctify anything we pledged in his house?"

"You know, brother, that the Holy Church has not considered me within its fold for some time, but I would guess that whether the priest accepted your pledge would depend on how you had sealed your vows." The smile became malicious. "Do you care to tell me, Andrew?"

When Andrew raised his eyebrow at his brother and laughed, a brief look of anger distorted Roberto's face. Then his usual carefree expression returned. "I think you may have a most interesting marriage." At the entrance to the stables he stopped, but Andrew knew his brother was studying him as he strode on to the stall where his brown gelding waited.

When he was riding along a path between the low coffee trees, he thought about Roberto's sudden anger and his interest in Andrew's personal life. Roberto probably knew Andrew no longer visited Lele. Did Roberto still blame him for installing her as his mistress?

He'd never told his younger brother that Lele had chosen him, rather than the other way around. When she'd come to his house one night and invited herself into bed with him, she'd made it obvious she wanted a man who could support her and not a seventeen-year-old still dependent on his father. She wasn't a virgin even then, and Andrew had seen no reason to reject what she so skillfully offered. He'd never been faithful to her as some men were with mistresses, but he had provided for her.

When the liaison with Lele began, Roberto seemed too sensitive and vulnerable; Andrew hadn't wanted to hurt him more by the knowledge Lele had scorned him. Now Andrew shrugged to himself and urged his horse to a faster pace. Roberto certainly wasn't sensitive or vulnerable now, and he had money to spend on a woman. If he wanted Lele, she'd probably take him. Whatever he did with his life didn't affect Andrew.

*   *   *

"Look out what you're doin', girl." Serena's voice was sharp as she pushed Scizira's hands away from the delicate veil and fastened the circle of sheer lace to the red-gold curls that had been arranged high on Julia's head.

Julia knew Serena's anger came from her distress that her mistress was leaving in this precipitate manner. When Julia had announced that she wanted a small June wedding, with only their closest friends, Serena had been as aghast as William. But despite her father's disapproval and Serena's uncharacteristic protests, Julia had remained fixed on the plan she and Andrew had decided a month ago.

From the absence of any sly looks, Julia had decided that Scizira, though she probably suspected Andrew's visit to Julia's room, had said nothing to the other servants. Gratitude for the unusual reticence, along with growing admiration for her maid's poise and intelligence, led Julia to ask Scizira to move with her. The black girl would pack Julia's possessions and go to Andrew's house to wait for her mistress to arrive from her honeymoon.

Though Brazilians customarily freed a favorite slave on the occasion of a wedding or other special event, Julia had hesitated to suggest that William, with his convictions about slavery, release Scizira. But he'd given the black maid to his daughter, and Julia planned to free Scizira as soon as she could.

It wouldn't be for the birth of a baby, she thought thankfully, at least not soon. Her monthly bleeding had appeared two weeks ago, relieving the anxiety Andrew's assurances hadn't dissipated.

She had missed her mother acutely the last month and wondered if Mama would have been pleased with her today. At least her wedding dress in pale yellow was beautiful. Beginning with a narrow ruffle at her throat, lace in a rosebud pattern covered her bare shoulders and arms and the tops of her breasts. The taffeta bodice clung tightly to just below her waist, where the skirt flared to a wide hem. The same lace covered the row of tiny buttons down the front and on her sleeves. She'd refused to wear a stiffened crinoline, determined that today she would give in only to the ultimate requirement that she marry at all.

A rap on the door preceded Sally's breathless entrance. "Julia, honey, Uncle William's waiting downstairs, and everyone's ready." In the ten days since she'd returned from her honeymoon, Sally had taken on a slightly superior air that indicated she occupied a position above her cousin. But she also seemed willing to learn the duties of being the mistress of the Rayford household, and Julia gratefully forgave the sometimes patronizing manner. They had not become closer, or more like sisters, but at least Sally and James seemed happily in love, and that satisfied Julia. Serena smoothed one last fold of the veil, and Julia took the small bouquet of yellow rosebuds which Scizira held out to her and followed Sally down the curving staircase to the tiled hall where William paced.

"Julia!" He stopped and took her hands, tears in his voice. "Mary would have been so proud. You're as beautiful a bride as she was." Then his usual teasing smile returned as he offered her his arm. "Well . . . almost as beautiful."

As they walked along the hall to the family sitting room, Julia allowed herself to wonder how she would have felt if she were marrying the man she'd chosen. Deliberately she'd resisted this thought the last two months, telling herself she only invited more regret by dwelling on Nathan. Now, with her vows of commitment only minutes away, she thought of Philadelphia and her youthful hopes. Suddenly she couldn't remember clearly just how he looked. She struggled to assemble brown hair, hazel eyes, a mouth she'd thought the gentlest she'd ever seen—but she couldn't put them into a face.

"Honey, what's the matter?" She hadn't realized she'd stopped until she heard William's voice.

"Nothing, Papa." Her distress faded as she walked on. It was nothing, had to be nothing—that she couldn't remember one man's face when she was about to marry another—but it felt like losing a part of herself.

Then a violin, played by a black musician, beckoned her into the room where the late-afternoon sun touched the waiting faces. The Scotts sat on one side, Mrs. Scott tearfully enjoying the sentimental loss of the bride she'd tried to make into a substitute daughter. Though Julia had refused to take on that role, she appreciated the warm intentions enough to include these former neighbors. William had suggested inviting the Bernanos family, but Julia resisted, feeling she didn't know them well enough, and also remembering Carlota Pereira almost with dislike. Andrew hadn't asked that any guests be included, and Julia didn't know whether that meant he had few close friends or he didn't want them to witness a marriage he had come to so reluctantly.

Andrew waited with the Reverend Shackelford; Richard and Roberto sat opposite the Scotts. When James and Sally took seats, Julia and William moved forward to join Andrew. His formal dark suit fit his tall, rugged frame almost as if it had been molded to him. Only the ruffled white shirt front disturbed the smooth lines of broad shoulders, narrowing to lean waist and hips, and muscular thighs. His black curling hair seemed part of his elegant attire; his intense blue eyes and tanned skin provided the only color.

Those cobalt eyes caught and held her as she walked toward him, as if he were claiming her in some elemental way, as the earliest men had captured their mates. Briefly she hesitated, and a shiver ran down her spine; then she took the hand which he held out to her and faced the minister, the warm grip suddenly representing safety, not conquest.

She listened to the familiar service as in a dream, hearing her father's words and Andrew's promises, repeating her own automatically. Then Andrew was sliding a plain gold band on her finger, and when he lifted the veil to give her a lingering kiss, suddenly the marriage ceremony—her marriage ceremony—was real.

As Andrew held Julia's trembling lips with his own, he felt as if some penalty had lifted, making his heart light and freeing him from the irritation and resentment which had dogged him the past two months. When he raised his head and looked into the gold-flecked depths of her brown eyes, he saw surprise, as if she'd expected some other ending. Then they were turning, accepting the embraces and handclasps of the others.

Roberto decided that his brother's new wife looked like a radiant bride, whatever unusual circumstances had motivated this marriage. When he stood in front of her in the receiving line, he said, "Welcome to our family, Julia. I never hoped for such a fair sister." He bent his head as if to kiss her cheek, but at the last minute caught her mouth instead, holding the kiss just long enough to savor without being obviously forward. As he laughed into her eyes afterward, he saw both that she realized his kiss had lasted a fraction too long and that she was amused rather than offended. He gave her his little-boy look and saw her mouth curve upward. He relinquished his place to Mrs. Scott, pleased that Julia regarded him with a promising degree of indulgence.

After the congratulations and the greetings outside from the assembled slaves, the wedding party went to the small dining room for champagne toasts and supper. Julia barely tasted the meats, though she did eat some of the avocados and oranges she loved. A crystal platter held some small molded sweets and candies she didn't recognize. As she was trying to decide whether to try one, Roberto spoke behind her. "My brother's cook made these for today. Would you like to know what their Portuguese names mean?"

Noticing the glint in his eyes, she nodded.

He pointed to the different shapes as he listed them: "Little kisses, the married couple, maiden's tongue, raise-the-old-man, and love's caresses."

She knew she should be shocked, but at his sly look she laughed and took one of the "little kisses," which turned out to have a tart flavor. Roberto chose a "maiden's tongue" and savored it slowly, his eyes teasing her as he ate.

She thought the champagne had not affected her until they all went outside for the fireworks display her father insisted they couldn't skip. When she tried to look up, she found herself swaying dizzily.

Andrew's strong arms circled her and his voice teased her ear. "What—a wife who drinks too much wine? Do you have secret vices you've kept well concealed?"

Grateful for a place to lean her head, she laughed, the dizziness growing pleasantly at the feel of his hard body against her back and the affectionate sound of his voice calling her wife. "Oh, many vices."

A soft poof announced another shower of green stars. She turned her face to his, and the sparks which disappeared above their heads lodged in her throat as his lips tasted hers. The last rocket exploded, and her father's delighted laugh broke their embrace.

They returned to the candlelit house for a final toast, and then she and Andrew mounted the stairs to her room. Tomorrow morning they would leave for Santos, but tonight they would spend here. The door closed behind them, and suddenly the furnishings seemed unfamiliar, the large bed awkwardly prominent.

She had refused Scizira's assistance with undressing tonight, and now she concentrated on undoing the tiny lace-covered buttons. She had finished her sleeves when long fingers lifted her chin.

"Let me help you."

His eyes followed the path of his fingers as he opened the lace and silk from her chin downward, brushing the cleft between her breasts, and finally slipped the elaborate gown off her shoulders. He still wore his black trousers, but light from a single candle shone on the sun-darkened skin of his arms and chest, with faint shadows marking the muscles which ridged the firm flesh. She wanted to rub her hand across the dark hair which curled around his nipples, but she felt suddenly shy when he slid her gown past her hips. As she stepped out of the pale yellow swirl of lace and taffeta, she put her hand on his shoulder to steady herself, and the heat of his skin seemed to sear her arm.

At the thought that soon her undergarments would follow the dress, she searched for some delay. "Andrew, I—"

He put his finger against her lips. "No words now, Julia. We do badly together when we talk, but this . . ." He drew her into his arms for a kiss so full of promise that she willingly abandoned whatever she had thought to say.

As he finished undressing her, and with her tentative

help shed the rest of his clothes, they fell together on the bed. With his hands and mouth he aroused her until she felt as if every nerve in her body led to that throbbing center that begged for surcease. When he reached the same pitch of intoxicated desire, he entered her, filling her with excruciating pleasure that was at the same time wild discontent. With each thrust her need grew until in his wild explosion she too was shattered and the promise of his earlier kiss fulfilled.

As she lay against him, gradually the outside world returned. From the windows she could hear faint music coming from the celebration in the *senezala*. No matter how modest a ceremony she and Andrew had chosen, the slave quarters had received their portions of special foods and of *cachaça*, the fiery liquor made from sugarcane.

Andrew's fingers lightly caressed the side of her neck. "No need for a visit to the *senezala* tonight," he murmured. As his hand moved downward to her breasts in tantalizing exploration, Julia thought that she had just performed the most sensual dance of her life and knew she was achingly ready to begin again.

James stood beside Andrew on the front drive, thinking that his new brother-in-law had surely pleased his sister last night. This morning, when she'd come downstairs on her husband's arm, she'd looked more radiant in her dark blue riding dress than in her bridal gown yesterday. From the way Andrew was watching her as she told Papa good-bye, he was as happy with his bride as James was with Sally.

For the first time in two months, the anxiety for his sister was completely gone. After the night he and Papa had found her in Andrew's room, he hadn't been able to escape the dread that she had somehow sacrificed her own happiness to his. But surely she and her husband wouldn't have that glow unless they loved each other, no matter how little they'd shown it before. Andrew obviously had difficulty keeping his hands from brushing her, and each touch between them brought more color to her face.

He thought of the rather aesthetic-looking man he'd met when he went to Philadelphia to bring Julia home. "Thank God she didn't persist in the idea she was going to marry Nathan Holt."

Andrew turned to look at James, and even before the taller man spoke, James realized he'd said his thought aloud. "Nathan Holt?"

"Why . . . ah . . . my Uncle Daniel's foster son." James could feel the hot color flood his face as his stumbling tongue betrayed his discomfort. "Julia met him when she lived in Philadelphia before the War. She thought she was in love—you know how sixteen-year-old girls are. But when we came here, I'm sure she forgot all that." He tried to laugh, but no smile answered him from the expressionless face. "Anyway, he's married now too, to a cousin. We heard about it just about the time you and Julia . . . well . . . decided to marry."

He saw a faint deepening of the lines around Andrew's mouth and miserably wished he'd not tried to explain that first accidental statement. With relief he heard a rustle that announced Sally and turned gratefully to greet her.

William released Julia, and James stepped forward to hug his sister, wondering if he should tell her what he'd inadvertently revealed. But as he felt her smooth face against his, he only said, "Be happy, Julia—as happy as I am."

Her convulsive embrace was her answer, and he

stood, Sally's hand in his, and watched the carriage, with Andrew's horse and Julia's riding mare tied behind, depart along the dusty road.

For several miles Julia and Andrew rode in the carriage, and then they changed to horseback. He was strangely silent at first, as if something were on his mind, but after they were on the horses, he seemed to relax. Perhaps he just needed activity, Julia decided, and grew warm under her snug wool jacket, thinking of the kind of activity that had occupied them last night.

They would not travel through São Paulo, so the route was new to her. As they rode, Andrew pointed out features of the landscape which she'd never noticed before, and she enjoyed the late-autumn sun and the sound of his deep-pitched voice.

The land undulated in irregular patterns, cresting at rounded summits, several hundred feet high, often with steep sides. At the base of these hills, groves of myrtle, scrubby pine, and the valuable hardwood *aroeira* with its bunches of crimson berries covered the rifts where the land had not been cleared for cultivation. Between fields of deep green grasses, so even some farmer might have scythed them, the earth looked wounded, its color a deep red, almost purple.

Just before noon they reached an area lumpy with mounds four to six feet high and almost as wide. "Andrew," Julia called, "what are those?"

He reined nearer to answer. "Termite nests."

"So large?"

"Yes. Once when a French naturalist visited me, he wanted to see the inside of a nest. It took four blacks half an hour, chopping at the shell with axes, to break it open. The inside was a maze of intricate passages." Julia shuddered, interested that he knew a French naturalist, but glad she hadn't seen the swarming white ants.

"Because of the termites," Andrew continued, "buildings in Brazil don't use wood on the ground floor."

Hoping to forget the termites, Julia asked, "Andrew, please tell me about your house." She couldn't think of it as hers also. "What is it like?"

He gave her a laughing look. "Let it surprise you. It's not as grand as your father's home, but I think you'll like it." When he would say nothing more, she gave up questioning him. He couldn't know what she would like, but she already suspected he could be obdurate and she'd have difficulty if she ever wanted to change his mind about something.

On the edge of a sugarcane field, workers, eating a midday meal, sat around a kettle which hung over an open fire. On the coals below the kettle a coffeepot simmered, and the drifting aroma reminded Julia how little she'd eaten either last night or this morning.

As if hearing her thoughts, Andrew halted in the shade of a bamboo copse, and Capitolino, the black coachman, brought the basket which Serena had prepared for them. Julia helped him spread a cloth, and she and Andrew sat on the ground for their meal of cold wedding meats and fruits. When Andrew offered her some of the sweet cakes, she decided from the smile around his mouth that Roberto hadn't been teasing about the names.

Through the afternoon they followed the rutted roads, constructed, Andrew explained, not for the convenience of travelers, but to transport the products of the large *fazendas* to the port of Santos. They passed trains of pack mules so loaded that Julia expected the animals to tumble over on the steeper slopes. Her sympathy for the burdened mules lessened when she got close enough to see their air of latent deviltry and the way they snapped viciously at each other's legs and ears.

Just before evening, they rode into a small town where they would spend the night. In the center of town were the municipal "palace," which was above the jail, a theater, and, to her surprise, a public library.

When they reached the roadside inn, Julia read the name, *Hospedaria Gratidão*, but as she looked around, she couldn't believe any guest was ever truly thankful to stay there. Beside its whitewashed plaster walls dogs and pigs sniffed for whatever they could find. Women and children of all shades of black, brown, and near-white seemed to be getting their evening's entertainment by watching the travelers.

Earlier arrivals were already setting up kettles over fires in the yard to cook their own food. While Andrew went inside, Capitolino took a similar kettle from the luggage section of the carriage, explaining that at such accommodations as were available in small towns, the wise traveler prepared his own food. Julia, feeling pleasantly useless, wandered around the building, as interested in the watching women as they were in her.

A young, almost white-skinned woman stared boldly at Julia, reminding her of the practices which resulted in such coloring. Brazil, even more than the American South, had a large mulatto population. Occasionally a white man might marry a black woman, and extremely rarely, a white woman and a black man might wed, but most mixed blood stemmed originally from liaisons between masters and their women slaves. And as in the South, the white mistress of the house could do little but ignore the children who looked so much like her own except for their darker skin.

As Julia turned from the stare of the young mulatto, she shivered. Would she see Andrew's face among the slave children on his *fazenda*? She didn't even know, she reminded herself, whether she would care.

When she hurried back to Capitolino, Andrew was just coming to search for her. "Julia, it's best for you to stay with Capitolino or me. Women here never go out unescorted."

With a flash of irritation, she recognized her husband was right, though she chafed at such restraints. She could have pointed out that colored women came and went freely, but she said nothing as she took his arm and walked with him to their fire, where the steaming kettle promised a savory mixture of pork with beans and peppers. Capitolino was obviously skilled at more than driving a carriage and handling horses.

Andrew had arranged for a cubicle in which to hang the hammocks he had brought with them. When they went inside, she washed off as much dust as she could with a basin of water, removed only her outer clothing, and climbed into the swinging hammock. She found she felt relieved that they had only enough privacy for a lingering kiss before Andrew settled in his hammock. Of all the things so new to her in the past days and weeks, the most unknown was still the heart of her husband.

Late the following afternoon they reached the ocean. Julia had assumed they would stay at one of the hotels in the port of Santos, but before the road reached the town which sprawled beside the curving bay, Andrew turned his horse off into a narrow trace barely wide enough for the carriage to follow. Where the ruts through the stiff grass widened, Julia urged her horse ahead until she rode beside him.

She had to shout against the breeze. "Where are we going?"

Andrew cupped his hand around his mouth. "To the

chácara of a friend, his country house." He pointed ahead to a tile-roofed building, crouching at the edge of the white strip of sand which separated the gray-green sea of scrubby plants from the gray-blue sea of restless water.

When they arrived beside the one-story house, Andrew helped her dismount. His hands dropped from her waist to the curve of her hip before he released her and said, "My business in Santos will take only a few days, but we'll stay here as long as we choose before we go back to the *fazenda*."

"Whose house is this?"

"It belongs to Sergio Roque de Andrade. Just now he's fighting with the emperor's army in Paraguay."

Julia had read in the newspaper of a war by Brazil and Argentina against their small neighbor, but it had seemed unimportant in contrast to the war she'd endured. "Is he a close friend?"

"Yes," Andrew responded as together they ascended the five steps to the veranda, which ran all around the house, and went inside.

The interior had a warm informality, with gaily colored cushions, settees made from jacaranda wood, and five bamboo cages for the noisy parrots so popular with Brazilians. At the sound of a soft Portuguese voice, Julia turned to find Andrew greeting a small black woman. Her gap-toothed smile beamed up at the face so far above her own. Behind her stood a slight black man.

"Julia, Baba and Rino will look out for us." His affectionate tone told her he knew them well.

Baba ducked a curtsy. "Senhora Langdon, I hope you will be comfortable."

This was the first time anyone had addressed Julia with the startling new name; Capitolino had called her Miss Julia, as had everyone at the Rayford home. Following Baba into a bedroom, Julia silently repeated the name. Was she really Senhora Langdon, or was it only a mistake everyone seemed to share?

In the center of the bedroom a young woman was pouring water into something shaped like a small canoe. Coming closer, Julia saw it was a bathtub. As the girl, who Baba said was her daughter, brought another bucket of water, Julia didn't care how the tub was shaped, and she tore off her clothing and gratefully sank into its reviving warmth.

When she finished soaking away the residue of two days' travel, twilight had stolen the sight of the ocean. Only the swelling hiss and crash of the waves told of the hidden sea. She stood beside the tub listening, holding a large linen towel around her, when Andrew entered, already loosening his shirt. Startled, she clutched the towel more closely around her. So far they had undressed only in very dim light, and she felt suddenly shy.

He paused, his hand halfway down the row of shirt buttons. "If possible, you're even more enticing with that towel than during the regrettably few glimpses I've had of you with nothing on. If I weren't so dirty, I'd make an exact comparison right now."

As she turned her back to hide her blazing face, he gave an exaggerated sigh, for a moment sounding like Roberto in one of his mock moods. "If you'll put on your robe, Rino will refill the tub for me." He came up behind her and slipped his hand around under the front of the towel, caressing her breast and fondling the nipple until it hardened against his fingers. She bit her lower lip to quell the gasp of excitement his touch drew from her. He lifted her damp hair and kissed the back of her neck. "Ah, Julia, you smell of roses, but I stink of horses."

He released her, and she forced her weak legs to the wardrobe, where Baba had already filled the shelves and hooks with her clothing. She held the towel while she pulled a shift over her head and then a robe before she turned to find Andrew still watching her.

"Unfortunately you managed that too well. Don't dress more, though. We'll be alone, and it would be a waste for such a short time."

She left before he could drop his trousers and reveal the source of the bulge in front.

As she lay beside him in the wide bed later that night, still faintly trembling from their passionate lovemaking, she thought again of how little they knew each other, despite their growing familiarity with each other's bodies. She resolved that tomorrow she would try to talk to him, to avoid the challenges which often sprang up between them, and to learn what sort of man she had married. Then she might discover exactly what she was beginning to feel about him.

10

A short distance south of the *chácara*, a mass of rocks thrust boldly into the sea. Huge white-capped waves thundered against the resisting granite, sending columns of spray into the air before falling back in defeat. Farther on, unimpeded swells rushed onto the curving sands of a small bay, victorious against the passive shore.

Walking on the beach after exploring the rocky point with Andrew, Julia remembered her resolution of the previous night. "I know so little about you, Andrew. Where were you born? Where did you grow up?"

He stood, looking at the water, his thumbs hooked under the belt of his worn leather trousers. When he faced her, his wind-ruffled hair softened his face, making him look younger, more carefree. How much he resembles Roberto now, Julia thought.

He took her hand as they walked on. "There's little to tell. I was born in Charleston in my grandparents' house, lived nearby until my mother died, then stayed with my grandparents, except for trips with my father and two years at the university, until I came to Brazil. I had the usual education, with perhaps a bit more music and art than otherwise because of my grandmother."

As they walked, the breeze blew her skirts against his legs. She asked tentatively, "But what about the War Between the States. You were in Brazil then. Did you think of going back to the South to fight?"

From the cynical arch of his thick eyebrows she could tell he considered her question naive, but he answered politely, "No—not at all. Realism has always appealed to me, and unless the Confederacy had won within the first year, their cause was hopeless. And though I take advantage of the slave-labor system here because it exists, I'm not committed to it; it's not worth my life."

She felt rising the antagonism she had determined to avoid. "I don't believe in slavery, but we fought for our freedom, not just to hold slaves."

In her agitation, she stopped, but he took her hand, propelling her onward again. "I think the conflict between North and South developed from many issues, but I didn't want to fight for any of them."

"What of your grandparents?" she asked hotly. "Did they and other relatives mean nothing to you?"

His voice took on an edge. "My grandparents died in a yellow-fever epidemic in 1859, and I have no other relatives. Both my father and mother were the only surviving children in their families."

His anger faded, and once again his face glowed with youthful enthusiasm. "Sometimes I think my life began when I came to Brazil. In a way, your father is right: there's much of the feeling of the American South here. But there's a difference. The Portuguese settlements are older than towns in the United States—São Paulo was founded in 1533, almost seventy-five years before the first English colonists settled in the South—but this is like a new country. A man can build anything here for himself if he's strong and smart enough and willing to work. South Carolina seems old by comparison."

His words took her back to the oaks which had sheltered her childhood, and she felt the homesickness which, though faded, could still bring tears. "But old things can be the best," she offered.

The wind caught her hair, whipping it around her head. When she pushed it back, she saw the now familiar darkening of his eyes. He grasped her hand and pulled her close against him so that her errant hair entangled them both. His voice held a husky tone of desire. "Today the past and the future don't interest me—only the present." He kissed her, his mouth sharing his growing passion until her heart began to thunder like the waves. "Come, Julia, let's go back to the *chácara* for better things than talking."

"But, Andrew, it's daytime. We can't—"

In answer he swept her up into his arms and started for the bungalow, her flowered dress trailing in the small showers of sand kicked up by his long stride. When he reached the veranda, she expected him to put her down, but instead he called loudly for Baba. When she opened the door, he brushed past her, ordering over his shoulder, "It's a beautiful day for a walk. Take everyone with you." He carried Julia into the bedroom and closed the door with his foot. Moments later the front door shut, and the house was silent.

He removed Julia's garments himself, kissing the skin revealed at each step. At first she wanted to shield herself from the light, but his ardent appreciation of her body released such surges of longing in her that she felt as if the ocean had invaded the room and were tossing her in its gigantic rhythm. Impatiently he pulled off his own clothing and then caressed all the secret places which excited her. She responded with her own exploration of his eager body, until finally he thrust inside her, filling her, and the waves of desire and passion crested with shuddering force before they receded. At the moment when she seemed to be drowning in her sensations, she heard him moan "Julia," and felt his name in her throat.

As they lay, still breathing in rapid unison, she thought that these were the first words they'd spoken in that moment of complete intimacy—not of love, but at least calling to each other.

Andrew raised on one elbow, and with a finger traced a scar down her belly to its ending in the damp tangle of curls. "How did you get this?"

"A silly fall—when I was doing something I wasn't supposed to. I had sneaked out wearing James's old breeches and fell down some rocks. A fit punishment, I guess."

He laughed. "I have the idea that if you bore a scar for every time you did what your parents disapproved of, you'd be covered."

Suddenly wanting reassurance, she ventured hesitantly, "I used to worry that a scar . . . there would . . ."

He leaned across her and brushed the faint line with his lips. "It doesn't make you less beautiful, if that's what bothered you." Then his lips descended past the marking on her skin, and she forgot anything she might have said as the elemental tide of passion enveloped them again.

When later that afternoon Julia sat in the steaming canoe-shaped tub and listened to Baba's friendly voice, she felt she should be embarrassed. But the old woman's face beamed approval. That Julia and Andrew had so obviously been making love seemed to loosen Baba's tongue, and as she set out soap and towels, she chattered happily, her use of the familiar slave addresses showing her acceptance of Julia.

"*Sinha*, how good to see Senhor Andrew happy. And to have him come with a wife—such a beautiful wife, with the long red hair. A man needs to be married and have many children."

Julia interrupted the flow of words. "Does Senhor Andrew come here often, then?"

"Oh, yes, often with Senhor Sergio, and many times also when *o senhor* is away."

The water suddenly seemed chilly. Would Andrew come to an isolated spot like this alone, or would his mistress—or had there been several?—be with him? The picture of Andrew and the beautiful woman in front of the flower stand in Rio returned to Julia as vividly as if she had seen them last week. Had Andrew lifted that other woman out of this tub and carried her to the large bed, still rumpled from an afternoon's lovemaking?

In that aftermath of their closeness today, telling herself his life before their marriage didn't affect her was useless. As she stood and let Baba rub her dry, Julia knew from the sudden silence that her distress must be showing. But she couldn't lift the black woman's spirits when she didn't know how to comfort herself.

Candlelight shone on Julia's hair and the thick red-brown lashes, now lowered so that Andrew couldn't see her eyes. She'd hardly looked at him all during supper, he thought, annoyed at a coolness the afternoon's love-making had led him to think had vanished. Could she still be embarrassed at making love in the daylight? Her initial shyness had certainly seemed to disappear quickly enough.

He watched her fingers twist the glass of wine and found that he was toying with his brandy snifter. She rose from the table, still not looking at him, and went to stand in front of the fireplace, as if the flames held some particular fascination. Or was she looking into the past?

The wind off the ocean whined past the house, momentarily obliterating the sound of the surf. He thought of James's obviously regretted reference to Julia's having been in love with Nathan Holt. He'd dismissed the conversation from his mind that day, but her changeable moods brought James's remarks back.

She leaned her forehead against the marble mantel, and he wished he could see into her mind. He'd have forgotten Nathan Holt's name entirely, he was sure, had it not been for James's saying Julia had learned of Nathan's marriage at about the time of the incident in the bachelor house. Could the two events have any connection? He remembered that in Rio she'd spoken of having a plan for returning to Hundred Oaks. If Nathan had been part of that plan, would she have needed a substitute?

The wind howled again, fitting the dark thoughts which wouldn't go away. The matter of the land in South Carolina which was part of her dowry suddenly seemed important. He couldn't sell it without her family's consent. Did she hope he would become so enamored of her that he'd return with her to the plantation that meant so much to her?

His early suspicions returned—that she'd deliberately forced him into marriage—and the independence he so fiercely prized brought back his distrust, reinfecting the contentment which had been building since their wedding.

Men's voices echoed from the marble walls and floors, multiplying the conversations in the center of the Santos Coffee Exchange, where a polished dark railing separated the coffee planters and their agents from the spectators. From one of the mahogany armchairs around the outer edge Julia watched as the men who acted as coffee factors bargained for the sale and resale of the aromatic beans. Despite their mostly Brazilian faces, they all wore dark frock coats and tall hats, like the British businessmen who had dominated Brazilian trade for so many years. She longed to join the carefully controlled excitement of that inner rectangle.

On the far side of the magic inner space, Andrew was speaking to a heavy middle-aged man whose graying side whiskers stood almost straight out from his generous cheeks. He was the coffee factor who handled the sales for Andrew's crop, and he was as important to a planter as his banker or lawyer, and at times almost like his priest. Though Andrew had explained to Julia that he grew many products other than coffee on his *fazenda*, most Brazilian planters, like Southerners in the American cotton belt, raised only one commercial crop. Once it had been sugar; in the São Paulo area coffee now predominated, and the coffee factors held great economic power.

Even though she was a spectator, Julia felt her spirit respond to the bustle and clamor of the Exchange Just walking through the loading area outside had been ex citing, past open sheds where muscular blacks staggered under the bulging bags and occasional rips spilled loose beans onto the floor. Over the whole area the heavy aroma of coffee clung, making her eager to accept one of the small cups of steaming liquid from a servant inside the Exchange.

Today she'd welcomed the excursion into Santos, since she'd been alone at the *chácara* for most of the last three days. After their walk on the beach and the afternoon of lovemaking, Andrew was preoccupied and distant, spending most of his days in Santos on unidentified "business" and returning just before the evening meal. Though they'd been physically intimate each night, he had almost seemed to revert to the suspicious stranger of the first days of their engagement, and Julia found she missed the teasing warmth that had developed between them. Nor had Andrew again called her name during the climax of their lovemaking.

At first puzzled and then hurt, Julia realized thankfully that Andrew's distant attitude protected her from what she decided would be a mistake: his lovemaking affected her so profoundly that she might have imagined he meant more to her than he did. Though she intended to be as good a wife as she could, she didn't expect the kind of marriage she'd hoped for with Nathan. She felt safer by not caring what Andrew did, since she didn't know how he felt about her—or she about him. Marriages of real love like her parents' were rare, Julia realized.

This morning she'd gladly left behind Carlyle's *French Revolution*, the only interesting book in English at the *chácara* but one she'd read before, to accompany Andrew to the port of Santos and the Coffee Exchange. Now she looked up to see him approaching beside the man with the abundant waist and whiskers.

"Julia, I wish to present Senhor Manuel Fonseca. Senhor Fonseca, this is my wife, Senhora Langdon."

Senhor Fonseca removed his hat from a polished bald head, and his chins and whiskers jiggled in rhythm when he bowed over Julia's hand. But shrewd-looking brown eyes and a charming smile denied his somewhat ludicrous appearance. "Senhora Langdon, I have already congratulated your husband on his good fortune in having such a beautiful wife. I add my most sincere wishes for your happiness. If ever I can be of any help to you, I hope you will call upon me."

Although Julia had heard the ritual words addressed to others dozens of times before, the rich tones of Senhor Fonseca's faintly accented voice gave them obvious sincerity, and she smiled with pleasure. "Thank you, and I shall take advantage of your generosity immediately. Please explain to me just what a coffee factor does."

For the next half-hour while Andrew went to talk to other planters, the genial man enthralled her with descriptions of the buying and selling of coffee crops. When he finished, she said, "Senhor, you are telling me that you are a gambler."

His laugh rippled down to his knees. "Yes, of course, you are exactly right, Senhora Langdon. It is the most exciting form of gambling anywhere."

Andrew returned, and Senhor Fonseca rose, bowing formally to Julia. Regretfully she said good-bye; too briefly he'd shared with her his world of work and commerce.

In the sunlight outside she wished she'd worn a lighter dress than the green velvet suit, with its long sleeves and jacket that buttoned tightly over the full skirt. Even at the beginning of winter, the humid air by the sea was warmer than the drier climate of the 2,500-foot plateau where São Paulo and the Langdon and Rayford *fazendas* were located. Andrew looked no more comfortable in his dark suit and waistcoat with the high stiff collar. He had turned to speak to someone, and suddenly she wanted to touch the thick black hair which curled over the white collar, to loosen his wide cravat and feel the muscles along the side of his neck.

Shocked, she clasped her hands tightly together, and she could feel her face flaming under the veil of her hat. Andrew turned back to her, and she saw a moment of surprise in his eyes before he spoke in Portuguese.

"Julia, may I introduce to you Senhor Luiz Henrique de Mello. Senhor Mello, Senhora Langdon."

A small, exquisitely dressed man in his early seventies kissed Julia's hand, and then looked at her with black, assessing eyes. Thick white hair topped a still-handsome face, but the blatant quality of his attention, which she had usually seen only in the faces of much younger men, often ones who'd been drinking, disconcerted her, and she had difficulty following the exchange of courtesies.

When good-byes had been said and they had walked far enough away that Senhor Mello could not hear, Julia asked, "Did I understand correctly—you agreed we would visit him at his home outside São Paulo?"

Andrew laughed, his face more relaxed than it had been since the first day at the *chácara*. "So you didn't care for Senhor Mello's appreciative glances?"

His lighthearted teasing brought an unexpected warmth to Julia as she laughed with him. "Appreciative! That's a polite word."

Andrew's eyes invited her to be embarrassed. "Would 'lecherous' be better?"

"Yes, definitely. But, Andrew, did you agree to visit him?"

Ahead of them Capitolino waited with the carriage, and he took her arm as they threaded through the sweaty men unloading bags of coffee. "Not only did I agree, but you also accepted his invitation."

At her questioning look, he laughed again, and handed her up into the carriage. "Some of those polite nods you were giving while trying not to blush indicated your wifely submission to your husband's plans."

As they settled on the black leather seats behind Capitolino, a visit to Senhor Mello suddenly seemed a small exchange for the pleasure of bantering with a more lighthearted husband.

The strenuous ride next day through the valley and up the slopes between Santos and São Paulo tired the horses and Julia, but she looked forward to seeing the city. Though she'd been there once before, it still seemed new to her. As they entered the outskirts of São Paulo, they passed low, poor dwellings—*porta e janella* houses, Capitolino called them, so named because they had only a single door and window. Farther on, large, roomy town houses displayed gilt pineapples on the roofs and birds of tile and mortar perched along the ridges. In the center of the city the streets were wide and paved with macadam, and she saw numerous shops, several large churches, and an obviously new large public market.

The Hotel Grande, to Julia's relief, bore no resemblance to the inn where they had stayed on the road to Santos. Andrew helped her from the carriage, and they ascended broad steps to a wide covered veranda, then across a high-ceilinged lobby. A smiling man with a thin mustache bowed and greeted Andrew by name before leading them up two flights of carpeted stairs to a large suite of rooms. On one side of the sitting room and bedroom, lace-curtained windows more than twice as tall as Julia overlooked the central park and square.

They had departed from the *chácara* at dawn, and Julia wanted most of all a bath and sleep. Andrew seemed tired as well, and after a light meal in their rooms, he joined her in the large bed, but only kissed her lightly before settling for sleep. The previous night, after the excursion to the Coffee Exchange, he had been less distant, but Julia thought sleepily that tonight, just relaxing against him without lovemaking seemed as intimate as anything they had done.

The next morning, after a late breakfast, they walked to some of the shops near the hotel, then stopped at the opera house across the square for Andrew to purchase tickets for a performance of *O Guarani*, an opera by a contemporary Brazilian, Carlos Gomes.

"The opera," Andrew explained as they started back to the hotel, "takes its plot from the first popular novel to have an Indian hero and describe the natives in admiring . . ."

At the break in his voice, Julia looked up from the cobblestones she'd been watching to avoid the puddles from a brief shower and saw that he was staring at the hotel entrance. Puzzled, she turned toward the front of the hotel and noticed a young woman walking away from the steps. A parasol blocked her view of the woman's face, but something about the figure jolted her with a chilling memory. She looked back at Andrew; his face had its usual expression, but his hand gripped her elbow too tightly as they continued across the paved square.

"You'll hear the story when we see the performance tonight," he finished as they mounted the stairs to their rooms.

Julia was pulling off her gloves when he said, in too careful a voice, "Julia, I need to call on someone here in São Paulo—a business acquaintance. Perhaps you'd like a *sesta*."

Her hands suddenly felt very cold, and she didn't look at him as she said, "Of course, Andrew. How considerate of you to think I might like to rest."

Andrew watched her go into the bedroom, and the firm snap of the door seemed to express the sarcasm which her words, if not her voice, had suggested. Damn all women, he thought as he left the room and strode angrily down the hall. If he could find her, he *would* be seeing a business acquaintance, because all that remained between him and Lele was the support he'd provided her. Damn Lele for being in São Paulo instead of Rio and for having the brazen gall to come to his hotel. How did she know where he'd be?

At the front steps he paused, wondering what he had planned to do. Search for her so he could tell her to leave him alone? But search for her where?

He took a thin cigar from his pocket and smelled the rich tobacco. He could go to the smoking room of the hotel and have a brandy and smoke his cigar and say to hell with all women. No—not all women. Feeling his muscles relax, he returned the cigar to his pocket and went back to the hotel desk to have his horse brought around.

For the next two hours Julia alternated between misery and anger—misery at the conviction that the woman leaving the hotel was the same woman she'd seen with Andrew in Rio, and anger that she would allow herself to be miserable because of it. Fool, she accused herself, you were absolutely right to be wary of him, but a few kind words, and here you are mooning over him as if what he does matters. Where's your pride, even if you don't have good sense?

She rang for a bath, and as she sank into the large tub, the ability she'd inherited from her father to laugh at herself shakily reappeared. Sunlight turned the teardrop crystals which surrounded each wall candlestick to flame and deepened the crimson of the velvet bed hangings. Roses, her favorite scent, perfumed the soap she was using in her bath. At least if she were to be unhappy with Andrew, he had enough money so that she could be unhappy in luxury.

When her fingers began to wrinkle in the cooling water, she left the tub and dried enough to put on an emerald-green dressing gown, then sat and leaned her head down so that her wet hair fell forward as she toweled it briskly. Suddenly strong hands grasped her shoulders and warm lips on the back of her neck sent sparks flashing along her spine.

She whirled, lifting her head and holding the towel around her hair, to find Andrew with his eyes fastened on the thin silk which strained against her upthrust breasts. Before she recovered from her surprise, he knelt beside her and pushed the top of her gown off her shoulders, baring her breasts, then bent his head to kiss an exposed nipple. She could smell the strong odor of brandy and the faint but unmistakable fragrance of lilac perfume.

Rage and pain knifed through her. Their honeymoon— and he was coming back to her and touching her with another woman's scent on him. How dare he humiliate her so! She pushed against him so hard that he fell back, only catching himself with one knee. She jumped to her feet, dropping the towel from her clenched hands, and her damp hair tumbled about her bared shoulders. Fury choked her, and she glared at the bewildered look on Andrew's face.

When his bewilderment changed to a smile, she erupted in a flame of wrath, raising her hand to hit him. Instantly he was on his feet, catching her trembling fist, pulling her against him.

"Let me go!" To her horror, she could hear the beginning of tears in her voice. She refused to cry from intense anger as she had as a child. That would be the ultimate humiliation.

"Julia, please . . . I'm sorry. I didn't mean to startle you."

Andrew looked down at the face where he could see tears forming in the gold-flecked eyes and rage in the lines of her trembling mouth. He recognized jealousy and was surprised he meant enough to her that she cared where he'd been. Or had he merely hurt her pride by leaving? For a moment he was tempted not to tell her; to enjoy the breaching of her seeming indifference to him, but jealousy was an ugly emotion he didn't want to inflict on her.

Gently he held her, enjoying the pressure of her heaving breasts against him, and he spoke soothingly. "I'm sorry I left you. I went to see someone I wasn't sure you'd want to meet, but perhaps you will if you understand."

As Andrew pulled her to the settee beside the windows, confusion began to replace the sick anger in Julia's stomach. He couldn't want her to meet a mistress; no wife would be expected to be that understanding. Had she only thought she saw the dusky woman she remembered so well?

She sat stiffly away from the arm which had been around her shoulders and pulled her silk robe tightly over her breasts, but she listened without objecting. "Julia, a woman lives in São Paulo whom I consider a good friend, but who is not accepted in what your family would call respectable society. I'd like to take you to meet her, but I want you to be aware of her position before you decide whether you'd be willing to do so."

"You saw her this afternoon?"

"Yes. Her name is Ellen Durr. She's English, a singer, and she's my father's mistress."

Julia barely kept her mouth from falling open. "Richard's mistress? I didn't think he loved anyone." As she realized what she'd said, she fumbled to remedy her words. "I mean, he just doesn't seem . . ."

Andrew's laugh verged on being grim. "Yes, it's surprising, but Father does love Ellen and would marry her, I think, if she'd consent."

Julia tried to rearrange her impressions of Richard Langdon from a coldhearted man, interested only in power, to a lover and a rejected suitor. She found she was intensely curious about a woman he would love but who would not want to marry him, but to meet a single woman who lived with a man would horrify almost everyone she'd known as she grew up. Even Uncle Daniel's family, with their unbiased attitudes to blacks, had refused to attend an abolitionist group which included a woman of "loose morals."

Still, Andrew wanted her to meet Ellen Durr, and Julia refused to be bound by all the rules that had governed her mother's life. When she did her father's and brother's work at Hundred Oaks, she'd stepped outside the acknowledged woman's role, though plenty of women in the South during the war had done the same. And when she'd been intimate with Andrew before marriage, she'd done what only their wedding had legitimized.

She turned to her husband and his waiting eyes. "Yes, Andrew, I'd like to meet . . . is it Miss Durr?"

He smiled, pleasure creasing the lines around his mouth. "No, it's Mrs. Durr. She's either widowed or divorced. I've never asked which."

He rose and pulled the silk wrap across her breasts again. "You'd better dress right away, though, or you'll tempt me to delay us until it's too late."

Not until they were riding behind Capitolino along one of the broad streets did Julia think to ask, "Did you also go to see a business acquaintance this afternoon?"

The sun seemed to accent the bronzed color of his skin as Andrew gave a curt "No," and Julia decided he didn't like her questioning him about his activities. She

understood that, because she didn't like to have anyone
check on what she did. It was too much like having a
parent, and much as she loved Papa, independence, as
she'd learned during the two years she'd really run
Hundred Oaks, was intoxicatingly sweet.

They stopped at a two-story white house on a quiet
street, and a maid admitted them to a small salon.
Through the windows Julia could see a tiny garden
where yellow and orange autumn flowers lingered. Soon
a short blond woman hurried into the room, hands
outstretched to Andrew, and greeted him with a kiss.
Then she turned to Julia as Andrew said, "Ellen, I wish
to present my wife, Julia."

The hand which gripped Julia's had slender fingers,
but it offered strength and warmth. "Julia, I am so
pleased to meet you." Julia felt as if she were assem-
bling the woman before her in sections: first the voice,
silky and golden, then laughing blue eyes over broad
cheekbones and a mouth that was red and full, the
scent of lilacs, and finally the small height and volup-
tuously curved figure. Ellen looked perhaps forty, with
laugh lines prominent around her eyes and mouth. Her
appearance surprised Julia; a modest dress of simple
lines, and hair drawn back almost severely from her
face, contradicted the gaudy effect Julia realized she
had expected. But when Ellen turned back to Andrew,
Julia saw that every movement radiated a sensuality
which must be enormously appealing to men.

"Andrew, you didn't prepare me for such a beautiful
wife." She looked at Julia again and added laughingly,
"And so slender. How I envy you. Come"—she indicated a round table beside a window with coffee cups
and a tray of small cakes on it—"you can eat anything
here, while I should pick and choose." She put her

head close to Julia as she led her to a seat by the table and whispered, "But I'll probably have one of each. I'm a real Brazilian when it comes to eating sweets."

Julia could hardly believe when an hour had passed. Ellen had chattered first about her current role in a musical comedy and then about the emperor's policies and the latest changes in São Paulo. From the discussion, Julia decided that Ellen must be acquainted with many of the important men in the city. "Really," Ellen was complaining to Andrew, "with twenty-five thousand people here, we certainly should have a railroad. Your friend Baron Saia should do something. And," she included Julia, "you must have the disposition of a saint to be willing to ride to Santos and back. I hate horses."

When they left, Ellen embraced Julia as if they had known each other for years and said, "If you have trouble with these Langdon men, let me know. They can be a difficult bunch."

Andrew laughed and hugged Ellen, but when he turned his back to get his hat, Ellen whispered to Julia, "I mean it," and Julia felt more cared for than she had in a long time.

As they rode back to the hotel in the growing dusk, Julia knew that when she saw Richard Langdon again, she would look at him with different eyes.

Half a day's ride from São Paulo the next day, Julia and Andrew reached the edge of the Mello property. In addition to her dislike of Senhor Mello's bold appraisal, Julia wanted to go on to her new home, but the invitation had been accepted, and she knew that both the giving and receiving of hospitality were sacred on the large *fazendas*.

After they started across the Mello land, they rode

for an hour through newly planted sugarcane fields. In the distance Julia could see crews of blacks. "How large is this *fazenda*, Andrew?"

"We'll cross only a tiny portion. Senhor Mello owns over twenty square miles, and he has at least two thousand slaves." He smiled at her astonishment. "He inherited much land from his father and his first three wives, and you'll see that he lives as the great landowners have done for centuries."

They passed outbuildings which included a sugar mill and a distillery, quarters for blacks, storehouses, and shops to supply the needs of the plantation. "Senhor Mello has his own domain here," Andrew explained, "and provides all his own services, as I do on a smaller scale."

Finally they reached the big house, a succession of low white buildings which enclosed an oblong divided into neat lots. Brown coffee beans, drying in the sun, covered most of the spaces, but the few uncovered lots were a dazzling white which Julia could hardly stand to look at in the glaring sunlight. "Andrew," she gasped, shading her eyes, "will . . . our home be surrounded by these?" She waved toward the coffee lots.

He took the leading rein of her horse and guided their mounts around the side of the building. "No—I use more modern methods of coffee production."

As they dismounted by an entrance, Julia thought that the first specific information about her new home only told her one thing it didn't have. A black butler in a red uniform weighted down with gold braid welcomed them and showed them to a room where Andrew left her to wash from the dusty trip. He returned to escort her to an enormous dining room where Senhor Mello came to greet them.

Beside the elderly man stood a young girl, obviously not over fourteen years old, whom he introduced as his wife. Julia covered her surprise by a curtsy before she went on to meet a covey of black-clad aunts and cousins of the present and deceased wives, as well as several sons and daughters, all of them older than their stepmother. In addition to the relatives, numerous guests chatted in the long room, including a couple who didn't know the Mello family but who had been passing, became ill, and stayed on at the big house for over a week. Julia decided any fears she'd had about needing to escape Senhor Mello's attentions had been unnecessary; he'd never see her again in the crush of visitors.

She couldn't resist murmuring to Andrew, "I read that the emperor worries because Brazil doesn't have a large enough population. He should visit Senhor Mello and be reassured."

His grin and the knowledge that the people near them didn't speak English emboldened her to ask, "Senhora Mello—is she as young as she looks?"

He glanced sympathetically toward their hostess. "Yes. Wealthy men often take very young wives, and many women die young. Her predecessors were no more than her age when they married, but Senhor Mello's third wife lived long enough to become a formidable lady."

As she moved with Andrew to seats near the head of the table, Julia thought with sympathy of the young bride, but she could see nothing to suggest the childlike wife was unhappy. She should be, thought Julia angrily, as her host's eyes found her and smilingly assessed her charms.

At the end of the meal, Julia tried to make conversation with her young hostess, but her American-accented Portuguese elicited only a childish giggle. When Andrew came with Senhor Mello, Julia rose gratefully to say good-bye. This time she listened carefully to what Andrew was saying, and when his graceful promises did not include any specific return visit, she smiled polite agreement.

As they crossed the front drive to a mounting block where their horses waited, Julia almost collided with a young mulatto woman hurrying across the yard. In her first surprise, Julia said, "Oh, please excuse me," and then realized that the slave didn't understand English. For a moment Julia stared at the young woman; her face, except for an unusual mouth, was exquisite and her body voluptuous. Even in the slave clothing, with her creamy skin and graceful form she was as beautiful as the most sought-after Charleston belle.

Finally Julia remembered her Portuguese and smiled and said, "*Desculpe.*"

The young woman's large eyes widened, then she bobbed her head and smiled—and her beauty disappeared. She was toothless.

Julia could not suppress her shocked gasp at the ugly transformation. A tan hand came up to cover the gaping smile; then the slave hurried on her way. Julia continued to the horses, her amazement growing. Often old blacks, like any elderly poor people, were missing some or all of their teeth, but she'd never before seen anyone so young without any teeth.

As Andrew helped her to mount and they rode away from the sprawling buildings, anger replaced surprise. On a rich plantation like this one, surely better care could be taken of the health of the slaves.

"Andrew, did you see that young slave I almost collided with?"

He slanted a quizzical look at her. "You mean the one without any teeth?"

"You noticed that."

"Hard to miss."

His casual remark added to her indignation. "But, Andrew, how can Senhor Mello feed his blacks so badly that a young woman like that would lose all her teeth? She'd be an extraordinarily beautiful woman if it weren't for that."

Andrew's voice had an edge. "I'm afraid you mistake the matter, Julia. It was her beauty which led to the loss of her teeth. The late Senhora Mello, perhaps because her husband appreciated that same beauty too much, had all the slave's teeth pulled."

In the shocked silence that followed, he added, "It's a common enough practice on the older *fazendas*, and I warned you that the Mello plantation is run as such places have been for several hundred years."

As if wanting to discontinue an uncomfortable topic, Andrew nudged his horse to a faster pace. Julia followed more slowly, unable to escape the memory of the slave's toothless smile. She couldn't imagine the kind of woman who could do such a horrible thing.

But as the afternoon shadows lengthened, Julia knew that although she condemned the brutality, she felt some kinship with the beleaguered wife. Senhor Mello's eyes told her that his wives undoubtedly saw familiar faces among the children in the slave quarters. Like Southern wives who knew of the nights their husbands spent in a slave hut, or who faced the threat of a black mistress to whom the white master openly adhered, this dead wife must have acted out of jealousy and rage.

Had her own anger been so different when she thought Andrew had left her to seek his mistress in São Paulo? Julia knew she would never treat another human being

the way the beautiful young mulatto woman had been
abused, but she shared with the dead Senhora Mello
some of the same dark feelings, and she shivered at the
knowledge.

11

February 1867

High overhead, fronds of giant bamboo clasped each other, shielding the avenue from the hot summer sun, reshaping it into an aisle in a shadowy cathedral. Julia loosened the collar of her light cotton dress and pulled off her wide-brimmed straw hat, letting the breezes rustling their way through the bamboo lift the damp wisps of hair which clung around her face.

When she needed someplace serene and restful, she avoided the garden with its uncontrollable riot of vines and blossoms and came here. The bamboo arch had appealed to her as soon as she saw it eight months ago after she and Andrew arrived from their honeymoon.

"*Sinhazinha.*" Julia tried to pretend she hadn't heard Scizira's soft call; she didn't want to return to the preparations for tomorrow's announcement of her father's betrothal to Carlota Pereira. Her maid persisted. "Quintiliana needs to know what you want her to do next."

"All right. I'm coming." Reluctantly Julia waved Scizira ahead, then followed her through the orangery, where she picked a tangerine before going down the slope to the graceful two-story building which was slowly becoming her home. Quintiliana asked directions only

220

when she absolutely needed them; one of the pleasures
of Andrew's household was having such a capable woman
as housekeeper. Now Julia could understand why a man
who didn't like to run a plantation would leave everything to an overseer; since she'd worked out the rou-
tines for the big house with Quintiliana, if she could,
she'd leave the house to the black woman and do what
she really wanted—learn about the field work.

She dallied along the covered brick walk which led to
the kitchen section of the building, pausing in the door
of a workroom to smile at the five black seamstresses
cutting out cotton clothing for the field hands. Scizira
went into the next room and sat down among several
black girls whom she was teaching to make lace. Julia
stopped in the pantry long enough to eat the tangerine
and rinse the juice which squirted over her hands before entering the long kitchen.

As usual Quintiliana wore sparkling white, from her
turban to the full cotton skirt and apron. She was a
Mina, one of the tall blacks whose spirit Andrew admired. When she turned, her dignified eyes were on a
level with Julia's. "*Sinha*, do you want me to make the
little sweets for the party—the ones I sent for your and
Seu Andrew's wedding?"

The cakes with the suggestive names for the dinner
to celebrate her father's coming marriage to someone
she disliked so much? "No. Just the usual assortment."

The middle-aged woman nodded and returned to her
work, and Julia left the kitchen and climbed the stairs
to the room she shared with Andrew. Restlessly she
went to the window and pushed back the white lace
curtains and looked out. Below her the quaint garden
reflected the tastes of the former owner; an iron bridge
led to a prim summerhouse on the islet in an artificial
lake. Farther on she could see palm trees and the fruit

orchard, and in the distance hazy lines of purple hills intersected each other in fading patterns.

How completely her life had changed in the year and a half since leaving South Carolina. Her mother dead, Sally and James married with a baby soon, her own marriage to Andrew—and now Papa's wedding soon to Senhora Carlota Pereira. How could he choose someone so coarse and conniving to take Mama's place? Couldn't he see Carlota was using him to escape her sister's household?

When Julia had received the letter telling her of the wedding plans, only Andrew's determined opposition had prevented her from rushing to her father's house to beg him to reconsider.

"Julia," Andrew had said sternly, "don't interfere. Your father will decide his own life." Though she'd resented her husband's peremptory tone, she realized he was right, and she'd painfully suppressed her protests.

A puff of dust on the road told her a rider was coming, and her heart lightened. It might be . . . yes, it *was* Roberto. Today she needed a visit with him! After a hasty brush over her hair and a pat at her chignon, she went gleefully to the sitting room to wait for him.

In a strange way, Roberto completed her marriage to Andrew, as if they were two aspects of the same man. The physical side of her life with Andrew remained as exciting as it had been at the beginning—perhaps even more as they grew to know each other's responses. The touch of his hand on her arm or his thigh resting next to hers in the carriage could make the blood surge through her veins and drive all thoughts away of anything but the powerful climaxes they reached together. The eagerness with which Andrew turned to her and the fre-

quency of their lovemaking convinced her she affected
him as strongly as he did her.

But other aspects of their relationship also remained
the same, as if some invisible wall stood between them
which Andrew wouldn't and she feared to breach. With
Roberto, however, she felt an undemanding ease. She
had to admit he was lazy, but if he worked as constantly
and as hard as Andrew did, he wouldn't be able to
provide the comfort and friendship she enjoyed. Though
she didn't believe most of what he said, his stories of
his adventures as a *bandeirante* in the *sertão*, the vast
hinterland, entertained and amused her.

She rang for coffee and turned smilingly to greet
him, then stopped at the sight of a cloth-covered cage
in his hand. "Roberto! Not another parrot. We have
one for every room now."

He set down the large cage and pulled off the cover
with a flourish. "Ah, but this fine fellow has a special
use. Just a moment and you'll see." He tapped the cage
sharply and called, "Carlos, Carlos."

The bird cocked its green-and-blue head on one side,
and then loudly but distinctly squawked, *"Vai pra inferno, puta."*

"Roberto!" Though she treated Roberto's pranks with
indulgence, Julia knew she couldn't keep a parrot that
said, "Go to hell, bitch."

Her brother-in-law leaned against a wicker table and
grinned wickedly. "Did you notice what I called him?
He only makes his little speech if he hears his name, or
the feminine form of it—your future mother's name—
Carlota."

He paused, and the parrot promptly repeated, *"Vai
pra inferno, puta."*

Roberto's black eyes danced with a mischievous smile.

"On other occasions, simply call him whatever you wish, and he's a model of decorum."

Despite her shock, Julia had to laugh. She'd tried not to discuss her feelings about Papa's marriage plans, but Roberto's skillful probing had uncovered the strong emotions she sought to conceal.

A maid brought the tray of coffee, and Roberto lounged companionably on a chair next to Julia. "Tell me the news, little sister. Are you increasing yet?"

"You are outrageous." Of all his teasing, Julia objected to only this kind of question. He talked freely about anything, so it wasn't the subject that bothered her but an uncomfortable feeling that the nature of her intimate life with his brother interested him too much.

"Well," he continued lightly, "I can tell you what to do. Get some *pombinha*—one of the old black women is sure to have some of the herb—mix it with the teeth of a dead man, and throw these on some hot coals. Breathe the smoke, and you'll soon produce another little Langdon."

Deciding that as usual the only way to handle Roberto in this mood was to ignore his comments, she asked, "Will you be here tomorrow for the dinner?"

The teasing smile left his face, and his dark eyes studied her sympathetically. "Do you want me here, Julia? Will I help you by coming?"

"Yes. I do want you to be here."

He took her hand and held it for a moment, the pressure of his warm fingers comforting. "Then I'll come."

Guests arrived about noon the next day; dinner would be in the early afternoon so they could return home by evening. Andrew stood beside Julia in the large parlor, welcoming the Southern families and the Brazilians who were William's and now Carlota's friends. The wedding itself would be at the Bernanos *fazenda*.

All the guests had arrived except his father when Andrew heard Julia sigh, then watched her cross the room to join William and Carlota, her smile concealing the distaste he knew she felt for her future stepmother. Her ecru lace dress, in the new fashion which had abandoned crinolines for a small bustle, clung to her as she walked, and the way it revealed her rounded breasts and slender waist and hips made him want to forget everyone else here and take her back to their large bed. She attracted him physically even more than when they married, and she had become an inventive and skillful lover. Though Quintiliana had always made him comfortable, everything in his household ran even more smoothly under Julia's efficient management. Anyone else would think his marriage extremely satisfactory.

But did Julia? And why did he work even longer hours than he needed to? That initial distrust remained with him still, the wariness of letting his wife become too essential to him. As he watched, Roberto joined the group around her, and he felt the irritation his brother invariably provoked. If his father expected Roberto to inherit any part of the large Langdon holdings, he should insist that his younger son spend his time on the land, not riding to Andrew's *fazenda* so frequently. If Roberto didn't neglect his duties so casually, Andrew wouldn't care what his brother did, he assured himself, but he hated laziness and inefficiency. One Brazilian trait he couldn't admire was the widespread contempt for work—an attitude his brother seemed to share unashamedly.

Dismissing his annoyance, Andrew resumed his role as host and started to join the unlikely group of Senhor and Senhora Bernanos and the Scotts, when he saw

Mrs. Scott's eyes widen and her mouth drop partly open. Behind him he heard his father's voice. "Julia, Andrew, please forgive our tardy arrival." He turned, and understood Mrs. Scott's fishlike look.

Beside Richard, in her usual restrained dress but with the senuous look she could never conceal, stood Ellen Durr. After his astonishment passed, Andrew felt a rush of anger toward his father for subjecting Ellen to the humiliating disapproval she'd receive in a group of this kind. He stepped forward, and found Julia before him, her hands outstretched to Ellen.

Julia's lilting voice held nothing but unembarrassed welcome. "Mrs. Durr, we are delighted to have you here." She bent and kissed the blond woman's face.

Richard, his face radiating pleasure, said clearly, "Julia, it is no longer Mrs. Durr. Ellen and I were married yesterday in São Paulo."

In the startled silence, Andrew reached Ellen and folded her in a warm embrace. She whispered in his ear, "Dear Andrew, I'm sorry. But nothing would do Richard but that he shock you all."

Muted exclamations broke the silence. Julia hugged Ellen, her feelings a mixture of delight and apprehension. She'd visited this woman whom she almost immediately loved twice since that first meeting, but always in São Paulo. Probably everyone here knew Ellen had been Richard's mistress; gossip among the inbred American community fed upon the ubiquitous servant network. How would she be accepted?

As Julia took Ellen's arm and began to make introductions, the answer to her question lay in the haughty nods and frosty responses which skirted rudeness. As she persisted around the room, anger tightened her voice until she wondered if she could continue. When she and Ellen approached Senhora Bernanos and Carlota and met the hostile eyes of William's intended bride, Julia felt her stomach begin to knot with rage.

"Julia, Quintiliana sent word that she must speak to you," Andrew said behind her, and he loosened her fingers from what she realized must have been a painful grip on Ellen's arm. He turned a charming smile to the Brazilians, and as he continued, Carlota's disapproval melted into the seductive look she often gave him. "I'm sorry to interrupt, but perhaps I can introduce Mrs. Langdon."

Julia managed a "Please excuse me," and realized from the sympathetic message in Andrew's eyes that she wasn't needed in the kitchen; he'd rescued her from a potential explosion she would have regretted. She fled past the cluster of men around Richard and William and along the hall to the deserted sewing room.

By the time Andrew found her a few minutes later, her anger had subsided, but when he took her in his arms, tears burned her eyes. "Oh, Andrew, how can people be so cruel? We can't let them hurt Ellen so."

He held her, rubbing her back, and she leaned against him, comforted by his strength. "We can't change them, and I don't think Ellen is really hurt."

"Well," she said fiercely, "if they want to be my friends, they'll have to be Ellen's too."

He tipped her head up and brushed away a tear that remained on her cheek. "Then, my loyal wife, we'd better go back and start making friends for her." His lips touched hers, and his hands cupped her buttocks, lifting her and pressing her into his thighs. "And let's get the party over."

As they returned to the salon, she felt a special warmth between them that seemed like a tender plant pushing up toward the sun.

By the time dinner and the toasts ended, Julia was

able to ignore the strained glances directed at her new
mother-in-law. Ellen seemed oblivious of the undercurrent of disapproval, but Julia wished Sally and James
were here; Sally's frivolous chatter could always divert
the conversation. However, their baby was due in March,
and they hadn't come, fearing the trip would be too
great a strain on Sally.

Julia smiled gratefully at Andrew when the men rejoined the women more quickly than usual after their
brandy and cigars. Then Mrs. Scott, her husband reluctantly trailing, started a conversation with Ellen and
Richard, and Julia relaxed; the genial South Carolina
woman was smiling and admiring Ellen's dress—Julia's
old neighbor couldn't be unpleasant to anyone for long.

Suddenly Julia felt she must get outside and find a
cool breeze, and she followed several guests on their
way to the garden. As she passed the small sitting
room, she heard Roberto saying, "Yes, Senhora Bernanos,
this is a new parrot, quite unusual-looking. Did you
notice the brilliant purple feathers in his tail, and the
green-and-blue head? Would your sister like to see
him?"

Suspicion halted Julia, and she turned to see Roberto, with a smile so innocent that anyone who knew
him would have been instantly wary, standing by Senhora Bernanos, the cover from the parrot cage he'd
brought her ,yesterday in his hand. Before Julia could
decide if she wanted to intervene, Senhora Bernanos
spoke to her sister. "Look at this unusual bird, Carlota."

As William's future bride peered at the cage, the
raucous voice squawked clearly, *"Vai pra inferno, puta!"*

Julia had only a moment to appreciate Roberto's pretended look of horror before she fled down the hall.

Andrew found her outside, still wiping tears of laughter from her face. When she told him of the incident,

he grinned and said, "A jest of Roberto's I wish I hadn't missed."

Two hours later, Roberto's last words to a departing Senhora Pereira repeated the apologies he'd offered her earlier. "I am at fault, Senhora Pereira, for giving the bird to my brother and sister-in-law, when obviously he had such a crude former owner."

Her smile to Roberto forgave him, but her good-bye to Julia sounded strained. Embracing her father, Julia found she had to suppress the laughter that threatened to return when she remembered Carlota's offended face.

Only the Langdons remained, and Julia had ordered coffee in the small sitting room when she heard a clatter in the entry hall. A maid came to the door, but before she could say more than "Senhora," a giant of a man ducked under the doorframe. He wore the green-and-gold uniform of the emperor's special troops, and his massive body looked as if he alone could defend Dom Pedro against any danger. Wild blond hair and a bushy beard completed his formidable appearance.

Andrew exclaimed, "Sergio!" and rushed to embrace the bear of a man. He must be seven inches over six feet, Julia thought, awed, three inches taller than her husband. Andrew turned to her, the blond man's enormous arm still resting on his shoulders. "Julia, I wish to present to you my friend Sergio Roque de Andrade. Sergio, Julia is my wife."

Sergio gave a bellow of pleasure and spoke in a voice which matched his size. "Andrew—with a wife—and a beauty too. My friend, you don't deserve such good fortune. I'm going to kiss your bride because I know I'll never get another chance." He enfolded Julia in a hug which she expected to crush her but didn't, and his mustache brushed her as he gave her a kiss with the same unexpected gentleness.

"Ellen," Andrew said, "Father, Roberto, you all know Sergio. And, Sergio, Ellen is now my mother."

In the congratulations and exchange of courtesies, Julia noticed that Roberto alone greeted Sergio unenthusiastically, and he looked almost hostile when talk turned to the war against Paraguay.

"Yes," Sergio was saying, "I returned with the Count d'Eu, the emperor's son-in-law, but we'll be going back to the field in another month."

"But why is the war taking so long," asked Ellen, "when Brazil has both Argentina and Uruguay fighting with her against such a small, poor country?"

"For one thing," Andrew responded, "Dom Pedro has refused to negotiate as long as Francisco López remains in power in Paraguay." Julia was surprised to hear a faintly disapproving tone in his voice; she knew he greatly admired the politically astute emperor, whose picture hung in the salon.

"But can you blame him," Richard argued, "when López closed the rivers to Brazilian shipping and then so brutally attacked Mato Grosso?"

Sergio boomed his great laugh. "Maybe it doesn't matter. Those Paraguayans are fierce fighters. Besides their loyalty to their country and to López, they're organized in squads of six men. Each man will shoot any of the others who might want to flee or give up. But not many surrender, because they know what will happen if they do. López and his mistress will publicly flog their wives or sisters to death." He looked at Ellen and Julia apologetically. "Please forgive me, senhoras. I've been with soldiers so long I forget that some topics should not be discussed."

Roberto spoke for the first time, his voice smooth and amiable. "But I hear that his mistress has organized the women and taught them to carry arms, and she's led them into battle on horseback." He gave his brother a mocking glance. "Surely we must all admire a woman who will even take over a man's duties when needed."

Julia spoke hurriedly. "When do you return to the army, Senhor Sergio?"

"Soon, unfortunately. There are plans for the siege of the fort at Humaita, which guards the river access to Asunción." He smiled with obvious pride. "I'll be on the staff of the Duke of Caxias, who commands all the Brazilian forces."

When Roberto rose to leave with Richard and Ellen, Julia said good-bye to him more formally than usual. She resented his sly implication that her interests in the running of a plantation were like women going into battle. At times it seemed he wanted to make trouble between her and Andrew. At the last moment, he flicked his eyes toward Sergio and whispered to her, "Such a great hero," and suddenly she wondered whether his bad humor was caused by jealousy of the impression Andrew's friend might make on her.

Andrew and Sergio went to Andrew's study for talk and probably brandy, and she slowly climbed the stairs. Having Ellen on the nearest *fazenda* would be a great pleasure, but it wouldn't assuage the restlessness Julia felt growing. She crossed the bedroom to look out where night hid all but the lanterns moving along the road, held by slaves lighting the way for the Langdon carriage and Roberto's horse. She wanted to at least observe how some of the crops were grown here; surely Andrew couldn't object to that.

From her own curiosity and restlessness, each day for the last month she'd taken one of the books on coffee production from the library and, with her Portuguese grammar, gone laboriously through it. She'd decided that though the *fazenda* produced many crops—cotton, wheat, grapes, sugar, cattle—their principal revenue came from coffee, and she would learn about it first. Now she wanted to see for herself how the processes she'd read about worked here on their plantation.

For the next several days, Andrew spent his waking hours with Sergio, not coming to bed until after Julia was asleep. Roberto didn't appear, and Julia's days seemed more unfulfilled than usual. Though she enjoyed Sergio's bluff humor, she waited impatiently for a chance to talk to her husband.

Sergio left early one morning, and before Andrew could depart for the day, Julia followed him to his study. He stood beside his desk, wearing the loose pants and shirt he used for riding around the fields. When she spoke, he looked up. "Andrew, do you remember when you asked me what I expected from marriage?"

He put down some papers and answered thoughtfully, "Yes, you said you didn't want a life like your mother's, but you've seemed content here."

"At first I had lots to learn about the house, but I don't now, and Quintiliana can do everything practically without help." She hesitated, not sure just how to continue.

He sat on the edge of the desk, one booted foot dangling, and a reluctant smile curved his mouth. "I think you're about to tell me you want to lead your own troops into battle."

She flushed, angry again at Roberto for suggesting the parallel and at Andrew for making fun of her. "I want to learn about coffee production. I've read some of the books you have here, but I want to know just what is done on our *fazenda*." With her eyes she dared him to object to her use of the word "our."

His smile disappeared, and his face gave no clue to his feelings. "You want me to show you?"

"Not necessarily. Senhor Oliveiro could do that." Julia didn't know the overseer well, but she didn't want her request to seem like a demand for Andrew's time.

"Very well. I'll tell him to be here early tomorrow so that you can go out with him before it gets hot."

Elation mingled with a queer disappointment that Andrew didn't want to teach her the work himself, but then he pulled her close so that she was trapped between his thighs, and the breathless excitement his touch aroused obliterated her other feelings. Half-seated on the desk, he was on a level with her, and his breath was warm against her lips when he spoke. "Did you hate having to ask me?"

She looked at his face in surprise and saw in the cobalt eyes an understanding she hadn't expected. Then his mouth touched hers, gently at first, then searchingly, and his hand slipped up under her left breast, rubbing it through the thin cloth, his fingers pressing the tingling nipple. When he pushed her dress down over her shoulder and bent to fasten his lips to the erect bud, she shivered and sagged against him.

Through her singing blood she thought of the open door and pushed at his head. "Andrew . . . the servants."

In answer, he released her, but only to close and lock the door, and then returned to strip her clothes from her trembling body. When his own clothes had been left on the floor, he pressed his naked body to hers, his penis, standing rigidly out from the mat of curling hair at his groin, hard against her belly. She stretched upward, wanting to feel him in her pulsing center; then he picked her up and carried her to the upholstered chair behind his desk. He sat down, and drawing her folded knees on each side of his waist, pulled her onto his hard shaft, holding her hips tightly as they thrust together in a spiraling ascent to the explosive crest that left her slumped, gasping, on his chest.

When their breathing quieted and he had turned her so that she sat across his thighs, she hid her head in the side of his neck. A laugh rumbled underneath her cheek as he asked, "What? Embarrassed at an early-morning ride?"

Without looking up, she waved her hand toward the shelves of books. "It feels as if they're all watching."

He laughed again, and lifted her head for a kiss. "Then we'd better get our clothes back on before they fall off the shelves in envy."

After he put on his own clothes, he fastened Julia's dress, and she went back to their room to recomb her hair. As he picked up his riding crop to go out to the stables, Andrew found he was happier than a passionate interlude with his wife or a recent visit with his closest friend would warrant. He realized that Julia's request had pleased him enormously; if she wanted to find out about growing coffee, she probably didn't intend to maneuver him into taking her back to South Carolina. Perhaps his distrust of her had been unwarranted all along.

He strode lightheartedly along the hall and outside, where Capitolino had his horse waiting. As long as she knew her husband ran the plantation, Andrew was content to let Julia play at raising coffee. With the kind of activity they indulged in constantly, she'd probably soon be raising children instead.

Upstairs, Julia heard the diminishing sound of hoofbeats and leaned out the window. "Capitolino, please saddle horses for me and you. I want to visit Senhora Ellen this morning." She found her hat and gloves, reflecting that while she'd asked Andrew about going around their land here, she'd decided to travel off the *fazenda* without consulting him. But ladies were supposed to visit, she concluded wryly, not learn about plantation management. Even that thought didn't dim her high spirits this morning; Andrew had not only agreed to her request, but he'd understood almost more about how she felt than she had herself.

At the end of the three-hour ride, Ellen welcomed Julia with a warmth that added to her special pleasure in the day. Without waiting for Julia to decide whether she could ask, Ellen explained why she'd agreed to marry Richard. "São Paulo and my career there didn't seem as important as they used to, and I do love Richard. Besides, he's agreed that I will be free to sing elsewhere at least part of the time if I wish."

Julia could feel her mouth falling slightly ajar at the thought of Richard agreeing to let his wife have a career of her own. She couldn't believe it. But when he joined them before *sesta*, every word and gesture he used showed his joy and pride in Ellen. Julia found she not only liked him, but she could see elements of both Andrew and Roberto in him. Maybe the power-hungry manipulator had been more her imagination than reality.

After *sesta*, when the day had cooled, she and Capitolino started for home. An hour's ride from the house, she saw Roberto and pulled her horse into the shade of a large myrtle tree to wait. "The national hero has left?" he asked when he stopped beside her.

She felt a moment of annoyance before her pleasure at her news banished it. "Yes, Roberto, and I have something so exciting to tell you. Tomorrow Senhor Oliveiro's going to begin teaching me all about our coffee production."

"Coffee production?" His black eyes looked disdainful. "Why do you want to learn about that? I've spent the last few years avoiding such lessons."

Irritation returned, mingled with a flat disappointment that her great news seemed so unpleasant to someone else. "Well, I want to learn, and Andrew understands how I feel."

His tan face paled, and he pulled his horse back so sharply that both mares danced nervously. He spoke coldly, his mustached mouth sneering. "Oh, yes, the virtuous, marvelous Andrew. Does he never do anything wrong?"

Shocked, Julia watched as he whirled his horse and galloped off, driving his mount furiously. She hadn't been wrong when she'd first met him; buried under the laughing exterior lay a corrosive bitterness Julia still did not understand. Slowly she rode to where Capitolino waited, feeling almost as if an enemy had replaced a dear friend. But, she decided, the joking, teasing Roberto who'd supplied the place James had always filled was real too. She liked him, and she didn't want to give up his friendship.

In the next few weeks Julia had little time to think of anything but the excitement of what she felt was the real world under the patient tutelage of Pedro Oliveiro. The large man with fair skin guarded by a floppy hat had worked as Andrew's overseer from the time the *fazenda* had first been purchased. He always wore high boots and a gray blouse, strapped around the waist by a broad black belt to which were fastened a powder flask and a knife. A bugle hung over his shoulder.

Julia rode with Pedro over the hillsides, seeing year-old plants, newly transplanted from the nursery, as well as the first sprinkling of berries on the three-year-old trees. In another area, exhausted plants which had borne coffee beans for thirty years were being torn out, their useful life over, and the field being manured to prepare for a different crop. Though she knew Andrew had fewer slaves than most *fazendeiros*, she was surprised to find two-thirds of his field hands were immigrants, mostly Italians.

As she followed the overseer along the roads which angled up the hillside, he explained that Andrew had put in these roads; the former owner had used ordinary ones which went straight up the sides of the hills between the lines of trees, gullied by every rain, so steep that even with eight or ten oxen it was often impossible to drive the clumsy carts up the slope; slaves had to bring a great part of the harvest down on their heads. Where the old roads had been, Andrew had planted orange trees.

Each night Julia returned to the books on raising coffee so that she would know as much as possible when harvesting time came in the fall. Andrew smiled at her diligence, but Julia noticed that he listened patiently to her excited descriptions of activities which he must have seen hundreds of times. He took pleasure in her enthusiasm. It seemed to her that he was less occupied with *fazenda* activities than he had been, and even occasionally had time in the evening to play his favorite Mozart on the piano.

After a week of absence, Roberto appeared one afternoon, again her lighthearted companion. She thought of asking him about his bitter words at their last encounter, but decided she had no right to pry into his feelings. She also tried to avoid talking of her consuming interest, but he insisted on hearing, laughing and saying, "If you keep telling me, you may make a coffee planter out of me when my father couldn't."

In March she returned to her father's house to be with Sally when the baby came. It seemed strange to

sleep in the room she'd used there, as if the person
she'd been had almost disappeared. She realized with a
shock that she no longer thought daily of Hundred
Oaks. Instead, she found she missed Andrew, wished
for him in bed at night, and stored up things to tell
him. When he rode over to spend one night, she found
she was waiting as restlessly for bedtime as she could
tell he was, from the abstracted way he was talking to
Papa.

The next morning she woke to find him already dressed
to ride back to their *fazenda*. Feeling suddenly shy at
the thought that someone might have heard her cries
during their lovemaking, she pretended to be asleep.
She heard him come back to the bed, hesitate, and
tiptoe from the room. Confused by her feelings, she lay
and watched the sun follow the same path it had almost
a year ago when she'd waked to the memory of having
been found in his room the previous night. She wondered if she loved him, if it was safe to love him.

The next two days and nights, James and Sally occupied all her thoughts and feelings. Sally's confinement
was long and difficult, and when the tiny baby arrived,
she lived only a few hours. Sally clung to James, crying
hysterically that she could not stay in this land where
everything died.

Trying not to think about what their departure would
mean to her, Julia remained with her family while
James and Sally made preparations to return to live on
James's portion at Hundred Oaks. Their plans renewed
for Julia the pain she'd felt at leaving South Carolina.
When William and Carlota's wedding was hastily moved
to the end of April so that James and Sally could be
present, Julia felt that now she truly had only one
home: Andrew's.

She hadn't realized that in some secret portion of her thoughts, she'd stored the comfort of knowing that if she couldn't have a happy marriage with him, she didn't have to stay. Now, unless she wanted to live on her brother's bounty or with a stepmother she was close to detesting, she must remain with Andrew. Though he had comforted her during the sad days of the baby's funeral and sustained her pride in concealing her unhappiness at her father's wedding, she felt dependent and vulnerable as she watched James and Sally's departure. As if Andrew sensed her uneasiness, he suddenly seemed distant again; the wall she'd thought was crumbling between them had returned.

When she went home with Andrew in early May, the coffee harvesting had already begun, and neither he nor the overseer had time to continue any instruction. The day started at four in the morning, with coffee at six A.M., and a breakfast of jerked beef, manioc meal, beans, and corn cakes at nine; noontime meant a dram of rum and a short *sesta*, then picking until dinner at four, followed by more work until seven, when the overseer blew his bugle to signal the end of the day. Andrew and Pedro Oliveiro kept to the same schedule as the field workers.

Julia rode out to watch, and she marveled at the sight of the workers, men and women both, with broad, shallow trays of plaited bamboo strapped over their shoulders and supported at their waists, gathering the coffee berries and unloading their baskets into carts stationed at the ends of the rows. She doubted that she could work as these women did, and in spite of her determination to learn the overseer's job, she wondered if she could keep up the grueling schedule Andrew and Senhor Oliveiro managed.

When the harvesting was finished, Julia discovered

why no glaring concrete drying beds surrounded their *fazenda*. Instead of leaving the berries in the sun for sixty days, Andrew used steam sheds to complete the drying in a few hours, and more machinery to burst the covering skins. Then the workers sorted the beans according to size and quality and sacked them. When Andrew had come to Hundred Oaks, he'd been on a trip to New York to purchase some of that machinery.

The first of the mule trains loaded with coffee beans had departed for Santos when Julia came back into the house on a chilly June afternoon from a visit with Ellen and was stopped by Scizira. The young woman's normally soft voice was agitated, and she clutched at Julia's hand. "Sinha Julia, I must speak to you. If you would please ask Seu Andrew to take Jora with him. He would be a good man for Seu Andrew—he would take good care of him in the war and see he was not hurt."

Julia stared at her trembling maid, trying to make sense out of her words. Jora was a young male slave who worked under Capitolino and had acted as their coachman on one overnight trip to São Paulo when Capitolino was sick. "Stop, Scizira, I don't know what you're talking about."

Scizira gulped, and her words came more slowly. "It's about slaves going to the war. The emperor said that any slave who goes to fight will get his freedom. If Seu Andrew would take Jora with him, Jora would come back a free man and we would marry."

Andrew going to the war? Andrew didn't fight for causes he didn't believe in, but Julia knew the speed and accuracy with which information passed through the servants' network, and a cold feeling of fear knotted her stomach as she hurried upstairs to the bedroom.

Inside, one servant was folding clothes into a small leather trunk while another pulled boots from the bottom of the wardrobe. Turning, she descended and went to the study, where she found Andrew sorting through papers, his pistols open in their case on the desk. A young black man she had never seen before, his travel clothes stained and ragged, stood nervously to one side.

"It's true? You're going to war?" Her voice echoed her disbelief. "But why?"

Andrew came and put his arm around her before he spoke to the black man. "Geraldo, please find Quintiliana. She'll provide anything you need. I'll be with you as soon as I can."

He led Julia to the chair and leaned on the edge of the polished desk as he spoke. "Geraldo has just brought word that Sergio was wounded and perhaps captured—or at any rate is missing in an assault on the fort at Humaita in Paraguay. I'm going to join the forces there to see if I can find him."

The fear in her stomach spread to the hollow that should have been her heart. "When did it happen?"

"Three weeks ago. Geraldo searched, and when he could get no help, he came for me, but it took him two weeks to get here."

"But what can you do? Won't the authorities look for him?"

Andrew's eyes hardened to chips of blue ice. "In a situation like that, no one cares enough about one individual. But I care, and I have money. Money can accomplish a great deal."

"Will you . . . ?" Her lips were too dry for her to continue. She moistened them and began again. "Will you be safe?"

His eyes melted as he drew her up into his arms. "I intend to be. Will you care?"

At the look on his face and the touch of his hands, she felt as if the heat which had melted his eyes was dissolving her bones. She whispered, "Yes," before his lips found her mouth.

When he released her, his voice reflected the tenderness of his embrace. "It's a good thing you wanted to learn about coffee. Did you arrange Sergio's disappearance so you could try your hand?" Then the teasing disappeared. "Pedro knows how to run everything, but I'll ask him to discuss things with you. And if he needs help, get in touch with the coffee factor, or Richard is available, though I think Senhor Fonseca can give better advice."

He touched her face lightly. "There's no time; I must finish my preparations."

As he turned back to his desk, she remembered and said shakily, "Could you take Jora with you? Scizira wants to marry him, and she says he'd be freed if he went with you."

He looked up, considering, then nodded. "Yes, he'd be useful. Have her tell him to come in here."

An hour later Julia stood in the front drive, her lips still warm from Andrew's good-bye kiss, and watched the three horses with two pack mules plodding behind disappear along the road. As she turned to go back into the house, she thought that now she had the freedom to do the kinds of activities she loved. But a lonely feeling inside her told her that she didn't want to pay the price that might be demanded for that freedom.

12

Outside, the September sun touched the trunks of trees that were sending shy leaves into the spring air. In the study the overseer rose from the round table where he and Julia had coffee each morning as they planned the day's work. "You want me to tell Capitolino to bring your horse, Senhora Julia?"

She smiled regretfully. "No, Senhor Pedro, I must work on accounts this morning. I'll ride out to see yesterday's planting this afternoon."

The burly man nodded and settled his slouch hat over his thick gray hair before striding out the door. Julia speculated on the age of the hat; it appeared to be the same one she'd first seen over a year ago, now slowly sagging under its accumulation of red dust.

She walked to the window and stared out over the pale greens of the spring morning, the question surfacing which always lay just beneath her other thoughts. Where was Andrew? When would he be back?

A wounded officer returning home to São Paulo had brought her a letter in late July. After a grueling ride across to the Paraná River, Andrew had traveled south on a riverboat to the Brazilian army headquarters but found no trace of Sergio. He'd heard that some wounded

Brazilians had been left behind after skirmishes, and he planned to use his status as an American citizen to search the surrounding countryside. No more messages from him had arrived in the past two months.

As Julia watched two black girls dawdling between the kitchen and the garden, she thought that except for missing and worrying about Andrew, she was happier than she'd been for a long time. Pedro Oliveiro knew his work well and at first consulted her only because Andrew had instructed him to do so, but now he obviously respected her grasp of *fazenda* activities. It hadn't taken Julia long to assume responsibility as she had at Hundred Oaks years before, and she felt useful and needed once again, leaving the household decisions to Quintiliana. The restlessness which had plagued her was gone.

Now Julia longed for something else. As if the two girls, giggling together in the yard below her, could see not only her face but also into her mind, she turned hastily away from the window, her skin burning with a vivid blush. She yearned for Andrew's touch. She missed his lovemaking desperately, sometimes pacing their bedroom during sleepless nights, shocked at the intensity of her desires, but unable to dismiss them.

Her fears about whether Andrew would humiliate her with a mistress had vanished. No child's face in the slave quarters resembled his, and the frequency of their lovemaking and the hours he spent working reassured her that he didn't have another woman. Wistfully she remembered the comfort he'd offered during her father's wedding and Sally and James's departure. In those last months before he left, after he'd agreed that she could learn about coffee production, a new and warm understanding had been growing between them. She wondered whether her marriage, which had begun with as much passion as distrust and antagonism, could nuture love within it. She didn't know, but she longed for Andrew's return; to know he was safe and to have him with her again.

Turning away from the window, she settled at the desk to go through Andrew's account books. Without him here to answer questions, she had been reading the records of his financial transactions to instruct herself. Usually she reserved the task for evenings, but yesterday Roberto had stayed beyond his usual afternoon visit, and she hadn't finished the pages she allotted herself daily.

Two hours later she heard shouting in the yard and went to the window. House servants clustered around one of the wooden field carts. Julia could hear Capitolino giving orders, but she couldn't understand his words. Hurrying feet echoed in the hall, and with only one sharp knock the door opened to Scizira's frightened face.

"*Sinhazinha*, come quickly. Senhor Pedro has been hurt."

Julia ran along the corridor and outside, where Capitolino was directing four black field hands in lifting the white-faced overseer from the cart to a leather litter. One leg was turned at a strange angle, and the injured man's groans changed to a scream as he was moved.

"What happened?" Julia asked Quintiliana shakily.

The tall woman's face looked gray. "An axle broke, and a cart rolled down a slope, hitting Senhor Pedro."

Capitolino had already sent a rider to Richard's *fazenda* to summon the doctor the two plantations shared. By evening the small middle-aged man had set the broken leg, but he could do little for injuries to the overseer's back and chest other than to dose him with laudanum.

"Senhor Pedro will be mending for a long time, Senhora Langdon," the doctor warned as he prepared to leave. "I have instructed your housekeeper as to his care, but he will be unable to perform his duties for many months." He kissed her hand as if he had made a social call instead of doing the job he'd taken because he was the sixth son in an impoverished family.

When he left, the smile at his courtly manners faded from Julia's face. Regardless of Senhor Oliveiro's injuries, the work of the *fazenda* must go on. Although Julia had learned a great deal about all of the activities, she realized that without a man's authority behind her, only a woman of long experience could take the place of a man as a direct supervisor. If Andrew were here, he would be his own overseer, but the workers would not accept her in Senhor Oliveiro's place.

Moonlight slowly crept across the braided mats on the study floor as she paced around the desk. She couldn't hire an overseer from outside because she wasn't certain enough of all the details to train someone new. She'd have to make one of the field supervisors a temporary overseer.

By the time she finally settled into bed in the big room upstairs, she felt confident she could solve the problems caused by Pedro Oliveiro's accident. Though she shuddered at his misfortune and wished she could spare his terrible suffering, she also felt a kind of shameful excitement at this new challenge. She reached for the empty pillow next to her and held it close, missing Andrew's warmth, his touch, the shivering pleasure he gave her, but she went to sleep ready for tomorrow, even without him.

Andrew sat tiredly on his plodding horse, wondering why he continued what was probably a futile endeavor.

In the two months since he'd arrived at the Brazilian encampment on the Paraguay River, he'd used the protection of his American citizenship to go on expeditions into the surrounding area. He'd been right that no one would look for a missing man, but also no one stopped him from his search.

The siege of the fortress of Humaita, which guarded the river approach to the Paraguayan capital of Asunción, had begun in July, and all energies and attention centered on this attack. The Paraguayan soldiers fought as fiercely as Sergio had said, and Andrew guessed that the siege might last longer than the Brazilian and Argentine commanders confidently expected. He knew he wouldn't be allowed to go upriver; the Brazilians had even refused to let Elihu Washburn, the United States minister to Paraguay, go to his post. Andrew would have to hope that Sergio might still be somewhere in this area.

At first he had searched futilely west of the Paraguay River in Argentina, thinking that a wounded Brazilian might have been cared for by people who were at least temporary allies. He'd shivered in the winter winds as he set out doggedly each day, questioning, paying to loosen tongues. Once, in late August, he heard of a village where a tall Brazilian had been left behind, wounded in a raid by Paraguayan soldiers. For half a day Andrew felt wild hope, but when he located the soldier, he found a ragged miner from Minas Gerais who'd attached himself to a household with two widowed daughters and had no wish to rejoin the army. Only grim determination had kept Andrew to his task after that painful disappointment.

Then two weeks ago he'd heard a rumor of dissatisfaction among the Guaraní Indians in the area of Paraguay west and north of the river junction. Leaving Jora behind at military headquarters, he'd hired as guide a young Paraguayan who knew the area and the native Guaraní language. Andrew had bribed their way across the Paraná River into the open savanna, where only clumps of palm trees interrupted the shoulder-high grasses. At first hopeful, he offered gold and silver for information about a giant of a soldier, but so far he'd learned nothing. A sensible man would give up, he knew, but a sensible man wouldn't have come in the first place.

As he rode toward a distant fan of waving palm trees where he could see a group of low buildings, he thought of his ties to Sergio. He couldn't ignore even a remote possibility of helping the man who'd been his best friend.

He thought also of his growing emotions for Julia. If his marriage prospered, it would have to survive separations, but Andrew had hated to leave her just when a new regard and concern had grown between them. He didn't know if he loved her, but their relationship had deepened as they trusted and understood each other more. And tired and anxious as he'd been on this trip, he missed her responsive lovemaking. Whores had never appealed to him, and all the women around the military camp looked unappealing when he remembered his wife's beauty.

He loosened his jacket, appreciating the warmer spring air. Since he wouldn't get home soon, he was glad he'd taken care of the business about Lele. A few days before he left home, his banker in São Paulo had written to ask whether he wanted to pay another year's rent on the house for Lele in Rio. With her beauty and skills, she should have found someone else before this; if he continued to pay her rent, he suspected he'd also be supporting some impecunious lover. He'd intended to

refuse, but when word came about Sergio, he'd hastily
sent a note to his banker to pay the rent. Remembering
Lele's unexpected appearance at the hotel in São Paulo,
he'd decided he didn't want to risk the possibility she
might go to the *fazenda*.

Now as he approached the palm trees, he forced
himself to forget home and concentrate on the scene in
front of him. Several crude houses huddled together,
their low clay walls reinforced by poles which leaned at
drunken angles. The people who lived there must have
seen him and Juan, his guide, because only a scrawny
rooster and two bedraggled hens roamed outside. He
sent Juan ahead to call to them and waited on his horse
while a bent old man hobbled out, soon followed by
three ragged women and a circle of naked children.

When Juan had finished his questions and received
the usual negative answers, he remounted his horse,
and said, "Señor, shall we go on north?" A wave of
discouraged anger made Andrew want to shout and
yell, but he only nodded, and urged his horse into a
trot.

When they had gone beyond hearing distance of the
huts, he heard a low call. One of the women who'd
stood silently while Juan questioned the old man panted
to a stop. The guide slid from his horse and stood
while she spoke nervously in Guaraní. Her hands waved
expressively toward Andrew as she talked, and he felt
his heart beat faster.

Finally she finished speaking, and Juan turned to
Andrew. "She says she knows where a giant man is.
Her sister and mother, who live in the next set of huts,
found him."

Andrew started to inquire if the man were Brazilian
but instead asked, "Will she take us there?" If it were
Sergio, he'd know soon enough. He waited, barely

breathing, until the woman nodded to Juan's question. Dismounting, he led his horse as the woman scurried before them.

Over his shoulder he spoke to Juan. "Did she say what happened—why someone looked after this man?"

"Not too much. She said something about all of the men from their family being taken for the army and one of them being killed by his commander." Though no one but the woman could hear them and she spoke only Guaraní, Juan lowered his voice. "El Presidente is a cruel man to anyone who makes a mistake."

When Andrew finally knelt beside the gaunt figure lying in the corner of a dark hut, he hardly recognized the skeletal face of his friend. The eyes flickered open and he heard a hoarse whisper. "No . . . it's a dream. You can't be here." A faint smile curved Sergio's lips before his eyes closed again.

During the long afternoon while Andrew waited beside Sergio for Juan to return with mules and a litter, he thanked God for the miracle which had brought him to this place. The women may have kept the Brazilian alive because of hatred toward the Paraguayan leaders, or perhaps they hoped he would stay here in this maleless household, but Andrew's gold should enable them to leave the area if they wished. First he'd get Sergio to a military doctor, and when his friend was well enough, they'd go down the Paraná River to Buenos Aires and from there to Sergio's home in Rio. He'd send a message to Julia; she could meet them there. As the thin hand reached for his, he felt tears spill from his eyes.

Julia studied the tall black man who stood before her, hoping he could fill the job of overseer. She'd already found out from interviewing them that neither of the Italians had sufficient knowledge of overall plantation business to take over Pedro Oliveiro's responsibilities. This free black looked at her with an easy intelligence that encouraged her. His height and bearing suggested he was a Mina, and something about him looked familiar.

"Your name is Tomaz?" she asked in Portuguese.

"Yes, Dona Langdon." His clear voice suggested that he only accorded her that title from courtesy, and she wondered if he would have been a member of the nobility in his own country.

As they discussed the plantation work, Julia's excitement grew. He could do the overseer's job—she felt convinced of that. She wouldn't have to depend on help from anyone else.

Fortunately Richard and Ellen had gone to São Paulo, or she suspected Richard with his overbearing ways would have been here as soon as the doctor had told him about the accident. Roberto had ridden to see her, but in true form he'd offered sympathy and comfort, but no advice. Papa would help, of course, but the one time she'd been back to his house since he'd married Carlota, her stepmother had made her feel like an unwelcome intruder. Sadly she'd kissed Papa good-bye that day, knowing that if he was as happy as he appeared, she couldn't speak against his bride, but she also couldn't share her concerns with him as she once had.

With Tomaz' help she'd be able to handle the *fazenda* on her own until Andrew returned. Smilingly she rose. "Tomaz, I would like you to take over Senhor Oliveiro's job of overseer until he is well again or Senhor Langdon returns."

To her surprise no responding smile answered her. Instead dark brows drew together in the handsome face. "I thank you for the honor, Dona Langdon, but I cannot do that. The white workers would not take orders from a black." He spoke matter-of-factly, without obvious bitterness, but his midnight eyes looked closed and unapproachable.

Anger replaced Julia's first startled reaction. Deliberately she used the term of respect she always used to the overseer, but she put all of her authority into her voice. "Senhor Tomaz, we pay our laborers very well to work here under the orders of whoever is chosen to direct them. You can, I believe, fulfill the duties of overseer; the two Italian supervisors cannot. I wish you to perform that job for the present."

For a moment she thought he would refuse again, but then, with what looked like a resigned shrug, he said, "Very well. When do you wish me to begin?"

"Come to the study in the morning." For a moment she hesitated, then smiled, dismissing him. She'd always shared coffee with Pedro Oliveiro as they discussed the work, but an unwelcome discomfort prevented her from mentioning that.

Her uneasiness increased when shortly after Tomaz' departure, Quintiliana asked to speak to her privately. When Julia closed the study door, she found that for the first time, the housekeeper's poise seemed shaken, and she almost stumbled over her words. "Sinha Julia, you must not make Tomaz your overseer."

Julia's anger rose more swiftly this time. After Tomaz left, she'd had time to think that never had she seen the whites and the black working together. In fact, she realized, she hadn't noticed the separation because she didn't expect to see them together. In spite of her pride in the ideas she'd absorbed from her Quaker relatives, she accepted the systems around her as readily as anyone else. Quintiliana's objection wounded her already damaged esteem.

Her voice carried an unusual sharpness. "In my husband's absence, I will make whatever decisions I think necessary."

She could see she had offended the proud woman. "Senhora Julia, I understand that, but Tomaz is my brother, and I do not wish to see him harmed."

Julia put her hand on the older woman's arm. "He will not be hurt, Quintiliana. I won't allow it."

Two nights later Julia remembered with bitterness her confident words as she watched Capitolino and the black servants putting out a fire which had badly damaged the overseer's house. Fortunately Senhor Oliveiro and his family were in two rooms in the big house, and Tomaz had not moved into the overseer's house as she had told him he could do. She clutched her robe around her and wished her head didn't ache so. When the two white supervisors had come to her in anger, she'd refused to listen to their protests. Now she had to recognize that Tomaz and Quintiliana had been right and she had been wrong. What should she do?

The next morning Richard stormed into the house before she finished her breakfast coffee, all the arrogance she'd distrusted when she first met him evident in his voice. "Are you insane, Julia, to attempt to put a black in charge of white laborers?"

She found herself standing with clenched fists, shouting back, releasing all the anxiety of the last few days on his head. "Why shouldn't whites work for a black, when he knows the job and they don't?"

He loomed over her, looking like a portrait of the Devil, with his beard and his slashing black brows over raging eyes. "Because blacks are not fit to rule whites, and anyone who doesn't recognize that is a menace to this society. If I had been here before you started this insanity, I'd have stopped it soon enough. I'll send over my overseer until we can arrange something different."

Fury exploded in her and she shook with its force. "You'll do nothing here. Your son left me to take care of *our* land, and I'll decide what to do without any interference from you."

He clenched his hands as if only tremendous control kept him from hitting her. "We'll see." His boots thundered along the hall, and the slam of the entrance door echoed through the house.

Julia groped her way to a chair and leaned her head on the desk, fighting to control the nausea which followed her rage. An amused voice brought her upright.

"Brava, Julia!" Roberto sauntered across the room. "That was a marvelous scene. I'd guess that no one has spoken that way to Richard for years." Amusement died from his voice. "Julia, you're not going to be sick?"

"Yes," she gasped, "I am," and reached for the clay pot she used for trash.

Roberto held her shoulders until the convulsions stopped, then led her to the small sitting room and had a maid bring water and a cloth. After she rinsed her mouth and washed her face, she lay on the settee, exhausted from the events of the past night and morning. Roberto sat beside her, his long legs stuck out in front of him.

"Feeling better, Julia?"

She nodded, but she didn't feel better. She closed her eyes against the light, wishing no cart had broken an axle, wishing whites respected blacks, wishing Richard were dead and Andrew were here. She felt a warm hand take one of hers and looked into Roberto's sympathetic eyes. "Well, dear sister, you will accomplish what Richard and Andrew have despaired of for years. You will turn me into something any good Brazilian would abhor—an honest, hardworking man."

Bewildered, she stared questioningly at him. A smile

curved his lips and crinkled his black eyes. "I, my dear, with your direction, will be your new overseer." He raised her hand to his lips and kissed it, and his touch soothed and comforted her.

Two months later the November morning had already lost its coolness by the time Julia and Roberto finished their coffee and discussion. Roberto rose to leave, but Julia touched his hand to stop him. "Roberto, I want to tell you something." She paused, momentarily embarrassed, then continued, determined to pay him the tribute she felt she owed him. "When we first met, I thought you never had a serious idea, that only frivolous pleasures interested you. I was wrong. I don't know how I would have managed without you, and I want you to know how grateful I am."

Roberto watched her soft eyes, looking at him with admiration in their golden-brown depths, and he realized how much the love he had come to feel for her had grown. From the moment he met Julia, he'd found her captivating. He'd flirted with her and silently gloated when he realized Andrew couldn't understand the friendship between his wife and his brother. Yet Roberto had never expected to fall in love this deeply. He knew Julia would be shocked if he revealed his emotions, so he forced himself to speak lightly. "But you weren't wrong. Then I didn't have a sister to inspire me. Now you see a reformed—or ruined—man before you whom my Brazilian relatives would recognize only with horror."

He took her hand for a moment, then released it so that he wouldn't pull her into his arms. "Besides, Julia, you provided the opportunity for me to prove Richard wrong—something I've wanted to do for years." He grinned at her wickedly. "And I get to eat Quintiliana's cooking and have your steady company, though," he added lightly, "if I had to choose between her meals and your charm, you might come in second." With that lie, he picked up his riding crop and left.

Julia looked after him thoughtfully, wondering if she heard a special warmth in his voice, but dismissing it as Roberto's naturally charming banter with all women. She hummed happily as she went to her desk and began her daily study of Andrew's accounts. She'd read everything up to just before they were married, and this self-instruction had been thorough. The accounts reflected pattern of plantation activity, and she felt she knew what would be a wise decision about selling any of the crops. Of course Senhor Fonseca, as coffee factor, could advise her about their most important crop, but by the time for the coffee harvest in the fall, Andrew would be home.

A brief message had come from him saying he had found Sergio and planned to take his friend to Buenos Aires and then to Rio. Their arrival in Rio depended on Sergio's health, but Andrew would get word to her in time for her to join him there. The thought that she would see him soon intoxicated her and made the nights seem less empty. With the knowledge he would return, and with Roberto to help her, she reveled in her current duties.

Remembering the friction between the half-brothers, she wondered how Andrew would react to the news that Roberto had taken over the overseeing of the *fazenda*. Richard had been furious at first and refused to speak to them, but Ellen had continued to visit and provide Julia with loving support. Gradually Richard had softened, and Julia could see a growing though unacknowledged pride in his son. Surely Andrew would understand also and be grateful to Roberto.

Indeed Julia felt confident Andrew would be pleased

with Roberto's work. He had put men to work repairing
the damaged overseer's house and had moved in there.
Julia actually saw little of him because of the long hours
he worked. Apparently he knew a great deal about
running a *fazenda* that he hadn't revealed before, but
the long hours in the saddle and the strain of putting
his observations into practice had exhausted him at
first. Now all the plantation activities went smoothly.
Though he occasionally argued with her, he welcomed
her appearance in the field and usually followed her
suggestions. Never before this morning had she wondered even for a moment if she meant anything more to
him than a comfortable sister and friend.

An item in the account book caught Julia's eye: the
sum of one thousand *mil reis* for one year's rental on a
house on the Rua Direita. Did Andrew rent a house
somewhere that he hadn't mentioned? And where was
the Rua Direita? When they traveled to São Paulo, they
always stayed at a hotel. She looked at the date, early
May of 1866, just before Sally and James's wedding.

Curiously she looked for entries for the same date in
1867 and found nothing, but flipping forward she found
a smiliar notation in June on the day Andrew had left to
look for Sergio. The amount had doubled to two thousand *mil reis*, undoubtedly because of the disastrous
inflation caused by the Paraguayan War, but the address was the same—number forty-three Rua Direita.

Why would Andrew rent a house which they never
used? A thread of fear she thought long buried chilled
her. Could he have another household where a mistress
lived? Immediately she recognized how farfetched her
suspicion was. Until he'd gone to Paraguay, Andrew
hadn't been away from her in the year of their marriage; he had no opportunity to visit a mistress. Though
he hadn't expected her to read his account books, he

hadn't forbidden it either, and the information certainly wasn't hidden.

The cloud over her happiness retreated. She felt ashamed she'd allowed something so unimportant to upset her and make her doubt him as she had early in their marriage; he deserved more trust than that. After he returned, she'd ask him about the entry if she remembered it.

The sounds of an arrival interrupted her, and when she went to the front entrance, she found the rotund figure of the coffee factor descending from a sturdy black coach. She ran down the steps to greet him. "Senhor Fonseca! How delighted I am to see you."

"And surprised as well, I'm sure, Senhora Langdon," he said as he bowed over her hand. "I hope you will forgive my coming unexpectedly, but I have a question that cannot wait for an answer, as well as a letter for you from Senhor Andrew."

When she'd seen to his comfort and he was resting, she excused herself and took the letter to her room where she could be alone to read it. The two sheets, covered with Andrew's forceful script, told her he and Sergio had arrived in Buenos Aires, but Sergio had become ill again, and they would wait until late November to go to Rio de Janeiro. He had booked passage on a ship that should reach Rio in time for the emperor's birthday celebration on December 2.

Though Senhor Fonseca waited for her, she reread the letter, and then the last two lines a third time. "I hope that nothing will prevent your joining me in Rio, my dearest Julia. I have missed you greatly these past months." Those sentences, and the closing, "Your devoted husband, Andrew," filled her with such gladness that she felt the heart really must be the center of joy and that hers might burst. From anyone else these phrases might seem only polite, but from her restrained husband the words sounded like a medieval love ballad.

She clasped the letter and whirled around in the center of her bedroom until her ruffled skirt flared high around her legs and strands of hair tore loose from her chignon. Five minutes with her brush and comb were needed before she could descend demurely to the small sitting room to join her portly guest.

After they exchanged pleasantries and she described the progress being made with Roberto's help, Senhor Fonseca's face became grave. "I see, Senhora Julia—may I call you that?—that you have managed excellently during your husband's absence. Now I fear I must burden you with another decision." He rested his spread fingertips against one another as he appeared to think how best to phrase his words. "I have been approached by an American who wishes to buy coffee beans now."

"But, Senhor Manuel, we will have no beans until May and June, nor does anyone else," she responded, puzzled.

"This gentleman wishes to buy future harvests, and he will pay very well." The coffee factor waved his hands expressively. "He represents the interests of a company in the United States which plans a new venture in selling specially powdered coffee and wants to purchase choice beans in advance to assure the amounts they will need for their new factories."

"Powdered coffee?"

He leaned toward her enthusiastically. "Yes. In Illinois a Mr. Borden has been experimenting with this idea for some years and just recently has marketed such a coffee."

The excitement in Senhor Manuel's eyes seemed to Julia to come from more than interest in a new coffee process. "Senhor Manuel, you told me once you are a gambler. I think you want my husband and me to gamble with you."

His side whiskers shook from his delighted laugh. "You are completely correct, Senhora Julia, and since you see through me so easily, I will come directly to the point. The purchaser offers an exceptionally good price for your future crop. If you accept his contract, you are obliged to deliver a specific amount of coffee. Should anything happen to your crop, you must still meet that obligation, by buying enough beans from other planters if necessary. I hardly need tell you that such purchases after harvesttime would be exceedingly costly."

Julia felt her spirits rising to match the coffee factor's. "So if we had a good crop, we could make a great deal of money, but if a bad one, we could lose just as much."

"Yes, that is exactly right."

She rearranged her napkin by her coffee cup, restraining her excitement so that she could consider his proposal carefully. Then the realization she had no right to make this decision stopped her. "When Andrew comes home, we will give you our answer," she said, trying not to sound disappointed.

"Senhora Julia, unless Senhor Andrew returns within the next week, I cannot wait for him. That is why I made this trip to see you now. The contract must be signed immediately; the purchaser will not wait. I plan to return to São Paulo tomorrow."

Julia's heart began to pulse with a mixture of anticipation and anxiety. Could she—dared she—make such a decision on her own? "Senhor Manuel, I would like to think about this tonight, but I will give you an answer before you leave in the morning."

While the coffee factor recovered from his jolting carriage ride, Julia spent the rest of the day and into the night poring over Andrew's accounts, averaging the coffee harvest for the last five years, mulling over possible outcomes. She could discuss this with Richard, but after their furious argument, she refused to consult him about anything less than a complete disaster. Since the *fazenda* sold products other than coffee, even with the worst results, they would eventually recover. She described the possibilities to Roberto, but he only smiled and shrugged, refusing to offer any advice.

By the time she went to bed that night, she had decided to gamble two-thirds of the coffee crop they could reasonably expect. The gain wouldn't be as high, but neither would a loss. Surely Andrew would understand that they shouldn't miss this opportunity. Would he also understand that risk appealed to a gambler in her she hadn't known existed before now? She was more like the Southerners who spent their evenings with dice and cards than she had realized.

Early the next morning she watched beside Roberto as the pleased coffee factor departed. On the strength of her word, he would sign the contract as Andrew's agent. She turned to go into the house, and found Roberto smiling at her.

"I see that you are glowing with pride in yourself, Julia," he teased, but she could see admiration in his face. "I hope that my brother appreciates all the qualities of his unusual wife."

A doubt insinuated itself into her happiness. Suddenly she wanted reassurance. "Do you think he'll approve?"

Roberto's warm laugh comforted her. "If he's not an idiot, he'll be delighted with you."

Gratitude for all Roberto had done for her filled her, and impulsively she threw her arms around him and hugged him. "Thank you, Roberto, for everything."

He stiffened, and she started to draw away, afraid she had offended him, but he pulled her close and she felt a kiss on her hair. "My dearest . . . sister."

A tremor began in her chest, and for a moment she wanted to press closer to him, as if Andrew held her and soon she would feel those wonderful sensations of making love. Shocked at her response, she hurriedly stepped away from Roberto. As she turned and went into the house, she couldn't look at him. Andrew, she thought confusedly, you've been away too long, and Roberto is too much like you. Thank God her husband would be returning soon.

13

Light skittered off the surface of the bay at Rio de Janeiro, leaving silver patches like floating pieces of ice, an illusion quickly melted by the noontime heat. Just two years before, Julia remembered, she'd first seen these mountains which fell so sharply into the sea. Fleetingly she thought of the unhappy girl she'd been, then forgot her in the excitement of looking for her husband.

Straining to see the figures on the dock, she shaded her eyes against the glare as the small coastal steamer jostled its way through the confusion of the harbor. When outlines and bits of color turned into top hats and bonnets, disappointment replaced the anticipation which had kept her sleepless in the hotel in Santos last night. No black head reached above the others; Andrew had not come to the dock to meet her.

When she could distinguish faces, she saw Jora, a wide grin on his face, waiting toward one side. Her spirits rebounded; probably Andrew hadn't been able to leave Sergio, but obviously he had planned for her arrival. She waved excitedly and pointed Jora out to Capitolino, who had escorted her to São Paulo, then on the long day's journey to Santos, and now to Rio.

The steamer finally nudged its way to a place beside the quay, and Julia, with Capitolino following, descended to Jora's enthusiastic welcome. "I've been meeting the ships from Santos each day, Sinha Julia. Seu Andrew left yesterday to see Senhor Sergio to his family's summer home in Petropolis. He said for me to tell you he will be at the hotel before evening."

As they drove through the streets, Jora pointed out the banners everywhere, left from the celebration of Dom Pedro's birthday two days before on December 2. "You should have seen the emperor," he chattered, "riding his white horse to the cathedral. His uniform had so much gold I hid my eyes. In the afternoon a big balloon went up into the air over the bay, and at night every window had a candle in it. Oh, it was a glorious day."

"Jora," Capitolino scolded, "stop that foolish talk and watch where we're going."

Julia laughed happily. "It's all right, Capitolino. Tell me, Jora, why didn't you stay with the army to get your freedom?"

The young man rolled his eyes. "I found out right away, *sinhazinha*, that I didn't want to be a soldier. That's a bad life." A wide grin covered his face. "But Seu Andrew freed me anyway, because I went with him and helped him with Senhor Sergio."

"Scizira will be so pleased."

The carriage turned into the Rua d' Ouvidor, passed a tree-shaded square and a handsome church, and stopped at a large hotel with pink walls and wrought-iron grilles over the windows. Next to the hotel Julia noticed delightedly a shop with a sign identifying it as a British subscription library; she could purchase some books during their stay in Rio, perhaps something new by Mr. Dickens.

A short man whose waxed mustache gave his face a perpetual smile came out to greet her and escort her upstairs to a large sitting room and bedroom at the back of the hotel. It overlooked a garden so crammed with marble statuary that flowers had to struggle to find a place.

Settling into her rooms and a leisurely bath occupied Julia until midafternoon. She thought of going next door to the library but knew she only pretended to consider it—nothing could get her away from the hotel until Andrew arrived. Restlessly she wandered around the room, looking down into the garden, taking up a Portuguese novel and abandoning it unopened. A packet on the writing table caught her eye. The hotel maid must have laid it there when she unpacked Julia's traveling trunk. Julia recognized the letters which she had picked up in São Paulo but had been too rushed and excited to open.

Happily she sat down at the small rosewood desk. Near the top of the pile she recognized James's handwriting and tore open the envelope: "My dearest sister, I hope this finds you well and happy and I apologize that my letter has been delayed because of my many tasks. Sally and I made our return trip in good time. We are looking forward to the prospect of beginning a family again and are happy and content in each other. But, Julia, I have no other good news to give you. Papa's decision to leave this land showed great foresight. You cannot imagine the terrible conditions here. Were it not for Sally's health and happiness, I would return immediately to Brazil. . . ."

Tears filled Julia's eyes as she read of the desolation he had found at Hundred Oaks, but she smiled at his closing words. "In spite of the problems we must overcome here, I get pleasure when I see trees you and I

used to climb, and yesterday I paused a moment by the
bank which you slid down one day, giving you an injury
which may mark you still. Someday when you visit
Sally and me and the family I trust we will have, we'll
go back to these places together."

Yes, James was right; she still bore that scar on her
abdomen. The letter fell to her lap as she relived excur-
sions with her twin, and she cried a little more at the
thought of their separation.

Shaking off her sadness, she looked through the remaining envelopes, most from business and political
acquaintances of Andrew's. A return address leapt at
her from a letter near the bottom of the stack—number
43 Rua Direita, with the additional notation of Rio de
Janeiro. The address covered the page in elaborate
scrolls and curlicues, in the style of the street scribes
who wrote letters for people who couldn't write for
themselves.

She stared at the envelope. It had never occurred to
her that the building on which Andrew had paid two
years' rent might be in Rio. She'd assumed it was a
house, but now she realized it could be a business.
No—a businessman wouldn't need a scribe to write his
letters, and Andrew's account book would have contained more information about a business. Perhaps Andrew kept a house here for the times he came to the
capital, though the cost seemed high when hotel rooms,
or even private houses, could be readily obtained. Who
had paid for a letter to be written to him? Maybe a
housekeeper. Perhaps the message concerned their using the house for this trip and they would move to it
from the hotel.

Despite the windows open to the breezes from the
bay, the afternoon seemed oppressive, and Julia could
feel a headache beginning. What I need is sleep, she

decided, feeling suddenly as if her eyes would not stay open a moment longer. Andrew would, she assured herself, explain to her all about the puzzling letter. Carefully she inserted the envelope into the center of the stack of mail and went into the bedroom. When she had removed all her clothing except her chemise, she lay on top of the bed and let a breeze cool her damp skin as she drifted into sleep.

Andrew took the stairs two at a time and tried to restrain himself to a fast walk along the hotel corridor. A grinning Capitolino had met him downstairs, reassuring him that Julia had arrived. It seemed like years rather than six months since he'd ridden away from the *fazenda*, and with Sergio safely installed to endure his family's cosseting, Andrew's responsibilities for his friend had ended.

A glance took in the empty sitting room, and two strides put him at the bedroom door. He halted, then continued softly to the bed to look down on his sleeping wife.

She lay on her side, her legs slightly bent, one hand nestled beside her head. Her hair drifted across the pillow in a red-gold fan; her thick lashes, a darker shade of the same brilliant color, rested against her cheek. He didn't need to see the enticing patch of hair at her thighs to remind him of its deep red, but she stirred and moved slightly, and through the thin chemise he saw the shadowed triangle. A lace strap had slid down her left shoulder, leaving her breast exposed so that part of a pink nipple showed. He could feel his erection beginning. How he'd missed his wife. As he studied her face, the stubborn jaw and mouth soft in sleep, more than passion stirred him, and he realized with tender delight that he loved her.

At what point distrust and suspicion had vanished and love taken their place, he didn't know or care. Remembering how things had been between them before he left, he was certain she felt the same toward him.

He leaned over to kiss her awake, then stopped. She slept soundly; he'd contain his desire a little longer. Quietly he returned to the sitting room, closing the door behind him, and went out to order a bath. When the tub had been set up in the sitting room and silently filled by two well-tipped maids, he stripped off his travel-dusty clothes and stepped into the steaming water.

Andrew's hand caressing the side of her face seemed like a dream, but when his lips kissed hers softly, then more insistently, Julia awoke. She opened her eyes to find Andrew's mouth teasing hers. "Andrew!" she gasped, and then he kissed her again.

He lay naked beside her on the bed, his arousal obvious in his stiff organ, standing out from the black hair at his groin. As he pulled her close, she managed only "Oh, Andrew," and clung to him, her heart racing, her breath coming in sharp gasps. They parted for him to slip off her chemise; then he leaned over her, one elbow on each side of her head, and traced the lines of her face, as if replenishing some image he carried inside him. He still showed the marks of his long search for his friend, but his body seemed more magnificent in its lean beauty than she remembered. Greedy now for the feel of him, she pressed close again.

"I didn't want to meet you at the dock, Julia," he said softly, rubbing his thumb gently across her cheekbone, "because I knew as soon as I saw you, I'd want to make love to you." His lips claimed hers, and her world narrowed to this room, to the sunlight slanting across the wide bed, to the man who was capturing her soul and binding them together with his touch.

With each caress given and received Julia felt as if she were floating in a space reserved only for lovers. His tongue danced inside her mouth and invited her to taste his. His breath teased her ear and she caught his earlobe with her teeth. While his kiss on the side of her neck sent shivers racing down her spine, her fingers tangled themselves in the hair on his chest. He drew her heart from her body as he caressed her breasts and suckled the nipples to an aching hardness. She made him release her so that she could kiss his shoulders and back, reveling in the feel of his taut body.

All was blindingly new, and yet familiar in taste, in feel of skin and muscles, in scent that could only be his. Her center throbbed with readiness before his fingers found her, caressed her, and she arched her back and hips to meet his touch. When she stroked his rigid penis, he groaned. His words came in a gasp. "Julia, I can't wait," and she parted her legs to receive him. When she felt him fill her, her spiraling excitement began, the pulsing waves of sensation building, until he shuddered with the release of his bursting seed.

For a moment she clung to him, searching for her own crest, still caught in unsatisfied desires. Lying above her, he buried his face in her neck and groaned, "Oh God, Julia—I'm sorry. It's been so long—and I wanted you so much." Though she still felt her own burning need, his words filled her with a new kind of pleasure. His voice and his rasping breath told her how intense his desire had been, and knowing that she had caused both passion and satisfaction gave her over-whelming contentment. She held him, resting against her, and knew that she loved him—so much that his pleasure meant more to her than her own.

He raised his head and smiled ruefully. "We'll have to wait a bit for me to recover from your charms." Then he moved downward, proving with his hands and mouth that he had lied, and she did not have to wait to experience a dizzying tumult of sensations. And as if her climax provided all the refreshment Andrew needed, his shaft hardened again and he moved on top of her, guiding her buttocks with his hands into a frenzied pattern. Julia groaned as she felt Andrew's mouth seeking her breast, teasing her nipple. She held his head close to her chest, then moved her hand down his back, entwining her legs around his as they reached another summit together.

When darkness forced them to light the candles, they put on robes and Andrew had dinner sent to their room. She expected him to ask about *fazenda* affairs, but he laughed and said, "Not tonight. It can wait until tomorrow. Now I want to make up for the long time away from you." But while they sampled shellfish from Rio bay and fruit from its gardens, she insisted on hearing about his trip, and he relented and talked of his search, making light of the frustrations but not able to conceal how discouraged he had been.

"So," he concluded, "I must believe in miracles, for Sergio is home and will recover, and you're here with me."

When they came together in bed again, Julia's discovery of her love for him enriched every embrace. His tenderness convinced her he cared for her as she did him, and she almost blurted out how she felt, but shyness made her want to wait for him to speak first. Before sleep overcame her, she curled contentedly against him. Tomorrow would be time enough for words, she thought hazily, and drifted into slumber.

Andrew held her, feeling her breasts soft against his

side, and wondered why he hadn't known before how much she meant to him. He would tell her, but as always the act of loving her seemed easier than the words. They would have a second honeymoon here, and he would find a time which would be just right to say he loved her. Maybe she already knew and wouldn't need the words. He felt sure Julia felt the same. She stirred and turned slightly, but he pulled her into his arms again as he settled himself to sleep as well.

When Julia stretched herself into wakefulness the next morning, she could see Andrew through the door into the sitting room, already dressed in a beige suit and sipping coffee as he read a letter. She put on a green robe over a nightgown she hadn't needed during the night before, brushing her hair and tying it back with a green velvet ribbon. When she joined Andrew, she saw the stack of letters in front of him. Shyly she approached him, and he smiled and pulled her into his arms.

"You look like a little girl, with your hair wild and loose," he teased, "except my exhaustion this morning tells me you are very much a woman." He kissed her and nuzzled his head against her neck before lifting her off his lap. "We'd better not get started now, though. I see a letter here from Senhor Fonseca which I don't quite understand. I'm afraid we must talk about the *fazenda*."

Her throat tightened uncomfortably at the uncertainty of his reactions, and though she knew herself cowardly, she protested, "I must have my coffee before I can remember my own name." She went to the table where the pots of coffee and hot milk steamed.

"Of course," Andrew agreed. "Will you excuse me if

I continue going through the mail until you finish your coffee?"

She smiled in answer, and he opened another letter while she dawdled over filling a cup and sipping slowly. When he tossed that letter aside, the next one he picked up had the distinctive calligraphy which told her it was from the Rua Direita. Holding her cup, she wandered to the window, but she could not keep from watching him surreptitiously. He frowned as he slit the envelope and took out a single sheet, and his mouth compressed into a harsh line. Carefully staring out the window, she ventured, "Will we be staying at this hotel the whole time we're here?"

He didn't answer immediately, then said abstractedly, "Yes, unless it displeases you in some way. Does it?"

"No, no. It's fine," she replied hurriedly. "I just wondered."

Trying to ignore the uneasy feeling which was growing stronger, she set down her empty cup and took a chair across from him. "What do you want to know about the *fazenda*?"

He smiled, but to her nervous gaze his smile looked strained. "Everything."

As she described events up to the time of Pedro Oliveiro's accident, she relaxed, and although Andrew didn't exclaim with the admiration she wished for, he smiled and responded with pleasant comments to her details of weather and crops. When she mentioned studying his accounts, he looked surprised and said, though it seemed to her a little grudgingly, "I know you're clever, Julia, and I suppose I should have expected something out of the ordinary from you."

At her description of the overseer's accident, he leaned forward, his face shocked and then concerned. "Is Pedro mending well? Did you get special medical attention for him?"

Happy she could relieve his distress, Julia reported, "He's improving steadily. Our doctor has taken good care of him. The whole process has been very slow, but Senhor Pedro will be well eventually, though he'll always have a limp."

Andrew rose and stood before Julia. "But how did you manage? I assume Pedro couldn't even advise you for some time. Did you go to my father?"

Julia could feel heat creeping from her neck to her face, and she stood also, feeling at a disadvantage when he towered so far over her. "No. Well . . . Richard and I had a rather violent argument after I . . . tried something that didn't work." Furious with herself for her stumbling speech, she felt her face grow hotter.

"What do you mean, something that didn't work?"

Her embarrassment became indignation. "I don't like your suspicious tone, Andrew. After all, you weren't there."

She saw a responding temper in the hardening line of his jaw as he replied, "For good reason. But you're right, I wasn't there, though I believe I had asked you before I left to go to my father if the need arose."

Her anger blossomed, and she answered without regard for diplomacy. "I am capable of thinking for myself, Andrew, without having to ask a man about every breath I draw."

Now he looked as angry as she. "Please just tell me what happened."

She saw how she had trapped herself, and the prospect of having to admit her blunder to him in his present unresponsive mood made her voice sharper than she intended. "I asked Tomaz to act as temporary overseer."

His voice exploded. "Tomaz! For God's sake, why?"

Her stomach knotted with fury, at herself for having made such a mistake, but more at him for the harsh indictment she heard in his voice. "Because neither of the Italian supervisors knew enough and Tomaz did."

He folded his arms across his chest and looked at her coldly. "And how did that work out?"

"It didn't work, as I'm sure you know very well," she said bitterly. "The whites wouldn't take orders from a black."

"What I don't understand," he said, in a voice that told her he would like to say something harsher, "is why the hell you ever thought they would."

She raised her chin defiantly. "Well, they should, when the black knows more than the whites."

He scowled, his thunderous eyes reminding her of the confrontation with his father. "Goddammit, Julia, that's not the world we live in, no matter how you think it should be. Are you sure you didn't just tell yourself this because you couldn't stand to give up being in charge?"

Furious at his voicing an accusation she'd tearfully made to herself after the fire, she almost shouted at him. "You'll be pleased to know that I had to find a *man*, a *white* man to give the orders."

"Since you say you quarreled with Father, I presume he didn't help you, unless you both had more sense than I would guess now. So who was the man?"

She held her hands clenched across her stomach to stop the churning which was bringing its inevitable result. "Roberto."

"Roberto!" Andrew looked stunned, then incredulous. "My brother?"

"Yes, and he's done a superb job. Even your arrogant father can see that now."

Andrew stared at her, his shock consumed in a flame of rage. He tightened his jaw, determined to keep his feelings under control, but he knew his voice betrayed him. "How did Roberto know what to do, and why would he take on the kind of job he's always carefully avoided?"

He could see a matching fury in Julia's eyes. "You're unfair to him. He's intelligent and observing and he knows all he needs to about plantation management. He made an excellent overseer, and together we took care of everything very well."

He stared at her, but he hardly saw her face. Instead Roberto's image filled his mind—laughing with Julia, teasing her, entertaining her with stories, and now leaping into the role of her heroic rescuer. Yes, Andrew though bitterly, his brother was willing to do labor he'd always scorned because he was working for something he wanted: Julia. Another picture rose before him, of Julia embracing Roberto, offering him her kisses and her body, and searing pain seized him. He tried to obliterate the image, but it persisted, and his fury overcame reason. "It seems you hardly need a husband. What other duties of mine has my dear brother taken over?"

For a moment she looked bewildered; then her face lost all color, and when she spoke, her voice shook. "That is a despicable thing to say."

Afraid of what he might do, he whirled, snatched his riding crop from the desk, and strode from the room.

At the slam of the door Julia wanted to seize something—the coffeepot, a candlestick—and throw it as hard as she could after him. She paced the floor, rubbing her knotted stomach, alternating between fury at him and a sick feeling that somehow she could have avoided the terrible quarrel. But she couldn't possibly

have guessed he would suggest that she and Roberto
had been lovers. At first she hadn't even understood
what he meant.

Appalled, she remembered that just last night she'd
thought she loved Andrew. She must have completely
forgotten what he could be like. God, she might even
have said it—she almost did. She sat down at the desk
and leaned her head in her hands. Despite her determination, tears filled her eyes and streamed over her
cheeks. She had been so happy when she awoke an
hour before. Now the morning lay around her in
shambles.

Tears fell on the desk, watering the pile of letters. The
one from the Rua Direita had been on top, but now she
didn't see it. She shuffled the envelopes, but the elaborately addressed one was gone. Andrew must have taken
it with him.

Her tears dried on her face as she restacked the
letters. Andrew had accused her of having a lover—
perhaps he was judging her conduct by his own. Determinedly she found her handkerchief and wiped the last
dampness from her cheek. He didn't warrant tears and
she would never, she promised herself fiercely, cry
over him again. But through the anger and bitterness,
she felt an aching pain.

The groom, his apprehensive glance telling Andrew
how his face must look, hurried away to get a horse.
Andrew schooled himself to conceal his emotions and
waited, but his blood still pounded and he had trouble
getting a deep enough breath. Never before had he let
anything affect him so much, not even during the youthful fights when blood had flowed.

Capitolino, not the hotel groom, brought Andrew's
horse. When he came close, his smile vanished, and he

hesitated before he asked, "Can I do something for you, Seu Andrew? Do you wish me to accompany you?"

"No!" Andrew swung up into the saddle, then looked back at the distressed face. He forced his voice to calm. "Senhora Julia may want the carriage. Please take her anywhere she wishes. I don't know when I'll return."

As he rode away from the hotel, he heard the crinkle of paper and remembered the letter from Lele that he'd slipped into his pocket earlier. He'd get great pleasure from breaking someone's head, and it would relieve his feelings to vent his anger on Lele. She had no business asking for more money and sending him a letter. He wondered if Julia had seen the envelope. He could have explained that he'd felt an obligation to provide Lele shelter for that first year, but he didn't want to mention Lele after the morning's quarrel. Julia wouldn't know whom the letter came from, and he didn't intend to justify his actions anyway.

He started in the direction of the street where he'd rented the house for Lele, then reined in his horse. He didn't want to see her. He thought briefly of finding a congenial place to drink, but he really didn't like liquor much, and especially not in the morning. Turning his horse, he headed for the beach. He'd go beyond Sugarloaf to a deserted stretch of sand he remembered and ride until he and the horse were exhausted, and maybe he could exhaust his fury as well.

Julia pulled on her gloves and inspected her face in the mirror. Her eyes still looked faintly red, but with her large hat pulled down, no one would know she'd been crying. Her yellow cotton dress felt warm, and she'd be more comfortable if she remained in the room in just a chemise, but Andrew might think her attire a request to make love if he returned. She didn't intend to offer him that invitation again! And she didn't want to hide in the hotel like a wounded animal.

In the door to the veranda she hesitated, and the hotel clerk with the waxed smile hurried to her side. "May I call your man, Senhora Langdon?" he inquired solicitously.

She forced her stiff lips to respond graciously. "Thank you, but I am only stepping next door." She ignored his faintly distressed expression and walked to the subscription library.

Half an hour later she went to the counter in the stuffy shop, Sir Walter Scott's *Ivanhoe* in her hand. Papa's copy had been water-damaged in transit to Brazil, and he would enjoy having the old favorite again. Nothing she'd seen had appealed to her, but she promised herself to return tomorrow when the books would surely seem more interesting.

Carrying her wrapped book, she went to the door, then stopped and returned to the counter where the slight mulatto clerk sat on a stool. "Excuse me, senhor, could you tell me where the Rua Direita is?"

He looked surprised, then uncomfortable. "Yes, senhora, but it is not a street where . . . ladies go."

"Why not?"

A voice at Julia's elbow interrupted. "Senhora Julia, I didn't know you had left the hotel. May I escort you somewhere?" Julia turned to meet Capitolino's concerned face.

She couldn't prevent the sharpness in her voice. "I'm quite all right, Capitolino, and I can certainly walk ten paces away from the hotel by myself."

As they left the store, she stopped. "Capitolino, please get the carriage. There's an address I wish to find on the Rua Direita."

Surprise, then dismay showed in the black face and

voice. He started to speak, then paused, obviously fumbling for words. "Senhora Julia, I will get the carriage, but would you not like to visit the Rua dos Ourives, which gets its name from the goldsmiths? The jewelry stores there are exceedingly fine. Or you might enjoy—"

"Capitolino, will you take me where I wish to go?"

He stood twisting his hat in his hands, his eyes on the ground, then meeting hers with unhappy determination. "*Sinhazinha*, I cannot take you to the Rua Direita."

Capitolino's distressed face confirmed Julia's suspicions and renewed her pain and anger. She handed him the wrapped book and spoke coldly. "Very well. Please take this to my rooms. I shall go for a walk." As he moved to follow her, she whirled on him furiously. "And you will *not* escort me. I am fully capable of walking by myself. Please go back to the hotel." Without waiting to see whether he listened, she turned and walked determinedly to the square, then along a tree-shaded path to the opposite side. Rules of proper conduct for ladies forbade her going out unescorted, but right now she didn't care.

Making sure Capitolino hadn't followed her, she hailed one of the carriages for hire, choosing a closed one despite the heat of the day. When she asked for the address on the Rua Direita, the driver looked first surprised, then familiarly amused, until her frozen stare restored a respectful demeanor.

When the carriage arrived on a quiet street of modest residences, she asked him to stop three buildings away from number forty-three. The houses all looked ordinary, but obviously the street had some kind of unsavory reputation. Now that she had found it, she couldn't explain to herself just why she had come or what she expected to do.

Her first outrage over the quarrel with Andrew had receded, and though he had angered and wounded her this morning, she realized now she wanted to mend the rift with him. A moment came back to her—of the fleeting embrace between her and Roberto just before she had left the *fazenda*, and the sudden warmth it had roused in her. Andrew knew more of the world and of human reactions than she; perhaps his suspicions were not as unreasonable as she'd first thought. Somehow, though, before she could talk to him again, she had to know more about the house here, and she didn't want to ask him. Nervously she peeled off her gloves and wiped her damp hands.

Two graceful trees shielded the front of the house at number forty-three, and Julia could see a vase of red flowers through an upper window. As she debated what to do, the front door opened and a young woman in a fashionable orange dress came out. She looked briefly up and down the street before she raised a white parasol and walked languidly toward Julia's carriage.

Though two years had passed since Julia had seen the beautiful mulatto, she recognized her—Andrew's mistress and, she was sure now, the woman outside their honeymoon hotel in São Paulo. Julia shrank back into the corner of the carriage, praying she wouldn't be seen. The young woman stopped and knocked at the entrance of one of the other houses. Another mulatto, dressed in a gaudy purple robe, opened the door. Julia could hear her high voice clearly: "Lele, come in."

When the door closed behind Lele, Julia rapped on the carriage window and motioned the driver to go on. At the corner he leaned down, and she directed him back to the hotel, no longer caring whether anyone saw her in a hired rig. As the driver clucked the horse forward, she sat rigidly, resolved to deny the pain which would flood her if she allowed it. Andrew isn't worth it, she told herself fiercely. Let him have his Lele.

By the time Andrew got back to the hotel, long shadows promised relief from the day's heat. During his ride, he'd faced the unpleasant realization that jealousy had motivated his outburst at Julia, and this knowledge appalled him. Though he didn't normally question his own feelings, he knew he'd never been jealous of any woman before. But Julia meant too much to him; grimly he wished now she didn't.

His behavior toward her had been unjustified, he knew, and recognizing it made him even more uncomfortable. He should have praised her resourcefulness, but, goddammit, she'd begun to sound like a man instead of a wife, and Andrew wanted Julia as his wife. Then, when he was having difficulty swallowing his pride over her accomplishments, she told him she'd turned to Roberto. If only she hadn't defended Roberto so quickly, Andrew thought, he might not have accused her so unfairly.

As he walked his horse around to the hotel stables and swung off the tired animal, Capitolino came to take the reins. Something in the black man's face, a reluctance to look at him, made Andrew ask, "Did you take Senhora Julia out today?"

"No, Seu Andrew. She . . . went walking."

"In this heat? Where did she walk?"

Capitolino had started to lead the horse away, but he paused, still not looking directly at Andrew. "I don't know. She would not allow me to go with her."

Andrew started to reproach Capitolino, then stopped himself, knowing he couldn't blame his servant because Julia had disregarded conventional behavior again.

In the hotel lobby, the clerk approached him, holding a woman's glove. "Senhor Langdon, I believe this belongs to Senhora Langdon. Apparently she dropped it in the carriage she hired today. The driver found it later and just now returned it."

Andrew took the glove and stared at it before putting it in his pocket. "Thank you."

As he slowly climbed the stairs, the phrases of apology he'd reluctantly assembled on his way back to the hotel crumbled. Did he really know what Julia thought or did? She hadn't denied intimacy with Roberto—only condemned the accusation. And where had she gone today? He paused at the door of the suite, pain and anger and suspicion all roiling in his mind.

When Julia heard the door open, she continued staring out the window, putting off facing him. The sight of Lele this morning had shattered her plans to seek a reconciliation with Andrew. Now she didn't know what to expect from him and was even less certain what she wanted. Slowly she turned around, and indignation stiffened her spine; Andrew looked cool and unruffled, as if their impassioned quarrel had been no more than a disagreement.

He crossed the room to the desk and put down his hat before he faced her. "Julia, I believe I owe you an apology. My remarks about Roberto were unfair." He paused, apparently waiting for her response.

His words confused her, and beneath her anger and hurt she recognized a desire still to listen to him, to accept his apology no matter how coldly delivered. But knowledge of the small house where Lele had obviously been living for all the time of her and Andrew's marriage kept her silent.

As if his words had been extracted reluctantly, he added, "I'm afraid I react badly to Roberto's activities. I'm sorry."

He looked at her for a moment longer, but she couldn't speak. The lines around his eyes and mouth hardened to a forbidding mask, and he picked up one of the letters from the desk. "We didn't get to an explanation of this message from Senhor Fonseca about a coffee sale."

Julia took one of the chairs and waited; she wasn't going to explain while Andrew stood over her like a prosecutor. When he also sat, she began, subduing her feelings in order to describe in a steady voice the sale of the future coffee crop. He listened silently, his face expressionless.

After she finished, he studied the letter again, then rose and said, "We'll see next fall whether you were wise." His mouth curved in a faint smile, as if mocking either her or himself. "You're more of a gambler than I thought. Perhaps that's why we're married."

Before she could decide how to interpret his last remark, he took something from his pocket and held it out to her. "You left your glove in the carriage you hired today."

Julia could feel her face grow cold and then intensely hot. To her dismay, when she reached to take the glove from him, her hand trembled. She forced herself to look directly at him. "Thank you." Unsaid words hovered in the air between them, and Julia felt as if she could hear them dying in the silence.

A knock sounded at the door, and when Andrew answered, a hotel messenger gave him a note. After reading it, he turned back to Julia. "Baron Saia is downstairs. He apologizes for disturbing us, but he says he needs to speak to me and asks us to dine with him in the hotel dining room. Do you wish to accept?"

Relieved that they would be buffered from each other

for a while, Julia responded, "Yes, but I need to change my dress."

Andrew nodded. "I'll go down and meet him now; please join us when you're ready." He didn't look at her as he left.

All of the dresses in the clothes press looked ugly to her, but finally she decided on a blue-and-white-striped muslin which left most of her shoulders and arms bare. She had dismissed the hotel maid, and as she brushed her hair, she wondered wearily what sort of marriage she and Andrew would have now. He had apologized, but that didn't erase his accusations about her and Roberto or her knowledge of Lele. She knew her unexplained carriage ride angered Andrew, but since he didn't tell her where he went, she decided to let him wonder what she did.

Julia joined Andrew and Baron Saia in the lobby. The baron greeted her with a bow and smile, the lines around his mouth even deeper than she remembered. They went into the high-ceilinged dining room and were seated at a round table near a tall front window. Although the baron's presence relieved the strain of being with Andrew, Julia only pretended to eat as she smiled and responded normally to anecdotes about life in Rio. Over coffee the talk turned to politics and the movement for a republican form of government.

"You oppose it, Baron?" asked Julia.

He tapped his fingers restlessly on the white tablecloth. "Certainly, Senhora Langdon. Though I know the United States has made great progress as a republic, we need our monarch and our monarchy." He glanced at Andrew, then added, "The republicans allow themselves to be used by men who join with them to oppose the emperor because of some of his goals, such as abolition of slavery. These allies, however, do not care about a republic, only about power for themselves. Brazil is an enormous country, loosely tied together; only Dom Pedro's wise political leadership has prevented large sections from trying to break away. That could lead us to the kind of conflict with which you are lamentably so familiar."

The looks exchanged between the baron and Andrew seemed to Julia to be part of another conversation which they both understood but from which they were excluding her. Andrew began asking of the prospects for a railroad to São Paulo, and she knew the two men wouldn't reveal what underlay the discussion of politics.

When they finished their coffee and went back to the lobby, Baron Saia spoke soberly to Julia. "Thank you, Senhora Langdon, for allowing me to intrude on you this evening. I'm afraid I must ask to detain your husband for a time. I have something I urgently need to discuss with him. Please forgive me."

"Of course, Baron Saia." Julia smiled, but after Andrew escorted her upstairs and then left, all the tension of the day returned. She felt unhappiness growing like an enormous weed inside her, and even the air oppressed her. How could she stay here with Andrew, enduring the misery of the strain between them, such a bitter contrast to her hopes and the pleasures of their previous lovemaking?

That night she slept fitfully in the bed, but Andrew didn't join her. Images plagued her, of Andrew's glowering face, of Lele's senuous walk, of the two of them inside that window behind the vase of flowers. As the night stretched on, another picture came to her, of Andrew, in some dark street, set upon by thieves. Finally just before dawn she rose and went into the sitting room to find him sleeping uncomfortably on the settee, his head pillowed on one arm and his feet hanging over the other end. The rush of relief she felt at knowing he was safe disappeared under a surge of renewed anger. She went back to the bedroom and finally fell asleep again.

The day's heat had already invaded the bedroom when Julia woke. Lying in the tumbled bed, she felt tears begin to form again and clenched her fists, dreading the coming day. Abruptly she rose and began to dress. She would suggest to Andrew that they return now to the *fazenda*, and he could see for himself how well Roberto and she had managed and how groundless his accusations were. Perhaps then they could talk, try to understand each other. But could she accept his continuing tie to Lele?

In the sitting room Andrew stood and stretched, then rubbed the back of his neck, trying to calm the ache from sleeping on the settee. He thought of what the baron had told him last night and silently swore. He'd speculated about his father's motives for encouraging the Confederate immigration, but he'd never suspected Richard of fomenting treason against the Empire of Brazil. He foresaw a confrontation with his father, but first he needed more information. He'd have to spend most of the next days seeking out the men who apparently shared his father's schemes to create a separate state if the emperor succeeded in having slavery abolished. How many, he wondered, of the American Southerners around São Paulo understood the role that Richard apparently expected them to play.

Looking toward the closed bedroom door, he cursed again, and realized his attention should be on his marriage, not on his father's insane schemes. But, he reminded himself, he had apologized to Julia yesterday. She'd barely acknowledged it and still hadn't bothered to explain where she'd gone. Andrew could feel his temper simmering. He knew he should be more patient, but his pride was too great.

Julia heard sounds in the sitting room and opened the door as Andrew put on his jacket. "Andrew, could we return to the *fazenda* instead of staying on here? I really wish to do that—tomorrow, if possible."

A muscle stiffened in his jaw, and his voice sounded cold and harsh. "I don't intend to leave Rio yet, but I suppose you can't wait to get back to your . . . *duties*."

Hearing the same word Andrew had used when he suggested she and Roberto had been intimate, Julia felt her stomach tighten. Her despair and fury, which had simmered for the last day, boiled over. "Yes, and you'll be free to spend your time on the Rua Direita with Lele."

For a moment he stood as if frozen; then fury blazed in his face. He strode to the door and pulled it open. Turning back, he said savagely, "Very well. You won't have to wait until tomorrow. I'll secure passage for you today and inform the hotel this room won't be needed longer. With our income gambled on the coffee crop, it would be foolish to spend money here when I have a perfectly good house and a welcoming companion elsewhere."

As the door slammed behind him, Julia felt sobs rising in her throat, and she couldn't tell whether her tears released rage or pain or both.

14

Julia reined in her horse at the top of the rise. The sun had fallen halfway down the afternoon sky, and in the distance she could see the red tiled roof of the *fazenda*. Her bones felt brittle with fatigue; she'd slept little the last two nights, first in Santos and then in São Paulo, and she had begun today at dawn still weary from yesterday's long ride between the two cities.

Jora stopped beside her in a cloud of red dust, his young face bright with impatience. "Sinha Julia, may I ride ahead?" She knew he was eager to tell Scizira of his changed status. When she waved his dancing horse on, he disappeared at a gallop. She glanced back at Capitolino, following with the carriage, then nudged her tired horse into motion again.

As she rode, she thought of Andrew's grim face when he'd escorted her to the dock in Rio. His last words before she boarded the coastal steamer for Santos had been that he didn't know when he'd be home, perhaps in two weeks. Since then she felt as if she had repeated every bitter word of the quarrels until they were engraved in her memory like the designs on the leather cover of a book. Briefly she'd considered going to her father's plantation, but Carlota's face rose before her, and she discarded that idea immediately. Besides, her pride wouldn't allow an estrangement with Andrew to defeat her.

She recognized the curves in the road, and a particular grove of cedar trees told her they were only a short ride from the house. The *fazenda* was truly her home now. By learning the work, by thrusting herself into activities outside the domestic life, it had become as important to her as Hundred Oaks. Andrew could force her to supervise only the household, but she wouldn't give up easily. She would allow him as many mistresses as he wanted; her life would be complete without him.

A horseman appeared over the next rise, and Julia felt her muscles tighten with apprehension. Although she'd been practicing what to say to Roberto, she still felt unprepared.

"Julia!" His voice, filled with cheerful pleasure, bridged the space between them even before he slowed his horse and turned to ride beside her. "Jora surprised everyone. We weren't expecting you so soon, though nothing," he added gaily, "delights me like your presence."

He looked around, and then turned back to her. "But where is the triumphant rescuer, my brother?"

Julia kept her voice steady and serene. "He had business in Rio that will take a week or two, and I wanted to be back home, so I came on ahead."

Disbelief raised Roberto's eyebrows and straightened his mustached smile. "You gave up the pleasures of Rio to come here? Julia, are you ill?"

She laughed, but she couldn't look directly at him. "No, certainly not. I just . . . knew you couldn't manage without me."

Even keeping her eyes ahead, she could sense his puzzled scrutiny of her, though he said, "Of course

you're right," in his teasing way. After a moment
he began to talk of what had happened in the few days
she'd been gone, commenting with his usual ironic
amusement on minor quarrels and irritations. "And
Quintiliana tells me Scizira has been completely useless. She's had all the little girls in the lace room in
tears every day. I don't know if she'll be better or worse
with Jora here."

When they arrived at the house, Roberto gave the
explanations for Andrew's absence, and gratefully Julia
managed a natural smile for him before she went upstairs. When she started into the large bedroom, pain
clutched at her so strongly she stopped in the doorway.
"Quintiliana," she said to the tall woman who followed
her, "this room seems so terribly hot during the summer months. I think I'll have my things taken to the
bedroom at the other end of the hall. It gets less sun."
As she left the room, she ignored the surprise in
Quintiliana's eyes.

A week later Roberto sat in the small sitting room,
both hands cradling a brandy snifter, watching light
from a single candle catch the golden liquid. Again he
pondered Julia's return and Andrew's continued absence. During the morning conferences, she listened to
explanations of the work almost desperately, and she
rode out to the fields each day, disregarding his objections to her riding so long in the sun. At other times
she avoided him and gave wooden responses to his
efforts at dinner conversation.

Obviously something had happened between Julia
and Andrew in Rio. She often looked unhappy, and
dark smudges under her eyes suggested sleepless nights.
Roberto tried to suppress the excitement this evidence
gave him, yet the knowledge of her misery couldn't blot

out the hope that she might turn to him. In the beginning of Julia and Andrew's marriage, he'd encouraged Lele to think Andrew would return to her and had suggested she go to São Paulo to try to see Andrew there. Since then he hadn't sought to meddle because Júlia's happiness had truly come to mean more to him than revenge against his older brother. If Andrew, however, had done anything to estrange himself from the woman Roberto revered over all others, he would help her in any way he could.

Roberto rose and walked to the window, looking out into the soft moonlit night. Two years ago he would have scoffed at anyone who suggested he might put someone else's feelings before his own. He laughed at the idea now, but his laughter derided himself.

The hall clock chimed ten o'clock. Outside he saw a woman cross the veranda and start along the path which led over the bridge to the quaint summerhouse. In the moonlight he recognized the dress she'd worn to dinner and her shining hair. What was Julia doing outside at this time of night? He put down his brandy to follow her.

The twisted railing on the iron bridge felt cool to Julia's hand. The tiny lake looked as if fairies or water sprites must surely live below its silver surface. She reached the island summerhouse and paced around its small octagon, glad for a change from the pattern she'd worn across her bedroom during the past week.

A footstep sounded behind her and she whirled to confront a tall figure. For a moment she thought it was Andrew, and a confusion of dismay and hope filled her, but when he moved forward, she recognized Roberto.

He spoke softly, his voice offering comfort. "Julia, why are you alone here at night?" He moved closer through a shaft of moonlight, and she saw concern on his face. "I know something troubles you. Please, can't you tell me what it is?"

His words hung between them, beckoning her to release the pain that felt as if it might suffocate her. She could feel sobs gathering deep in her chest, forcing their way upward, bursting the dam of her restraint. Then strong arms enfolded her, absorbing the wild tears that drained her, holding her until her weeping exhausted itself.

With her face buried against his chest, she could feel as well as hear his words. "Julia, I want to help you. Did something happen between you and Andrew?"

As if her sobs had tapped such deep anger that it had its own voice, she cried, "I hate Andrew. I hate him," and knew it was only half-true, because she loved him as well.

She clung to Roberto and wept again until she was empty, and only his support held her upright. Numbly she let him lead her back to the house and into the sitting room. At the candlelight, she hid her face in her hands until he snuffed the single flame, then guided her to the sofa.

He brought her a glass. "Drink some of this, Julia." She recognized the odor of brandy and took a fiery sip, but he insisted on a second swallow before he would let her put it down. Then he sat beside her.

In the dark he became an anonymous listener to whom anything might safely be said, and when he urged her to reveal her troubles again, she began to talk. As if in a trance, she told him of the entries in Andrew's account book, of arriving in Rio and finding the letter. In the same disembodied way she described Andrew's reaction to her problems at the *fazenda*, only faltering when she came to his accusation about Roberto.

Realizing how forbidden such a topic was, she said

chokingly, "Forgive me, Roberto. I shouldn't tell you this."

Roberto kept his voice calm. "I won't misunderstand, Julia. I hope you can say anything to me without worrying," but a dozen emotions warred in him. He wanted to protect her, to reassure her, but just as strongly he wanted to shout that Andrew could never love her as he did, that she should forget his brother and that he would take care of her and cherish her always. Even in the midst of his turmoil he felt a cynical surprise at his own restraint.

"And after he left, I hired a cab and went to that address, and I saw her—the woman I'd seen with him in Rio when I first came to Brazil, the same woman who came to the hotel where we stayed in São Paulo." Anger laced through her voice. "She lives in that house, where Andrew's paid the rent for another year. Roberto, you must know—you seem to know about everyone. Is Lele still Andrew's mistress?"

He sat almost without breathing, his clashing emotions now in full battle. The temptation to say yes, to drive a wedge between her and Andrew which they might never overcome, assailed him so strongly that he thought he had said it until he realized Julia still waited for his answer. To his astonishment he heard himself say, "No, Julia. As far as I know, Andrew hasn't seen her since before your marriage. As you know, he rented a house for her for a year." Not the most altruistic urging of his little-used conscience would make him add that Andrew only did the gentlemanly thing by such provision for a former mistress. He was glad he could honestly add, "I didn't know he'd paid a second year's rent for her, or why."

Julia continued, this time with as much sadness as anger. "I told myself he wouldn't have a mistress in Rio

whom he'd practically never see, and I can even understand why he wouldn't explain to me about the rent.
I know I goaded him by bringing up the house at the
last, but he practically said he'd stay with her after I
left." Sorrow disappeared from her voice, leaving only
refueled anger. "That doesn't excuse his suspicions of
me. He had no justification for the things he said. His
pride—his blown-up male pride—couldn't stand having
his wife and his younger brother manage without him."

She rose and lit the candle, then stood before Roberto, her face flushed, sparks flashing in her eyes. "I
lost my temper and said things to him I didn't mean,
but I can't pretend to be a simpering female. *You* don't
get upset because I'm not meek and mild."

Roberto got to his feet and said slowly, "But what you
do doesn't reflect on me, Julia." Giving her a rakish
smile to cover his astonishment at his own nobility, he
added, "If I were your husband, I'd probably lock you
up with embroidery and a bunch of brats."

The unintended intimacy of his words hovered between them; he could see a faint flush in her face and
had to fight down the desire that surged through him.
"Thank you for telling me, Julia. Take heart. Even my
thickheaded brother will probably come around eventually, provided you sheath your claws occasionally."

He cherished her answering smile before she vanished up the stairs, then cursed himself for a weak fool
who was losing the opportunity he'd longed for. Well,
he jeered at himself, you've been honorable for the first
time, how does it feel? As he went out to the overseer's
bed, he knew it felt desperately lonely.

Scizira and Jora stood before the traveling Portuguese priest, she in a white muslin dress and a veil of
lace she had made herself, Jora in a white linen suit.

Julia would have liked to provide a more elaborate dress for Scizira, but Jora had been home two weeks, and the excited young woman didn't want to wait. Despite Andrew's continued absence, they had gone ahead with the wedding. Quintiliana had supervised the decoration of an altar in an alcove of the large drawing room, a common practice when the *fazenda* did not have a separate chapel.

Julia didn't like the priest's manner. To her and Roberto the priest was polite, almost subservient, but with Scizira and Jora his manner just escaped being insulting. Though he mumbled his words during the Mass, once he scolded Scizira for not speaking loud enough, and in a rough voice he ordered her and Jora to kneel at the altar for a blessing which sounded more like a curse. Julia could feel her temper rising, and only Roberto's hand on her arm restrained her from interrupting. Finally the priest's voice stopped, and Scizira and Jora rose and smilingly ran outside to showers of rose petals.

Frostily Julia paid the priest, noticing how grimy his garments were. After he departed, she asked Roberto, "Why does the church tolerate men like that?"

He took her elbow, and they walked toward the back veranda, where the sounds of the wedding celebration had begun. "Probably it doesn't, but the big land owners, not the church, have the real power in Brazil. Years ago the Jesuits tried to reform the church and make the priests behave, but they didn't get far. This sorry man is an old-style plantation priest, who answers only to the *fazendeiros*, and he probably hates blacks. Dom Pedro's made changes in the cities, but out here . . ." He shrugged.

On the terrace, palm fronds formed shelters over long tables where house servants were already helping themselves to food and drink. Grateful for Scizira's loyalty, Julia had decided to have a full day's wedding celebration at the big house. Though Andrew hadn't objected when she'd freed Scizira, Julia wasn't sure he'd have agreed to arrangements normally made only for whites, but he wasn't here to question her judgment. At one side five black players had begun the music which would continue into the night. Julia knew an even more boisterous celebration would occur in the *senezala*, and perhaps in the cluster of houses where the Italian workers lived.

She greeted Pedro Oliveiro, seated beside his thin wife, his foot propped on a bench. In the late-morning sun his face still looked pale, but he smiled heartily at her. "Before long, Senhora Julia, I shall be able to do my work again. I've been riding a little each day."

"Yes," she assured him, "but you mustn't do too much or worry. We're getting along well, and soon Senhor Andrew will be home." He nodded, and she moved on, concealing her humiliation that she had to pretend she knew her husband's plans.

As morning changed to afternoon and then stretched into the long twilight, Julia made herself forget her cares and enjoy the lighthearted celebration. The laughter and the joking companionship of the servants she knew so well enfolded her as if barriers between white and black had dissolved. She tried the *aluá*, that fermented rice-and-pineapple drink which she'd discovered at James's wedding, and found it tasted even more delicious than she remembered. In the mellow mood produced by the drink, dignity seemed unimportant compared to the freedom from her anxieties and frustrations. Happily she listened to the music and visited with the overseer and his wife and Quintiliana, though even in her hazy pleasure she didn't give in to her desire to join the dancing. Roberto spoke to her occasionally, but most of the time he moved among the celebrants, a drink in his hand, laughing and joking.

Since the night Julia had cried out her story to him, a special ease had existed between them. At first their strangely intimate moment had bothered her, yet they hadn't spoken again about her two days in Rio, and Roberto's manner to her remained cheerfully teasing. She felt that by sharing her pain with him, she'd somehow eased it. When she went to visit Ellen and Richard, she'd felt no need to confide in her mother-in-law, saying only that Andrew had remained in Rio on business.

Now, as the sunlight faded on the wedding celebration, her carefree mood began to evaporate. Suddenly she wanted the silence of the empty house. When everyone else seemed occupied, she rose to go inside, and stumbled over the leg of a table. A black hand gripped her arm, keeping her from falling. Quintiliana said, "Sinha Julia, are you all right?"

"Yes . . . I think so," she said, but her muscles contradicted her. She swayed, and again the strong hand supported her. "I'm afraid," she whispered, "I may have had too much *aluá*."

A rare smiled creased the housekeeper's face. "I think you are right, *sinhazinha*."

"I believe," Julia said carefully, "I'll go in and rest for a few minutes."

"Do you wish me to go with you?"

"No, I'll be fine." Slowly she climbed the stairs in the deserted house and went to the small bedroom where her clothes hung in virgin loneliness. The room still held the day's heat, and she pulled off all but her thin shift, loosened her hair, and fell across the bed, which seemed to tip and rock from the effects of the *aluá*. She sat up again.

Only a few days until Christmas, and she didn't know if Andrew would be home by then, or how she could explain if he weren't.

She ached inside and, slipping on a light cotton robe, padded barefoot along the hall to the room she normally shared with Andrew. In one wardrobe part of her clothes rested familiarly; she opened the other, and in her melancholy mood, the scent of Andrew's clothes seemed to fill the room with his presence. She went over to the bed and touched it, but it looked empty and forbidding.

A sound from behind pulled her around. In the doorway stood Roberto, his light jacket discarded and his ruffled white shirt open at the throat. He moved toward her and spoke, his voice slurred. "The party—no fun without you, Julia." The unsteadiness in his walk told her he felt the effects of the day's drinking even more than she.

He stood in front of her, swaying slightly, his eyes alive with an emotion that warmed her even as she tried to deny it. The air between their bodies vibrated like a water-saturated cloud, waiting for lightning to release its tension. He raised his hand and his fingers lightly stroked her cheek. Her whispered "No, Roberto," shivered through the silence.

He withdrew his hand, but his voice still caressed her. "I want to touch you . . . hold you. Please, just this once. No one's here . . . two of us . . . alone. Can't bear it . . . unless I can have . . . something."

His stumbling words captured her breath and sent ripples down her spine. Fuzzily she knew she shouldn't let him speak that way, but she couldn't make her feelings obey her mind. He had sustained and comforted her; he'd been her friend, almost like a brother. Now suddenly he was much more—a man who desired her, who made her feel desirable, whose longing reached out to her and soothed the ache and humiliation of her husband's absence. She looked into his face, so uncannily like Andrew's, but alive now with the passion she'd yearned for during the months of Andrew's absence.

She tried to laugh but made only a choked plea: "Roberto . . . you're drunk."

"You're right. My excuse. Not so drunk I can't see you . . . so beautiful."

She backed away from him, protesting, trying to clear her head. "Roberto, don't say that. We've both had too much to drink. Tomorrow you'll be embarrassed."

He closed the space between them, and they stood, their bodies not quite touching, the tension growing, and then he pulled her into his arms. His kiss felt like lightning racing through her; the frantic beating of her heart seemed a thunderclap. His mouth released hers, only to cover her eyes, her cheeks, the line where her hair sprang away from her forehead, and then her lips again.

She struggled to escape his caresses, but at the same time her wounded spirit welcomed the medicine of knowing herself loved and desired. She put one hand over his mouth. "No—it's wrong."

He ignored her gasped words, kissing the hand with which she tried to deny him. As his mouth moved to her throat, her blood pounded, releasing her from the sorrow and denial of the past two weeks, greedily mirroring his desire. He cupped her face in his hands and groaned. "Julia . . . let me love you. I said one touch. I lied . . . it's not enough. I want you . . . want you so much."

Feverishly he strained against her, his kisses seeking, demanding her consent. She struggled to regain her control, pushing him away from her, but though her mind and clenched fists said no, her senses cried to accept the response his passion demanded. Dizzily she accepted her own building sensations as his hands pushed aside her robe and found first the straps of her shift and then her breasts.

It seemed to her she was both the woman in the arms of the swaying man and an observer who watched dreamily as they fell backward onto the bed. As if from a distance she felt his hands pulling off her clothing, then fumbling as he unsteadily removed his own clothes. She saw rather than felt his lean body, hardened from the months of work, naked now against her own.

They lay together on the bed, his body partially covering hers, his head buried in her neck, his breathing heavy. Then he raised his head and spoke haltingly. "Julia . . . can't help myself. I love you." His words slurred in his mouth, but they cherished her and comforted her, and she realized more painfully than ever before that Andrew had never spoken these three words to her. Images of Andrew loving Lele crowded her mind.

Roberto rolled to one side and murmured, "Must look at you . . . all of you . . . see how beautiful." His fingers traced her throat, her breasts, her belly, wavered along the faint scar and stopped at the red pubic hair. His kisses followed the path of his fingers, and his mouth and hands fed her passion. Then he lifted himself over her, his rigid shaft pressing against her thigh, his face above hers.

The sight of his black eyes pierced her like another flash of lightning, and reason began to reclaim her. Words thundered in her head: this is Roberto, not Andrew! As if the silent scream of names woke her from a dream, she stiffened and jerked away, and she heard his anguished words, "Oh, God! Oh, God!" and he shuddered as his seed burst from him against her thigh.

He lay above her, his gasping breaths slowly subsiding. "Julia . . . sorry. Too soon for you." He groaned again. "Hold me. Rest a minute. Love again." His hand stroked the side of her face and neck, then rested on her throat.

Frozen, she felt his breathing slow and gradually take on a regular rhythm. With unsteady hands she pushed against him, but he didn't move; all his weight still pressed heavily against her. Urgently she said, "Roberto. You must get up." She pushed at him again and realized he couldn't respond.

Using all her strength, she pulled herself from beneath him, trying to calm herself and think what she should do. Shakily she slid from the bed and pulled on her clothes. After she tied the belt of her robe, she looked around and only then realized the door to the room was partly open. Horrified, she rushed to shut it and leaned against it until her trembling subsided.

My God, how close they'd come to disaster! Only her return to sanity—and the amount Roberto had drunk that day—had saved them. She covered her burning face with her hands. Until that last moment, she had allowed and almost welcomed his embraces, and she couldn't escape that shameful knowledge. Her unhappiness, her gratitude to Roberto, and even the real affection she felt for him couldn't excuse her behavior. She, who'd been so proud of her independence and control, hadn't been in charge of her own emotions.

Roberto gave a half-groan in his sleep, and then lay still again, and Julia realized that they had not been spared disaster after all. Horrified, she stared at his naked figure, sprawled on the bed. He mustn't be found here like this. Going quickly to his side, she

grasped his shoulder and shook him, then said in his
ear, "Roberto, Roberto," but he slept on. Fearfully she
went back to the door and opened it a crack to listen.
Sounds of laughter and music still came through the
windows, but the house remained silent.

Again she tried to rouse Roberto, but he only shifted
his weight slightly. She'd have to leave him here, but if
she could at least get some clothing on him, the maids
would think he'd come in and passed out from drink.
They might wonder why he hadn't gone to his own
room, but since she no longer slept here, she'd have to
hope they wouldn't connect it with her.

Sweat was dripping from her by the time she had
managed to get his underwear and trousers back on.
She gave up and left his shirt and boots on the floor,
hoping it looked as if he'd partly undressed in the heat.
She moved him enough so that she could sponge away
most of the stain from the spilled semen. Closing the
door behind her, she hurried to her room and washed
herself, then put on the dress she'd discarded earlier.
Her hands still trembled as she combed and repinned
her hair, but she managed a silent descent to the hall
and out the front entrance.

When she circled to the back terrace, the dancing
and singing masked her return. To her relief, only
Quintiliana spoke to her. "Are you feeling all right now,
Sinha Julia?"

Julia forced a smile. "Yes—all I needed to do was
wash my face and rest a few moments. I've been walking in front, and the fresh air made me feel better. Now
I'm hungry." The housekeeper nodded, and Julia went
to the table where maids kept platters filled with meats
and fruit. She arranged slices of turkey and pork on a
plate, fearing for a moment her stomach might rebel,
and sat down, as if she planned to eat. Had she con-

vinced Quintiliana she'd been outside? After a while, she hid her plate with the untasted food under a chair and joined Pedro Oliveiro and his wife.

After night darkened the sky, she watched the fireworks. Then, feeling too exhausted to stay longer, no matter what the consequences, she gave her last congratulations to the bride and groom and went in to the house. As she passed the master-bedroom door, she stopped, but noises downstairs told her others had left the celebration also, and she feared to open the door and look inside. She listened for a moment, and silence reassured her.

Just before dawn, after many bitter tears had passed, she finally slept. As she had realized after Andrew first made love to her, she couldn't change what had happened, no matter how much she regretted it. She could only go on.

A timid knock roused Julia a few hours later. "Sinha Julia." She recognized the voice of Luzia, the girl who had taken Scizira's place, since Jora and Scizira planned to farm a small acreage Andrew had promised Jora as a wedding present.

Julia pulled herself up in bed and called, "Come in." The shy black face appeared around the door; then Luzia brought a tray with steaming coffee and milk and put it beside the bed.

"Quintiliana thought you might like your coffee here this morning." Luzia busied herself picking up Juila's discarded clothes while Julia gratefully sipped the hot beverage and tried to ignore her aching head.

Keeping her voice casual as she rose and let Luzia help her dress, Julia asked, "How is everyone after the big party?"

Luzia gave a little giggle, then covered her mouth

with her hand before answering primly, "Fine, *sinha-zinha*."

Julia gave the maid a teasing smile, but her heart was pounding so hard she thought the girl would hear it. "No one who celebrated too hard?"

Luzia busied herself with brushing Julia's hair, but her giggle broke out again. "Well, I heard that Seu Roberto—"

Quintiliana's stern voice interrupted from the doorway. "Luzia, if you are to be a maid and not just a silly girl, you must not repeat foolish stories."

The smile fled from the young black face, and she finished Julia's hair with a subdued air. When she had left, Julia asked Quintiliana, "Has something happened to Roberto?"

Quintiliana's impassive face looked more expressionless than usual as she answered, "Senhor Roberto may have drunk more than he realized, and he fell asleep in one of the upstairs bedrooms."

"Is he all right?"

"I believe so; he is in the study now, waiting for you."

Avoiding Quintiliana's eyes, Julia said, "Thank you," and nodded without listening to the housekeeper's suggestions for using the leftover food from the wedding. When Quintiliana finally left, Julia stood, quelling her trembling. She felt relief that nothing in the housekeeper's demeanor suggested suspicion or censure, but the idea of facing Roberto made her a coward. She chastized herself, because avoiding Roberto would only result in more time for apprehension and regrets she'd have anyway. Desperately arranging a pleasant expression, she went downstairs.

*　　*　　*

Roberto tried to study the notes he'd made two days ago about *fazenda* affairs, but the words blurred before his eyes. Savagely he threw the paper on the table. If his head didn't pound so, he'd laugh, but it would be bitter laughter. He rose and wandered around the study, looking blindly at the books on the shelves, asking himself if there were a philosopher who would console him this morning. But the irony of what he'd won and what he'd lost seared him too painfully for cold words to assuage his misery.

Julia's eyes would tell him how she felt about last night. He heard her footstep and turned to face her, waiting to see if she was his savior or executioner.

Her heart pounding, Julia closed the study door behind her and stood, her hand resting a moment on the knob, looking at Roberto. In his taut face and questioning eyes she saw hope, then watched it die. He put on his mask of unconcern, but the tiny lines etched around his mouth and the opaque blankness of his eyes revealed his anguish. She realized that in spite of the liquor, he had meant all he'd said yesterday, and she wept inside for the affection she had for him and the pain she must cause.

His voice was husky. "It was a mistake, wasn't it?"

Tears trembled in her throat, and her words came out in a whisper. "It isn't a mistake that I care about you, Roberto. But it was wrong."

"Wrong because you're married to my brother or wrong because you love him?"

"I'm not sure, but both, I think."

They stared at each other, and control wavered, until he turned and stood with his back to her. When he faced her again, mockery armored him, giving her a painful safety. "Very well, Julia, don't worry that it will

happen again. And you needn't wish I'll be punished
for my misdeeds. I already have been."

He laughed, but the bitterness of his laughter made
it gallows mirth. "You must share this final irony,
Julia—my Julia for such a brief time. Then I'll never
mention it again." He took a step toward her, and she
shrank closer to the door, almost frightened by the
intensity of his gaze. "I've wanted you almost since I
met you . . . to see you naked and beautiful . . . hold
you that way. I wanted you even before I loved you.
Now I know your kisses, how your body looks and feels,
all but the last moment of possession."

She stared at him, uncertain what he meant. Was he
saying he couldn't recall everything?

He laughed again, and the insane edge of his voice
appalled her. She held out her hand to him. "Roberto—"

As if she hadn't spoken, he continued, "That must be
the ultimate punishment—to drink until I sought you
out, but so much I can't remember the final prize."

Speechless with dismay and shock, she stared at him.
He didn't know what had happened at the end! With an
effort she recovered her voice. "But we—"

He put his hand against her lips, and the crazy laughter drained from his face. "No—don't say anything,
Julia. No one will ever know, and I'll never bring it up
again." He put his arms around her, and she could feel
him trembling with repressed emotion. "You don't know
what it means to me, even if I have only partial memories, to know that once I possessed you. That for one
brief time you belonged to me."

He rested his cheek against her hair, then released
her and stepped away. A tumult of emotions kept her
silent, and he spoke again, but calmly. "Years ago Andrew took a woman I thought I loved and wanted—
Lele—and I hated him for it. Now he has you, Julia,

and I know what it's really like to envy him, but strangely enough, I don't want to get even with him anymore, because it might hurt you." Under his mustache his lips twisted in an ironic smile. "My God—I hardly recognize myself. See how you've reformed me?" He attempted to laugh in his usual lighthearted way, and Julia felt as if her heart were bleeding.

She couldn't tell him what had happened and humiliate him. It wouldn't change the fact that she had surrendered, to both the physical desire he'd aroused and to her anger and hurt at Andrew. Only her last-minute realization of what they were doing had prevented a culmination Roberto believed had occurred. Her wretchedness and resentment over the estrangement from Andrew and her real affection for Roberto had made her vulnerable. As the thoughts whirled agonizingly in her mind, she realized she'd used Roberto to get revenge on her husband, and that knowledge shamed her more than the adultery that had come so close.

She held out her hands to Roberto and whispered, "Please forgive me," and hoped that he'd never know what kind of forgiveness she asked for.

When he pressed her hand and hurriedly left the room, she stood for a long time wondering how she would live with herself, and with Andrew. That uncertainty was her punishment.

15

"Are you trying to blackmail me?"

"No, Father, I'm trying to protect you." Andrew stood facing his father across the office in Richard's house, hearing in the accusing words the rage he'd expected but hoped to avoid.

"Protect me!" Richard's hands clenched with a fury Andrew had seen directed before only at a black who had dared to cross his father, and once at his brother. "You come here, having gone behind my back to my associates, and threaten me with deportation!"

Fatigue and worry about both his father and his wife frayed the last edge of the temper Andrew had been holding in check. "I'm not threatening you. Your plans are delusions, and I'm only trying to make you see that." Furiously he matched his father's shout. "Your republican allies want no part of schemes to divide Brazil. If they knew your real aims, they'd denounce you immediately. And don't look for support from the slave owners. The big planters have never been able to decide on a concerted action, and the Confederate immigrants won't fight again here."

Richard advanced threateningly. "What did you tell the people in Rio?"

Disgusted with his father and with himself for failing to control his temper, Andrew replied more calmly, "I told them nothing. I sounded out their feelings, more intelligently than you apparently have. And how do you think I heard about this? Others—men in the government—will be watching to see what you do."

He took his riding crop and broad hat and strode to the door, then turned to add wearily, "Abolition will come, not next year, but before long. The British and the emperor are both determined on it, and most Brazilians agree. Slavery is a doomed system, and your coterie of slave owners should use their energies to get compensation, not on futile opposition." He paused, his anger softened by regret for the resentment he knew his father would continue to feel. "It's Christmas Eve, Father, and I haven't even been home yet. I came because I care what happens to you, whether you believe me or not."

As he made his way to the entrance hall, he met Ellen, her face distressed. She held out her hands to him. "Andrew, I heard the shouting. Can I help in some way?"

He kissed her hands, then shook his head. "You were right when you warned Julia about the Langdon men. We're a hardheaded bunch. I'm afraid there's nothing you can do. Just make Father's life happy here; I know you've done that already."

She smiled lovingly at him. "Dear Andrew, can you stay for refreshment?"

"Thank you, Ellen, but I must go. I want to be home before dark. If I'm welcome here after tonight, I'll come back soon. Otherwise you must visit Julia and me."

She pulled his head down to kiss his cheek. "Merry Christmas, Andrew."

He hugged her. "Merry Christmas, Ellen." She followed him outside to where his new groom held his horse, and his last backward glance found her still looking after him as he rode away.

The dusty smells of late afternoon wafted around Andrew, the resinous odor of pine that had warmed all day in the sun reminding him how glad he was to leave cities behind. His throat felt dry, and he'd have liked to accept at least a drink of water from Ellen, but that would have meant staying to talk to her, and his need to reach home was greater than his thirst.

How would Julia greet him? Had her nights been lonely, and had she also regretted the words with which they'd savaged each other? He wished he hadn't implied he'd be with Lele. He hadn't gone to his former mistress, but he'd still been too angry before Julia's ship left to deny his earlier words, nor had he written. A letter wouldn't let him see her response.

To one side of the road a crooked pine reminded him of a spring in the small draw which ended at the bent tree. He spurred his horse up a sharp slope, then through scrubby brush to a pocket where water bubbled up through gray sand. Behind him thudded the hoofbeats of his groom's horse and the pack mule. He dismounted and cupped his hands, first to drink and then to splash his hands and face.

While he waited for his black groom to do the same, he saw a flash of pale yellow plumage on a small bird in a nearby acacia tree. It reminded him of the dress Julia had worn the first evening when they talked on the veranda at Hundred Oaks. When he'd listened to her then, he'd admired her spirit and her interest in activities most women ignored. Her determination last fall to learn about coffee planting had pleased him. Yet when she'd told him about her management of the *fazenda*, he'd felt upset and uncomfortable even before he knew about Roberto's help.

As he mounted and rode back down to the road, he recognized clearly what he'd only begun to understand during the almost three weeks since their argument in Rio. It wasn't, as he'd briefly considered, that he really cared what people might think if his wife seemed unwomanly, for in his struggle not to allow his father to dominate him, he'd learned to disregard the superficial opinions of others. What he did care about—what he wanted—was for Julia to be dependent on him.

Their marriage had begun with so much uncertainty and suspicion that he'd grown to love her without acknowledging it to himself. For her to act as if she could get along without him—or with his brother's help—had roused rage he'd never experienced before. He didn't really care that she'd made a mistake about Tomaz; her unrealistic view of blacks and whites probably hadn't done any lasting harm. But her innocence about Roberto's motives and feelings could leave her unprotected. Even if Roberto didn't intend to seduce her, they'd been thrown together constantly, and her warmth and beauty would rouse almost any man's desire. And, Andrew realized, when she'd goaded his already lacerated feelings, he'd foolishly sent her right back to his brother.

Ignoring the fatigue which he knew his horse felt as keenly as he, he pushed his mount to a faster pace. He must overcome his pride and mend things between them. Then he could hold her and love her as he longed to do.

"*Sinhazinha*." Luzia's excited voice roused Julia from her copy of *A Tale of Two Cities*. "Capitolino says he sees two riders with a pack mule, and he's sure it's Seu Andrew!"

Julia felt as if she'd swallowed a lump of lead, but her trembling legs held her as she put aside her book and rose. "Thank you, Luzia. Did he say how far away they are?"

The shining black face seemed an enormous smile. "No, but I think he saw them coming over the last hill."

Julia hurried up the stairs to the small bedroom and the oak-framed mirror. Her flushed face stared back at her above the white cotton dress with its low neckline and short sleeves. She wished that today she hadn't put on the casual clothing Brazilian women wore inside the house in warm weather. Did she have time to change?

She gripped the edge of the dresser so hard that the wood pressed painfully into her palms. What would she say to Andrew—how could she face him?

As he'd promised, Roberto hadn't spoken again of their aborted lovemaking. They had conferred each morning, but she'd felt too distressed to ride out into the fields with him, and after each evening's uncomfortable dinner, he had gone promptly to the overseer's house. From his appearance in the mornings she suspected he regularly took a bottle of brandy with him at night, but the surface calm between them was too fragile to risk offering him any comfort.

In any case, she didn't know what she could offer that would help him more than the gift he didn't know she'd given—that of letting him think they'd consummated the lovemaking.

"Sinha Julia. Here they come!" Luzia appeared in the doorway and then disappeared as if she were a puppet on a string.

Julia pulled the pins from her hair so forcefully they showered with tiny clicks on the polished wood floor. She tugged the brush through her heavy hair and listened with a pounding heart to the clatter of horses' hooves below. Through blurred eyes she looked for the scattered hairpins and stooped to retrieve them.

Slowly she straightened and reached for a ribbon to tie back her hair, which would have to remain loose instead of in its usual chignon. Forcing a deep breath into her tight chest, she turned and started downstairs.

Halfway down to the entrance hall she paused, the fear she'd tried to forget encasing her with ice. What if he'd spent these weeks with Lele? Pain lodged in her stomach, but she stiffened herself against it. If he had, she would have to endure the torment, because he'd have done only what she'd come so close to doing herself.

She took another step, then stopped as the door opened and Andrew's tall figure filled the entrance. He looked up and halted also, as if the two of them were figures in some frozen tableau. In his face she saw lines of strain and fatigue, and in his eyes a question, but not the coldness or anger she'd feared.

Behind Andrew Capitolino beamed, his grin stretching across his wide face. Quintiliana stood next to Andrew, her dark eyes glistening with tears. Then she looked up at Julia and her expression changed, the lines of joy disappearing in an impassive watchfulness. Julia's breath seemed to stop in her throat as she waited to see how Andrew would greet her in front of the servants.

"Julia." Andrew's husky voice sounded more sweet to her than a flute playing the most exquisite music, and her heart swelled with hope. She felt almost giddy, as if she would fall, and then he slowly mounted the rest of the stairs and caught her close in his arms. She swayed against him as his lips touched hers.

Trembling, she drew back. Since he stood below her, she could look directly into his eyes, and what she saw there made her hope he too longed to heal the breach between them. He took her face between his hands, his thumbs caressing the edges of her mouth. "We have so much to talk of, Julia." His next gentle kiss set her blood racing through her veins, but guilt returned to dampen her passion, and when she pulled away, she felt lines of strain subduing her smile.

Andrew sensed that Julia's first spontaneous response had changed, and he couldn't prevent a feeling of disappointment. He hadn't intended to approach her immediately, but the sight of her in the soft dress, with her red-gold hair curling around her face and loose down her back, had destroyed his restraint. To expect her to forget how they'd parted wasn't reasonable, he reminded himself, and at least she wasn't angry. Surely she wanted to work out their difficulties.

Her face looked pale, and he realized her informal dress meant she had been staying inside. Masking his concern, he teased, "Are you well, Julia? I half-expected to find you out in the coffee fields."

Her smile didn't quite reassure him. "I've felt a little extra tired recently and stayed in. And tomorrow is Christmas; there's much to do here." Behind him he heard more excited voices and turned, still holding her hand, to descend and greet the growing throng of household servants.

Julia went down the stairs by Andrew's side, realizing that part of her explanation was true. She had felt more tired than usual the last week and exhausted by her inner turmoil since the encounter between her and Roberto. Christmas had hardly entered her thoughts; she only hoped Quintiliana had been as efficient as usual about preparations.

Capitolino waved his hand toward the back terrace. "Seu Andrew, the field hands working near the house have heard about your return and are gathering outside."

Andrew turned to Julia. "Would you excuse me while I speak to them?"

"Of course. I'll go upstairs and change. I imagine Senhor Pedro and the supervisors will be here to see you soon also."

He smiled and squeezed her hand before going outside, and she turned and hurried back up to her room.

While she put on a flowered muslin dress and buttoned the snug bodice, she tried not to think about the time when she and Andrew would be alone. Her hair resisted the efforts of her nervous fingers to confine it. When she finally twisted it into the bun at the back of her neck, she slowly turned from the mirror to look at the small room. Would she spent the night here, or in the large bedroom where she was sure Andrew's saddlebags were being emptied? Thrusting the question aside, she went downstairs to find Andrew in the small sitting room with Jora and Scizira.

"We thank you for our land and the fine wedding, Seu Andrew," Jora was saying. A smiling Scizira clung to his arm.

"A fine wedding, you say," Andrew responded, and sent Julia an amused glance. "It was just what you deserved."

As the young couple left, Pedro Oliveiro limped into the room and greeted Andrew with a sober restraint that was belied by his wet eyes. "I'll be able to return to my duties very soon," he proudly assured Andrew.

"And I'll welcome that," Andrew replied, "but don't jeopardize your health. I expect you to oversee our land for many years, so take time to recover completely."

Julia thought the tears were going to break through the overseer's crusty exterior as he pumped Andrew's hand.

Pedro had just left when Julia heard the jaunty step

she'd been dreading. Slowly she turned to see Roberto in the doorway, his usual unconcerned smile on his face.

"Well, my wandering brother has finally returned to reclaim his kingdom." Though Roberto's tone was light, Julia flinched at the interpretation which his words could have. Hardly breathing, she looked at Andrew.

Her husband's expression told her nothing, and his voice sounded natural, even warm, as he held out his hand. "Roberto, I owe you a large debt for all you've done while I was away. Though words seem inadequate for my gratitude, I do thank you." The brothers shook hands, and Andrew turned to the decanter of brandy on a side table. "Will you share a glass with me?"

"Did you ever know me to refuse?" Roberto asked. "Your homecoming is certainly . . . an occasion for celebration."

If Andrew noticed the flicker of hesitation in Roberto's reply, Julia could not tell it in his face or voice as he said, "Julia, a glass of sherry?"

"Yes, please."

When they each held a glass, Julia sat down quickly and took a sip of her wine, hoping to avoid any sort of toast. To her relief, the two men sat also.

Roberto held his brandy in front of him, swirling it as if savoring the aroma, waiting for his stomach to unclench. He'd almost hoped for Andrew's return so that he could leave and end the torture of seeing Julia each day without being able to touch her. But watching his brother brush her hand as he gave her the sherry raised such pain that Roberto would willingly have gone back to the strain of the past few days. Tomorrow was Christmas. He had no reasonable excuse for leaving until at least the day after, when he could go over records with Andrew, but he must get away before he exploded.

The sip of brandy seemed like water compared to the fire of envy and longing in his gut. He'd told Julia he didn't want to get even with Andrew because he didn't want to hurt her. He hoped he could keep his word.

Andrew looked into the golden liquid to avoid seeing the shadows on Julia's face. He was determined to conquer his jealousy toward Roberto, to assume that nothing had happened between them. If he were to resume his marriage, he must believe in Julia. Seeing her confirmed even more strongly than all his thinking in Rio that he wanted her as his wife, responding to him, depending on him, but at least with him. Her eyes when they'd met on the stairs and her soft yielding to his kiss spurred him to overcome his resentment of Roberto and to express the thanks to his brother he was trying to feel.

As she watched the two men together, Julia realized that she'd been weak once, but now she must be strong. Unable to stand the silence, she said, "Roberto, you can tell Andrew better than I just how the work is going." In Roberto's face she saw a momentary expression of relief she wouldn't have recognized before she'd come to know him so well.

"Do you object to serious talk, Andrew?" he asked, and without waiting for an answer, began to describe recent activities.

When Capitolino came to announce dinner, the atmosphere between Andrew and Roberto had eased, and Julia found she could eat with some appetite. Knowing the foods Andrew loved, Quintiliana had prepared a particularly spicy sauce for the *feijoada* of pork, beans, and rice. At her direction the maids had set the table with the English bone china. Pedro Oliveiro and his wife joined them, and the happy faces of all the ser-

vants supplied a festive air. Soon after dinner the
Oliveiros went to their room and Roberto left for the
overseer's house. Her heart beginning to pound, Julia
started to precede Andrew to the sitting room, but his
hand on her elbow halted her.

"Julia, we must talk, but where we can be completely
alone."

As she looked up at him, he added, "I'd suggest our
bedroom, but from what I understand, I'm not sure
which room that is."

She felt a blush heat her face. "It was warm, and I
didn't want to—"

He interrupted her stumbling explanation. "It's not
important. Come, let's go outside."

Twilight still distinguished colors that would soon be
only different shades of gray. Silently they walked across
the terrace. At the path beyond, Andrew asked, "Shall
we go to the summerhouse?"

For a moment she hesitated, remembering the night
Roberto had found her there, then started toward it. As
they crossed the bridge and went up to the small shelter, she reminded herself that if she couldn't speak to
Andrew here, she'd never be able to join him in their
bedroom. And she knew that more than anything else
in the world, she wanted to be his wife, to love him and
be loved by him.

As she sat on a bench along one side, she vowed that
if Andrew wanted her again, she would bury deep
inside her the guilt about Roberto. Even if Andrew had
slept with Lele, he probably wouldn't forgive his wife's
behavior. It was unfair, but society led men to demand
fidelity from their wives that they didn't expect from
themselves. To tell Andrew about Roberto might ease
her remorse, but it would be an indulgence that could
destroy them, and she must be strong.

In the silence she heard the whir of tiny insects and the plop of a frog slipping into the little lake. A vine of Spanish jasmine trailed a perfumed message in the air as it climbed one of the supports of the octagonal roof. Andrew's voice seemed gentled by the peaceful surroundings. "When we parted in Rio, we had said angry words to each other—words that I at least didn't mean." He sat down beside her and leaned forward, his hands resting on his knees, his eyes holding hers. "I didn't see Lele while I was in Rio. I had never any intention or desire to see her. My words, which I regret, were in response to yours, but that doesn't excuse them. I did pay the rent on the house where she lives, at first because I felt I owed her that much, again because I didn't want to risk her bothering you while I was away. It meant no more than that."

At his explanation, the fear about Lele which had tormented her died in a great surge of relief. She started to speak, but he stopped her. "Please, Julia, let me finish before you say anything." He rose and paced a few steps, then turned back and sat beside her again. "Apologies don't come easily to me, Julia. I tried to apologize to you that day in Rio, but I'm not sure if I meant it then. I was still too angry."

He took her hands, and she could see from the deep line around his mouth that he spoke with difficulty. "You see, Julia, I had just realized how much you mean to me—how much I love you—at the same time that you were telling me how well you could get along without me."

His words began to grow inside her, like streaks of sunshine breaking through dark clouds. At his next husky question, wild rainbows arched inside her. "Can you forgive me, Julia? Can we put aside our quarrels and begin now as we did when I found you sleeping that first afternoon in Rio?"

She lifted a trembling hand to his face and whispered, "Can you forgive me? I, too, said things I didn't mean. You see, I realized I love you, and it frightened me, made our quarrel more dangerous."

"Julia . . . Julia!" He stood and pulled her to her feet, then into his arms. She could feel his heart thundering against her throat as she pressed close against him. When he tilted her face up and captured her lips in a kiss, she felt as if she had exploded in surging colors, like the fireworks at their wedding.

His hands sought to rediscover every curve and contour of her face as she explored the geometric planes and surfaces of his shoulders and back. The buttons of her dress proved no barrier to his fingers, and his hand on her breast sent tremors of passion and joy racing through her veins. When she pushed aside his shirt to fold her arms around his warm chest, she felt the shudders her touch produced.

When he pulled away, she gave a soft cry and snatched at his shoulders, unwilling to lose the magic of his touch, but he laughed shakily. "If I don't stop now, I'll have your skirts over your head right here where anyone could come by. But I can't wait long. Shall we go to the bedroom and lock the door?"

Her buried guilt threatened to rise. "Not yet. Is there anywhere else—not in the house?"

In answer he took her hand and pulled her with him back across the bridge and along the path to the stables. "Where are we going?" she asked when she could manage enough breath.

"You'll see." In the empty stables he left her while he led out the brown gelding. After he saddled the patient horse, he attached a rolled blanket and an unlit lantern to the back of the saddle, then swung up and held out his hand to her. When she took it, he lifted her up in front of him, settling her across his thighs. As he held the reins, his arms encircled her, and she leaned against him.

From a window in the main room of the overseer's cottage, Roberto watched them ride away in the deepening twilight. Around him the whitewashed walls and crude furniture seemed as ugly and empty as his life, and the single decoration, a crucifix above a picture of the Virgin and Child, meaningless. He looked at the half-full brandy bottle, then with a savage blow knocked it off the table. The bottle crashed against the tile floor, and the pungent liquid spread in a widening stain. He turned and groped his way into the bedroom. From the bottom of the wardrobe he dragged his saddlebags and began to stuff clothing into them. Pedro Oliveiro had ridden out enough that he could tell Andrew everything necessary. By tomorrow morning, Roberto promised himself, he'd be in São Paulo, ready to join the Devil, the only fitting companion for him now.

As Julia rode, sheltered in Andrew's arms, the motion of the horse jostled them together and heightened her growing excitement. At the same time the memory of his words in the summerhouse brought an aching tenderness. She knew him well enough now to understand how difficult it had been for him to apologize— the same kind of pride governed her actions more often than she wished. But he loved her, and he'd spoken the painful, wonderful words which opened a new life for her. When they reached a sheltered spot beside a small stream, she was almost sorry for the ride to end.

Enough light remained to see the lazy water, softly winding its way through the small clearing, surrounded by a screen of bamboo and ferns. Colors had faded to grays and muted purples, with only hints of green. Andrew unrolled the blanket and stretched out, pulling her down beside him. The whisper of the water sliding over rounded stones, the snuffling of the horse at its nearby tether, filled the air with subtle sounds of tenderness. A single note reverberated from the ringing of a bell, as if a curtain separated her and Andrew from ordinary activities, sheltering them for a time in a world of their own.

They turned to each other, to touch and taste and renew their mutual knowledge. For a brief moment Julia feared the encounter with Roberto would somehow be communicated through her skin, but the familiarity of Andrew's body, melding with hers, banished all thoughts except of him.

At first the night air felt cool to her nakedness, but Andrew's touch and the heat of the passion between them created its own fire. She lost herself in the aching pleasure of his mouth tugging at her breast, the feel of the muscles of his thighs and buttocks beneath her hands, of his kisses arousing her to a frenzy of desire. When she felt she couldn't wait longer, he thrust into her, filling the emptiness she'd felt so long and propelling them both to a shuddering fulfillment.

When she returned to the world, night had released the first stars, and as she lay with Andrew's arm around her and her head on his shoulder, she felt as peaceful as the shy sparkles which were joining their bolder luminaries. Andrew rubbed his jaw against her hair and said softly, "It's almost Christmas. Will you accept as my gift to you my promise to make this a new beginning?"

In answer she turned and pushed herself up to trace the lines of his face—the strong jaw, the well-defined eyebrows and straight nose, and finally the wide, sensuous mouth. "Yes, if you'll receive the same from me." He drew her head down for a kiss that sealed both their promises.

They rode slowly back to the house with the lantern hung on a pole sticking out from the saddle to light the way. After the horse had been stabled, they slipped up the stairs to their bedroom, Julia giggling at their stealth but sharing Andrew's wish to be completely to themselves.

Not until Christmas Day did Julia know of Roberto's gift to her—his silent departure.

Three weeks later the morning was half-gone when Julia woke to Luzia's soft knock. Sleepily she called for her maid to come in. Andrew had risen hours ago and would be out with the overseer by now. Somehow she couldn't force herself to leave the comfort of their bed, and Andrew seemed to approve of her indulgence.

Distastefully she eyed the tray of steaming coffee and milk. "Luzia, I think I don't want coffee in the morning in this warm weather. It doesn't seem to agree with me. Maybe something else instead, like . . ." She frowned, unable to name something that didn't make her feel faintly queasy to think of. She wondered if she could have some slight illness that bothered her in the mornings and accounted for the exhaustion she often felt by evening.

Luzia gave her high-pitched giggle. "*Sinhazinha*, I think Scizira will be happy."

"Scizira will be happy because I don't want coffee in the morning?" Julia got out of bed and stretched, then pulled on a robe. "You are a goose, Luzia. What are you talking about?"

"The baby."

Julia picked up her brush before giving Luzia a puzzled look. "What baby?"

Luzia put her hand over her mouth, and her wide eyes looked distressed. "Oh, Sinha Julia, I thought you knew. Scizira will be very angry with me."

Startled, Julia put her hand on the slight shoulder. "For heaven's sake, Luzia, what's wrong?"

Tears glistened in the fearful eyes; when sobs began, Julia spoke impatiently. "Luzia! Stop your crying and tell me what you've done."

"The baby—Scizira bought a spell from a *macumbeiro* to get a baby. But I thought you knew."

From time to time Julia had seen a *macumbeiro*, or love sorcerer, usually an old black woman who traveled between plantations, selling prescriptions for attracting a lover or preventing a husband from finding out about infidelities. "So Scizira spent her money for a spell," Julia said with amusement, "and does she know so soon that she's going to have a baby?"

The young maid's answer was almost too low to hear. "Not Scizira's baby—your baby." Julia stared at the downcast eyes in disbelief before the explanation for her feelings fell in place. Pregnant—she was pregnant, and from some wisdom Luzia possessed but Julia didn't, the girl had known.

Luzia knelt and pulled a small bag out from under the mattress and held it out to Julia, who opened it onto the stand beside the bed. Inside were a crumpled piece of paper with minuscule writing on it and two thin strands of braided hair, one black and curly and one long and red. A dark brown powder covered the paper and clung to the hairs.

Still dazed by Luzia's revelation, Julia struggled to speak naturally. "Luzia, what are these?"

"The hair from you and Seu Andrew. The prayer is to São Gonçalo, the saint for loving and having babies, and the powder is dried toad's blood," Luzia replied in a trembling voice. "Shall I help you dress?"

Julia stared at the little bag, then said, "No—just take the coffee tray."

When Luzia left, Julia sank back onto the bed, stunned that she, who'd learned so much about raising coffee, had paid so little attention to the processes of her own body. The recent tenderness of her breasts, as well as the morning uneasiness, was a sign she should have remembered from discussions with Sally when her sister-in-law was pregnant. When she thought carefully, Julia realized she'd had no monthly flow since late November, two weeks before she'd met Andrew in Rio. In the distress of subsequent events, she hadn't noticed its absence. She must have conceived that first night in Rio.

A welter of other emotions made her heart pound and her head whirl. What would having a baby be like? What would it mean to Andrew? Would he be happy? A baby would change her responsibilities, confine her. Suddenly another thought chilled her. If she and Roberto had completed the sex act that day, she might not know which man had fathered her baby—Roberto or Andrew. Since the two brothers looked so much alike, she might never be sure.

Slowly she rose and dressed, overwhelmed by gratitude for having escaped the torment that too easily could have been hers. As calm returned, she thought of the new life growing inside her, life made possible by the love between her and her husband, and she knew that whatever changes a baby brought, it could also bring a new and wonderful happiness.

If Luzia had observed the signs of pregnancy, probably Quintiliana suspected also. Though the housekeeper would say nothing, Luzia wouldn't keep such interesting news to herself. Julia knew she must tell Andrew right away, before he heard hints from one of the servants.

Turning back to the bedside stand, she looked at the crumpled paper, but the Portuguese script was so small and smudged she couldn't read it. She gathered the paper and strands of hair and put them back into the bag, which she slipped into her skirt pocket.

She waited until evening when she and Andrew were in the small sitting room, he with a glass of port and she with sherry. He'd come in before dinner in time for half an hour playing the piano, and he was relaxed and happy. But then, Julia thought as she watched his expressive eyes and mouth, he seemed content with her all the time now, despite their occasional disagreements about minor matters. The anger and distrust between them seemed to have finally been banished. Surely a child would only add to their love for each other.

He looked at her, his eyebrows raised, and gave her a teasing smile. "I have the feeling you're about to tell me something. Let me guess—you've been reading one of my journals again before I even get to see it. What innovation in planting are we going to argue about tonight?"

She laughed, but finding the right words seemed suddenly difficult. "No new plans for the field work to suggest." She rose and stood beside him, her hand resting on his shoulder. "I do have something to show you, though."

He pulled her down into his lap and nuzzled the side of her neck. "Hmmm—the smell of roses," he murmured against her. "Maybe we should go to bed early again tonight. I think it has a marvelous effect on my health."

She pushed his head up and tried to laugh. "It's

already had an effect on mine." Before he could ask the question she saw in his eyes, she pulled the small bag from her pocket and opened it.

He took the paper and tiny braids from her hand. "Looks like a charm. Where did you get it?"

"First—your Portuguese is better than mine. Can you read the paper?"

He shifted her weight slightly so he could hold the wrinkled scrap closer to the kerosene lamp. "It's a verse, addressed to São Gonçalo." He studied it for a moment, then translated, " 'Get me a lover, get me a lover; little Gonçalo, hear my plea; that is why I pray to thee, friendly little saint.' " He quirked an eyebrow above teasing eyes. "Now you must tell me where this came from. I certainly don't want my wife praying for a lover."

She put her arms around him and caressed the thick hair curling at the back of his neck. "I already have the lover I want." When he put the charm aside and started to kiss her, she drew back. "According to Luzia, Scizira put this under the mattress in our bedroom. Apparently she thought we weren't doing enough about . . . getting a baby, and she bought something from a *macumbeiro* she thought was supposed to help us."

Andrew's eyes held hers, the intense blue deepening as he asked, "And even though it was the wrong charm, did it work?"

Julia felt a surprising shyness and knew a blush was coloring her face. "Yes—we're going to have a baby."

As if he couldn't quite believe what she'd said, he stared at her for a moment longer. Then he caught her to him in a wild hug, holding her so tightly she felt almost crushed. "A baby! Our baby. Oh God, Julia." When he released her, she saw tears in the blue eyes. He cupped her face between his hands and said tenderly, "I thought since I came home that I couldn't be happier, but now I am." His kiss confirmed his words, and as Julia rested in the protective strength of his arms, she gave another prayer of thanks at knowing the joy of Andrew's love.

16

At the sound of Ellen's melodious laugh, Julia put aside the letter she was writing and ran to the front entrance. In a whirl of ruffles and fringed shawl, the two women embraced. "Ellen, I was afraid you might not ride over today. It's so cold for May. Come into the small sitting room. I had a fire lit in there this morning."

When they were settled in the cushioned chairs with cups of hot coffee, Ellen picked up a tiny dress from the top of a rosewood sewing cabinet. "For the little one, I see." She held it up to look at the beginning of embroidery around the hem. "I think you're farther along with the baby than with this decoration."

Julia wrinkled her nose. "Yes—I never liked sewing."

Ellen laughed, then asked, "Where is Andrew—out working as usual?"

"Yes," Julia replied. "He watches the coffee crop more intently than a mother bird with eggs. This sudden cold weather worries him—and me too, since I'm the one who agreed to the advance sale."

Ellen smiled at Julia. "I think Andrew will be happy with you, no matter how the coffee sale comes out."

The maid came in with an assortment of sweet cakes. Protesting that she shouldn't have any, Ellen took two.

After they finished eating, Julia asked, "Does Richard know you visit us?" Though she knew she should call him "Father," she hadn't been able to.

Ellen glanced at the tray of cakes, then determinedly set her plate aside. "Yes, though he pretends he doesn't." She sighed, and added, "He'd like to see Andrew, but his pride won't allow it."

Julia thought of her husband's distress over his father's activities. "Andrew has that same kind of pride, but I think that in spite of their clashes, Richard does matter to Andrew."

"Yes," agreed Ellen, "and Richard's sons mean more to him than he'd ever acknowledge. I'm sure he misses Roberto; he was so proud of the job Roberto did for you."

At the thought of her brother-in-law Julia felt both relieved and sad. "Do you know where Roberto is?"

"Yes," Ellen answered, "he's sent me a few brief notes, and a friend told me of seeing him. He's in Santos—living with some woman, and drinking too much, I suspect."

A flare of something unpleasantly like jealousy startled Julia. She sat silently, uncomfortable to realize how much she'd thought of Roberto as hers. If she hadn't met and married Andrew, she might have fallen in love with Roberto—at least with the more responsible and caring man he'd shown himself to be when he helped her.

Wanting to dismiss those thoughts, she asked, "Do you think Richard will relent and visit us when the baby comes?"

"Maybe. Grandchildren can be very important."

A wistful note in Ellen's tone made Julia look at her questioningly. "Do you already have grandchildren, Ellen?"

The older woman hesitated, then replied, "My grand-daughter is three years old, and my grandson must be five months by now, but I've never seen them."

Julia leaned across and put her hand on Ellen's arm. "Please—don't talk about it if you don't want to."

Ellen squeezed Julia's hand. "I'm glad to tell you, as an example of folly. You see, I married very young, to someone older and 'suitable' from my parents' point of view, which means he had money and position. My family was poor, and I thought I wanted wealth and respectability. But my husband and I didn't get along. Even before our son was born, he had mistresses and I didn't care."

She gave a sad laugh. "In English society, liaisons outside of marriage were common, so I thought I could have a lover also. But I made the mistake of falling in love with the wrong man—someone who managed a theater. If he'd been from my own class and I'd been more discreet . . . but I made the additional error of being discovered. So my husband divorced me, and I wasn't allowed to see my son again."

Horrified, Julia could only say, "Ellen, how terrible. And how unfair."

Ellen's eyes glistened with unshed tears. "It's the way things are arranged, Julia. Men can do as they wish with wives, and I should have known that and been more careful. Fortunately the housekeeper felt sorry for me and has written to me all these years and told me of my son, and now of his family."

She refilled her coffee cup and said, "So I married my lover, John Durr, and became a singer in the the-ater. A divorced wife has nothing to lose, so she might as well employ herself as she can. When he died, I took jobs which suited me, and eventually I came to Brazil, liked it, and stayed. I never intended to marry again, but Richard finally wore down my resistance."

Her face lightened. "There's a dangerous streak in Richard—and in his sons. Richard conceals it by blustering, and Andrew keeps it more controlled than his brother, but it's in all of them. And I confess it appeals to me."

At the thought of how much Ellen must have suffered, Julia put her hands protectively over her rounding stomach. Already she felt a fierce attachment to the son or daughter who grew inside her, and couldn't imagine how she could survive that kind of loss.

When Andrew returned to the house in time to give his departing stepmother an affectionate good-bye, Julia stayed close by his side, as if to guard the love that bound them together and let nothing come between them.

The late June sunshine slanted across the desk in the study. Julia put down James's letter and picked up the one from Philadelphia, but her mind was still in South Carolina. Sally had miscarried the baby James wanted so much, and he worried about her health and spirits. The last cotton crop had shown a minuscule profit, but the struggle to manage under the difficult conditions made James sound like an old man.

Sighing, she opened Purity's letter. Since Purity and Nathan's marriage, Purity had written every few months, and usually Nathan added a greeting. They now had twin boys, a year old, and most letters had been full of anecdotes about the babies that, until her own pregnancy, had bored Julia. But the first lines of this letter captured her startled attention. Nathan was moving his family to California!

Soon after the twins were born, Uncle Daniel had died. Nathan had continued to manage his father-in-law's importing firm, but he wanted to return to practicing medicine. In San Francisco, Purity said, he could join a doctor he'd known in the army. They would travel by way of Panama. Purity made no attempt at cheerfulness, covering three pages with her fears. In contrast, the note at the end in Nathan's scrawl sounded exuberant.

A door slammed, and Julia could hear Andrew's shout before he reached the study. "Julia—it's finished! The last cart of coffee beans went to the steam sheds an hour ago." He picked her up from her chair and swung her around before giving her a sweaty kiss.

"Andrew," she protested, laughing, "you're squeezing me and the baby."

Instantly he put her down, but his wide grin remained as he enfolded her more gently in his arms. "How will we spend all the money you've made for us, my gambling wife?" He threw back his head and laughed. "My God, I'll have to endure all my neighbors congratulating me on my wife's shrewdness. Well, let them— we'll even have a party to show you off."

"But we can't—the way I look now."

For answer he just patted her cheek. "I think they all know babies aren't discovered in cabbage patches, love. You won't shock them."

Though Julia still felt self-conscious, she did as Andrew asked and sent invitations to all of the American expatriates nearby and to the Brazilian families who had become their friends. Andrew's willingness to acknowledge her part in their success filled her with pride and a great burst of love for him.

When guests crowded the candlelit salon two weeks later, she decided Andrew hadn't been completely correct about the acceptability of her appearance. Several women obviously disapproved, though she had thought her loose high-waisted dress and draped shawl dis-

guised her pregnancy quite well. But with only two
months until the baby's birth, her bulk couldn't be
completely concealed. Even Mrs. Scott had looked at
Julia a little sadly, as if after such a disreputable beginning, Andrew and Julia couldn't be expected to behave
in orthodox ways. Julia took wicked pleasure in a disdainful glance from her stepmother, Carlota.

Ellen and Richard had come today, delighting Julia at
this first softening of Richard's attitude to Andrew. The
two men had greeted each other stiffly, but the silence
had been breached. She and Ellen had stifled their joy,
allowing only their eyes to tell each other of their
pleasure.

Across the room she saw her father standing by himself, lines of strain around his mouth and eyes as he
looked at something beyond her. She turned, following
the direction of his gaze.

Carlota, her hand on Andrew's arm, was standing so
close to him that she almost leaned against him. Andrew's dark head bent down to hers as she said something into his ear. Then she laughed and touched his
cheek with one finger, a gesture of practiced seduc-
tiveness.

Though Julia knew Andrew disliked Carlota, she felt
jealousy flame up in her like a newly struck match.
Underneath the security of the love she and Andrew
shared, she knew dark feelings could exist which even
the thought of him and another woman could trigger.
She and Andrew were no longer able to make love in
the usual way, and she knew he missed the more fulfilling sexual climaxes they'd had before. If he sought the
arms of someone else, no matter how casually, she
couldn't bear the pain. He glanced up now and in the
love for her she saw in his eyes, she knew how foolish
such fears were.

As quickly as it had come, her jealousy died away, but concern for her father remained. She knew it must be terrible for her father to witness his wife's flirtations. Carlota practiced her arts indiscriminately, including even scrawny Mr. Wetherly and Duncan Scott, only now broadening to his adult male size.

Quickly she crossed to her father and took his arm. "Come, Papa, I want Andrew to have to tell you all over again how much money we'll make from our coffee." She pulled her father determinedly with her. "Andrew needs a little humbling occasionally. Otherwise he'd be impossible to live with."

When she reached her husband, she could see from his smile his relief at being rescued. Though she spoke politely to Carlota, she really wanted to shout her anger over William's unhappiness. How fragile marriage could be, she thought as the two men jested together, and she felt a deep gratitude for the happiness she and Andrew shared.

That night when they were alone in their bed Julia nestled against Andrew's shoulder, Papa's strained face still in her mind. "I wish Papa hadn't married Carlota," she murmured, more to herself than to her husband.

Andrew gave a sleepy laugh. "Would you have liked anyone your father married?" he teased.

"It's not just jealousy," she protested. "How would you like it if I flirted with every man in sight?"

He turned and drew her as close into his arms as her bulk would allow. "You know the answer to that. Unfortunately you've found out how angry and unforgiving I can be."

In his deep voice, Julia heard a note of pain. She caressed his face, contrite for having recalled a shadow of their old estrangement to hurt him. She covered her remorse with a light tone. "You know that no one else

is worth flirting with when you're around." All her love
went into the kiss she offered him.

By the first of September, Julia knew she couldn't
possibly get any bigger, but the child inside her seemed
to have his own schedule. Finally, on an evening in
mid-September, her labor pains began. Ellen had been
staying with them for the past week, and Julia found
comfort in her mother-in-law's serene presence.

As dawn lightened the sky, Julia lay exhausted, her
newborn son cradled against her breast. Andrew, refusing to wait longer outside the room from which he'd
been excluded through the night, held her hand. In the
clear air all the bells on the *fazenda* vied with each
other to announce the birth. She and Andrew had
already decided on a name—Paul, for the grandfather
with whom Andrew had lived, and Francis for one of
Julia's dead brothers.

Paul Francis Langdon—it seemed wildly inappropri-
ate for such a tiny red-faced bundle, but Ellen had
already assured Julia he was large for a newborn. Best
of all, he screamed with the cry of a strong, healthy
infant. The memory of Sally's frail baby had haunted
Julia through her own pregnancy. Sleepily she touched
her husband's strong hand caressing her cheek, and felt
supremely blessed.

Andrew watched Julia's eyes droop, and gently he
reached for the tiny blanket-wrapped child. Moving
softly, he went to the window to look again at the
wrinkled face and the thatch of black curls. "My son,"
he whispered, and again, "My son." The world could
hardly hold more joy.

In the months that followed, Andrew's delight in his
son grew. Usually Paul was happy and smiling, though
he could scream lustily when he was hungry. Julia
claimed he looked just like his father, and he certainly

had the dark curly hair of all the Langdon men, but his eyes were his mother's golden brown. Maybe, Andrew hoped, next they'd have a red-headed girl with blue eyes.

To his delight, though Julia still wanted to know all about the running of the *fazenda*, she seemed content to discuss it with him and busy herself with the baby. That might not last, he realized, but for the present he enjoyed her preference for more usual female activities.

The *fazenda* thrived as well. Thanks in large part to the coffee sale, 1868 had been a very profitable year. Andrew signed a second contract for the 1869 coffee crop, and through the summer months of January and February, weather proved ideal for prospects of a large harvest. Andrew felt that he had everything he could want, except perhaps more children.

On a night in mid-March, rapping on the front door pulled Andrew awake, and as he rose and pulled on his trousers, he heard soft voices below. Julia asked sleepily, "What is it?" More alert, she said, "Is it Paul?"

"No—stay here." He lit a candle, but before he went down the stairs, he glanced briefly into the room next to theirs and saw his six-month-old son sleeping peacefully on his face, his rump slightly raised under the covers.

In the entrance hall Capitolino's candle lit the anxious face of Richard's groom. "Senhor Andrew, Senhora Ellen asks that you come right away. Seu Richard is ill."

Andrew turned and mounted the stairs, knowing Capitolino would have his horse saddled and ready by the time he'd dressed. In the bedroom, Julia sat up as he entered, her long hair tumbled around her bare shoulders.

"Richard is ill, and Ellen has sent for me," he told her as he pulled on a shirt and jacket.

"Oh, Andrew—do you want me to go with you?"

He stamped into his boots, then leaned over her to kiss her. "No. It's only a little after midnight. No point in getting Paul up in the middle of the night." He touched her breast teasingly. "And we can't take this away from him yet. I'll send a message later if you need to come."

He kissed her briefly, then raced down the stairs and out into the night, where his horse waited beside Richard's groom. Capitolino's sleepy grandson, holding a lantern, sat astride a small mare. Andrew touched his heels to his horse's side, and they started toward Richard's plantation.

Andrew curbed his impatience as they rode, knowing that trying to hurry in the darkness could result in injury to horses and riders. He tried not to worry about his father. Though he and Richard spoke now, he knew his father had never forgiven him for his interference. Just by talking to some of the advocates of republican government, Andrew knew he had in effect caused them to regard Richard suspiciously. Though he regretted hurting his father, he would do the same again, and still didn't understand how someone as shrewd as Richard could ever have harbored such insane plans.

When Andrew saw the lights from Richard's house, he risked a gallop over the last half-mile. Throwing his reins to the grooms, he bounded up the steps and found Ellen waiting at the door.

"Thank God, Andrew." She hugged him and they hurried up the stairs. "The doctor thinks Richard has had a mild stroke. We were . . . talking earlier, when Richard stopped, then swayed and fell. His face flushed almost red, and when I asked how he felt, he couldn't seem to answer. I had to get the servants to help him upstairs. Now he's in bed and resting, but his speech is confused and—"

A stroke! The word chilled Andrew. Had his actions in thwarting Richard's ambitions led to his father's illness? He put his arm around Ellen's shoulders. "Don't say more. We can talk later."

When Andrew reached the bed, Richard's eyes were closed in what appeared to be normal sleep. Andrew stared at the shadows over the deep-set eyes and bearded face.

"He'll sleep for some time, I believe," the doctor observed. "I'll be here with him, and perhaps you could stay with Senhora Ellen. She is greatly upset."

"Yes, of course," Andrew agreed. He led Ellen from the room and down the stairs to the small salon, where he found a decanter of brandy. Pouring two glasses, he gave her one. She smiled faintly at him before sinking down on a brocade-covered sofa and taking a sip.

"Ellen . . ." He stopped and had to clear his throat. "I may have contributed to this illness of Father's. He's never forgiven what he sees as my interference."

"Oh, Andrew!" She put her glass down on a dainty cherrywood table with a shaky hand. "You mustn't blame yourself. If anyone is responsible, it's I."

"You! How could that be?"

She rose and walked nervously around the room, her full skirts swinging around her plump figure. "No, Andrew—don't get up. I just can't sit right now. Did Julia tell you about my son and grandchildren?"

"Yes."

"Since Paul arrived, I've felt I could hardly stand not seeing them, and I decided I must go to England. My first husband died recently, and I think his family won't prevent my visiting."

She returned to rest her hand on Andrew's shoulder.

"Richard is opposed to the idea. He says the scandal might not have been forgotten, that I might be badly treated. Really, I think he's jealous of any attachment I might have to anyone besides him."

"Father—jealous of your grandchildren?"

The beginning of a smile curved her lips. "Yes. After all, they're my family by another man. You Langdon men all feel intensely—whether it's love or jealousy."

"You're right," Andrew admitted, and thought of the emotions which had torn him at even the possibility of Julia's interest in Roberto.

Ellen sat and took another sip of brandy. When she put it down, Andrew saw that her hands were trembling again. He reached across and took them, holding them gently. "But how could this have caused Father's stroke?"

"Today I received a letter from the theatrical manager with whom I originally came to Brazil. He expects to be in Rio soon and wants to see me. He's offered me a job in England, and I'd travel with him. Tonight I told Richard that if he didn't agree for me to go, I would go to England anyway. He became very angry . . ."

Tears overflowed her eyes, and she added in a whisper, "It was right after that—the stroke . . ." Andrew put an arm around her shoulders, offering comfort to this special woman.

Julia, with Paul and Florella, the nursemaid, arrived in the early afternoon the next day. By then a physician who had been summoned from São Paulo had confirmed the *fazenda* doctor's diagnosis of a stroke and warned Ellen and Andrew that Richard would need several months—perhaps a year—without responsibilities. After Julia nursed Paul and left him in the care of the nursemaid, Andrew explained to Julia what Ellen had told him. When the physician left, the two women and Andrew met in Richard's office.

Julia hugged Ellen close. "Dear Ellen, what a difficult time for you as well as Richard. What will you do about England?"

Though Ellen's eyes had circles of fatigue, she spoke serenely. "Of course I can't go now, with Richard ill and the plantation to be looked after."

"I can divide my time between the two *fazendas*," Andrew offered.

She smiled, but said firmly, "Thank you, Andrew, but I can't agree to that. Richard probably would feel upset if you were supervising. As we discussed last night, he's still very sensitive about the part he thinks you played in his affairs. Even if that weren't true, it's not fair to you, or to Julia and Paul, for you to spend so much of your time away from home."

"But, Ellen, Father will need someone here." He glanced at his wife. "Julia did very well while I was away, but even so, she couldn't manage alone."

A suggestion of the sparkle which usually animated Ellen's face returned. "And you're too polite to tell me I'm not as capable as Julia. But I have in mind the same solution as when you were in Paraguay. I'll ask Roberto to take over the management here while Richard recovers."

Julia's stomach tightened with apprehension at the thought of Roberto nearby again, and then she felt ashamed. Roberto had kept his word and said nothing to reveal the intimacy which had developed between them. If he had the full-time supervision of his father's lands, he'd be too busy to visit their *fazenda*, and she and Andrew seldom came here. But her heart beat too rapidly as she looked at her husband.

He frowned, then said slowly, "Of course—that's the

logical thing to do, and he did very well when he acted
as our overseer. Do you think you can locate him?"

"Yes," Ellen replied. "He's in Santos. I can send a
message today, and he should receive it day after tomorrow. Or would it be better for you to write a note to
him?"

Andrew's face was too carefully expressionless as he
said, "No, Ellen. You should send the message on
Father's behalf. It would probably be better if Julia and
I went home before he arrived—let him take over
without an older brother around."

Not until the next day, when Andrew and Julia were
on their way home, did Julia have a chance to bring up
what she had been thinking about. They rode the horses
while Capitolino drove the carriage; Paul slept on the
seat between the nursemaid and the groom.

Feeling she must know how Andrew felt toward Roberto now, Julia nudged her horse closer to him and
asked, "Andrew, does it bother you that Roberto will be
managing your father's property?"

The clop of their horses' hooves mingled with the
creak of the wheels behind them. When Andrew didn't
respond, she regretted her words. "Maybe I shouldn't
have asked."

"No, it's all right," her husband reasssured her. "I'm
trying to answer you honestly. I'd like to be able to say
it doesn't bother me. I appreciate what Roberto did
while I was gone, and the competence he displayed.
But things between us have never been easy. It's as if
we've been in some kind of contest most of our adult
lives."

He was looking straight ahead, and the line of his
straight nose and strong mouth and jaw seemed more
forceful to Julia than usual. "When he's not around, I
don't think about him, but when we're together, the

competition seems to begin again. I'd like to regard him as you do James, but it doesn't seem likely."

When he turned and looked at her, he smiled, and his sensual mouth and inviting eyes made her long to be alone with him in their room. "Under the circumstances, we probably won't see him or Father much. But with you and Paul—and the children we could go home and work on having—I don't need other family."

At his loving look, Julia determined to banish the anxiety the prospect of Roberto's return had aroused. She and Andrew had been so happy for over a year. Their marriage had a firm foundation, one that wouldn't easily be shaken.

Roberto leaned back wearily in the chair in Richard's office. He'd been at his father's *fazenda* for a week now, and he hadn't adjusted to the change from his indolent life in Santos. At this hour he'd have been playing cards or preparing to bed either the woman who was keeping him or someone else. He certainly wouldn't have been going over account books. But it didn't feel bad to be here.

He yawned and started to pour himself a glass from the decanter of *cachaça* on the bottom bookshelf, then stopped. For the first time in over a year he didn't feel like drinking. He smiled wryly. If he weren't careful he'd be so respectable none of his friends would know him.

Putting a marker in the account book, he closed it and blew out the lamp. Soft moonlight silvered the floorboards as he started along the hall to his room, then impulsively turned and went out the front doors.

A cool breeze reminded him that summer was ending, and by the time he found his way around this plantation again, he'd be into the coffee harvest. He'd be busier than he'd been since the first days of working as Julia's overseer.

Roberto was pleased that he'd stayed in Santos and not gone to Rio, since it had been easier to reach him. The realization of why he'd stayed in the port city instead of choosing the more sophisticated pleasures of the capital forced itself to the surface of his mind. Though he'd cursed himself for a fool, he hadn't been able to go farther away from Julia. For years he'd lived only for himself, cared for no woman except to satisfy their mutual lusts—and then fallen in love with his sister-in-law.

He looked along the road that led toward his brother's home, and the images he'd been trying to blot out flooded his mind. Julia asleep, her hair fanning out over the pillow. Her body with its high breasts, just the right size for his hand, and her taut belly with the faint scar which led to the triangle of curls.

He groaned and closed his eyes as if to shut out the picture, because he knew that her husband lay beside her, and nearby—perhaps in the next room—an even more forbidden image formed in his mind. It was an image without a face, because he'd never seen the child, had tried never to think of him—because to think meant more pain than Roberto was sure he could stand.

Despite the cool night, he could feel sweat beading on his forehead. Maybe he would decide to go back and get that drink now he had earlier resisted. Halfway to the office, he stopped. Drinking an ocean of whiskey in Santos hadn't helped, and it wouldn't do any good now. He had to forget, and someday he wouldn't care that Julia's son might be his instead of Andrew's. But, God—let that day come soon.

17

By late April the bright red coffee berries gave arrogant notice that it was time for the fall harvest, and Julia couldn't resist riding out to the fields. As she watched the workers strip the berries into baskets, she felt her old restlessness returning. She couldn't carry the heavy sacks of beans on her head as could these women and men, but she knew how to do the planning and solve the problems of making their labor profitable. Andrew's exhausting schedule prohibited her from talking to him then about her ideas, but she decided that when the mules started toward Santos laden with their sacks of dried and hulled beans, she would raise the subject of her activities.

But when the harvests finally ended, Paul fretted with a childhood fever which kept Julia absorbed in caring for him. Not until an afternoon in early July did she find a good opportunity to tell her husband what she had been considering. Andrew lay on the braided rug in the small sitting room; Paul, tired from tussling with his father, slept beside the tall man he came to resemble more each day.

"Andrew, I want to discuss something with you."

His answering "Hmmm?" sounded little more awake than his son.

She picked up the sleeping child and called Florella. When the black nursemaid had taken Paul, Julia closed the door and turned to find Andrew still lying on the floor, his head resting on his crossed arms.

"It must be something serious," he teased. "Are you planning to join me here? It's a little hard, but soon it wouldn't be the only thing that way."

She looked down at him, at the muscular yet graceful body, and the sensual eyes which invited her to forget everything but him. Half-irritated and half-aroused, she nudged him with her foot. "Sometimes I think you have only two things on your mind—raising coffee and making love."

He sat up and pulled her down onto his lap with one hand and slid the other under her skirt and up her thigh. "I like to plant both the land and you."

She pushed aside the fingers which had already opened two buttons at her neck. "Andrew, stop. I want you to listen to me."

"I am listening," he murmured as he stroked her thigh with one hand and brushed her nipple through her light wool dress with the other.

Pushing against him so forcefully that he fell back on the rug, she scrambled to her feet. She glared down at him. "You're not listening!" To her amazement, she felt tears begin to gather. "This is important to me."

He rose from the floor and pulled her to the settee, then sat beside her. "Sorry, love. Tell me now. I promise to pay strict attention."

"Andrew, I would like to manage the cotton crop."

She saw surprise, then understanding mixed with disappointment in the strong face, before he asked, "Why?"

"Because—as you've always known—that's the kind of work I love. You have only a small part of the land in cotton, so it wouldn't take all my time, and though I don't know much about wheat or cattle, I do know about cotton from the years at . . . Hundred Oaks." Out of childhood habit, she had almost said "home."

He looked at her for what seemed a long time before he responded. "What about more children? Pray God nothing happens to Paul, but children don't always survive." He touched her chin and gave her a part-teasing, part-serious look. "When will we have that red-headed, blue-eyed girl?"

"I want more children too," she defended herself, "but we were discussing the cotton crop."

He smiled and pulled her into his arms. "How can I refuse? You know I want you to be happy."

"And you also know I can do a good job with the crop, or you wouldn't agree, no matter how happy it makes me," she insisted.

"Yes, that's true."

When he finished kissing her, she said, "After Paul's first birthday in September I'll quit using the sponge when we make love. But," she reminded him, "we didn't conceive him until we'd been married a year and a half, and you'd been in Paraguay. Maybe I just don't get pregnant easily."

He held her close in his arms. "I'm not willing to be away for almost six months ahead of time to ensure each child. Perhaps Scizira could get us another charm."

His hand found her buttons again, and this time she didn't protest. He had opened the bodice down far enough to reach one breast, when a knock and Capitolino's voice interrupted. "Seu Andrew, excuse me, Senhor Pedro wishes to speak to you."

Andrew swore softly in Portuguese and set Julia on

her feet. "Very well, tell him I'll see him in the study,"
then muttered in her ear, "Go get your damned sponge.
I'll be upstairs as soon as possible."

Julia turned her back to the door to refasten the
buttons, smiling at the impatient sound of his footsteps
leaving the room. Before her marriage she would have
been shocked by the idea of discussing contraception
with her husband. How naive she had been then. On
the other hand, from women's gossip she knew that
many wives never talked to their husbands of their
intimate life and knew nothing of birth control.

After the first year of marriage, when words had been
so difficult between them, and since they'd made up
their terrible quarrel, Julia had been honest with Andrew about all aspects of their life—except the one
thing she'd resolved she could never tell him.

She went to the window and looked out toward the
hills which separated Andrew's land from his father's.
Since Roberto had taken over managing Richard's *fazenda*, he hadn't come to see Andrew and Julia. The
few times they'd ridden over to see Richard and Ellen,
Roberto hadn't appeared. Richard had improved more
rapidly than the doctor had first feared, but his illness
still limited his activities, and Roberto worked long
hours.

Julia first thought he might be intentionally avoiding
her. Gossip repeated by the servants told of a woman
from São Paulo established in a small building near the
senezala, so maybe, Julia realized, he simply didn't care
about her any longer.

In September a family gathering would celebrate Paul's
first birthday, and Roberto would certainly attend. Julia
didn't know how she felt about the prospect of seeing
him. She was only sure she was relieved by his disinter-
est, and intensely grateful for his silence.

*   *   *

To Julia's surprise, William and Carlota arrived before noon on Paul's first birthday. Her father greeted Julia and his grandson with his old exuberance, and he looked delighted as he held out his arms to catch Paul's wavering steps. The one-year-old had just discovered the pleasures of climbing the stairs, and William patiently held the small hand for countless trips up and down. Carlota watched with evident boredom and retreated to the small dining room for coffee. When Andrew joined them, Carlota brought out her seductive smiles, but William appeared not to notice. Well, thought Julia, Papa has made some changes.

The perfume from blossoms in the orangery saturated the September spring air, and Julia had a table set up on the terrace for the midday meal. She had just checked the arrangements when she heard the rattle of carriage wheels and the stamp of hooves. That would be the arrivals from the other Langdon *fazenda*, and though she had prepared herself for this meeting, she found her heart racing.

By the time she reached the front entrance, Ellen was standing on one side as Andrew and Capitolino helped Richard from the open carriage. When Richard was on his feet, he motioned to Ellen, who handed him a stout cane. Impatiently he pushed Capitolino's hand away, and leaning on Andrew, made his way inside. Ellen gave Julia a hurried kiss and followed.

In her surprise at watching Richard accept help from Andrew, his "traitorous" son, Julia had noticed only the scene between them. Behind her she heard the familiar jaunty voice. "Julia . . . hello."

She almost let a betraying hand clutch her throat before she turned. Roberto stood easily, his only motion a gentle tapping of his riding crop against his leg.

He looked thinner than she remembered, the lines of his face leaner and more intense. Then he smiled, and she recognized the carefree expression that she associated with him. Relief let her match his lighthearted manner.

She held out her hand to him. "We're so glad you could take time to help us celebrate today."

Roberto bowed over her hand. "I couldn't miss congratulating you on the birthday of your son."

Until he saw her, Roberto had almost convinced himself he was recovering from the madness of loving Julia. That conviction had enhanced the charms of the *mameluca*, the part-Indian woman he'd installed on Richard's *fazenda*. The pleasures he'd enjoyed with her last night had, he'd been sure, fortified him against Julia's charms. But as he followed Julia into the main salon, trying not to watch the way the small bustle swayed with the motion of her hips, he knew he'd been fooling himself.

It wasn't Julia's beauty which transfixed him, for he saw her with such an inner vision that he wasn't even sure she would look as exquisite to anyone else. And though images of her body invaded his mind, more than lust caused the pain he felt at the futility of those pictures. He wanted to make love to her, but also to take care of her, to live with her for all their lives.

He heard a happy chortle and saw William carrying a black-haired child into the room. Slowly he crossed to them, watching the chubby hand clutch his grandfather's neck. "This must be my small nephew," he said.

William's eyes sparkled, and he laughed. "Big enough to wear you out, if you let him lure you to the stairs. Would you like to hold him?"

"Oh no," Roberto assured William, "he looks too happy with you."

As if to contradict anyone else's judgment of his desires, Paul immediately squirmed protestingly. William set him on the floor, and he stood, holding William's pants leg, staring up at the tall man who looked so much like his father.

Mesmerized by Julia's eyes in the Langdon face, Roberto crouched before the child. Paul pointed at him and said, "Ba-ba."

Momentarily Roberto feared he couldn't speak, but then he said, pleased at his casual tone, "I don't know what you're saying, but I'm your Uncle Roberto."

"Ba-ba is what he calls Andrew," William explained, "and you look so much like your brother, he must think the name fits you also."

Pain knifed through Roberto, but he denied it and laughed. "Well, I've been taken for Andrew before."

Julia's special rose fragrance told him she had joined them even before she picked up her son. After William excused himself and went outside, Julia said, "Paul doesn't have much of a vocabulary now, but he'll soon learn to call you Uncle Roberto."

Roberto wanted to rail at her, refuse the title, but he only responded lightly, "He probably won't see enough of me to remember the name."

Julia hesitated, so briefly that were he not tuned to every nuance of her, Roberto wouldn't have noticed. She smiled and said, "We hope that's not so."

Paul leaned his head against his mother's neck and stuck his thumb in his mouth. He still looked at Roberto, but with droopy eyes.

Reaching for protection, Roberto lied, "I don't care greatly for children—maybe because I've never been around them much. And keeping ahead of Richard's complaints doesn't leave me time for anything else."

Looking at the two faces, the sleepy child and the

serene mother, Roberto suddenly found the bitter taste of resentment in his mouth. He didn't expect her to say, "Thank you, Roberto, for not breathing your possible claim to my beautiful son," or even, "I understand your pain," but he felt she must know what his silence cost him, and he wanted her to give him some tiny indication of gratitude. Instead, though no one watched, she just looked at him politely, as if he had never been more to her than the frivolous companion he pretended.

"Julia," William called from the door to the terrace, "Ellen and Richard are seated out here and would appreciate your bringing Paul to see them before he falls asleep."

As Julia smiled and moved off, Roberto felt words choking him, but he clamped them inside. He joined William and asked, just like one of the planters he'd always derided, "How is the spring work going for you this year, Mr. Rayford?"

During the meal and for the two hours afterward he felt he must stay, Roberto managed to avoid talking to Julia alone again. He also pretended concern about William's affairs and, to his surprise, found that world coffee prices seemed more interesting than he'd ever thought them before. But when the nursemaid brought a newly awakened Paul out to the terrace, Roberto decided to leave, alleging the deliberately vague excuse of "a problem to check on."

"What problem?" Richard asked. His hesitant speech didn't obliterate his customary arrogance.

"Richard, Roberto doesn't need to explain." Ellen put her hand soothingly on Richard's arm, but he shrugged it off impatiently.

William smiled as if he understood the reason for Roberto's departure, and leaned across to say softly to

Richard, "We were young men once, too." Richard subsided at the suggestion the "problem" was female.

Andrew, escorting his brother to the front entrance, realized that today he hadn't felt the subtle competition that usually underlay meetings with Roberto. Working for his father couldn't be easy, he knew, and he felt a new sympathy for his younger brother. While they waited for a groom to bring Roberto's horse, Andrew asked, "How are you and Father getting along? He can be difficult."

Roberto grinned. "Not 'can be.' Richard *is* difficult. When Ellen can't keep him inside any longer, we'll probably kill each other. But," he admitted, "even so I like what I'm doing. Probably crazy. If he weren't sick, Richard wouldn't trust me with taking care of the chickenhouse."

Andrew heard the tension in Roberto's voice. Mockery? Or bitterness? He watched Roberto swing up into his saddle and for almost the first time in years wanted to say something "brotherly." A little uncomfortable with these new feelings, he remarked, "In a way you're working for yourself, because someday the land will be yours. Thanks to my grandfather's money, I have my own property."

Roberto felt a confusing rush of pleasure at his brother's words. Andrew wasn't mentioning all the work that had gone into enlarging his holdings far beyond his inheritance, an effort that until recently Roberto hadn't been willing to make. But Richard's lands from his Brazilian marriage were a large portion of his present *fazenda*, and Andrew was suggesting that Roberto was earning a position equal to his. Despite his envy of Andrew and the pain of accepting Paul as Andrew's son, Roberto realized how much he liked the idea that his brother might admire him. With a heart lighter than anytime since he'd arrived at the birthday celebration, he raised his riding crop in salute and cantered away.

Julia, coming out in time to watch Roberto ride off, took her husband's arm. "I'm sorry—Paul delayed me. I didn't get to say good-bye."

Andrew smiled down at her. "You look happy."

"Yes, I am," she agreed, and knew Roberto had helped make her happy by treating her so casually. After all, she thought, that one afternoon was so long ago now. Though she hoped she and Roberto would always be friends, nothing remained of that intimacy to tie them together except a memory which must have faded as much for him as for her. She pulled Andrew's face down and kissed him before they went back to their son's party.

Through the spring and early summer months of November and December, Julia supervised the cotton crop, finding in the remembered tasks a special happiness, as if Hundred Oaks had in a small way been recreated here in Brazil. She and Andrew occasionally quarreled—with their mutual pride, she supposed they always would—but they tried not to wound each other, and reconciliations soon followed. Paul delighted both of them, growing from baby toward small boy. Julia was not yet pregnant again, and although she saw Andrew's disappointment each month, she didn't want anything to change her present happiness.

Andrew, however, longed for more children, and as he rode toward his father's house on a hot January afternoon, he wondered whether it was the woman or the man or just chance which caused some women to have a child each year.

Shrugging off the question he couldn't answer, he thought of his father and his brother. Though he hadn't completely changed his opinion of Roberto, Andrew had come to admire and like him more than he would ever have expected several years ago. The lands were prospering under Roberto's management, and it amazed him that Roberto had accomplished this while tolerating his father's overbearing manner and temper.

Andrew glanced at the sun and realized the afternoon was half over and he was still three-quarters of an hour away from Richard's house. He nudged his horse to a faster pace.

A gust of wind sent a whirl of red dust around Roberto's boots as he walked from the stables to the big house. He glanced up at the brilliantly clear sky and frowned; no rain had fallen for several days. He hoped 1870 wouldn't be a dry year.

Ordinarily he would still be out in the fields, but this afternoon he needed to speak to his father about the cattle. Three of the cattle were sick, and though Roberto planned to contact a new veterinarian in São Paulo, he knew Richard would want to think he'd made the decision.

Since his father's stroke Roberto had worked ceaselessly, surprised by his own energy. As Richard improved and became more autocratic, demanding an accounting of his son's activities, Roberto found he could accede to or ignore his father's wishes without more than an occasional loss of temper. Gradually, he felt confident, his father was coming to respect his abilities.

With work absorbing almost all of his time, he hadn't seen Julia or Paul since September, and he thought he had successfully buried his feeling about them. He'd chosen, however, to avoid the Christmas family gathering by going to São Paulo to visit cousins with whom he used to spend many hours drinking. But he found their company bored him, and he'd returned to the *fazenda* early the following morning, almost as astonished by the changes in himself as were his relatives.

This afternoon he half-expected to see Andrew's horse in the stable since it was time for a visit, but obviously his brother hadn't arrived. The new ease between the two brothers pleased Roberto. He knew that some of his old envy of Andrew remained, but he no longer wanted to goad his brother at every opportunity. He laughed at himself—at the reformed and virtuous brother and son—but he didn't jeer at the image as he once would have.

Grinning at his own thoughts, he strode along the hall to Richard's office and was halfway through the door before he heard Richard's angry voice.

"We settled this last year. You are not going to England."

Roberto stopped at the sight of his father, hands clenched, face distorted, facing an equally infuriated Ellen. Though she spoke more softly, her words sounded emphatic. "No, it was not settled, only postponed. You are well enough to accompany me if you wish, but if you do not, I am going anyway."

His first impulse was to back out of the room, but when he saw Richard's clenched fists, Roberto moved across the room to stand beside Ellen. Ignoring him, Richard thundered, "I forbid it."

"You cannot. But we don't have to quarrel—you can go with me."

Alarmed by the color in his father's face, Roberto said, "Richard—"

Richard snarled at Roberto, "Get out—this doesn't concern you."

"Yes, it does," Ellen declared, sounding more composed now. "Roberto can manage everything here perfectly well while you go with me, just as he has been doing."

"Yes," Roberto affirmed, "I'll be glad to take care of the work."

The red color in Richard's face changed to white, and his rage turned from his wife to his son. "Yes, you'd like that—to get your hands on my land. Well, you won't. If you want land, get your own, if you're man enough. Worthless—that's what you've always been."

Roberto felt as if someone had clubbed him in the stomach. At the unfairness of his father's charge, an answering fury exploded inside him. "My sweat has been worth a lot to you this year," he ground out. "And part of this *fazenda* was my mother's land."

Richard took two steps forward until he was directly in front of Roberto and snarled, "But it won't be yours. Everything here goes to Andrew."

Years of envy at the favoritism shown his older brother returned to envelope Roberto in choking bitterness. Only some residue of sanity kept his hands from his father's throat. Through a red haze he heard Ellen's horrified voice. "Richard, you don't mean that."

Past his murderous rage Roberto grated, "Yes he does. Andrew—always everything for Andrew."

"And why not?" Richard shouted. "He's proved himself—and he's given me a grandson to carry on my name. If you have any sons, they're bastards."

Roberto felt as if all the blood in his body had turned to fire, yet when he spoke his words came out like daggers of ice. "And what if the grandchild you so proudly call Andrew's son is one of those bastards?"

After one shocked gasp from Ellen, silence hung between them, as if Roberto's question had created an unbreachable void. Then from behind them a voice as

cold as Roberto's ordered, "You will retract your words."
Andrew, his eyes like granite, stood in the doorway.

The anguish and rage that filled Roberto blocked out
rational thought. Andrew and Richard—even Julia and
her child—seemed equally his enemies. "No, I won't
change anything I said." He was shaking now. "Paul
could as easily be my son as yours."

Andrew crossed the room in one bound and seized
Roberto by the shoulder, his low voice more deadly
than a shout. "You son of a bitch—you'll do anything to
hurt me. You despicable liar."

Roberto threw off the hand, his muscles so tight with
fury he felt they would break. "You're so sure—always—
of everything. You don't have to believe me. Ask Julia."

"I wouldn't insult her by asking."

The scorn and loathing in Andrew's words felt like
knife wounds in Roberto's flesh. Cauterizing hatred
swept him. "Are you afraid that your beautiful wife with
that scar along her belly that ends at—"

Andrew's fist smashed into Roberto's jaw at the same
moment that Ellen screamed. Roberto rocked back,
and then he leapt for Andrew. Dimly he felt the edge of
a table and heard a crash and the crack of splintering
wood as he and Andrew fell sideways, clawing at each
other. They rolled together, straining, hitting. He felt
Andrew's hands at his throat, squeezing, cutting off his
air, and he lashed out, his fist striking against flesh.

Dimly he heard Ellen's hysterical cry, "My God. My
God. Anselmo . . . stop them."

The vise around his throat loosened, then was gone.
Black hands dragged him to a sitting position, and he
saw two more servants pulling Andrew away. Painful
breaths forced air into his heaving lungs, and he struggled to his feet.

Blood trickled from the edge of Andrew's mouth, and

Roberto felt a stinging below one eye and blood seeping from his nose. Richard sagged in a chair, his face white and old.

Her voice trembling, Ellen told the blacks, "You may go."

When they left, Andrew spoke, his voice rasping with deadly calm. "Because you're my brother, I won't kill you. But that's the only reason." He turned and left.

Richard straightened and said shakily, "Roberto—"

Furiously Ellen rounded on him. "Don't say anything. You've done too much harm already." She began to weep, and between sobs she gasped, "Roberto, how could you? How could you?"

Despair settled in Roberto's heart so black it could encompass all the misery of the world.

At the last rise before reaching home, Andrew reined in his lathered horse. He must walk the rest of the way to cool the heated animal, and to tame, if possible, the chaos of his thoughts. Through his mad ride home he had held himself in check, tried to keep Roberto's accusation at bay. Once before he had judged Julia without listening to her. He would not do that again.

He'd arrived to hear Ellen's suggestion that Richard go with her to England, Roberto's agreement, and then his father's cruel response. He could force himself to understand the rage both men felt—Richard at what he would see as Ellen's betrayal, and Roberto at his father's rejection. Briefly he thought of his father's gray face and the possibility of another stroke, but right now he couldn't care. Richard had unfairly attacked Roberto, and Roberto had responded. Andrew wanted to believe Roberto had lied, but he couldn't forget the sound of truth in his brother's voice.

Unwillingly he remembered that night at the Rayfords'
almost four years ago, when he'd found Julia in his
room. She'd never explained the circumstances, and in
the happiness of their marriage, he'd almost forgotten.
Had she deceived him then, and did she still?

The question seared his soul: was Paul his son, or
Roberto's? He must ask Julia, yet the thought raised
such anguish that only iron control kept Andrew from
forcing his mount to a more punishing pace. But steely
resolution couldn't keep Roberto's last words from Andrew's mind, and he hadn't been able to escape a
second torturing question: how did Roberto know about
Julia's scar?

Another thought haunted him. Julia's only pregnancy
had followed his absence. Lele had never conceived by
him, and though he'd taken precautions with her, preg-
nancies often occurred anyway. Nor had any other of
the women he'd bedded over the years charged him
with fathering a child. Did this mean Julia had not
become pregnant earlier in their marriage because of
some lack in him? He cut off his speculations and
concentrated on getting home.

He'd stopped at the spring and washed the blood
from his hands and mouth, but he knew the side of his
face must be swollen, as was his left hand. His shirt
gaped from a tear near the left shoulder and clung to
his sweat-drenched chest and back. Everyone would
know immediately something had happened, but by the
time an account of the fight reached the servants here,
he and Julia could present a united front to gossip.

Slowly he started down toward the buildings and
trees where the last of the twilight shrouded the dying
colors. Agonizing doubts accompanied him, of whether
he and Julia would be united after they talked. God, he
prayed so.

*   *   *

Julia made the last entry in her cotton ledger and returned it to the desk drawer reserved for her papers. A partly written letter to James lay on top of a stack of envelopes. Tomorrow she would finish it and begin a letter to Purity and Nathan in San Francisco. Guiltily she chided herself for not writing to Purity more often. After more than a year in California, her cousin still longed for Philadelphia, though Nathan's hurried notes at the end of the letters sounded excited and happy.

I'm selfish, thought Julia as she climbed the stairs to the bedroom, because I know how miserable homesickness can be and I should try to comfort Purity. Yet since Andrew was visiting Richard, Julia could have the evening to herself and appreciate the luxury of being alone. Andrew might return by dark, but sometimes he spent the night at his father's house. The nursemaid had put Paul to bed after Julia read him a story, and he was asleep by now.

Feeling almost like a child herself, she closed the bedroom door behind her. Quickly she undressed and put on a pale yellow negligee. After she loosened and brushed her hair, she picked up Charles Dickens' latest book, *Our Mutual Friend*, from the small bookstand in the corner of the room, lit the kerosene lamp on the table beside the bed, and settled herself against the pillows.

Before she had more than opened her book, she recognized Andrew's footsteps in the hall. She waited for the doorknob to turn, but the steps stopped before reaching the bedroom, and she heard another door opening. He must have gone into Paul's room. She rose and went barefoot into the hall and to the open nursery door.

Beside a hammock where Paul slept, Andrew stood,

holding a branched candlestick with two candles. For a moment she watched, savoring the picture of the tall man leaning over the child whose face was already taking on the strong contours of his father's jaw and mouth. Then Andrew made a soft sound, almost like a groan, and straightened, and she saw that the right side of his face was swollen. At her gasp of alarm, he turned, and the anguished look in his eyes frightened her even more.

"Andrew, what's wrong? What happened?"

Without answering he blew out the candles and put down the candelabrum. The waxy odor drifted in the air between them. Silently he crossed the room and waited while she preceded him into the hall. His hand on her elbow felt icy as he guided her inside their room and shut the door behind him.

In the brighter light she could see a cut at the corner of his mouth as well as the swollen area along his cheekbone. Dried blood stained the front of his shirt. "Andrew, you must tell me. Did you have an accident? I'll get something—" She started toward the washstand, but his voice, harsh and flat, stopped her.

"Is Paul my son?"

Bewildered, she turned back toward him, not believing she had heard him correctly. "What do you mean?"

The light from the lantern struck his face from the side, illuminating one eye and the cut on his mouth, shadowing the other as if he were concealing some terrible dark side of himself. He took two steps toward her, and she could see his chest rise and fall with his rapid breathing. "Is Paul my son?"

His question didn't make sense, but his tone, harsh and implacable, created an icy pool of fear within her. "Of course he's your son. I don't understand." She could hear her voice rising hysterically. "*You must tell me*. What has happened? Why do you ask me that?"

"Because Roberto says Paul could be his son instead of mine."

Understanding blazed through Julia's mind like lightning over a nightmare's landscape. She strangled on a cry and covered her mouth. Because she knew the truth, it had never occurred to her that Roberto might think he could have fathered Paul. Terror washed over her, and she held out her hands to Andrew. "No . . . no. It's not true. Paul is your son—our son."

He didn't take her hands, and she saw his body quiver, as if all his muscles had tightened. "Why would Roberto say . . . think it?"

The guilt and shame of that long-ago afternoon silenced her, and in Andrew's hardening face she saw her world shattering.

The hope which Andrew had kept alive on the ride home died to bitter ashes as he watched Julia's stricken eyes and mouth. Her hair floated around her head, and in the light from the lantern he could see the dark shadows of her nipples and the patch of pubic hair through the thin robe. He thought of the marking across her abdomen which he'd traced so many times with his lips. Grimly he probed his own wounds. "How did he know about your scar?"

Her eyes—those sherry-colored eyes he loved so much—grew dark and large. When she finally spoke, each word seemed jerked out of her. "It was a long time ago—when we'd quarreled, and you stayed in Rio. The day of Scizira's wedding." She moistened her lips, and desperately he waited for her to offer some miracle that would prevent the admission he was demanding. "We—Roberto and I—had both been drinking, and we were alone . . ."

She stopped. Tortured, he guarded himself against her beseeching eyes. "Where? Where were you?"

364   *Barbara Keller*

"Here."

He tried to ignore the picture she created, but it was printed on his vision, so that Roberto was in the room with them—perhaps would always be with them. He could see tears in her eyes, yet he couldn't let himself comfort her. Julia's words stumbled on, dragging them both toward disaster. "We started to make love, but I realized what we were doing and how much I loved you and I stopped. Nothing more happened. You must believe me."

"Nothing *more!*" He clamped his lips against the obscenities his mind wanted to vent, and said hoarsely, "If nothing more happened, why does he think Paul could be his child?"

Her face flushed red, and Andrew's heart plummeted, the last cold ashes of hope destroyed. Pain rushed into the void in his chest, and because the pain was unbearable, anger began to surround it, like warriors guarding a too vulnerable castle. She twisted her hands together, and finally replied, but so low he could barely hear, "He'd been drinking, and at the last . . . Oh, can't you guess? Must I tell you?"

"Yes, you must."

From Andrew's voice Julia knew her explanation was hopeless. Anger had destroyed his willingness to listen and believe her. Shame and embarrassment made her voice wooden as doggedly she continued, "At the last I pulled away . . . and he came before . . . before he was actually . . . inside." Her last word choked on the sobs rising in her throat. "And then he passed out."

Andrew's voice cut cruelly through her beginning tears. "But he didn't know this sordid ending to your interlude?"

An answering bitterness began to replace her guilt. The scorn in his voice, as well as his words, added to the humiliation she already felt. The telltale nausea that accompanied rage began in her stomach. "No, he was too drunk—he didn't remember."

"And you didn't explain?"

She pushed the hair away from her face and stiffened her back. They had become enemies now. "It seemed important to him to think we'd . . . I couldn't tell him."

His fury erupted. "Important to him! But when I came back like a lovesick calf, begging your forgiveness, that wasn't important enough to be honest with me."

For a moment the rush of Julia's blood blotted out speech and sound so that she could only stare at him wordlessly. Then she spat, "And how would you have acted if I'd told you then? Just like now?"

His voice dropped to icy coldness. "I wouldn't have believed you any more then than I do now. Do you think I'm an idiot, to accept such a story?"

"Yes . . . no," she cried. "I haven't lied to you. I didn't tell you, but I haven't lied."

He seized her shoulders, holding her in a relentless grip. "And that night on your father's *fazenda* when you came to my room. Did you ever tell me the truth about that?"

Stricken, she couldn't answer. It was so long ago she'd forgotten that once she'd feared to tell Andrew why she'd been in his room, to reveal James's vulnerabilities. Andrew released her and stepped back, contempt in his eyes and rock-hard voice. "We've had a marriage that began with a lie—and how many since? And now this. I was a fool to believe in you. Never again."

"But . . . Paul . . ."

"Don't worry—he's not to blame for his mother . . . even if the identity of his father is questionable."

He turned and went to the door. At the sight of his

implacable stride, Julia's fury burst. "I know I was wrong, but does that mean everything else we've shared doesn't count? Because of one incident, does all the rest of our marriage mean nothing?"

He stopped, but he didn't look at her. "This isn't just 'one incident.' Without trust we don't have a marriage."

The door closed behind him, and Julia knew he was shutting her out of his life.

18

Spreading trees and large ferns crowded both sides of the road that zigzagged down the escarpment from São Paulo to Santos. The air of the drier plateau had held the autumn chill of May, but it had given way to more tropical warmth. The carriage gave a sudden lurch, throwing Julia sideways against Ellen. Straightening up, Julia asked, "Are you all right?"

"As well as I'll ever be until we get to Santos," Ellen responded with uncharacteristic irritation.

"But at least you're not on horseback," Julia offered sympathetically.

Ellen shuddered. "Thank God. I'd never get to England if I had to start out on one of those beasts. At least I don't get seasick." She closed her eyes and leaned her head against a pillow in the corner of the coach.

Julia's thoughts returned painfully to the *fazenda*. Her existence now seemed like a Chinese puzzle with carved pieces of wood fitting together to form one large cube. She still had the separate parts, but she couldn't match them to make a whole life because the piece which had become the center was missing. Andrew had shut her out of his life.

They still shared the house and sometimes the evening meal, but not a bed. Andrew had moved into a room at the opposite end of the house. In the four months since he had closed their bedroom door behind him, they had attended a few uncomfortable social gatherings together, but otherwise they led separate lives. He didn't even discuss her management of the cotton with her, as if it weren't important enough to warrant the contact joint decisions would require.

She had tried twice to talk to him. The first time he'd appeared to listen, but the clenched muscles along his jaw said he wasn't truly hearing her. After agonizing nights when remorse for that afternoon with Roberto alternated with fierce resentment of Andrew's unforgiving anger, she approached him again. But he had not relented, and at the end, in the face of his silence, she could only cry, "What can I do?"

He looked at her coldly and said, "Apparently Scizira got the correct charm after all. You did find one lover. Perhaps you should consult a *macumbeiro*."

She flew at him then, her fists pummeling him in hate and rage. He swore at her—ugly words, created by pain—and she saw underneath his rigid calm a torment as great as hers. She fled from his room and, unwilling to humiliate herself again, had not tried to reach out to him since.

When Ellen asked Julia to accompany her to the ship at Santos, Julia had agreed, glad to be away from home for these several days, even though she hated to leave Paul. Richard, hardier than he looked, had begun managing his lands after Roberto's departure and therefore stayed home. Yet Julia suspected the real reason Richard wouldn't go to Santos was because he was still angry at Ellen for going to England.

Ellen said softly, "It will be all right, Julia."

"How can it, when Andrew won't even talk to me? And I'm not sure I want him to. He's so unforgiving."

"Fatherhood and the sanctity of marriage—or at least of wives—are extremely important to men. Perhaps," Ellen suggested dryly, "because a man must take the woman's word that he's fathered their children. Andrew has more pride than most men, and Richard has fostered bad feelings between his sons as a way of manipulating them. But Andrew has a more understanding and loving nature than his father."

"Your first husband never forgave you," reminded Julia.

Ellen sighed. "Yes, but he didn't love me as Andrew loves you."

The coach stopped, and the groom opened the door. "Excuse me, Dona Ellen. Santos in half-hour."

Ellen leaned back. "Thank heaven."

Two days later, after seeing Ellen off for Rio to get passage to England, Julia returned to the Santos hotel. When she approached the door of her room, she saw a tall black-haired man, and her heart stopped, then began to beat again, but it was Roberto, not Andrew.

She almost turned to run, but he held out his hand to her. "Julia . . . please. I must talk to you."

As if he recognized her unspoken fears, Roberto added quickly, "I made sure no one saw me."

And what difference would it make? she thought. But she hurried to unlock the door, and he followed her into the sitting room. She gestured to a chair, "Please sit down." Her fingers worked with unaccustomed clumsiness to remove her hat before she sat across from him.

He wore the casual black clothes he liked; his face, though thin, was tan and his moustache and hair more closely trimmed than usual. He smiled and said with his old lightness, "You must be wondering how I knew you were here. I still have informants everywhere."

The smile disappeared. "Julia, forgive me for following you, but I had to tell you how sorry I am. Please believe me, I never intended to say anything, ever. I admit that I wanted to make a claim to your son— possibly our son—but until that day I was sure I wouldn't."

He rose and paced back and forth, his steps punctuating his words. "I think I was almost out of my mind that afternoon. It's no excuse, I know, but . . ."

She could hardly bear the anguish in his voice. "Roberto, I understand. Ellen told me what your father said."

His pacing stopped, and he looked at her longingly. "Can you forgive me, Julia?"

She raised her hands in a despairing gesture. "It's the other way—I should ask your forgiveness. I should have told you the truth long ago."

"The truth? What do you mean?"

Her throat felt dry, and she wanted to push him out the door, or hide. Instead she forced herself to look at him. "The afternoon when we made love . . ." She could feel her face flame as she blurted the rest. "We . . . You didn't complete the . . . the part you don't remember in the way you assumed, so you couldn't be Paul's father."

His face turned as pale as hers was flushed. "My God, Julia. You let me think . . . Why didn't you tell me?"

She covered her throat, holding back the hysterical laughter. "That's what Andrew said. The difference is that he didn't believe me, and I can see you do."

He crouched in front of her and took one of her

hands. She could feel the tension in his grip. "Why?" he insisted. "Why?"

"Oh, Roberto," she said in despair, "I'm not sure. It seemed as if it would be cheating you. And I was ashamed I'd behaved so badly to you."

"Cheating me! For God's sake, Julia, you haven't cheated me."

She began to laugh, a high, bitter sound releasing the tension she held within. "Julia," he commanded, "stop it!" and shook her until the laughter became sobs. With a groan he pulled her from the chair into his arms.

Though she knew she should push him away, she couldn't. When her tears stopped, he held her, gently smoothing her hair. Finally she moved away, and they sat on the floor looking at each other.

"I'm sorry, Julia. I didn't mean to touch you." Lines of pain deepened around his mouth. "I'll go to Andrew, tell him I don't remember, that I was wrong."

"No," Julia gasped; then, more quietly, "No. It wouldn't help. He wouldn't believe you now."

Painfully, as if some ailment had crippled him, Roberto rose from the floor and walked to the door. He put his hand on the latch, then turned back. "Julia . . . I love you and I'd do anything I could for you." Momentarily an ironic smile curved his lips. "Except control my temper." His mouth thinned to a determined line. "Divorce, though difficult, is possible. Nothing would make me happier than to have you for my wife, and Paul for my child, even though . . . I'm not his father. Will you remember that?"

She nodded, unable to speak. His old mocking smile returned. "I have a job—as an overseer. Can you believe that? It's on the Portella *fazenda*. Senhor Fonseca could tell you how to reach me if you ever wished to."

He stared at her almost hungrily, then opened the

door and looked outside. He turned back, attempted a nonchalant smile, and was gone.

She sat on the floor until the tears which fell on her clasped hands had dried. Finally she rose and began to prepare for an early-morning start, for she was impatient to return to the *fazenda*. Although Andrew might not care if she came back, Julia was going home to Paul. At least she had him.

Two days later Julia arrived home in the late afternoon and hurried upstairs to the nursery. She opened the door, calling, "Paul, I'm . . ." and stopped. The room was empty, the floor bare, the wicker toy basket and wooden rocking horse gone. Stunned, she ran back down the stairs to the kitchen wing. Quintiliana sat at a table in one corner of the room.

Julia checked her breathless rush. "Where is Paul?"

The tall woman rose. "He has been moved to the room next to Seu Andrew's."

"Why? I gave no orders for that."

In the other woman's eyes Julia saw an expression that resembled pleasure; then the black face had its usual impassive demeanor. "Seu Andrew ordered it."

Stunned, Julia stood for a moment. Then she was racing back upstairs to the room next to Andrew's. When she pulled open the door, she saw the black curly hair flipping back and forth as Paul rode his wooden horse. At her entrance he cried joyously, "Mama," and half-fell, half-scrambled to the floor. They met in the middle of the room, and she hugged him fiercely before she carried him back to the bedroom which was now hers alone.

As she held him and listened to his jabbering words, a new fear chilled her, and she snuggled the warm body close. Men controlled the fates of both their wives and children. Andrew had the power to take Paul away from her if he chose. Surely he would never do that—but what did she know any longer of his thoughts and purposes?

She kept Paul with her for his supper and rocked him until he fell asleep. After she carried him across the house to his bed, she went into Andrew's room. The scent of his clothes, the small cigars he occasionally smoked, and his woodsy fragrance so distinctive to him, almost forced her to retreat. But grimly she settled to wait for him.

Andrew climbed the stairs, exhausted by the long harvest day he made even longer in order to delay returning to the house. He knew Julia had come back from Santos, and in the upper hallway he hesitated. Then determined not to give in to the desire to see her, he turned toward what was now his end of the house. At the next-to-last door he stopped and opened it softly. In the light of one sheltered candle he saw Paul's head buried among the covers. Nearby the nursemaid, Florella, slept on her pallet. He eased the door closed.

As soon as he entered his room, the fragrance of roses told him of Julia's presence. Before he could guard himself against his response, his heartbeat quickened. She had on a high-necked dark dress which hugged her breasts and waist before flaring in smooth lines to the floor. Her hair was drawn back severely, except for a few escaping wisps. Her face was thinner than it had been a few months ago, making her eyes with their heavy lashes larger and more luminous, giving her a fragility that tore at him.

Reminding himself how easily she could deceive him, he said coldly. "Do you wish something?"

"Yes, I want Paul moved back to the nursery."

Anger rose to help him control his longing for her. As if giving no particular attention to her, he took off his dusty work jacket before responding. "Why don't you bother to ask why I had him moved?"

Her head rose defiantly. "Very well, why?"

"The first night you were gone, he had a nightmare. At this distance I didn't hear him. Florella couldn't quiet him and brought him to me. I decided it would be better to have him next door."

"Yes . . . I see. But you didn't need to have all his furniture moved as well. Now that I'm home to hear him at night again, I'll have his things returned to his regular room."

She started past him but stopped when he remarked calmly, "No. I've decided to keep him here."

In her golden-brown eyes he saw a flash of something that might have been fear.

Anger flared in Julia's eyes, and she spat, "I know why. You want to punish me by keeping my son from me. Because of one afternoon."

Pained by the dishonorable accusation and furious that she still had tried to deceive him, Andrew retaliated. "I know it was more than 'one afternoon,' so don't bother to lie about that. Your wild imagination is distorting my motives: you have Paul all day while I'm working; I want him near me at night. After all," he went on coldly, "I would think you'd welcome my concern, considering the uncertainty that I'm his father."

Her face lost all color, and she cried passionately, "If there is a bastard in this house, it's you . . . you . . ."

" *Filho da puta'* are the words you're looking for, I believe," he offered.

She stared at him, her face rigid with emotion, before she whispered, "Yes—you are a son of a bitch."

When the door closed behind her, Andrew stood,

staring after her. Slowly he pulled off the rest of his
clothes and began to wash. After he finished and blew
out the light, he lay on the bed trying to blot out Julia's
face, but he was no more successful tonight than most
nights.

If she'd been unfaithful only once, he thought for the
hundredth time, when she'd believed he was with Lele,
he wouldn't be so bitter toward her. After his first rage
had cooled, he might have been able to accept her
transgression—even accept the man being Roberto. Or
at least he would have understood enough to try to
make something of their marriage. If he hadn't overheard Quintiliana confirming what he most feared, he
might have tried to reclaim a life with Julia.

But he remembered Quintiliana's words as vividly as
if he'd heard them last night, not months ago. A few
days after the fight with Roberto and Julia's admission
of their intimacy, Andrew had been in his study late
one night, and had felt he couldn't stand his own company any longer. He knew Capitolino and Quintiliana
often stayed up in the small room off the kitchen, and
he'd walked along the hall to her office. He hadn't tried
to be quiet, but they must not have heard him, for just
before he reached the partly ajar door, he heard her
say, "Capitolino, you must not speak to Seu Andrew."

Something in Quintiliana's voice made Andrew stop.
He heard Capitolino's question, "You mean about Seu
Roberto and Sinha Julia? Yes, yes—it's not my place to
say anything. But I saw how careful they were to stay
apart, all the time the master was away."

At Capitolino's words, Andrew felt hope well up inside him, but it died with Quintiliana's response. "I
know it's fretting you, so I made up my mind you'd
better know. I saw them together many times—Roberto
and the mistress. In the summerhouse, and in the

house when they thought no one was around." Her voice dropped. "I even saw them that day—the wedding—in the bedroom, laughing and loving. Long loving."

Andrew had turned, not bothering to soften his footsteps, and gone back to the study for a bottle of brandy. Since then he'd kept his defenses against Julia intact. But countless nights, when he couldn't drug himself with work, he'd almost gone to her.

What he needed was a woman. Arturo, one of the Italian supervisors, had a daughter—good-looking and old enough—who always managed to be in view when Andrew stopped by Arturo's house to talk to him. She'd made it clear that if Andrew were interested, she'd be happy to oblige him. He didn't like men who bedded other women under their wives' noses, but a small house could be arranged, discreetly distant from the big house. After all, he'd been cuckolded in his own bedroom, so Julia would have no right to complain. He dismissed his lack of enthusiasm at the prospect of the buxom young Italian woman. She'd be able to relieve him, and he'd no doubt enjoy her.

Again he settled himself to sleep, trying to relax his tired muscles, but images of Julia haunted him. He didn't want the Italian girl. He wanted a woman who had lied to him, been unfaithful to him with his own brother, had probably given him a bastard child. Julia hated him for his coldness; he hated himself for his weakness.

Julia was already awake the next morning when she heard the bugle sound for the long day to begin. Hurriedly she rose and dressed, then went downstairs to find Quintiliana. During the night she had determined she would not accept Paul's new room. Andrew's explanation sounded reasonable, but the vision of Ellen setting off to see her son, a stranger to her for most of his lifetime, haunted Julia. She must stand up to Andrew now, let him see she wouldn't be intimidated as far as Paul was concerned.

She found the housekeeper in the door of her office, tying a fresh white apron in place. "Quintiliana, I wish to speak to you."

"Certainly, Sinha Julia," Quintiliana replied, but something in her tone sounded faintly contemptuous.

Not letting her voice show any hesitancy, Julia announced, "When the servants have time this morning, I wish all of Paul's things moved back to his old room."

Quintiliana's eyes were expressionless, her voice equally devoid of emotion. "I cannot do that. Seu Andrew has ordered that Nhonho Paul will stay where he is."

For a moment the black woman's face seemed to Julia to hold an emotion stronger than contempt—almost like hatred. The expression disappeared so swiftly Julia wasn't positive of what she'd seen, and again the housekeeper appeared the impassive servant.

"Then tomorrow you'll receive different orders," she replied, more confidently than she felt.

"Yes, Sinha Julia," Quintiliana responded, but as she turned away, Julia saw a flicker of triumph in her face. Julia returned upstairs to Paul's new quarters. She couldn't suppress a fear of the woman she'd depended on so long, and she couldn't understand why Quintiliana would hate her.

Through the long morning Julia tried unsuccessfully to banish the black woman from her mind, but her anxiety plagued her. She became convinced that Quintiliana had taken some action to harm her, but before she spoke to Andrew, she would find out what. Julia realized the other blacks in the household probably knew, yet no one would tell the white mistress.

Scizira! The land she and Jora had been given was close by. Scizira came to the *casa grande* frequently and still instructed several girls in lacemaking. She would know what happened in the household, and her loyalties to Julia might be stronger than her ties to another black. Julia knew she must at least try to get Scizira to talk to her.

When Paul was settled for his afternoon nap, Julia rode her mare to the modest whitewashed building where Scizira lived. Her former maid welcomed her with obvious pleasure, and showed Julia to the main room of the small house, where they could visit undisturbed. Trying not to show her nervousness, Julia curbed her impatience and described Ellen's departure and listened to news of Jora's accomplishments.

Julia's distress must have shown in her face, because Scizira finally fell silent, and Julia plunged into her words before she could lose courage. "Scizira, I must ask you a question which I know you may not want to answer. If you do, I swear I will never tell anyone else what you've said. I wouldn't ask if it weren't so important to me—and I can't go to anyone else."

For an instant Scizira drew back in fright; then her eyes softened. "*Sinhazinha*, you have been very good to Jora and me, more than anyone else ever has been. I will tell you anything I can."

Julia let out her breath. "Thank you, Scizira." She clasped her cold hands against her skirt and continued. "I want to know what Quintiliana may have said or done against me."

Scizira looked down, and the silence lasted forever before she looked at Julia again. Her voice dropped to a whisper. "I can only tell you what the servants say, but

I think it is so. Quintiliana has bragged that she managed so that Seu Andrew overheard her tell Capitolino . . . that you and Seu Roberto had been lovers many times."

Shock held Julia in paralyzed silence. She recalled Andrew's words the previous night—"I know it was more than *one afternoon*"—and now she understood them. He thought she'd deceived him often—had lied when she said she'd been with Roberto only once. No wonder he'd refused to listen to her further attempts to talk to him.

Anger flamed, releasing her voice. "But why? Why would Quintiliana lie about me?"

Scizira hesitated, and Julia could see uncertainty in her troubled face. Perhaps she too believed Quintiliana's lies. Her voice barely carried across to Julia. "She blamed you for making her brother an overseer. She said you didn't care what would happen to Tomaz because he was black, and that he would have died in that fire if she hadn't warned him not to go to the overseer's house."

Julia shuddered, appalled at the hatred that had festered so long, waiting for an opportunity to vent itself. From Seizira's strained face, Julia knew she could ask nothing else. The black woman's loyalties had already been severely torn by saying this much.

Julia rose and took Scizira's hands, clasping them gratefully. "Thank you, Scizira. I know you didn't want to tell me this."

Scizira's voice trembled as she asked, "You won't let Quintiliana know what I said? She's very clever, and I'm afraid of her."

"No, of course I won't." Julia would have hugged Scizira, but she could tell that the young woman had retreated into a distance that would probably always be maintained now. She'd violated loyalty once, and Julia must not ask more of her.

As Julia rode back to the *fazenda*, she felt as if the despair inside her was so heavy that her mare must feel the difference. Her first impulse was to confront Quintiliana, but Quintiliana had left her no weapons with which to fight. The black woman had served Andrew for so many years that he wouldn't question her loyalty. Even if Julia could tell him what Scizira said, when he questioned the housekeeper, Quintiliana only needed to deny her words. And Julia didn't doubt the black woman's intelligence—the denial would be made in such a way as to convince Andrew that she was trying to protect her mistress.

Desperately stemming bitter tears, Julia knew Andrew must hate her, and he'd never give in about Paul. He'd never know she was innocent of all but that one afternoon.

She knew that she might pay all her life for one hour of weakness. Andrew didn't want her for a wife now, and Quintiliana had done her best to make sure he would never want her again. And she might lose Paul as well.

Quintiliana had become a fierce and effective adversary. Julia realized she'd made two terrible mistakes. The first, over Tomaz, she'd almost forgotten. But that mistake, to her so much less important than the second, she would pay for just as bitterly.

During the winter months, when the plantation work lessened, Andrew spent many daylight hours with Paul. On Paul's second birthday in September Andrew gave his son a pony and began teaching him to ride. Each time Andrew took Paul away for the day, Julia felt her apprehension growing.

For Paul's sake she tried to welcome his attachment to his father, but the childish sentences about "Papa" brought a specter of her own loss closer. She told herself she worried needlessly, and she knew she needed more to do. Quintiliana hardly bothered to consult Julia about household affairs, and Julia couldn't bring herself to seek out the black woman. This time of year the cotton required little attention.

On a morning in October Carlota and William came to visit. Andrew had gone to São Paulo for a few days, and Julia had roused from her lethargy and kept Paul with her at night, taking pleasure from the small body next to her in the empty bed. William had come often during the past months, usually by himself, but always at a time of day Andrew would be away from the house. Her father had never spoken to Julia about her problems, but by his visits she knew that whatever he might think she had done, his love and loyalty to her remained unchanged.

Today she greeted him warmly and felt able to tolerate Carlota alone while William took Paul for the horseback ride he begged for. After coffee had been served in the family sitting room, Carlota smiled in the exaggerated way which Julia knew meant she had something malicious to say.

"Dear Julia, how difficult for you to be alone so much. When will Andrew return?"

Julia forced an equally false smile. "Not for several days."

Carlota's sly look became triumphant. "Then he must have taken his little Italian girl with him. I hear he can hardly bear to be away from her."

Carlota's words thrust deep into Julia, and in the void where her heart had been the wound began to bleed slow, bitter drops. But her determination not to show

382   *Barbara Keller*

her pain to her stepmother was as fierce as the hurt. "Your sources, Carlota," she asserted, proud of how indifferent she sounded, "are not as accurate as you think." Some of Carlota's smug pleasure faded as Julia added, "You might consider the results if you made trouble between Andrew and me."

"But, Julia," Carlota fluttered, "I wouldn't ever want to cause difficulty. I thought you knew all about Andrew's *amante*."

As if her stepmother hadn't spoken, Julia continued. "If I were unhappy here and left Andrew, the natural place for Paul and me to go would be to Papa." She smiled sweetly at Carlotta as she delivered her blow. "And you and I both know how much Papa would welcome me. Since you have done little to make him cherish you, I think I would soon be the real mistress in his house again, as I was after Mama died. Would you like that?"

Carlota's face blanched, and her coffee cup rattled against the saucer when she set it down. Her voice, which she usually kept seductively low, shrilled at Julia. "You misunderstood me, Julia."

Julia didn't bother to hide her anger. "I offer you some advice, Carlota. If you like the position Papa has given you, you had better try much harder to make him happy. The Rayfords do not, even from a sense of gallantry or duty, let themselves be mistreated or scorned for long."

When a smiling William and a subdued Carlota departed a few hours later, Julia kissed her father with special warmth, clinging to him for a last hug. He held her close in return; in his tenderness she felt the concern he hadn't put in words.

*   *   *

While Paul lay napping on her bed that afteroon, Julia thought about her threat to Carlota. Her stepmother's words about Andrew and a woman still twisted their sharp blades in her heart, but her own words had begun to cauterize the wounds. When she spoke of the Rayford pride, she described not just Papa but also herself.

What had happened to her pride and spirit? she asked herself angrily. Overwhelmed by her own guilt and remorse, she'd cowered, waiting humbly for Andrew to decide her and Paul's fate. She wasn't even running her own household. But no more! Even if Andrew didn't have a mistress now, he would eventually. Most men managed to satisfy their physical desires, and society recognized and covertly sanctioned their methods. Julia knew enough about physical needs to understand their pressures, even though women weren't supposed to feel such strong passions.

But the pain welling up within her told her that though she might understand why Andrew would seek another woman, she could never meekly accept it like the Southern and Brazilian women who pretended to see nothing. She remembered the toothless slave girl on the Mello *fazenda* and found in herself the same vengeful feelings that must have motivated Senhora Mello.

For so long, even underneath her rage at Andrew, she had hoped they could have a marriage again. As she knew she couldn't accept Andrew's having a mistress here, perhaps he couldn't ever overcome his feelings about her and Roberto. But she wouldn't let Andrew crush her spirit—she would take Paul and leave.

She would have to go far away, where he couldn't find them. He didn't want her, but Andrew loved his son and wouldn't give him up. Neither would she. Paul stirred on the bed, thrust out a hand, then slept again. She looked at him, and for a moment doubted. Was it fair to keep him from his father?

Carlota's words strengthened Julia's resolution. If Andrew had a woman he could "hardly bear to be away from," he'd soon have other children. He could divorce Julia for desertion, marry again, and he'd forget her and Paul. Not able to bear that thought, she turned to planning.

She still had the money which had come to her on her twenty-first birthday from Great-Uncle Francis' estate. It was in a bank in São Paulo. She couldn't go to Papa, for then Andrew would have Paul back immediately. Nor would Hundred Oaks be safe. That was the first place Andrew might look, and laws in South Carolina wouldn't protect her.

Nathan—Nathan and Purity! They would welcome Julia and Paul, and Andrew didn't know where they were, or even that she corresponded with them. Once, long ago, she'd talked about Nathan when he and Purity still lived in Philadelphia, but Andrew had seemed uninterested, so she'd never mentioned Nathan again. She and Paul could stay in San Francisco until she decided what to do.

For the first time in months Julia felt real hope. She knew it would be difficult, but she'd sheltered herself in Brazil long enough. She thought of Roberto, of his offer, and of the real affection she had for him. But if she went to him, Paul would be within Andrew's reach, and she would still be depending on a man to fight her battles. Ellen had courage enough to defy Richard and look out for herself; Julia could do the same.

She realized she'd have to leave before Andrew might return and guess what she planned to do. She would pack only essential clothing and take the carriage. Someone would have to go with her, she could manage the equipment by herself, but not when she had Paul also. Then she could send the horses and carriage back from Santos.

Capitolino's grandson, Beto, had become a good coachman. She'd see him tonight, have him get the horses ready to leave at dawn. She'd say she was going to visit her father, and Quintiliana would be pleased, thinking Carlota's gossip had driven Julia away. After they were started, she'd tell Beto where they were going.

The only risk might be in going to the bank in São Paulo, but she'd just have to be careful. Andrew would probably be busy, maybe entertaining his Italian mistress.

Resolutely closing her mind to all but her preparations, she first collected Purity's letters, then began to search through her clothing to choose what she would need. She'd have time later for tears over Andrew—if she were foolish enough to shed them.

At the familiar sight of the *fazenda*, Andrew began to lose some of the tension that had driven him to a bone-shaking pace on the ride from São Paulo. During the week he'd spent in the city, he'd made the arrangements for another advance coffee sale, but he'd also drunk far too much and had too many hangovers.

When he reached the stable, he turned his weary horse over to his groom. Though the brown gelding was the sturdiest riding horse he had, he shouldn't have pushed the animal so hard. At first he'd planned to be home early enough to see Arturo's daughter before he went to the big house. She'd hinted she wanted to go with him for the week in São Paulo, but he'd ignored her. Today on the ride to the *fazenda*, he'd told himself he wanted to visit her as soon as he arrived, but he hadn't kept up that pretense long.

After deciding in May to accept her invitations, he hadn't arranged a house for her until July and had visited her only a few times since a first encounter. As he'd suspected, she wasn't a virgin, and her sexual skills showed considerable expertise. She must, he thought wryly, be ambitious, to go about bedding the plantation owner so determinedly. He didn't object to her using him, for he did the same and would have recoiled from anything that seemed like real intimacy. But except for a measure of physical relief, he found little pleasure in visiting her. Despite his decision that he had a right to take a mistress, he felt as if he were dishonoring Julia.

Angry with Julia, and even more with himself for not being able to ignore his feelings for her, he started for the house. At least he had Paul, the source of the only real pleasure in his life. Though Paul might not be his own son, he loved him as much as he could ever love any child. The question of who had fathered Paul still caused Andrew deep hurt, but it no longer diminished his feelings for the small boy.

He took the back stairs to the upper floor and went to the room next to his. The emptiness at first disappointed him, and then, as he noticed Paul's favorite stuffed toys were gone, shocked him. He raced down the hall to Julia's bedroom to find the same chilling absence. Returning downstairs, he sought out Quintiliana in her office and demanded, "Where are Paul and Senhora Julia?"

For a moment her face held an unmistakable look of triumph, which smoothed immediately to respectful concern. "They left four days ago, to go to stay with Senhor Rayford, she told me. Beto took them in the carriage, but when he didn't return, Capitolino went to inquire about him. Senhora Julia and Nhonho Paul had not gone to the Rayford *fazenda*." That strange, almost malicious pleasure broke through to her voice as she added, "This morning Senhor Rayford arrived. He's in the sitting room, waiting to talk to you."

William met Andrew in the hall. "Thank God you're back, Andrew. But where are my daughter and grandson?"

"I don't know. Please." Andrew gestured toward his study.

William waited until Andrew closed the door, then said, his voice hoarse with obvious strain, "I don't intend to pry into your life, Andrew, but I must tell you something. Carlota and I visited Julia five days ago, and my wife has since admitted to me that she said some upsetting things to Julia while they were alone. Carlota suggested that you had taken a woman with you to São Paulo, someone whom you installed as a mistress and couldn't bear to leave behind."

Andrew felt a rock in his stomach that grew heavier and colder as William continued. "I'm not trying to judge what you do, but I am greatly concerned. I can assure you that my wife will never again say anything to hurt Julia." He stopped, then burst out, "I've seen how unhappy my daughter has been. Though I do not listen to gossip, Carlota does, and apparently even your housekeeper has spread malicious stories about Julia."

Andrew momentarily put aside that information. "I assure you, Mr. Rayford, that I plan to locate Julia and my son immediately, and I'll see that no one in my household says or does anything to harm her. I'll inform you as soon as Julia returns."

Only after William departed did Andrew's thoughts return to Quintiliana. As he soaked in a bath and then had his saddlebags packed, he remembered the look on the housekeeper's face today. He also recalled that on the evening he'd overheard her talking to Capitolino,

he'd made no effort to disguise the sound of his footsteps. Capitolino was slightly deaf, so he wouldn't have
heard Andrew, but Quintiliana, Andrew now realized,
must have known when he approached.

Silently Andrew cursed himself for being so absorbed
in his own feelings that until today he'd assumed
Quintiliana was telling the truth. She'd been with him
for so many years that it hadn't occurred to him she
might be lying. He'd believed his servant when he
should have believed his wife. And now, because of an
involvement with a woman he didn't want, the woman
he did want had left him.

By evening Andrew had given Pedro Oliveiro instructions and ordered clothes and gear assembled for a
dawn departure the following day, when he heard voices
below and recognized Beto's tenor tone. Moments later
he was downstairs and questioning the tired young
man.

"I left Sinha Julia and *o senhorzinho* in Santos yesterday morning. I didn't want to come back without them,
but the mistress made me go. She was staying at the
brown hotel near the docks."

When Andrew reassured Beto he didn't blame him
and dismissed him, he found Quintiliana waiting in the
hall. He motioned for her to follow him. Inside her
office he closed the door and faced her, studying her,
saying nothing. Beads of perspiration appeared on her
forehead, but her expression didn't change as she waited.

He felt fury so strong he thought it would sicken
him, but his anger included himself as much as her. He
didn't need to question her; he knew, looking at her,
that she'd lied. "Why, Quintiliana?" he demanded.

She didn't pretend to misunderstand. "Senhora Julia
tried to harm Tomaz."

For a moment Andrew didn't understand, until he

remembered Julia's attempt to make Quintiliana's brother
the overseer. She had nursed hatred for so long!
Quintiliana must go, but because of her years of loyalty,
he'd find a place for her elsewhere when he returned.
"Quintiliana, you'll stay here for now, but if you ever
again say one word against my wife, you'd better leave
immediately, because if I find you, I might kill you."
Without waiting for her response, he left.

When Andrew started out the next morning, he had
to force himself not to push his and his groom's horses
too fast. But his heart raced far ahead of the steady pace
of the animals, urging him onward toward the two
people he wanted desperately to find.

Julia sheltered Paul between her body and the ship's
railing as the curving shore of Rio bay disappeared
behind the rocky points at the harbor entrance. She
watched until she could no longer clearly see the green-
and-gold flag above the fort which guarded the approach to the capital. Around her sailors went about
their work, and Paul's excited chatter brought smiles to
sea-weathered faces.

She thought back over her departure. She'd had no
trouble withdrawing her money in São Paulo. Andrew
wouldn't find out, she was sure, what ship she'd taken.
For the two days in Rio she'd stayed at the hotel on the
Larangeiras road where her family had spent their first
days in Brazil. Fortunately, this small brig, the *Cortes*,
was leaving for California immediately, and she had
obtained a cabin which had been intended for a businessman who had become ill.

Captain Judkins, a fierce-looking but kindly man, had
hesitated to take a woman and child traveling without a
man. But with a silent request to Nathan to forgive her,
she'd given her name as Mrs. Holt and said she was

journeying to her meet her husband in San Francisco. She assured Captain Judkins she would look after herself and Paul, and he finally accepted them.

On the same day the *Cortes* sailed for California, two steamships had also left, one going to New York and the other to New Orlenas. If Andrew traced her to the hotel, he would probably think she'd taken one of the steamers.

She looked toward the Organ Mountains, lifting themselves sharply upward, like a huge green dinosaur that had crawled out of the sea and lain along the shore. But across the widening distance, she no longer saw them clearly through the blur of tears in her eyes.

The odor of fermenting sugar hung over the sparsely furnished office where Andrew waited. He paced around the edges of the room, too tense to sit on any of the bamboo chairs. Two weeks had passed since he'd returned home to find Julia and Paul gone, two weeks of futile searching in Santos and Rio, which had finally brought him here, to the overseer's office on the Portella *fazenda*. He felt almost sure Julia had gone to Hundred Oaks, but before he followed her, he had steeled himself to this final inquiry.

Roberto came in and closed the door behind him, then looked unsmilingly at Andrew. "Senhor Oswaldo told me you were here, but I thought he must be mistaken."

Andrew reminded himself he had resolved to control his temper and said, "I still feel toward you as I did before, but I need to talk to you, if you're willing."

Roberto gave a grim laugh. "Unrelenting as ever. Go ahead."

Painfully Andrew forced out his question. "Do you know where Julia is?"

Around the black mustache deep lines marked Roberto's mouth. "No—though God knows I wish I could say yes. But she wouldn't come to me. She has too much honor—more than you or I."

Andrew had both hoped and feared that Roberto had heard from Julia, but now despair filled him. At that moment he would have accepted Julia in Roberto's arms to know she and Paul were safe. "Yes . . . I've finally learned that much," he managed.

"You don't have any idea where she is?" Roberto asked.

Recognizing that he owed Roberto what information he had, Andrew said, "I know where she and Paul stayed in Rio and when she left the hotel. Also what ships sailed that day. Her name wasn't on any of the passenger lists, but she may have used another name. She has money . . ."

Unable to say more, he started to leave, but Roberto's voice stopped him. "Before you go . . . I did see Julia in May, when she was in Santos with Ellen." Andrew turned, anger flaring despite himself, but Roberto added quickly, "She didn't expect or want to see me, but I had to apologize."

The silence lay thick between them, as if the weight of their hostility to each other had condensed there. Roberto finally went on, his voice bleak. "She explained why I couldn't be Paul's father. I offered to tell you I couldn't remember everything that happened that day, but she refused. Said it was no use. From what I hear of the bastard you've been, she was right."

Andrew felt his muscles knot with the effort to hold himself back. But hitting his brother would solve nothing—and Roberto had only stated the truth. Slowly Andrew responded. "Maybe then, but I'm not so unrelenting as you think. I realize now she told the truth, and I hope I understand the circumstances. I wronged her, but that doesn't make you less of a son of a bitch."

Roberto laughed with bitter mirth. "You're right. You and I are true sons of Richard, that prince of bastards." He walked to a tray and picked up a decanter of *cachaça*. He looked questioningly at Andrew, and at Andrew's shaken refusal, poured one glass and held it up. "Confessions require a toast. And I confess that for as long as I can remember, I've had my greatest pleasure from making trouble for you. I'd have been in bed with Julia the week after you married her if I could have managed it."

Only by remaining silent could Andrew keep himself from lunging at his brother, so he waited as Roberto continued. "Then I had a disagreeable surprise. I fell in love with your wife. I didn't want to hurt her, so I couldn't hurt you. Whether you believe it or not, my getting into bed with her at all was an accident. I was drunk. She was unhappy—for which you, my brother, were responsible."

A reluctant admiration for Roberto's honesty forced its way into Andrew's mind, and he had to acknowledge, "Yes, you're right."

"If I were Julia's husband," Roberto vowed, "I'd search for her until I found her, and if she wanted me, no matter what she'd done, I'd never let her go."

Andrew looked at Roberto, and despite all the antagonism between them, he felt the beginning of respect. "That's what I intend to do." He started to leave, then turned back and said, "I'm glad you're not her husband, Roberto. Because I'd want her, and I don't think I'd get her away from you." The two men stared at each other, and then Andrew went out and closed the door behind him.

19

During the night the sky cleared and the seas calmed; directly overhead the four stars of the Southern Cross shone brightly. At the first streaks of light, Julia left Paul sleeping soundly and slipped out of the stuffy cabin. The winds had finally sent the brig around Cape Horn to the Pacific Ocean, and Julia had crossed off the date, November 13, 1870, on the calendar she'd begun when they left Brazil.

The gray sea spread before her, as smooth as its name suggested. Just breaking the top of a long, low swell, a shoal of whales lay sluggishly in the water, heaving in slow, lazy breaths. At the cry for the change of watch, she hurried below. She looked down at her still-sleeping child and wondered if he would ever see the Atlantic Ocean again.

Andrew sailed from Rio in mid-November and arrived in South Carolina after a month which seemed to him the longest he had ever spent. In Charleston he rented a horse and departed immediately for Hundred Oaks. As he approached the plantation, the bare trees reminded him that here December meant the coming of winter. Against the gray sky the immense oaks looked as bleak and tired as the people he'd seen on the impoverished lands he'd ridden through.

He reined in his horse in front of the plantation house. Except for fresh white paint on the tall front columns and a new door, it looked the same as it had five years ago. He hadn't sent word ahead of his arrival, for fear that if Julia were here, she'd flee without even seeing him.

Andrew also realized that if James knew of his sister's marital problems, he might not welcome his brother-in-law, whether Julia were here or not. Instead of going to the stable, Andrew walked his horse to the side entrance, dismounted, and tied the reins to a post.

An astonished voice exclaimed, "Andrew!" James stood in the side doorway, the surprise in his gray eyes changing to pleasure as he came down the steps. "Good God, what are you doing here? No matter—it's wonderful to see you." At James's unqualified welcome, disappointment flooded Andrew.

James's face was marked with lines of fatigue and worry. His thin frame had broadened in the three and a half years since he and Sally left Brazil, and in the rough jacket and pants, James looked as if he managed all of the heavy plantation work. But his delighted smile held the youthful charm Andrew remembered.

"I'm just as glad to see you," Andrew responded, bracing himself for James's next words.

"Are Julia and your son coming too, Andrew?"

Andrew suppressed the questions he hoped James could answer and replied, "No—they're not with me."

During the day Andrew kept to himself the painful explanation he must give his brother-in-law. He visited with Sally, now well-rounded with the child they expected in February, but seeming as frivolous as ever. In the afternoon he surveyed the plantation with James, listening to the sober, sometimes bitter account of the struggles to work the land with uncertain labor. Not until evening when the two men sat in the study did Andrew say, "Julia has taken Paul and left me. I don't know where she is. I thought she might have come here."

The shock in James's face slowly hardened to accusation. "Why, Andrew? She's my sister. I have to ask you."

"We quarreled over something which was both our faults. I'm sorry, James, but I won't tell you more, except that I'm to blame for her leaving. I intend to find her and Paul. I want them both back with me again."

The pendulum of a clock on the wall swung back and forth, its ticking the only sound until James asked, "If she won't go back to you, will you take Paul away from her?"

That question had occupied Andrew for sleepless nights aboard the steamship to Charleston. He missed his son desperately, and taking Paul might bring Julia back for the sake of her child. But Andrew wanted her love, not just her presence, and he couldn't hurt her so much again. So his answer was easy after all. "No."

Andrew waited, seeing the struggle in James's eyes, then the slow relaxation of the jaw which had the same determined lines as Julia's. "I believe you, and I'd help you if I could, but I don't know where she is."

On other painful nights aboard ship, Andrew had thought of a further question. "At the time of our marriage, you mentioned someone Julia had once considered marrying, a cousin. I believe his name was Nathan. Would she have gone to him?"

"Nathan Holt," James exclaimed. "I don't know. I haven't heard from him in years."

Holt. Andrew had remembered only "Nathan," and now the surname nagged at him. Several times he'd gone over the lists of passengers leaving Rio in the days after Julia had checked out of the hotel. On one of them, he felt sure, "Holt" had appeared. "Where does he live?"

"In Philadelphia, the last I knew. He married our cousin, Purity Townsend."

Pushing aside the thought that Julia might not only have gone to another man but also used his name, Andrew decided, "Then I'll go there. I intend to find her."

Julia rose and dressed herself and Paul. From habit she crossed off the date—January 19, 1871—on her calendar. It was just three months since they'd left Rio, and today they would arrive in San Francisco.

After the difficult rounding of the Horn, the voyage had passed uneventfully. The *Cortes* had made two stops, at the island of Juan Fernández, a military post off the coast of Chile, and at Acapulco. Julia had been treated with careful respect by the men aboard ship, including three other passengers, but she followed Captain Judkins' advice and stayed on the ship at both ports.

Now the familiar cabin suddenly seemed like home. Here she and Paul had celebrated his third Christmas with a plum duff and a toy ship carved by one of the sailors.

A chubby hand pulled at her skirt. "See Papa soon?"

She looked down at the face, already so much like Andrew's except for the eyes, and winced at the need to lie again. Since she'd told Captain Judkins she was going to meet her husband, she'd felt she must tell Paul the same. He'd begun to repeat every word she said, the formal sentences disconcerting in the childish voice. "I hope we'll see Papa very soon," she responded.

"I hope we'll see Papa very soon," he repeated happily, and hugged Uma Orelha—One Ear—his stuffed mule. Scizira had made it for him, and it had soon lost one ear and looked as travel-stained as the animals that plodded the back roads of Brazil. He carried it everywhere Julia would allow.

This morning she couldn't take it away from him. It might comfort him in this strange place, she thought, and realized it was she who needed the comfort for Brazil seemed like the home she should return to, and California the exile. Taking Paul's hand, she left the tiny cabin behind, drawing courage from knowing that at least this time she had made the decision for herself.

Fog hovered over the land, but soon the morning sun attacked it, vanquishing the last white fingers. A shy young man named Mr. Baker, the supercargo, stopped beside Julia at the rail and pointed to a strait between steep rocks. "That's called the Golden Gate, and beyond is the bay. All the ships in the world could anchor there."

After the *Cortes* negotiated the channel, Julia saw an expanse like a large placid lake stretching out of sight to the north and south. Scattered over the water, steamships and sailing ships rocked on their anchor chains. On the hills south of the Golden Gate, buildings sprawled in a jumble of gabled roofs and flat housetops with white railings; lightning rods probed the air like slender imitations of the bare masts which swayed in the harbor.

When the *Cortes* finally lay alongside one of the wharves, Julia half-expected to see black workers in white shirts and pants. Instead a few men in tall silk hats watched while others in billed caps and rough jackets transferred cargo to rail cars on trestles above the wharf.

A gruff voice asked, "Will your husband be meeting you, Mrs. Holt?"

Julia turned to the whiskered face of Captain Judkins. "No, he didn't know just what ship I would be on."

The captain hesitated, then offered, "I could perhaps spare a man—"

"Oh, no, Captain Judkins, I know how busy you are. I'll find a cab to a hotel, and then send a message to my husband."

Behind the captain one of the other passengers, Mr. Hayward, a middle-aged leather merchant, said, "I am going to the Imperial Hotel, and if Mrs. Holt would care to stay there—it is respectable in every way, I assure you, madam—I would be happy to escort her and the young gentleman."

At the relieved look on the captain's face, Julia smiled and said, "Thank you, Mr. Hayward."

"I'll have someone bring your trunk up right away," the captain promised before he hurried on.

The rotund leather merchant had been in San Francisco many times, and he provided a travelogue as their carriage jostled its way along Market Street. He explained that long wooden poles propped across the boardwalks supported the fronts of buildings damaged in an earthquake. Although, according to Mr. Hayward, the city had not quite 170,000 people, Julia thought it seemed more bustling than Rio. Everyone, from men in formal coats and beaver hats to bearded miners in denim pants and muddy boots, appeared to be in a hurry.

When they arrived at the hotel, a four-story building with ornate decorations around every window, Julia thanked Mr. Hayward and happily said good-bye, de-

clining his invitation to accompany him to the Poodle
Dog restaurant.

The next morning Julia felt apprehensive, despite all
her resolve. Concerned that Purity and Nathan might
be shocked by a runaway wife, Julia looked through her
limited wardrobe for her most conservative dress. She finally chose a two-piece dark blue serge with a high
neck and straight skirt, gathered modestly in back.
Since it was Sunday, she waited until church services
ended. Then she hired a cab and set out with Paul for
the address from Purity's most recent letter. They left
the business part of the city behind and climbed several
hundred feet to a hillside residential area.

The cab stopped on a street of tall, narrow houses, so
close together that a large man could hardly walk between them. Only the colors and the trim distinguished
one house from its neighbors as they stood in an as-
cending row, like soldiers at attention. On each a flight
of eleven steps led to a covered porch beside a dormer
window, with a balcony and another dormer window
above. A small window of an attic room nestled beneath
the gabled roof.

The driver climbed down and opened the door. He
pointed to a gray house with blue trim. "That's your
address, ma'am."

Now that she'd arrived, Julia dreaded having to explain why she'd come. On the voyage she had decided
to say she and Andrew had quarreled seriously so she
couldn't stay in Brazil. Since the descriptions of California had interested her, she had impulsively decided to
try San Francisco instead of returning to South Carolina. It was all true, except it left out the causes, but
they concerned only her.

Taking Paul by the hand, she asked the cab to wait
and climbed the steps to the blue door, which had two

oval glass panes. She rang the brass bell. The door opened, and Nathan, looking at first polite, then shocked, faced her.

His brown hair had thinned somewhat at the temples, and he had a silky brown mustache and beard. Small lines around his hazel eyes reminded her she hadn't seen him for almost ten years. He was shorter than she remembered, but otherwise he looked remarkably like the medical student whom she'd thought she'd fallen in love with in Philadelphia.

"Julia?" His voice sounded heavier, older. "Yes—it has to be Julia. No one else could have that red hair."

A shrill voice called, "Nathan, who is it?" and Purity appeared behind Nathan, looking like a faded picture of the girl Julia remembered. She wore a dark purple dress that made her pale skin look sallow. Her blond hair, once soft and shining, lay around her narrow face in dull waves, and her mouth drooped in a petulant line. Only the light blue eyes, at first frowning, then surprised, seemed familiar.

She pushed past her husband. "Julia . . . Julia! Can it really be you?"

In her cousin's embrace, Julia felt an almost hysterical welcome. "Yes, it's I," she affirmed. A tug at her hand reminded her, and she gently pulled the small boy from behind the shelter of her skirt. "And this is my son, Paul. Paul, these are your cousins, Mr. and Mrs. Holt."

Purity nodded briefly, but Nathan leaned down and extended his hand. "I am delighted to meet you, Paul, and I would like you to call me Uncle Nathan."

Paul shook the offered hand and asked, "Is my Papa here?"

Nathan glanced at Julia, then responded, "No, but we have two boys who would like to meet you."

"Julia," Purity interrupted, "come in. It's just like Nathan to keep you standing outside." She looked out the door. "Is that a cab waiting?" She sounded almost alarmed as she pulled Julia into the entrance hall. "But you're going to stay with us, aren't you? Nathan, send the cab away. Julia must stay here."

"My trunk is at the hotel—" Julia began, but an almost frantic note in Purity's voice stopped her.

"No, you're my cousin, my family, just like home, and you have to be with me. I won't hear of anything else."

"Is that all right, Julia?" Nathan questioned. She hesitated, then nodded. He smiled delightedly and said, "I'll dismiss the cab. Later we can take my man to the hotel and collect your things."

During the afternoon they visited in the parlor, where sunlight crept through the lace curtains on the front dormer, brightening the green-velvet-covered chairs and sofa and the oak paneling. Nathan and Purity's sons, David and Cecil, almost four years old now, came in. Their brown hair and blue eyes combined their parents' features in identical faces above stiff white collars and matching suits. Paul smiled, but they seemed not to know what to make of him, so he retreated to a place beside his mother and finally fell asleep.

When Julia, concealing her nervousness, explained her reasons for coming to San Francisco, Nathan looked startled, then sympathetic, but Purity seemed uninterested, returning almost immediately to the topic which Julia had already discerned must be Purity's primary subject of conversation: the difficulties of life in San Francisco.

In the late afternoon Nathan summoned Joe McMalley, a small, wiry man with an Irish brogue, and took Julia in the carriage to collect her trunk. They had almost reached the house again when Nathan said, "Julia, it would be generous to Purity and me for you to stay with us as long as you can. Purity . . . has not been well since we moved from Philadelphia, and it would cheer her immensely to have you here." Julia knew she couldn't refuse such a request.

Two weeks later Julia again considered her decision to stay as she stood at the window of her bedroom on the second floor. Beyond the city the familiar masts crowded the harbor. Farther across the bay she saw the smoke from one of the ferries which made three trips a day across to the busily growing village of Oakland.

Even in this time she'd become convinced she would make no difference in her cousin's feelings about California, and sometimes Julia felt she couldn't stand Purity's unceasing complaints. Only when they talked of Philadelphia did Purity's mouth lose its petulant expression. Even with her sons she seemed discontented and indifferent. She had a full-time housekeeper, Mrs. Steel, an amiable widow with dyed black hair, so Purity had little to keep her occupied.

Nathan and Paul made it posible for Julia to stay in San Francisco. Julia realized she had probably never loved Nathan—compared to Andrew, he seemed tame and unexciting—but he was wonderful to Paul. And Paul responded lovingly, running to meet Nathan when he came home at night, crowing at being lifted high in the air, crawling into Nathan's lap whenever David or Cecil would allow. After some initial jealousy, the twins had accepted Paul, often ignoring him but letting him watch as they played together. And they tagged after Julia, begging her to read aloud or play games with them.

Julia could also see how much more relaxed Nathan

looked than when she had arrived. He worked hard, building a practice among people who could afford to pay him, but also spending one day each week at a clinic in an area of shanties south of the city where the black people lived. Evening calls kept him out for several nights in a row and Julia knew Nathan was grateful for her sheltering him from the demanding boys during those harsh hours. The cook, Mrs. Campbell, who, along with a scrawny girl named Bessie, came in during the day, provided delicious dinners, but Julia could imagine that the evening meal must have been dreary with a daily list of Purity's discontents to be heard. Now after Nathan listened patiently to his wife, he and Julia talked of events that had been reported in the *Alta California* or the *Evening Bulletin* and Nathan seemed happier after each meal.

"Mama." Paul's voice interrupted her thoughts and pulled her away from the window. His happy face under the black curls appeared in the doorway, then disappeared, with only the words floating back, "Come see."

As Julia followed her son to the playroom, she thought that her decision to remain with her cousin for a time might not help Purity, but it couldn't hurt her. And it gave Paul a chance to get used to San Francisco as part of a family while she decided how to make her own way.

Andrew loosened his jacket as he strode along the dock at Rio, thanking God February meant summer in Brazil, for he had nearly frozen in the snow and sleet of Pennsylvania. Perhaps he wouldn't have hated it so much if he'd found Julia, but he'd spent a futile three weeks in Philadelphia before taking passage back to Brazil.

He'd soon found out that the Holts no longer lived in Pennsylvania, but dogged searching turned up little else. The Townsend importing business had been sold in 1868 and the new owner knew nothing of Nathan. No one, even in the Quaker meeting which the Holts had attended, remembered where they had gone. After searching the neighborhood where they'd lived, Andrew had finally found an old woman who said the Holts went west, she thought to California.

With that vague and disappointing knowledge Andrew had returned to Brazil, to look at the passenger lists again and to see about his own business. Pedro Oliveiro had never fully recovered from his injuries, and leaving him longer with the sole responsibility for the running of the *fazenda* would be unfair. No matter what Andrew discovered in the port office, he'd have to return home, and he couldn't leave again until he found someone else to take care of his lands.

Dodging a large cart stacked with oranges, Andrew entered the port authority building. A bored clerk listened to his request, then left and returned with a perspiring man in a crumpled suit. "Ah, Senhor Langdon. You wish to see the passenger lists yet another time." He gestured to the clerk. "Get the senhor what he wishes."

Several polite exchanges later, Andrew escaped to a counter and read the lists again. For the *Cortes*, sailing October 18, 1870, he found the name Teixeira with a line through it, and after it written "Sa. Holt," followed by a small "f." The clerk supplied the information that the small letter indicated Senhora Holt had been accompanied by a son or daughter. The ship's destination was San Francisco.

"Thank you, senhor," he told the clerk, "and please express my thanks to Senhor Boaretto."

"Will that be all, Senhor Langdon?" asked the clerk.
"Yes," Andrew responded. "I found what I wanted."

By March Julia began to think her visit was helping
Purity after all. Though Julia didn't want to spend any
more of her savings than necessary, the two women
visited a dressmaker at Purity's insistence. Since this
activity roused Purity to a more cheerful frame of mind,
Julia decided it was worth the money.

With Julia's encouragement, Purity decided to enter-
tain another couple for dinner, the first time in almost a
year. Nathan was clearly delighted, and this made Julia
feel she was repaying him for the attention he gave
Paul. The evening of the dinner, Purity took extra care
with her appearance, wearing a blue dress which emphasized her eyes. Feeling fesitve, Julia allowed herself
a russet silk gown with a tight bodice and modestly
revealing neckline.

The guests were Nathan's partner in his medical practice and his wife. Hiram Wilson, a short, plump man,
had a bushy blond beard and flaring mustache which
made up for an almost complete lack of hair on his
head. His wife, Ann, a small woman with dark brown
hair, worked as receptionist and nurse in the office the
two men shared in the center of the city. The Wilsons
laughed readily, with an amiability to which even Purity responded.

Purity introduced Julia as her cousin, visiting from
Brazil, leaving the impression that Andrew might arrive
anytime. Julia was slightly uncomfortable with that description, but she realized her position as an unaccompanied wife might embarrass her cousin.

As Ann and Hiram said their good-byes and went
down the steps to their carriage, the short woman took
her husband's arm. He pulled her close and whispered

something, and she laughed lovingly. An intense longing swept over Julia as she remembered that it had
been over a year since she and Andrew had last made
love. She had been so very long without Andrew, and
with no outlet for the strong passions he had taught
her.

"Julia," Nathan inquired, "are you all right?"

"Yes . . . fine," she managed, and put on an outward
smile.

"Good, because next Sunday I want to take all the
family—you and Paul are part of our family now—to
Woodard's Gardens. Purity agrees. We'll include Bessie to help with the children."

In Purity and Nathan's warmth and the affection she
felt for them, Julia's pain diminished, and she smiled.
"Of course. What is Woodard's Gardens?"

Nathan put his arm around Purity as he answered.
"It's an enormous pleasure garden, with a skating area,
concert stage, an art gallery—too much to describe.
Last summer every weekend featured a balloon ascen-
sion."

On Sunday Nathan and Purity had not come downstairs when Bessie, in a brown taffeta dress that was too
big for her, arrived. She sat stiffly on a chair while Julia
tried to quiet the impatient children by telling them
the story of the elves and the tailor. Finally Nathan, the
lines of his face rigid, came downstairs. "Purity doesn't
feel like going to the Gardens today," he announced
grimly.

The boys' wails expressed the disappointment Bessie's face showed. Nathan looked at them and then at
Julia. "Mrs. Steel will stay with Purity, but if you're
willing, Julia, I think we should go anyway."

Looking at the anxious faces turned her way, Julia
agreed. She'd been careful never to be alone with Na-

than or to seem to usurp Purity's place, but she couldn't disappoint the children or Bessie, who was almost a child herself. Even Joe McMalley, waiting in front with the carriage, had slicked back his hair and worn his best tan suit today. She smiled and said, "Of course—let's go."

Behind the high walls of Woodard's Gardens delights waited for both children and adults. A curved "boat" which moved by means of sails and oars around the edge of a lake, like the rim of a wheel, brought exclamations from them all, and Cecil and David wanted to stay there all afternoon, until they saw the zoo. Paul preferred the stuffed animals, particularly the tigers. Everything enchanted Bessie, and Joe had to watch over her as well as the boys.

Every other favorite was forgotten, however, when they saw the Chinese Giant. Dressed in a blue brocade mandarin coat and hat, he towered over the awed children. "How tall is he?" asked Julia, having a hard time remembering to be dignified and not stare.

"He's eight feet and three inches tall," replied an amused Nathan.

Finally Joe and Bessie took the children, sated with wonders, to the playground while Julia and Nathan sat at a table in one of the pavilions. They had ordered coffee when Julia heard a male voice exclaim, "Mrs. Holt." She looked up to see Mr. Hayward, the leather merchant from the *Cortes*.

Nathan rose, and Mr. Hayward offered his hand. "You must be Mrs. Holt's husband."

After only a moment's hesitation, Nathan said, "Yes."

Mr. Hayward beamed. "Excuse my speaking, but I was glad to see your wife again. Let me introduce myself—Jasper Hayward. I was a passenger with Mrs.

Holt and your son on the *Cortes*. Fine boy, Mr. Holt. How is Paul?"

Julia could feel a brilliant flush creeping up her neck as Nathan said calmly, "He's fine, Mr. Hayward, thank you."

Mr. Hayward tipped his hat and walked on as the waiter returned with the coffee. When the waiter left, Julia began, "I'm so very sorry, Nathan, to embarrass you. You see, I was afraid the captain of the *Cortes* wouldn't take me unless he thought I was joining a husband here, and I . . . didn't want to use my own name, so . . ."

Nathan covered her hand with his own, his skin warm against hers. "Julia, you didn't embarrass me. I understand that you had to leave Andrew, and you needed a name, so you posed as my wife." He stopped, and then spoke so low that Julia could barely hear him. "It ought to be true. I wish it were."

Startled, Julia pulled back her hand, and heard a breathless voice call, "Mama. Mama." She turned to catch the small body throwing itself at her knees. "Snakes. We saw snakes. Come look at snakes, Mama."

Bessie and the twins all had adventures to report, and in the bustle of a last round of sightseeing and the tired trip home, Julia could ignore the apprehension Nathan's words had roused. Only after she had checked on an irritable Purity and helped bathe the three children and put them to bed did she face how well she'd fooled herself.

Clearly Nathan and Purity had an unhappy marriage. For Julia to stay here, reawakening memories of the youthful infatuation she and Nathan had shared, invited trouble. But she'd let her uncertainties about how to manage, and Paul's need for a father's affection, blind her to reality.

She'd vowed to be on her own, to take care of herself and Paul, but instead she'd slipped into a woman's role in another man's household—a role that belonged to his wife. She must leave, find a boardinghouse, and get employment as soon as possible.

But the next morning Paul was feverish and coughing from an infection in his chest, and concern for him banished all other worries. Julia followed all Nathan's instructions with rigid care, but during the next week he grew steadily worse until the skin on his face began to look translucent. In his illness Paul called to her, but also to his father, and Julia could only hold him, gripped by terror and guilt.

During that terrible week, Nathan spent every possible moment with the ill child, using his skills as a physician, and responding to Paul's cries for "Papa" with soothing words of love. At Nathan's request, Hiram Wilson also examined Paul and agreed they were doing all they could.

Then Julia woke early one morning at her son's bedside and found Paul looking at her with clear eyes. "Where is Uma Orelha, Mama?" he asked, and, tears streaming down her face, she gave him the one-eared mule.

Paul improved steadily, but Julia's terror over losing him had been so great that if he stirred during the night, she woke instantly and got up to look at him and listen to his breathing. One evening when she yawned over dinner, Purity scolded, "Julia, you're foolish about that boy. If you fuss over him so much, you'll get sick yourself." Her voice sharpened. "Then Nathan will have to spend all his time looking after you."

Uncomfortable at Purity's tone, Julia replied, "You're right, Purity. And I'm sorry Paul took so much of your attention, Nathan."

Nathan gave his wife an angry look. "No need to be
sorry, Julia. A doctor expects to spend time with any
patient who needs him. But Purity's right. You need
sleep."

Julia knew she should bring up leaving now, but in
the face of Purity's frowns, her own fatigue, and Paul's
need for a complete recovery, she couldn't. Instead she
smiled at Purity and forced herself to pretend enjoyment of the rest of the meal.

In spite of her resolve to sleep that night she woke
when Paul stirred and had to make herself lie in bed.
Downstairs a clock chimed two o'clock, and she tried to
go back to sleep. Then she heard what sounded like a
moan from Paul's cot and rose instantly. She lit a candle, and shielding the flame, bent over his face. He
turned restlessly, then subsided.

Feeling foolish but relieved, she lifted the candle to
blow it out, when she heard a soft tap on the door.
When she opened it a crack, Nathan, in a long blue
robe, stood outside. "Is Paul all right?" he whispered.

"Yes, and I'm ashamed for disturbing you. I'm too
anxious, I know."

"You didn't disturb me. I had a late-night call and
was on my way to bed when I saw the light under your
door. If I may come in, I'll check him."

She realized she had only her nightgown on. "Just a
moment," she whispered, and quickly slipped on a
wine-red wrapper and tied her loose hair back with a
ribbon before she opened the door.

Nathan touched Paul's forehead and listened to his
breathing, then turned to Julia. "He's fine, but I think
you aren't. A glass of brandy will help you sleep. Come
with me."

He took her firmly by the elbow and led her downstairs to his study at the back of the house. It had a

worn desk and an old leather couch and matching chair, discarded from the first office he and Hiram had shared.

He moved a stack of papers from the chair to the desk. "Please excuse the mess. If I let Bessie in here, she ruins everything, so it's dusty. But I have here the best brandy and the best view in the house." He motioned toward the large window at the back, then took out a bottle of brandy and poured two glasses.

Julia took her portion and breathed the pungent fumes before sipping the amber liquid. She felt self-conscious about her nightwear, though while Paul had been very ill, she'd worn her nightgown and wrapper and seen Nathan in his robe many times without thinking of how they were dressed.

"Was your call tonight anything serious?" she asked.

He looked down at his glass, and even under his beard Julia could see the twist to his mouth. "Not really," he reflected. "About on the level of most of Purity's complaints."

Uncomfortable and unable to think of a response, Julia put down her glass and went to the window. A few lights still flared in an area where gambling halls and brothels stayed open all night. The city looked sad, like a tired lady who had shed her daytime mask of gaiety.

Behind her Nathan said softly, "When I knew you ten years ago you were a beautiful girl, sometimes lively, sometimes serious. Now you're a woman, even more beautiful, and with all a woman can offer."

Trying to avert an expression of the longing she heard in his voice, she protested lightly, "You don't know know how impossible I can be."

"I know I see passion in you. I meant what I said at the gardens. You should have been my wife."

She turned in alarm. He lifted her hair, stroking the

tender skin of her neck. She jerked away. "No, Nathan. You mustn't say that. You mustn't even think it."

He captured her face between his hands. "I can't help but think about you. All the time." His voice, low and hoarse, reached into her heart, finding the loneliness and pain of her long estrangement from Andrew. "Do you know how desirable you are, Julia? How much I love you? How much I want you?"

His breath warmed her cheek, and his silky mustache brushed across her lips like a question. "Julia, Julia," he murmured, "I've thanked God every day because you came, and I've cursed every night when I couldn't touch you."

She pushed at his hands. "Nathan. Stop! You must stop."

He seemed not to hear her. His mouth found hers, kissing her with increasing intensity, one hand at the back of her neck, the other finding the front of her robe, slipping inside to caress her waiting breast. For a moment her body, starved for the sensations he was creating, responded with deep pleasure, and she leaned into his hand.

Then reason broke the spell his hands and her own sensuality had been creating. She struggled, trying to get her arms between them, pushing against his chest. This couldn't be Nathan, the gentle friend who treated her child so tenderly. But it was Nathan, transformed by passion. As if he were beyond thought, he covered her face with kisses, his body pressing her against the wall. Through her robe and gown she could feel the pressure of his erection. His hands found her breasts again, but now they roused fear instead of desire.

She wrenched her face sideways, straining to escape him. Urgently she gasped, "Nathan . . . you don't know what you're doing. Let me go. You must let me go."

His labored breathing and clutching hands told her words were useless. She flailed at his shoulders, but he seemed not to feel her fists. Sobbing now, she felt her clothes pushed up, then his hand on her thigh.

Panic and fury gave her strength, and she thrust frantically against him. He stumbled backward to the side of the desk. As if finally aware of what he was doing, he stared at her, his breathing labored, his eyes stricken. "My God, Julia . . . what am I doing?"

He staggered to the chair and slouched down, his head in his hands. Gradually his breathing slowed. "Julia," he muttered, his words barely understandable, "I can't tell you . . . I never intended this to happen . . . right here in the house with Purity."

His obvious distress mitigated some of her anger. She pulled her clothes together and sat on the couch for fear her legs wouldn't support her. He looked at her and said hoarsely, "Please believe me, Julia, I would never dishonor you and Purity this way. Just, suddenly, tonight . . . I couldn't control myself."

She moistened her lips, reminding herself this was Nathan, who had cared so lovingly for Paul. Shakily she said, "I . . . I think I can understand. Maybe I'm to blame too. I knew I should leave, but Purity begged me so, and then with Paul sick . . ."

He moved across and sat beside her on the couch. "No, Julia, you mustn't blame yourself. It was up to me to be strong. But we'll work everything out." He took a deep breath and seemed to regain his composure. "I've already located a house, not far from my office, and close to a park where Paul can play. I can come over during the midday hour and after I've been out on a night call. I'll find a way to spend the whole night sometimes. It will be all right—not like tonight, with Purity upstairs."

Julia felt as if ice had replaced the blood in her body. No, she thought, I'm hearing wrong. She concentrated on keeping her voice steady. "Then you're sorry for . . . losing control when we're in the same house with your wife?"

"Julia, I've explained. I intended to wait until it was reasonable for you to leave, so we could make love in our own place. Not like tonight, in this room. I'm appalled at myself. Please understand." He took her hand, but she jerked it back, the ice inside her turning to blazing rage.

She jumped to her feet, standing over him, her fists clenched. "Understand! Nathan, we didn't make love tonight. You were *forcing* me. Do *you* understand that?"

He rose also and grasped her shoulders. "My God, Julia, be quiet. Someone will hear you. What do you mean, forcing you?" Though his voice sounded calm, his rigid stance told her of beginning anger. "Julia, I know you're upset now, and I've apologized for the circumstances, but I felt your response."

She held herself stiffly erect, determined not to let her fury bring tears. "Yes, I did respond at first. I can feel passion as much as any man, but that didn't give you the right to assume I wanted to make love. Or think I'd be your mistress."

His anger was obvious now. "My God, Julia, you left your husband. You came here by yourself. What else should I think?"

Thunderstruck, she stared at him. This was the man who'd offered his life to oppose slavery for blacks. "Doesn't a woman have the same right as a black—to be free?"

As if making that accusation had exhausted all her rage and strength, Julia turned and fled back to her temporary room to prepare for still another flight.

20

"Mrs. Langdon, may I have a word with you?"

Julia paused at the foot of the boardinghouse stairs and turned to face the heavy woman in the parlor doorway. "Of course, Mrs. Jennings."

She followed the landlady into the small room, crowded with furniture rescued from some more spacious house. "Has Paul been all right?" she asked.

Mrs. Jennings, panting a little as she settled herself on the sofa, replied, "Yes, indeed. He's asleep upstairs now. Polly's keeping an eye on him."

Relieved, Julia let herself sink tiredly onto the worn plush. Her afternoon's search for employment had been as fruitless as on other days during the past two months. She struggled for a smile. "What did you wish to talk to me about, Mrs. Jennings?"

"A gentleman was here today, asking for a red-headed woman with a young black-haired boy."

Before Julia could smother it, hope flared. Could it be Andrew? Then as swiftly hope turned to apprehension. "Did he say who he was?"

"He said he was Dr. Holt."

Disappointment and relief mingled equally before dismay swallowed both. Nathan was still pursuing her.

Within a week after the incident in Nathan's study, Julia had moved to a rooming house. Purity hadn't objected; she must have guessed her husband's feelings. But Nathan had not left Julia alone, appearing at unexpected times, unwilling to believe Julia's refusal. Though she hated to move Paul again, Julia had finally left that rooming house for one in the North Beach area.

"What did you tell him?" she asked.

Mrs. Jennings reached across and patted Julia's hand. "Nothing, my dear. I haven't lived fifty-three years without learning when to keep silent. I thought if you wanted to see this Dr. Holt, you'd have been in touch with him yourself."

On top of all the frustrations of the last two months, this kindness seemed almost more than Julia could bear. She barely managed "Thank you" before her tears began to fall. As she fumbled for her handkerchief, she felt herself pulled against a soft and ample bosom.

One of the unexpected blessings of the move had been Mrs. Jennings. The widowed landlady had hair like Papa's—faded red mixed with gray. Her sympathetic nature reminded Julia of William also, and gradually she had confided some of her circumstances to the understanding listener. Mrs. Jennings had taken to Paul and helped immeasurably by caring for him while Julia looked for employment.

When she had spent her tears, Julia pulled upright. "I'm sorry—I'm not usually so weepy."

Mrs. Jennings waved a dismissing hand. "No need to apologize. We all need a bit of comfort now and again. Had a bad day, I venture."

Julia smiled ruefully at the round face. "Everyone seems suspicious of a married woman alone. I've decided I need either a husband or a death certificate.

Though once I tried to say I was a widow, and that just brought two proposals of marriage before I could get out of the bank—and no job."

A chuckle jiggled the chins below the sympathetic face. "San Francisco has too many men and not enough women. Even I could get married ten times over."

"Apparently I'm not respectable enough to be a teacher," Julia concluded. "I've thought about working as a housekeeper. I'm certainly not ready to take something in a bar or gambling club."

Mrs. Jennings looked shocked. "I should think not. But you must realize, dear, no woman with a husband's going to hire a housekeeper with your looks."

The phrase brought back to Julia the news that Nathan had come here today. How had he found her? He must have seen her in this area. Distressed, she realized she would have to move again. "Mrs. Jennings, I'm grateful for all you've done, and especially for protecting me today, but I'm afraid I'll have to find another place to live." The tears she thought she'd exhausted threatened again.

The middle-aged widow hesitated, then said tentatively, "I know of a job you could have teaching school."

"Teaching school! That's the first thing I thought of," Julia exclaimed, then remembered, "but I'm not respectable."

"No one would ask questions in the job I'm thinking of," Mrs. Jennings rejoined, "but it's in a place not many women would go. My niece, who's visiting my sister, lives in Aurora, and they just lost their teacher. It's a mining town, on the other side of the mountains."

"A mining town," Julia exclaimed. "What is it like?"

"Cold winters and mostly rough men, but the families want education for their children, and they'd be good to you and your boy. My niece and her husband will be going home in a few days. If you're interested, you could meet them tomorrow. Wouldn't a soul know where you were unless you told him."

Mrs. Jennings' words raised painful thoughts. Julia knew if she went that far away, Nathan couldn't find her, but no one else would either. Although she'd concealed her departure from Brazil, a faint hope that Andrew would somehow find her had been buried inside her. Resolutely she asked, "What time should Paul and I be ready tomorrow to meet your niece?"

The teamster Reason Barnes negotiated every curve in the Sonora-Mono wagon road as if the six-horse team were his extra arm or leg. Under his disdainful stewardship, the Concord Coach climbed along the Stanislaus River beside peaks still snow-covered in late June, crested the Sierra Nevada at Sonora Pass, and descended to the desertlike eastern valleys, all in not quite two days. The names of the stage stations entranced Julia—Strawberry Flat, Leavitt Meadows, Fales Hot Springs, and Mormon House at Bridgeport, the last stop before their destination. As they neared Aurora, Julia looked out at the barren hills where scattered scrubby pines and cedars clung to small canyons, and felt as if she'd traveled to the moon.

She shifted Paul's weight where he slept, half on her lap. Beyond him Peggy Wright smiled at Julia, her plain round face showing her relationship to Mrs. Jennings and the same good nature. That warmth and friendliness had won Julia's affection, and the obvious honesty of Gilbert Wright had secured her trust. The school would open the first of August, so Julia had decided to accompany the Wrights back to Aurora. She would stay with them until she found a place to settle herself and Paul.

Nathan hadn't come to the rooming house again before she left San Francisco, so she was certain he wouldn't follow her. She didn't want to worry her father any longer, so Julia had written to him, explaining where she would be, asking him not to tell Andrew. Not, she thought, that Andrew would care by now.

"We're almost there," Peggy Wright said, and pointed to a scattering of stone huts with canvas roofs and a few tents. Outside of these rude shelters men stood or lounged, taking their Sunday ease. Partway up the hillsides large structures crouched below tailing piles, the stamping mills where the quartz was powdered and then treated to yield its gold and silver. The coach slowed at a frame shanty with a sign, "Haskell's Tollgate," but a man standing in the door waved them on. Wood buildings appeared, with an occasional two-story brick building mixed in, as they reached the center of town.

The coach pulled up at the stage office, where a large group of men waited. When Gilbert Wright took Julia's hand to help her down, she nodded toward the gathering and asked, "Is today some special occasion?"

He gave a booming laugh. "Three things bring out a crowd here, Miz Langdon—a fire, the stage comin' in, and a good dogfight."

From the interested stares Julia was receiving, she decided that the arrival of a female on the stage must add to the excitement. A murmur of voices accompanied the looks sent her way, and a tall thin man with a drooping mustache lifted his hat and bowed to her. Hastily she turned to help Paul down, and when she faced the crowd again, she noticed disappointed looks directed at the small boy. One man, whose frock coat and tall silk hat indicated he was not a miner, stopped and spoke to Gilbert Wright, but his bold glances at her showed that his interest was on her and not Mr. Wright. She smiled but stayed well back to avoid an introduction she didn't want to receive. To her relief Mr. Wright spoke only briefly to the man and nodded to the others before starting up the dusty street.

Paul clutched her hand as Julia followed the Wrights. For a moment doubt made her want to run back to the stage. Then her resolution to make a new life for herself and her child returned.

In muggy July heat, Andrew paced up and down the terrace of a hotel in Acapulco. He'd left Rio in early April on a steamer which was supposed to take him to San Francisco in two months. It had been three and a half months, and he still wasn't in California. He scowled in frustration. He ought to have been able to row to California by now!

One problem after another had plagued the ship—vicious storms around the Horn, engine trouble when they finally reached the Pacific. They'd been in this Mexican port for two weeks making repairs. Each day the captain had assured him would be the last, and then only a week to San Francisco.

His fellow passengers apparently enjoyed gambling with the Indian men in the square and spending their nights with the prettiest of the women. But Andrew yearned for only one woman, and he feared that with each day, she might be farther away from him.

Three days later the ship finally departed, and within another week Andrew had arrived in San Francisco and located Nathan Holt's office. Below the brass name plates beside the door, another, smaller sign invited anyone to "Come In," and Andrew entered the reception room. A woman and a girl in black dresses sat on a bench along one side of a small room. A young man, his arm in a sling, occupied a chair. From behind a desk a dark-haired woman asked, "May I help you?"

Andrew crossed to the desk and said, "I'm Andrew Langdon. I wish to see Dr. Holt about a personal matter."

A smile lit up the face in front of him. She stood and held out her hand. "That's why you look so familiar. You're Paul's father."

Andrew felt joy flood over him and knew his smile must be so broad as to look foolish as he bowed over her hand. "Yes. You've met him and my wife?"

"At the Holts'. I'm Mrs. Wilson. Unfortunately, Nathan's not here now, but let me give you his address. I'm sure you'll find Purity at home."

Half an hour later Andrew tied the reins of his rented horse to a post in front of a blue-and-gray house. It had been nine months since he'd seen Julia and Paul. His son wouldn't look the same, but would she? Would she welcome him?

Andrew mounted the steps and pulled the bell. In a few minutes a middle-aged woman opened the door. When she saw him, her face showed first surprise, then something else—perhaps pity.

"I'm Andrew Langdon," he explained, "and I would like to see Mrs. Holt."

She hesitated, then said, "Please come this way." Andrew followed her into the parlor, his expectations somehow chilled by her expression.

In a few minutes a thin blond-haired woman entered. "Andrew Langdon?" Her tone seemed more accusation than a question. She didn't wait for him to answer before she said, "I'm Purity Townsend Holt."

"Mrs. Holt." Andrew bowed over her hand. "Thank you for seeing me."

"Please sit down," she said, and in almost the same breath, "Julia's not here."

Though the servant's reaction had prepared him, Andrew had to smother a first thrust of despair before he could ask, "Can you tell me where she is? I understood from Mrs. Wilson that my wife and son were visiting you."

"They were, but I don't have any idea where they are now," Purity retorted, then added, her voice thin and spiteful, "but you can ask my husband. He probably knows."

Andrew's heart chilled further. He compared Julia's vibrant beauty to this pale woman with the pinched mouth, and knew Nathan Holt must have made the same comparison. Had he come so far to find Julia established with another man?

Grumpily Purity offered, "Nathan will be home soon. If you want to stay to see him, you're welcome." A glint of something like satisfaction appeared on her face. "You're big and handsome. Nathan won't like that."

The incongruity of this comment from the disapproving mouth struck Andrew, and for the first time in days he laughed. "Thank you, Mrs. Holt."

It was the only humor he found that day. Nathan returned and, obviously uncomfortable, insisted he didn't know where Julia was—that she'd decided she must be on her own, but then had just disappeared. Andrew didn't quite believe him, but he couldn't say so.

He declined a reluctantly offered dinner invitation and returned to his hotel. Julia and Paul had to be somewhere nearby, and most people remembered a woman with her beauty and coloring. If he had to search every lodging house in the city, he would find them.

*   *   *

"Mama, see my dog."

Julia finished washing the slate chalkboard on the
schoolroom wall and looked down at the drawing of a
circle with two points for ears and a wavering line
which she judged must be a tail. "It's Woeful," added
Paul, naming a droopy-eared hound who had become
his constant companion. If possible Aurora had more
dogs than sagebrush, and Woeful was only one of the
canines Paul would have adopted had Julia allowed.

She hugged Paul. "I like your drawing," she commented safely.

She and Paul had a room with the Butlers, across the
road from the brick schoolhouse. Sam Butler was the
blacksmith and had a large house; Mrs. Butler was
happy to have Julia and Paul board with them for ten
dollars a week. This left over half of Julia's monthly
hundred-dollar salary to add to what she had left of her
legacy. In the mornings Paul came to school with her
and during the afternoons stayed with Mrs. Butler until
the pupils left.

School for forty-two children had started at the beginning of August, and the first few weeks had been
difficult. The previous year the regular teacher had left,
and four different parents had tried to manage the
school. This year the children had arrived wary and a
little wild, testing whether Julia would last. But she
found she enjoyed the teaching, and by now, the third
week of September, she easily maintained order with
the proper combination of authority and humor. Even
the boy who still seemed determined to cause trouble
had softened a little toward her. The eager responses of
most of the children gave her a feeling of accomplishment and purpose.

Julia thought she could hardly have picked a place
more different from Brazil. Everything seemed raw and

unfinished. Yet, surprisingly, she already felt at home here. She had never before lived in a small town and didn't know what to expect, but the people of Aurora had welcomed her and Paul warmly, and even the roughest of the miners respected "the teacher."

Her growing affection for Aurora was partly due to Mrs. Butler's mother, Mattie Weber. The small wiry woman immediately involved Julia in recording a history of Aurora. At first Julia could hardly believe it possible to write a history of a town only a little more than ten years old, but Mrs. Weber's enthusiasm and her colorful anecdotes made the task appealing. Her seventy-six years showed only in her deteriorating eyesight. "Everywhere I live," she informed Julia, "I write the history, but because of my eyes I need help now."

So every Saturday afternoon Julia spent an hour or more transcribing tales about Aurora. She learned that already its population had peaked and was now declining. Silver and gold production had dropped off suddenly in 1864, and many of the miners drifted away, a few to nearby Bodie, others to faraway silver strikes they'd heard of.

Mrs. Weber told Julia that at first Aurora had been considered part of California instead of Nevada. In those years supporters of the Union or Confederate side in the War Between the States had participated in their own clashes in the small mining town. The Confederate sympathizers voted in Nevada elections, while Union supporters voted in California, and some men voted twice. In 1863 a survey put Aurora three miles inside Nevada.

Julia also learned that a favorite Sunday sport was a badger fight, that all lawyers were called Judge, and that at one time men had been shot for as little as throwing bricks at someone else's house. "A body for breakfast" was what the town called the almost nightly killings, until a citizens' committee established law and order in 1864. Aurora still had twenty-two saloons and only two churches, and gambling was the favorite entertainment, but the town was now safe for families.

Though the landscape at first seemed bleak and desolate, Julia liked the pungent odor of sagebrush and the rich smell of the claylike earth on rainy days. When plumes of cloud trailed over the jagged peaks of the Sierra and the chill winds swept down, a feeling of exhilaration came with them. Then she would take Paul and climb one of the nearby hills to refresh herself with the austere beauty.

Now Julia picked up her quill pen and sharpened it for tomorrow while Paul contentedly began to draw again. Despite the strange surroundings, she had made a place for him that depended on her own efforts—a place that benefited the children of Aurora. The pleasure of that accomplishment helped to conceal the lonely sorrow that crept over her when she allowed herself to listen to her heart.

The late September weather was warm for San Francisco when Andrew entered Nathan Holt's reception room, glad to see only a single man waiting. Mrs. Wilson smiled and rose to greet him. "How pleasant to see you, Mr. Langdon."

"I would like to see Dr. Holt."

"He has a patient now, but if you could wait, I'll tell him you're here." She waved her hand toward a chair before exiting to an inner room.

He walked back to the window, too restless to sit. He had been in California for two months without finding Julia. He'd canvassed every hotel and lodging house in San Francisco and even across the bay in Oakland. He couldn't search all of California, but before he would give up, he'd speak to Nathan Holt again.

Two women, the older leaning on the younger, came through the door at the back, followed by Mrs. Wilson. She motioned to Andrew and led him to an inner room where Nathan turned from a washbasin, drying his hands. "Andrew, I didn't know you were still in San Francisco. Please sit down."

"Thank you, but I won't take much of your time." He studied Nathan's face, deciding that his eyes looked as if he were carefully concealing his thoughts. "I'll speak frankly. I haven't located my wife and son, and I had the impression when we talked before that you may have some idea where I might find them."

Nathan flushed. "I assure you, I do not know where they are."

"Yes, but I think you could tell me more than you have."

The hazel eyes looked hostile now. "Perhaps Julia doesn't want you to know."

Andrew clenched his hands at his side to keep from trying to shake the information he wanted from Nathan. Just now he cursed his size, which would make any physical attack unfair. He put his frustrated desire to strike the smaller man into his voice. "I assure you she will have complete freedom to return with me to Brazil or not as she chooses, but I must find her, and I think you can help me."

The resistance died in Nathan's face, and he said stiffly, "I can tell you the street in North Beach where I glimpsed her once last May. No one in the three lodging houses nearby admitted seeing her, but I suspected that one landlady knew more than she would say."

So, Andrew thought, Julia had been hiding from Nathan as well as from him. He burned to know why, but he couldn't take time to find out. "Thank you," he said coldly, "I'd like that information."

It took Andrew less than an hour to locate the address Nathan had given him, and he now faced the buxom landlady whose eyes assessed him. She looked kindly, but kind or not, Andrew was determined to find out anything she knew.

Mrs. Jennings studied the tall man sitting in her parlor and considered what she should do. When he'd come asking about Julia in August, he'd accepted her denial, but she knew from the line of his jaw and the tense posture of his body that this time was different. More than his determination made her reluctant to lie to him again. Underneath his strong exterior she sensed a sadness like the sorrow she'd seen in Julia. The glow in the dark blue eyes when he mentioned his wife proclaimed an intense love for Julia, and whatever had happened between them in the past, Mrs. Jennings concluded, he'd never hurt her now.

"Yes, Mr. Langdon, I know where Julia is," she said, and was rewarded immediately by Andrew's brilliant smile.

He only said, "Thank you, Mrs. Jennings, for trusting me," but she could see the charm that had made Polly blush when she announced him.

Restraining an almost forgotten flutter in her breathing, she warned, "You'll have to hurry, though. The passes sometimes close by the end of October."

The wind sent chilly fingers under the collar of Julia's jacket and whipped her skirts around her ankles. Holding Paul's hand tightly, she hurried through the swirling dust of the road. At more than seven thousand feet, winter arrived early, and tomorrow would be the first of October. Only the weeds and flax grasses had turned

gold, but the scrubby evergreens looked faded, as if
dreading the coming cold. Even the piano music that
drifted from the hotel lobby as they passed sounded
plaintive, without its usual boisterous thumping.

Before she went to the Butlers', she needed to re-
plenish the food she cooked for Woeful. With three
dogs of their own, the Butlers had no scraps for the
hound that had adopted Paul. Since today's stage had
arrived, she would also inquire about mail. It probably
wasn't time for a letter to have reached Papa and an
answer to return, but it made her feel closer to him to
ask.

In the recessed entrance to Meredith's General Emporium, which also had the post office in the back, she
paused to brush away some leaves which clung to her
skirt. Across the road two men stood beside one of the
white posts which supported the balcony of the brick
courthouse. She recognized one of them as "Judge"
Reddy, onetime saloon keeper and gambler until he
lost an arm in a shooting and turned to law. He defended the poor and the most notorious criminals, but
his lost arm always made her think of James, and she
couldn't help liking him. The other was "Uncle Billy"
O'Hara, the local restaurant owner and money lender,
and one of the few black men in Aurora. The men
tipped their hats to her, and she nodded before obeying
Paul's impatient hand and going inside.

She could see William Meredith in the door of his
office and mail room at the back. Two Paiute women
stood at one of the long wooden counters, fingering
bolts of colorful calico and holding it up against a dressmaker's dummy. Dick, the clerk, stood behind the tall
coffee grinder with its faded pictures of exotic ladies
holding steaming cups. He was maneuvering a sack of

beans into place under the counter. "I'll be with you in a minute, Miz Langdon," he assured her.

"No hurry. I just need something for dog food when you're finished there." She went back to the section by the bins of oats.

Paul stopped in front of the glass-fronted counter. He pointed to a miner's metal hat with its well for a candle on top. "Look, Mama. I want a hat like that." She reached down and ruffled the black curls.

Mr. Meredith's voice called to her. "Mrs. Langdon, I'm glad you're here. I was just about to give this gentleman direction to the Butlers'."

She turned and her heart began to beat in a wild, erratic rhythm. Behind the store owner, having to duck his head to get through the doorway, was Andrew.

As if some photographer, hidden under his black cloth, had caught them all inside a gilt frame, Julia froze, her hand on Paul's head. Across the scuffed wooden floor Andrew stood, a heavy jacket making him look even broader than she remembered.

His deep voice shattered the picture. "Hello, Julia."

She tried to speak, but nothing could get past the constriction in her throat.

He closed the space between them and crouched in front of Paul. He spoke slowly, carefully. "Hello, Paul."

Again the ghostly photographer framed them. Paul turned and pulled Julia's head down. His whisper echoed in the space around them. "Who is this, Mama?"

Andrew rose, and Julia saw tears shimmering in his eyes. Her heart felt wrenched apart between the tall man before her and the small boy at her side. She looked down at the puzzled face turned up to hers, and words came from deep inside her. "This is your papa."

21

Julia heard Andrew thanking Mr. Meredith for his help, and listened to her own meaningless exchange of greetings with him, which betrayed nothing of the chaos inside her. Only when Andrew offered Paul his hand, which Paul hesitantly accepted, and took Julia's elbow, did his touch transform the dream to reality. He was here; he had come to find them and Julia realized she had wanted this to happen though she had not admitted it. No inner warning that he might want Paul and not her could prevent her wild excitement. Only pride and a shred of caution helped her preserve an outward calm.

As soon as they stepped outside to go to the Butlers', Julia knew the town's communication system was already operating. Across at the courthouse two more men were staring at the Emporium doorway. Farther up, three boys with assorted dogs obviously waited for the schoolteacher and her newly arrived husband to pass them. Another boy skidded around a corner and stopped, setting the dogs barking.

Andrew looked at her, a crinkle of laughter lightening his face. "You must be a figure of interest in Aurora."

That familiar teasing tone touched her heart, breach-

ing her reserve. "It's you who are providing the excitement," she responded lightly.

Paul tugged at Andrew's hand and gave a smile that
made them unmistakably father and son. "Do you want
to see Woeful?" he asked.

"I don't know," Andrew responded as they started
along the edge of the road. "What or who is Woeful?"

"Woeful is my dog," explained Paul, and added shyly,
"Papa."

"Then I certainly want to see him," Andrew assured
his son, and his voice held a tenderness which at once
wrenched and delighted Julia.

As they passed the hotel Julia noticed that the piano
music had stopped. Several faces peered through the
dusty windows, and three men were standing in the
doorway. After they walked on, a voice followed them
on the wind. "Waal, guess she had a husband after all.
God damn. I figured she just said that so's she could
look us over."

Someone else ordered, "Shut up, Limpy. She warn't
gonna look at you anyhow." Andrew gave Julia an amused
glance, and her heart beat even more rapidly.

Paul's steady chatter kept Andrew occupied, with
every sentence beginning or ending with "Papa," and
Julia was grateful to be spared having to speak and
display her trembling emotions. Across the road a trail
of boys matched Andrew and Julia's progress up the
sloping road past the schoolhouse. Paul patted the brick
wall and said proudly, "Papa, this is Mama's school. I
work here too, Papa."

At the far edge of the building more boys and a few
girls had gathered. Julia smiled at them and said hello.

"Hello, Miz Langdon," a chorus responded.

Beyond the cluster of children a sandy-haired boy
stood, his hands in his pockets, his frown proclaiming

his disdain for the others' interest. Surprised but pleased, Julia called, "Hello, Benny."

Though she knew he must have heard her, the boy turned and kicked his shabby boots in the dust, then ran off through the resulting cloud. "That's Benny," Paul volunteered. "He's mean."

From across the road a dirty yellow dog assaulted them, circling with yips and whines. Paul managed to clasp the wiggling dog, receiving enthusiastic kisses in return. "As you must have guessed," Julia said, "this is Woeful."

Other dogs and children ran out from the Butler house, and by the time they were all inside and introductions completed, Julia could safely excuse herself to wash and set the table for supper.

As Andrew watched Julia moving quickly around the room, he reminded himself he must be patient and not rush her into a decision—or the intimacy he longed for. She needed time to get over the shock of his arrival. Many things must be settled between them, but until the right opportunity, even a serious discussion between them must wait. Forcing himself to outward calm, he visited with the Butlers during the meal and evening, supplying the latest news from the San Francisco papers.

Mr. Butler was disgusted to hear that British Columbia had become a Canadian province. "Ought to be part of the USA," he grumbled.

He showed the most interest in the struggle over emancipation in Brazil. The Butlers had come from Virginia, and his Southern sentiments were still strong.

"The Brazilian emperor, Dom Pedro," explained Andrew, "favors emancipation. He freed all his own slaves thirty years ago, but he hasn't forced his views on the country. Instead he promotes immigration as a way of solving our labor problems."

"Do you hold slaves, Mr. Langdon?" the blacksmith asked.

"Yes, though only a few now. Our principal house servants are all freed blacks. Most stay on with us, though not all." Andrew looked at Julia, sending an unspoken message. "Our housekeeper recently left to work in Rio, where many blacks go from the plantations."

Paul had spent the evening on Andrew's lap, and when he lost the struggle to stay awake, Julia went to take him as Andrew said, "The Brazilian legislature has just enacted a law declaring that all children of women slaves born after this year will be free. The mother's owner must provide for the children for eight years. Then the owner can receive six hundred dollars from the government or keep the child's services to age twenty-one."

"Six hundred dollars!" Mr. Butler exclaimed. "Not much money."

"You're right," Andrew responded. He rose, still holding Paul, and said to Julia, "I'll carry him to bed."

As he followed Julia into the small bedroom, he savored the feeling of his son against him. He watched silently while she undressed Paul, holding himself under rigid control to keep from pulling her into his arms. When they finally embraced, he wanted her to come to him willingly.

Julia recognized the distinctive scent of Andrew's skin and clothes that had always been able to arouse her. When they both stood beside Paul's bed as he burrowed under the quilts, she was acutely conscious that her own bed lay just behind her, and she felt as if her breathing had stopped.

So far she and Andrew had said nothing personal

other than the information exchanged at supper that
William and Richard were both well and that Ellen
would be returning to Brazil in December. Now she
both longed and feared to break that silence. Andrew
turned her face up toward him, and tremors raced
through her at his touch.

His eyes were as blue as the center of a flame and
she thought he trembled, but the force of her own
emotions shook her so that she couldn't be sure. Huskily he said, "We must talk, but this isn't the place or
time." His head bent slightly, and for a moment she felt
his breath on her forehead. Her heart strained upward,
anticipating his kiss, but he moved back, and her spirit
plummeted.

Abruptly he left the room, and over the thunderous
beating of her heart she heard Mrs. Butler's voice.
"We'd be happy for you to stay with us, Mr. Langdon.
We could move things around and find a place for you."

Julia heard Andrew answer, "Thank you, Mrs. Butler. You and Mr. Butler have been most generous to
me and my family since they've been in Aurora, but I
can't impose more. I'll stay at the hotel tonight."

Composing herself, Julia returned to the main room.
Andrew already had on his heavy coat. "I'll see you
tomorrow morning, Julia," he said. "Thank you for supper, Mrs. Butler, Mr. Butler." He took Julia's hand for
a moment, almost destroying her calm, before he accepted the loan of the lantern Mr. Butler offered and
was gone.

As soon as possible Julia escaped to her room, but
sleep evaded her. Away from the almost overwhleming
appeal of Andrew's presence, the fears which had led to
her flight returned. Had he come for her—or just for
Paul? Did he have a mistress waiting for him at the
fazenda?

Andrew's laughter and the varying expressions of his sensual mouth had reawakened images from the past. Seeing his coat stretch across his wide shoulders and unable to ignore the way his trousers fitted over his thighs, Julia felt tormented with remembered passion. She pictured his naked body and dug her fingernails into her palms until tears of frustration and despair overflowed onto her pillow.

The weeping brought her some release, and she felt able to consider more calmly what tomorrow might bring. Until she knew his feelings, she couldn't plan what she would do or say. She forced herself to think of the school, of the work for the next day, and the children whose lives she'd begun to share. The image of Benny Gardiner, wanting as much as the others to see the schoolteacher's husband, but unwilling to admit it, occupied her thoughts.

Until recently, Benny had rebuffed all her efforts with sullen hostility. Though he was easily the brightest pupil in her class, Julia suspected he wouldn't be in school at all if it weren't for the threat of a beating from his stepfather. More than once he had come to school with black eyes and bruises, but none of the other children teased him about it. Large for a ten-year-old, he was already dangerous with his fists.

Just the last week Julia had sensed a change in Benny's attitude to her and to school. Her books clearly fascinated him, and he could read better than any of the older children. But he had refused to attempt spelling or arithmetic, and his writing was crude. Though Julia had grown to care about most of her students, helping Benny seemed particularly important. If only, she thought, she could win his confidence, he could learn so much—prepare himself for more than the often poverty-stricken life of a miner.

Concentrating on Benny, she felt her mind grow hazy, and she finally drifted into sleep.

The contingent of girls who came early to school the next morning, begging jobs to do, was larger than usual. When Julia rang the bell, she saw curiosity on the children's faces. She had just given assignments to the older children and collected the younger ones around her when she heard Paul's voice in the back of the room where he had a small table for his favorite occupation of drawing. "Papa," he said excitedly, and Julia looked up to find every head turned toward the tall man closing the door.

Andrew said, "Please excuse me for disturbing you. I came for Paul." His words roused a flash of her old fears, but it quickly died. Somehow she knew he wouldn't just take Paul and leave.

She could see she would accomplish nothing until she satisfied her pupils' curiosity. "Children, this is my husband, Mr. Langdon."

Andrew smiled and said hello, receiving shy responses except from Benny, who sat stony-faced, staring at a book in front of him. Paul left with Andrew, and when the commotion died down, the day continued as usual. At the noon recess, Benny bolted before Julia could speak to him, and he did the same at the end of the day.

Soon after the pupils left, Paul and Andrew arrived, Paul chattering breathlessly about all the places they had explored together. Watching the small boy cling happily to the tall man, Julia wondered how she could have separated them, yet she knew she could not bear to part with her son herself. Determinedly she pushed away her gloomy thoughts. Soon it would be time for appraisals, but until then she would relish the pleasure of being with the two people she most loved.

That evening was much like the one before, with Andrew answering questions about Brazil, and the blacksmith in turn describing the discovery of silver and gold which had led to the simultaneous founding of Aurora and the smaller town of Bodie. Mr. Butler loved a good anecdote, and Aurora's early undisciplined days supplied many. Paul again fell asleep on Andrew's lap, but this time Andrew let Julia put the child to bed by herself and offered only an impersonal "Good night" when he left for the hotel.

Despite her determination to enjoy the present, Julia found her fears returning. Though she felt an intense longing for Andrew's touch, she wasn't sure about his desires. When she finally slept that night, nightmares of strange landscapes where she was forever searching and forever lost plagued her.

The next morning Andrew came for Paul before it was time for Julia to cross to the schoolhouse, and she left them in Mrs. Butler's kitchen. The demands of forty-two children prevented her from thinking about anything else when she was in the classroom. Tomorrow would be Saturday—no school. Then she would have to face her feelings, but not yet.

That day Benny used every opportunity to create disturbances, from tripping the girls walking past his desk to starting fights with the larger boys. Determined to talk to him, Julia captured him before dismissing the others at the end of the day. She saw Paul and Andrew at the door and went to speak to them.

"I'll be a few minutes longer. Could you come back in a little while?"

"But, Mama," Paul protested, seizing her hand and pulling at her, "we have a surprise for you."

"Not so impatient," Andrew interrupted, and swung Paul up onto his shoulder. "We can wait." With a smile for Julia that made her breath come faster, he turned and walked down the hill. She could hear Paul's laughter as she closed the door.

Benny slouched in his seat, refusing to look at her as she sat at the desk next to him. "Benny," she began, "you know I can't let you behave as you did today." When he said nothing, she continued, "I had thought you were doing so much better."

Still not looking at her, he muttered, "Just go tell my maw."

Julia kept her voice even, trying to reach to the child she knew was hidden under the defiant manner. "I don't want to talk to your mother. I want to talk to you. I want to help you be as smart as I know you can be."

He half-turned toward her and said sullenly, "Won't matter anyhow. You'll just leave." He jerked his hand backward toward the door. "You're gonna go with him."

Now she understood. He was angry because he was afraid of losing something he was starting to value. Was he right that she was leaving? She didn't know, but she must say something.

"Benny," she told his still partly averted face, "I'm here today, and I'll be here next week, and I want you to be the best pupil in this class. I know you can be, but not if you're using all your time to tease or fight and be punished."

Slowly he turned and looked directly at her, as if weighing her words, trying to decide whether to trust her. Almost shyly he asked, "You think I could be the smartest in the school?"

"Yes, Benny, I do—if you work. Will you?"

In his face she could see the struggle between fear and the desire to believe her. "Well . . . I guess maybe I might try."

She wanted to hug him but feared to disrupt his

tentative acceptance. "Good, Benny. I'll see you on Monday, and we'll work together. You may leave now."

He rewarded her with the beginning of a smile before he was out the door and running wildly up the hill.

Paul and Andrew arrived a few minutes later. "We were watching for Benny to leave," Paul announced. "Come on now, Mama, hurry!"

Outside, Paul, with Woeful following boisterously, started to run down the road, then stumbled and fell.

In two strides Andrew had picked up his son and turned, grinning, to Julia. "Come on, slowpoke," he called. Laughing at their excitement, Julia followed.

She caught up with them at the cross street beside the courthouse. They turned and continued along Pine Street, past a house with a glass enclosure where a few plants found shelter from the wind, until they were opposite the Methodist church. Andrew stopped and put Paul down. Without waiting, Paul opened the sagging gate of a latticed fence and ran up onto the wooden porch of a weathered building. He turned and called to Julia, his voice high with excitement, "See, Mama. It's ours. Our house."

"Ours for now," corrected Andrew, and held the gate aside for Julia to go through.

"You mean this house is empty?" she asked incredulously.

"Mr. Butler told me about it," Andrew explained. "The owner had to leave suddenly, and for enough money, it was available."

The porch where Paul waited was at the front of a single-story house with narrow wood siding and a gabled roof. Andrew took a large key from his pocket and opened the door. In a small living room an ancient tan leather couch sat uncomfortably with a high-backed rocker. Along one wall two wooden chairs and a stool waited beside a round table, and a fire already burned in a potbellied black stove.

"At the back is a dog run to the kitchen lean-to," Andrew said, "and here are the bedrooms." Through a door in the back wall of the living room Julia could see a bedroom with a braided rug and a washstand beside a large bed. A smaller bedroom opening off the larger one held a washstand and two narrow beds. Beyond an open door at the other side of the big bedroom Paul was clattering along the dog run.

Then Julia noticed that clothes already hung from pegs on the bedroom walls, Andrew's in the larger room and hers and Paul's in the small bedroom. Disturbed, she turned to him. "But you've already moved our things."

He flushed slightly. "Yes—I realize I didn't ask you, but I found out this morning we could rent this house and I had to take it before someone else did. Having a place to ourselves seemed too important to wait." His voice deepened. "We couldn't sort things out with you at the Butlers', Julia. We must be alone."

Alone. The word suddenly seemed the most sensuous Julia had ever heard. It filled the space between them, reaching from him to her like a caress. She felt it bring heat to her face, vibrating in her breasts.

Paul broke the spell, running back to them. "Come see the kitchen, Mama. Mrs. Butler sent some food. It smells good. I'm hungry. Can Woeful come in too?"

"No, Woeful stays outside." She followed Paul, afraid to look longer at Andrew for fear he would see her waiting for his touch.

The kitchen had a small cooking range and an ill-assorted collection of pots and dishes. The stew Mrs. Butler had sent filled the room with a welcoming fragrance, and the meal at the round table was a happy one.

Exhausted by the strain of the past few days, Julia agreed to Andrew's suggestion that the washing-up be postponed until the morning. After Paul and Andrew arranged a place for Woeful in a shed behind the house, Paul climbed onto Julia's lap where she sat in the rocking chair. Andrew sat across from them, his eyes looking midnight blue in the lantern light.

She realized that she hadn't asked Andrew the most obvious questions. With Paul's weight and warmth soothing her, she began with the easiest one. "When did you leave Brazil, Andrew?"

"The end of March, this time."

He stretched his legs out, the toes of his boots resting next to the feet of the stove. "Last year, when you left, I went first to South Carolina."

A ghost of the old homesickness returned to Julia. "You saw James and Sally—and Hundred Oaks."

Julia rocked slowly as Andrew described the changes and difficulties at Hundred Oaks. "James wrote later to tell me their baby arrived—a girl, and a healthy one. I had the news when I got back home from Philadelphia."

"You went to Philadelphia?" Julia's heart began to beat faster at the approach of the more difficult questions. "That's how you knew to come to California?"

Andrew rose and put more wood on the fire before he answered. "Yes and no. Someone there told me the Holts had moved west. When I returned to Rio, I checked the passenger lists again and found the name Holt on a ship bound for San Francisco."

The knowledge that she had used another man's name caused Julia to pause before she moistened her lips to speak again. "Then you've been away from . . . home a lot. Who's taking care of the *fazenda*?"

"Roberto."

Julia stopped rocking. "Roberto!"

Andrew laughed. "You're no more surprised than he was when I asked him. I didn't know how long I'd be away, and he was the best person for the job." He hesitated, and the laughter left his voice as he said, "I saw that I'd been partly mistaken about him."

Paul stirred, and Julia glanced at him, but her thoughts circled around Andrew's words. She didn't know what he meant. She looked back at Andrew and asked, "How did you trace us here?"

"Dr. Holt finally suggested I see Mrs. Jennings." Andrew's dry tone made Julia wonder what he'd said to Nathan. "She told me you had come to Aurora."

Across the shadowy space between them the invisible strands which had entangled Julia in the bedroom caught her again. Andrew's deep voice tightened them. "Mrs. Jennings knew I would never do anything to hurt you or Paul again."

He rose abruptly and picked Paul up from her lap. Above the sleeping child his face looked tired. "Perhaps we've talked enough for tonight, Julia. We have tomorrow."

She stood also, not sure whether she felt relief or disappointment. "Yes, I think that's best." She followed him into the small bedroom and began to undress Paul.

Andrew watched until Paul was in one of the narrow beds with Uma Orelha tucked in beside him under the covers Mrs. Butler had lent them. "I'll check around outside and see you in the morning," he said.

"Yes," Julia managed. "Good night."

Andrew breathed in the cold air and wondered how many more nights like this he could get through. It had been hard enough to leave Julia and go to the hotel.

Tonight she would be just next door. But he'd seen the exhaustion in her face and the lines of her body and knew he must be patient. But, God, how desirable she looked—even in the high-necked black schoolteacher's dress with her red hair slicked back. Paul had pulled some of the strands loose as Andrew yearned to do but hadn't.

Overhead, stars crowded the sky, and the Big Dipper reminded him of how far he was from home. With things unsettled, he still didn't know how long until he would see the Southern Cross again.

He wasn't sure whether he had been considerate of Julia's fatigue tonight, or if he was avoiding what she might tell him. She may have left him because of her stepmother's tale about a mistress—his futile and unsatisfactory effort to find a substitute for Julia—but she could have gone to her father. Instead she'd made a long and dangerous trip to reach Nathan Holt. Andrew knew he must ask why, but he also knew the answer might destroy his hopes. She'd come to Aurora, he was sure, to get away from Nathan, but that could be because he was married and she loved him too much to remain near him. After all, she was a beautiful and passionate woman who knew how to satisfy a man's desires and had great capacity for sexual pleasure herself.

Slowly Andrew turned back to the house, steeling himself to another lonely night and wondering whether the next day would end or prolong his unhappiness.

Julia heard Andrew's quiet footsteps and the rustle of his clothing in the next room. She felt as if everything inside her was waiting—her heart to beat, her lungs to breathe, her blood to bring warmth back to her body. Then the bed on the other side of the wall creaked, and she knew Andrew was settling himself for the night.

Until then she hadn't known how strong her belief had been that, in spite of her clothes hanging here with Paul's, Andrew would want her in bed with him. Foolish expectations! He hadn't said he desired her—only that he wouldn't hurt her again. What did that mean? That he'd move his mistress to São Paulo and only visit her surreptitiously?

To keep the misery of this thought away, Julia fed her anger. She'd taken his son from him, but they'd had months before she left Brazil when she'd tried to talk to him and he'd refused to listen. He could have had a dozen mistresses in the time since she left—a man with his physical appetites probably had. He might even be comparing her, with her drab, "respectable" clothes, to the beautiful women he'd been bedding.

The anger died under Julia's realization it couldn't prevent her pain. And though pride might conceal her hurt from Andrew, she wouldn't lie to herself. It may have been wrong to tear Paul away from Andrew, but it had taken courage to leave Brazil, and again to leave San Francisco. She'd begun a new life for herself, one that mattered to these children and their families. If Andrew didn't want her, she'd fight for Paul and have the strength to go on here.

But Paul's first words to her the next morning tested her bravery. He crawled in bed beside her and asked softly, "Mama, is this our home?" Without waiting for her answer, he went on, "Do I have a real papa now?"

She hugged him fiercely, barely keeping the tears from her voice as she assured him, "You've always had a real papa, and now he's with you."

Paul took his clothes and scampered out to the living-room stove, but Julia shivered into her dress in the cold bedroom, self-conscious about the intimacy of her night-wear. Coffee smells tantalized her, and when she finished dressing, she found breakfast on the round table and Andrew filling cups from an enamelware pot. Determined to display an easy manner toward him, she teased, "Mrs. Butler again, or have you learned to cook?"

"Wrong about both," he responded. "It's from the boardinghouse next door."

"I'm hungry," announced Paul, and scrambled up onto the stool.

Paul provided the center for the morning spent exploring the town and the surrounding hills. Julia found she could talk easily with Andrew as long as they stayed with neutral subjects, and he seemed as glad as she to avoid anything serious. He seemed interested in her job here, and she described her days in detail, including her problems with Benny and her hopes for change.

They were standing on the slopes above the graveyard when Andrew remarked, "You sound excited about the children, particularly Benny, and about teaching."

"Yes, I am. It surprises me a little. Sometimes it's just terribly hard work, but most days I love it—and I feel really useful."

Below them Woeful began a mad chase after some small animal, and Paul started down. As they followed him, Andrew observed, "You used to feel that way about growing coffee and cotton."

Afraid to spoil their ease, Julia responded lightly, "Maybe this is cultivating children," then said more earnestly, "When I came here, people welcomed me, made me feel part of the town. When I help a child, I feel I'm repaying them—doing my share."

Andrew called, "Paul, wait," and the boy and dog slowed a little.

"Would you like to come with me to see Mrs. Weber

this afternoon?" Julia inquired. "I'm helping her write a history of Aurora."

"A history of this town?"

Julia laughed. "That's what I thought at first, but Mrs. Weber makes it fascinating. She'll want to meet you, and maybe you'll understand better from her that it's a real community."

When Julia and Andrew arrived at the Weber house where Mattie lived with her son, Paul stayed in the yard playing with Woeful. Mrs. Weber welcomed Andrew with a smile that was almost flirtatious.

After tea, Julia got out her notebook and Mrs. Weber recounted two faintly scandalous incidents in 1863 which Julia recorded and to which Andrew responded with intermittent chuckles.

When they'd said their good-byes and collected Paul, Andrew asked Julia, "And stories like those make you love Aurora?"

"Mrs. Weber was just showing off for you today," Julia defended herself. "Most of the people here are kind and friendly." He looked skeptical.

In the excitement of the day, Paul had protested against a nap, so supper, again from the boardinghouse, was barely over before his eyes were drooping. "To bed for you," Julia insisted, and soon he and Uma Orelha were settled. Andrew said a last good-night, and as he followed Julia back into the living room, she knew that the waiting was over. If anything of their marriage could be restored, they must begin now.

She stood beside the stove until Andrew asked, "Do you have to defend yourself against me? Can't we at least sit down together?"

Slowly she faced him, and she hoped he didn't hear the shakiness in her voice. "I'm not sure. Do I need a defense?"

The same pain Julia felt showed clearly in Andrew's eyes before he ground out, "My God, Julia, do you still think I would hurt you? I love you too much to ever want to do that again."

His words exploded like a flare which was so bright she couldn't look at it. She stared at him, wanting to believe him, but not sure whether to give up the protection she'd reached in last night's lonely bed. If he loved her, why had he tormented her? The tension of the last days erupted in something like rage, and her voice shook. "Damn you. You can see I love you, but you haven't touched me. If you care so much, why won't you go to bed with me?"

For a moment he looked stunned, and then he gave a shout of laughter. "Of all the things I've imagined you'd say to me, I never thought it would be that." His laughter died, and the look of hunger in his eyes told her what he hadn't yet been able to say. "No, Julia—I didn't know whether you still loved me, though God knows I wanted it to be so. And how could I make love to you until I knew?"

Though he didn't move toward her, she felt the distance between them narrowing as he continued. "I long to touch you, hold you, but I must know how you feel first. I'd like to say that we'll just begin from this moment, forget what's past, but it isn't so easily forgotten."

She then believed completely that he loved her, but she knew she must make the first gesture. Slowly she reached for his hand and drew him to sit on the sofa with her. The feel of his warm hand against hers sent a current through her so strong that she trembled as she admitted, "I love you, Andrew, but I'm still a little afraid. It's been so long."

"Believe this first, Julia. I love you more than any-

thing else in my life, even more than Paul. I know
Quintiliana lied, and I've hated myself for ever believing her. No other woman means anything to me. No
other woman has since I found you in my room that
night on your father's *fazenda*."

"Andrew, I want to explain that—"

He put his hand against her mouth. "No—not now.
But I must know what . . . Nathan Holt is to you."

Fleetingly Julia thought of the night in Nathan's study
and gave silent thanks that she'd resisted successfully.
"Nothing—Nathan means nothing to me except the
memory of a friend from years ago."

Andrew's face tightened. "Then why did you go to
him? I think I understand why you left me, but why
didn't you stay with your father, or go to Hundred
Oaks?"

"I didn't really go to Nathan," she explained. "I
chose California because it was far enough away I thought
you couldn't find me and take Paul."

"Take Paul?" At first Andrew couldn't make sense of
her words, and then understanding cut into him. "You
thought I would take him away from you?"

He saw her face flush deep red and then lose all color
except for her sherry eyes. "Yes. Men have such power,
and I was afraid."

He'd thought he'd already felt the pain of her departure, but her words created a fresh wound as she went
on. "Ellen was leaving to visit a son she hadn't seen for
most of his life. I thought you had . . . someone you
really wanted . . . and once I wouldn't have believed
you'd keep Paul from me, but I didn't feel I knew you
any longer."

As he watched her, tears filled her eyes. He pulled
her gently into his arms and was rewarded by the brush
of her hair against his face and the familiar scent of

roses. "Yes," he soothed her, "I think I can see how you might feel. We've hurt each other too much, Julia. Can we stop? Begin from now?"

Her face raised to his shone, not just with beauty, but with love he could feel.

In his embrace Julia felt her spirit open like a desert plant that, drawn in on itself during the dry period, opens and blooms with the rain. His kiss watered her parched heart until it overflowed. And with the release of her soul came the reawakening of her body. As he held her close, she pulled his hand to her breast, and she could feel the tremor of laughter in his lips.

"Will you let me take my clothes off before you attack me?" he teased, and in front of the fire they undressed each other, feasting on the sight and feel so long denied. All the sensations Julia had tried to forget flooded over her, as new as the first time he'd come to her bed, and yet recalling all the other passionate couplings they'd shared. She shivered at the sight of his naked shoulders and ran her hands over the strong muscles along the side of his neck. The flare of passion in his eyes as he pulled her chemise away from her bare breasts excited her further and she unfastened the buttons of his trousers. Her hands trembled as she slid the clothing down across his lean waist, releasing his penis from the strained cloth, and then past the hard surfaces of his thighs and calves. His hands made an equally unsteady path down her body as he stripped her of the last barriers between them. As they stood holding each other, the heat of their naked bodies greater than the radiation from the stove, he pulled the pins from her hair. "I've wanted to do that all day," he whispered, and carried her to the large bedroom.

In the borrowed bed they renewed the magic between them. Gently he touched her as she'd longed for him to do—his mouth reintroducing his tongue to hers and her lips to the shape of his. The special scent which was his alone invaded her senses, leaving her quivering and ready for him. He tasted every part of her face and lingered over the edge of her eyelids and the line of her jaw until she could wait no longer to rain her own kisses on the angular lines of his face. More frantically his mouth moved to her breasts, reawakening her nipples to a spiraling pleasure that was almost pain. She pulled away, leaning over him to find the wonderful saltiness of his neck and back before he knelt to trace with his hands and then his mouth the scar from her navel to the dark red curls and sensitive center beneath. Her now urgent hands relearned the feel of his firm muscles and the matted hair of his chest before seeking the throbbing heat of his erect penis.

His voice, hoarse with passion, repeated a litany of love and desire. "Julia . . . I love you. God, you're wonderful—I can't get enough of you."

She felt such intense love for him that her voice trembled in response. "And I love you, Andrew, more than I can say."

When she thought she could not contain the exploding sensations within her, she cried out to him, and with an answering groan he thrust into her, filling her, shutting out everything but the bursting passion they shared. When their shudders stilled, she lay spent, with him still inside her, and felt a joy so great that it overwhelmed the memories of the torment which had separated them for so long.

Andrew pulled the quilts around them and held her close against him, stroking the dampened hair away from her face so tenderly that she felt cherished by every touch of his hand. As they drifted into sleep, she wondered how she could have survived so long without Andrew's gift of love.

22

The hand on her breast seemed part of a dream, and she resisted waking, not wanting to lose the wonderful sensation. A mouth replaced the hand, and cold air on her shoulders dragged her from sleep, but the tremors which radiated from the pull on her nipple continued and grew. The quilts bunched around Andrew's head at her breast, and beneath the covers his hand moved up her thigh.

She clutched at his head, and he left her breast, finding her lips instead. His hard shaft pushed against her abdomen as he held her fitted to him, his tongue tasting her mouth. The quilts slid farther down, and Andrew raised his head. "Damn!" he complained. "It's easier to make love in a warm climate." Then his hands, on her back and buttocks, slipping between her legs, proved that they could provide their own warmth.

The delicious spiral started, and then a voice said, "Mama, I didn't know where you were." Paul stood beside the bed, his one-eared mule clutched in his hand.

Andrew gave a groan and rolled onto his back. In spite of her own disappointment, Julia couldn't stifle a giggle. "Laugh, will you?" he muttered. "Just wait."

Paul regarded his father with a suspicious frown. "Why is Mama in bed with you?"

A smile softening his face, Andrew reached out one arm and pulled the small boy closer. "That's the way with mothers and fathers. Most of the time they sleep in the same bed."

Slowly Paul's frown smoothed. "I like having a papa," he offered a little doubtfully.

"Good," responded Andrew huskily. "Jump back in bed where you'll be warm, and we'll have a fire going right away."

As Paul scurried back to his bed, Andrew sat up and began to pull on his clothes. Julia stifled another giggle as she suggested, "But not the kind of fire you were starting."

He reached back under the covers and slapped her bare bottom. "I see I'll have to teach you a lesson tonight."

"Promise?" she asked, letting the quilt slip to expose a bare breast.

Leaning down, he kissed the exposed nipple. "If you behave. Otherwise our son may get an immediate demonstration of just why you're in this bed."

On that promise Julia floated through the day. She could hardly keep her attention on the church service, feeling sure everyone must know just what the smiles meant that she couldn't restrain. Though Andrew teased her, she insisted on an attempt at cooking, and laughter flowed out of her constantly.

In the evening after Paul was asleep, they spread quilts on the floor in front of the stove and made love there, slowly, savoring each step of remembered pleasures. Then they bundled together on the old sofa and talked.

Julia described what happened that night, over five

years ago, when she'd returned to Andrew's room for Sally's shawl. "I thought I'd be betraying James if I told you about Sally and his fears over having only one arm," she explained. "You seemed like a stranger still. Later I forgot that we'd never talked about it."

"I never told you, because I didn't realize it then," Andrew disclosed, "but I first made love to you to ensure that you'd marry me. Though," he teased, "I didn't have to work very hard to seduce you."

"And I didn't understand until now," she said wonderingly, "that when I left Brazil, I only partly believed you might take Paul away from me. I think I ran away because, even with your having a . . . someone else, I was afraid if I saw you, I might go back to you." He started to speak, but she continued softly, "Then I would have hated myself. And what I think about myself matters almost as much as your feelings about me."

She could hear the emotion in his husky voice as he said, "I did try to . . . forget you with another woman, but it didn't work." He brushed her hair away from her face and kissed her. "I hope you know it will never happen again."

"Yes, I know," Julia responded, and she did.

He drew back a little. "Julia, there's something else I need to know. When you left San Francisco, you obviously didn't want Nathan Holt to know where you were. Did he . . . injure you in any way?"

Without hesitating Julia replied, "No. He and Purity were very good to Paul and me, but he began to think he was still in love with me. It didn't really mean anything, but he and Purity aren't very happy together. So I decided I'd better leave San Francisco, and this job seemed the answer."

"Will there be any trouble getting another teacher here when we go back to Brazil?" Andrew asked. "I understand the mountain passes close soon, so we can't stay much longer."

"I . . . I don't know. I hadn't thought about that yet."

Later that night when Andrew lay sleeping beside her, his question returned to Julia. Of course Andrew expected to return to Brazil as soon as possible. But who would take over her job here? She knew from the previous year's problems with a teacher that none of the parents had been able to manage the school adequately. What would happen to the children, and especially to Benny?

During that next week the question came often to her mind. To make her uncertainty more painful, Benny responded to her efforts with an interest that amazed her. It was as if he'd been coiled inside himself, waiting for someone to lift the lid so that he could jump out. He had rebellious moments, and it would take much more work for him to catch up, but he had made a start.

Paul and Andrew appeared at the school door each day as soon as the last children had left. On Friday while Julia straightened her desk and Paul went to his table to draw, Andrew paced restlessly across the front of the room. He stopped beside her and asked, "Did you speak to Mr. Wright today about getting a new teacher? You did say he's head of the school board, didn't you?"

"Yes, he is," Julia responded, trying to ignore a growing tightness in her stomach. "I didn't see him today."

"Then let's go by his brickyard when we leave here," Andrew suggested. "If he's not too busy, you can talk to him now."

"I suppose so," she said slowly, and went to get her hat and long coat. "Is it cold outside?"

"Yes. Looks like snow coming—so Mr. Meredith tells me." He beckoned to Paul, and Julia thought she heard a note of impatience as he said, "Come on, Paul. No more time."

That phrase settled in Julia's already clenched stomach as they walked to Gilbert Wright's brickyard. She never wanted to be separated from Andrew again. And yet Aurora had become important to her; had given her a special feeling of responsibility and pride when she needed it.

Gilbert Wright greeted Andrew and Julia heartily and invited them into his office. Andrew declined, saying he would stay outside with Paul. The office shut away some of the noise, but a fine red dust covered everything. Julia sat on the edge of a chair and Mr. Wright on another.

"I'm afraid I know what you're here for, Miz Langdon," he said.

"Yes," she affirmed, "my husband wants us to return to our home in Brazil as soon as we can."

He sighed. "Keepin' a teacher here is mighty hard, an' I'd hoped we'd have you all year. But I understand— after all, a woman's family comes first." The lines between his eyes deepened to a frown. "Frankly, I don't know anyone we can get, this time of year. Guess Miz Carver might try it again," he finished, his voice expressing plainly his doubts about that solution.

Julia felt as if she were strangling on guilt. "I'm terribly sorry, Mr. Wright," she finally got out. "I had no idea my husband would . . . be able to come here. I really feel very bad about not fulfilling my responsibility."

He looked hopefully at her. "Don't suppose you could just stay till January? Snow gets too high most times then to hold school for a spell." Then his face settled back into resignation. "Naw—probably have to stay till spring if you did that. Practically no way to get out of here in winter."

All she could manage was to repeat, "I'm so sorry."

He rose and escorted her to the door. "Don't you worry, now, Miz Langdon." He tried to smile, but he looked too doleful for the smile to succeed.

They exchanged polite good-byes before Julia found Paul and Andrew and the three of them started toward the small house on Pine Street. As if he sensed her distress, Andrew didn't ask about her conversation with Mr. Wright.

That evening the Butlers came to visit, and not until they had left and Paul was in bed did Julia and Andrew have time to themselves. They stood in front of the potbellied stove, and Andrew drew Julia into his arms. She rested against him, savoring the feel of his strong body against hers, his chin resting on the top of her head.

He said above her, "You've been very quiet since you saw Mr. Wright today." His hand caught her face, tilting her head back until she looked up into his eyes. "It bothers you, doesn't it—to leave the school here."

In the lantern light his blue eyes looked almost as dark as Roberto's, and she thought how desperately she loved him. But she couldn't deny her other feelings. "Yes. I feel that I'm breaking a promise to them—an important promise. Not that I'm such a special teacher, but I took on the responsibility, and I don't like running out on them."

A muscle along his jaw clenched, but he said lightly, "You took on a responsibility to me and Paul first. They can get along without you, but we can't." He caressed the side of her neck, and his voice sobered. "I've been away a long time. No matter how competent Roberto is, he can't make all the decisions for me."

She smiled at him, but she could feel tears behind her eyes. "Yes, I know."

When he kissed her, with its inevitable result, she lost herself in the whirling world he could create for her. Only later, when they lay together, did her earlier distress creep back. Silently she chastised herself; she was making too much of her feelings about the town and the children.

Andrew didn't accompany her to see Mrs. Weber the next day. When Julia finished writing, Mrs. Weber said quietly, "I think you're troubled today, Julia. Can you tell me about it?"

It was a relief to explain her feelings to someone other than Andrew. She finished by saying, "I want to go with my husband. I love him very much. But I also want to stay here until my job is over."

Mrs. Weber smiled wryly. "Women usually choose to do what their men tell them, and that's probably best." Something about Mrs. Weber's voice made Julia suspect the older woman didn't necessarily agree with her own statement.

That night Julia and Andrew took Paul to the box supper and dance at the Miners' Union Hall. Some of the older people didn't dance, so someone was always available to look after the children while their parents enjoyed themselves. Julia wore her one colorful dress, a bright blue, and let her hair fall in curls from a ribbon at her neck instead of confining it in a bun. Andrew's fitted frock coat emphasized his broad shoulders and lean waist and hips, and Julia noticed that he received as many admiring looks as she did.

She had been to such town entertainments before, but she'd always felt self-conscious about being alone and had stayed on the sidelines with Paul. Now she danced every set, both with Andrew and with other men, surprised at how many people seemed like close friends.

On the way back to their house, the snow Mr. Meredith had predicted began to fall. By the middle of Sunday morning it had melted, leaving puddles to remind Julia how little time remained for them to leave.

But on Monday, duty seemed unclear again. The day began well; Benny relinquished a book in order to take a spelling test. Though he spelled only seven words correctly, Julia thought she wouldn't feel a greater triumph had he just been accepted for Harvard. And the whole class worked hard so as to have time to prepare a play they were to give at the Miners' Union Hall the following week.

The children were leaving for the noon recess when Julia heard Elizabeth Carver brag, "I'll get the best part next time 'cause my mother'll be the teacher."

Her friend, a plump eight-year-old, protested, "You're lying. Miz Langdon's our teacher, not your old mother." She turned to Julia, her voice dismayed. "Aren't you?"

Beyond the girls' upset faces Julia saw that Benny had stopped and was looking at her, his rigid body telling her he was waiting for a blow—one she realized she couldn't give. A cold knot grew in her stomach as she said calmly, "Yes . . . I'll be your teacher."

The relief on their faces didn't make up for the terrible pain in her heart. How could she make Andrew understand? She loved him, and yet she had taken on, for herself, a commitment she must honor. Now would she be risking all she'd just regained?

She got through the afternoon somehow. As soon as Andrew arrived with Paul, he asked, "What's happened?"

She couldn't tell him in front of Paul, so though she knew it was cowardly, she said, "I'm fine." He didn't look as if he believed her, but he said nothing more.

That evening he didn't sit by the warmth of the stove in his usual relaxed way. Instead he waited only until Paul was asleep before he said, "You might as well tell me."

A hopeless feeling, almost like terror, choked her, and she had to fight against the tears which would be unfair to use. "Andrew. . ." She spread her hands in appeal. "I can't leave the school here now. I must stay a while longer."

Grimly he pointed out, "You say 'a while longer,' but that means the winter."

His truth silenced her. "Why, Julia? Are these children more important to you than Paul? Than going home with me?"

"No . . . no, they aren't." She tried to express clearly how she felt so that she, as well as he, could understand. "But what I feel I ought to do is important. Can't we stay here?"

A distant look she'd hoped she'd never see again tightened the muscles of his face. "I've explained. I need to go home, and I thought you loved me and wanted to be with me."

Her tears grew dangerously closer, but she fought them back, determined not to make a weapon out of that kind of weakness. "I do, I do. But I must do what's right in other ways too. As you had to go look for Sergio."

"That's not quite the same thing."

Hopelessly, she gave up her explanation. When they went to bed, they lay silently at first, not touching. Then they turned to each other, making love with fierce urgency, as if it were for the last time.

Julia managed that next morning at school, but she didn't quite know how. During the noon recess she didn't go across to Mrs. Butler's for a meal as she usually did, sending a message that she had work. Really she feared she might be sick if she tried to eat. Nor did Andrew or Paul come to the schoolhouse, and she felt relieved, not yet ready to face them.

Alone in the clutter of desks and books waiting for the children to return, she faced the conclusion she'd been evading. She must tell Andrew to take Paul and go back to Brazil. When she could leave in the spring, she would follow. Though she would miss Paul, it wouldn't be fair for him and Andrew to be separated again.

She stopped her pacing around the room. What if Andrew didn't want her if she refused to behave as a wife was supposed to? She couldn't make that kind of sacrifice in order to stay here. But slowly the thought became clear in her mind. To be an obedient wife of the sort her mother had been perhaps was impossible for her. If Andrew insisted on that kind of a wife, their marriage might founder eventually anyway. He'd understood her needs for doing more than a wife's usual activities before. She could only hope he would now.

The afternoon finally ended, but for the first time Andrew and Paul didn't appear for the walk back to the little house. She waited a few minutes, then, her anxiety building, hurried down the hill and along Pine Street. When she reached the house, she didn't hear voices, and the door was locked. Fumbling in her bag, she found the key she'd never used before and unlocked the door.

Cold and empty rooms confronted her. In her chest a terrible certainty began to squeeze her heart. This was Tuesday—one of the days the coach left for San Francisco. Nothing had prevented Andrew's meeting her after school before. He must have taken Paul and left.

Momentarily she thought that for the first time in her

life she might faint. Then she clutched her heavy coat around her and started out the door again. She couldn't give up hope without going to the stage office to check. Fear hurried her feet along the road, dodging the mud still left from the weekend's snow.

As she came to the corner above the hotel, a block from the stage office, she slowed, wanting to know, yet terrified to know. It seemed strange that everything around her looked so normal. Overhead, clouds raced across the fading sky. Two men walked their horses toward the livery stable. In the front of Meredith's Emporium three women had stopped, apparently to exchange gossip. Even the piano music coming from the hotel carried its usual boisterous melody.

The roistering miner's tune ended, followed by clapping, and then she heard the lyrical notes of a Mozart piano sonata—the Sonata in F major—one of Andrew's favorites. The sound pierced her, absorbing all her senses, flooding her with exquisite hope.

As if carried on those notes, she found herself at the entrance to the large main room of the hotel. She had never been inside, and realized without caring that an unaccompanied woman undoubtedly shouldn't go inside, but she opened the door.

Her eyes skimmed over the room, seeing every detail but at the same time hardly aware of them. Along the right wall men lounged on a battered green sofa and several mismatched chairs. To the left a long table held crockery, apparently in readiness for an evening meal. Several men with bottles or glasses stood at a counter in the far right corner. Against the faded paper flowers on the back wall was an upright piano. Seeing it, she came alive again.

Paul stood beside the piano, and Andrew sat on a stool, his back to the entrance, playing the Mozart as he had so many times on the *fazenda*. Such joy filled her that she could only cling to the side of the doorway and listen. Nothing she had ever heard had sounded so sweet.

One of the miners touched Andrew on the shoulder. Over the music she heard him say, "Mr. Langdon, Mrs. Langdon is here."

Andrew stopped abruptly and turned on the stool, pulling out his pocket watch. The faces of the other men turned toward Julia, and one bearded man rose quickly from the sofa and came to the door. "Mrs. Langdon, ma'am, please come in." -

His watch still in his hand, Andrew met her halfway across the room, with Paul following close behind. "Julia, I'm so sorry. I forgot the time."

One of the other men at the bar said, "Excuse me, Miz Langdon, but that was a right nice tune. We hope your husband'll stay and play the rest. Be a shame to leave it in the middle."

Andrew looked at her questioningly, and at her "Of course," returned to the piano. The room quieted instantly, and while Paul held Julia's hand, she listened as Andrew began the sonata again. In spite of the poor quality of the piano, he made the notes sing. At the end she joined the almost shy applause.

After Andrew responded to urging that he come back to play again with an assurance that he would, he took Julia's arm and they went out into the beginning twilight. Paul ran on ahead of them as they started toward Pine Street. "I am sorry I let the time to meet you get by," he said, "but it's been a long time since I played the piano. If I'm going to spend the winter here, I'll need more to do than split firewood, though I can see we'll need lots of that." He grinned down at her. "Maybe

I'll get a job playing the piano at the hotel. Would it be proper for the teacher's husband to do that?"

Julia thought she had never known before this instant how full of love she could feel. He was willing to do this for her! She wouldn't tell him of her fears—they shamed her now—but she must say what she'd decided earlier. "Andrew," she began, pulling at his arm to stop, "if you want to go back to Brazil now, you can take Paul, and I'll follow you in the spring."

Andrew looked at the face he loved so much, at her eyes reflecting equal love for him, and he knew she was offering just as much as he. He wished she felt right about going home now, but she might not be the woman who satisfied him so completely if she could. He touched her face and vowed, "No—no separations, Julia. The *fazenda* will have to wait. This time."

A malevolent gust of wind caught them, flipping up the edge of his coat, and he felt winter in its bite. "But don't ever again expect me to live in a place like this." He let his teeth chatter loudly. "Come on, woman. You still owe me a red-haired, blue-eyed daughter. Let's get home out of this wind so you can start doing your duty."

He took her hand and pulled her along so fast she had to run to keep up. Home to a tiny rented house in a town neither of them had ever heard of a few months ago. But she'd realized something important, and she was sure Andrew had learned it too. Home meant being together, sharing their life and love. Julia heard joyful laughter, and it was her own.

About the Author

Barbara Keller was born and raised in Southern California, and despite stints of living elsewhere, again makes her home there. History has always been one of her passions, and with her husband, a chemist, she seeks out the early stories of the places where they travel. THE EXILED HEART is her first novel.